The Chronicles of Ratha:
Book 1

Children of the Noorthi
Erica Lawson

The Chronicles of Ratha:

Book 1

Children of the Noorthi

Erica Lawson

Affinity
eBook Press
NZ
2014

The Chronicles of Ratha: Children of the Noorthi
© 2010 by Erica Lawson

Affinity E-Book Press NZ LTD.
Canterbury, New Zealand

Edition 2nd

ISBN: 978-1-927328-13-2

All rights reserved.

Editor: Nat Burns
Cover Design: Irish Dragon Designs

Dedication

To E, wherever you are.

Table of Contents

Also by Erica Lawson

The Chronicles of Ratha: Book 1 Children of the Noorthi

The Chronicles of Ratha: Book 2 Lion Among the Lambs

Out of Retirement

Miss-Match

Reflected Passion

Possessing Morgan

Soulwalker

Chapter One

Of All the Bars in the Universe
She Had to Step into Mine

This had to be one of the seediest spacebars I had ever been in. Located on the outskirts of the spaceport of Aldronicus VII, it was crowded with the worst beings the universe had to offer. I was seated near the rear of the establishment sipping my one very inexpensive, unpronounceable drink. In fact, the fuel running my ship tasted better than this crap.

I had been waiting for a few hours for my next job to turn up, but it looked like this was another wasted trip. I drained the liquid in my glass and winced as the ethyl alcohol burned my esophagus on its way down to melt away my stomach lining.

"Jordana!"

My head rose at the mention of my name, and my hand instinctively reached for the laser pistol strapped to my thigh.

"You still alive, you old bitch?"

Charming. The owner of that voice was someone I really wasn't in the mood to deal with right now. "And you still have the manners of an Agarian warthog, you old bastard," I replied.

The behemoth of a man sat down uninvited, spilling his equally large drink over the tabletop and almost into my lap. "Sorry, J. What you doing here?"

"Waiting for a client to turn up, but it looks like a no-show."

"Too bad. I'm about to head out to the outer rings in a few hours."

The inebriated mammoth in front of me was happily pouring alcohol down his throat like water. In his state, he would be lucky to find the spaceport, let alone his ship.

"What do you want, Chase?"

"Can't a guy say hello to the most delicious female in the place?"

"You've said hello, now go."

"Come on, what are you doing the rest of the night? No job, so how about some fun?"

I watched him with amusement. "You couldn't find your own dick. What makes you think I want to find it? Go away."

"Aww, you know you're the only one for me."

"You're wasting your time. Go home and get some sleep, because that's about all you're going to get tonight."

"You've gotten real boring in your old age."

"I'm not getting older. Just choosing a better class of men."

"Hey!"

I glared at him. If he had looked in the mirror, he would have seen what I was talking about. "Get out of here, you crotchety old grunt. You've had enough," I said more forcefully.

He pushed himself to his feet, swayed slightly for a moment, and staggered back to the bar. His forward motion was stopped by the heavy plastic platform that ran the length of the room, and his expansive waist rippled with the force of the impact. His head bobbed on his trunk-like neck as he surveyed the other residents at the bar, and he made a beeline toward a lone female a few seats down.

"Hello there, sweetheart. Lonely, are we?" Chase's voice boomed over the din.

I imagined his smelly breath as it assaulted her delicate senses. She drew back in reaction, and I couldn't quite hear her response over the noise in the bar, but I watched in case she needed assistance. Chase was mostly harmless, but when drunk, he became a little too pushy.

"Aww, come on sweetheart, your loser friend ain't showin'. How about you and I hook up tonight for some fun?"

Sighing, I stood to lend my assistance and strode over to the confrontation. "Hey, Chase, call it a night, okay?"

"Butt out. She ain't your type. I'm just keeping the lady here company. Ain't I, doll?"

It was now time to put myself into intimidation mode. I was as tall as he was wide, so I was able to tower over him and give him my best glare. "Go home. Now."

Indecision showed in his eyes as he sized up his chances of beating me in a fight. He apparently wasn't too drunk to realize he was outmatched. He backed away with what pride he could muster, but anyone within hearing distance knew it as the back down it was.

"I'm sorry," I said to the woman he'd been bothering. "He's harmless most of the time, but when he's had a few he thinks he's Koran Andover as far as females are concerned."

She blinked coyly at me and sibilantly whispered, "Thank you, kind lady. He was a bit of a bother."

"May I buy you a drink?" Something about her had caught my attention.

"Yes, thank you. A Pluuvian Twist, if you please."

I waved to the bartender, indicating two drinks. Hell, my stomach lining was nearly gone, anyway. "This is a bit out of the way for you, er..." I hesitated in the hope of a name.

"Andrissa. Andrissa Mandoorva."

"Jordana. At your service, ma'am." I gave her my best courtly bow, respectfully showing her the top of my head. "What are you doing here? This isn't exactly the nicest part of the port."

"I was here to see someone about a delivery, but I can't seem to find him," she whispered.

"A job?" Was this my client? "What sort of job?"

"It's the delivery of a small item. No questions asked."

"Who were you supposed to meet?"

"Someone named J. Laren," Andrissa said.

I smiled. "Well, that's me. Jordana Laren. Come. Let's sit in the back there where it's quiet." I snatched the two drinks off the bar and motioned for her to lead the way.

3

As she proceeded ahead of me, I watched the hypnotic sway of her hips. I was mesmerized by this intoxicating creature and was helpless but to follow her toward the table I had just vacated. She was about to sit down in the chair with the puddle when I spoke. "No, take the other seat." I put the drinks down on the wet table, pushed one tall glass toward her, and sat in the one other dry chair. I positioned myself to have a full view of the room. "Now, what can I do for you?"

"You were recommended by a mutual friend who said you were... discreet."

"Discreet is my middle name, ma'am," I said casually, giving her an impression of mild unconcern. I was interested in her, and I wanted to gauge if there was any reciprocation. A smile touched her lips. It gave me some hope. "Just tell me where and when, and I'll be there."

"And the price?" She batted her eyelashes at me.

"That depends on what I'm delivering and how much the authorities want it."

She took a sip from the glass then regarded me. What was she thinking? Was I going to lower my price just because she flirted with me? I knew that look. Other women had tried it on me. For some it worked; others it didn't. Numbed by her hypnotic eyes staring into mine, my thoughts were slipping away.

"I'm the package." She waited, apparently for some reaction from me. When she received none, she added, "And I would say that the authorities probably want me pretty badly."

It took quite a bit of concentration on my part to bring my attention back to the conversation. "In that case, for you, twelve hundred credits," I said, maintaining a professional demeanor. What did anybody want with her, besides the obvious of course? She was a hell of a looker.

"Twelve hundred?" She frowned. "That's an awful lot."

"We are talking about the Consortium here, aren't we?" When she nodded, I said, "Then it's twelve hundred." Hell, if she was interested in this deal, I'd drop my price, but I was going to start high with the haggling.

She sipped her drink while she contemplated my offer, her eyes never wavering from me. "If you can get me to Covaris in three solar days, I will pay you twelve hundred."

Covaris? It was going to take some serious flying to make that destination in that short a time. It could be done, as long as the Consortium left us alone. "Agreed." And then I caught myself, but not in time to retract. What had I gotten myself into? I sipped my long, tall drink and tried to concentrate on Andrissa's soft tones as she explained the politics of Covaris. In reality, I couldn't have cared less about Covaris, let alone its politics, but this young lady had me believing it was the centre of my universe.

"Let me at least buy you dinner," I said. "My ship's being refueled. We can't leave until that's finished, and once we take off... well, I'm not going to have time to cook."

She looked around the room, probably in an attempt to decide if the quality of the cuisine could be gauged by the quality of the room and its inhabitants. Her gaze returned to me, and she raised an eyebrow in question.

"The food's not too bad. Almost edible. But we don't have time to make an appointment elsewhere, so we either eat here or we don't eat at all."

She picked a dish from the menu illuminated within the table, and I left to place the order with the barkeep and get another round of drinks in the process. While I waited, I watched her. Even her attempt to wear common clothes so as not to draw attention to herself couldn't hide her high-class demeanor. Her ramrod posture spoke volumes. This was a creature of high-bred status stuck in a dive of a bar having to grovel to a nobody like me. Under any other circumstances, we wouldn't have even been on the same planet, let alone in the same room. I probably would have been the mud on the bottom of her expensive boots if the Consortium hadn't intervened somehow and thrown us together.

Despite myself, I responded to the twinkle in her eye when she looked at me. Perhaps it was my loneliness that was calling to me. Who knows? But I felt I had to give myself a chance. After all, everyone deserved some happiness now and then, didn't they?

I wove my way through the deafening crowd back to her and deposited the damp glasses on the table with a thud. There was a shove in my back, and I swiveled, fists at the ready, as a fight broke out on the floor. "Hey! Watch who you're shoving!"

"Get out of my way, bitch!"

"Who are you calling bitch? Dickhead." The epithets rolled off my tongue with practiced ease.

Despite his obvious confusion over my quaint dialect, this guy didn't know when to leave well enough alone and took a swipe. The crowded floor cleared, and soon we were facing off against one another.

The barkeeper called out, "J, don't take too long, okay? Dinner is nearly ready." A wave of laughter rolled around the edges of the circle.

"J?" His eyes opened in doubt as he said my name.

"Jordana to you, numbskull."

He glared. "Are you insulting me?"

How could I explain in two words what had happened about ten years ago? I fell in love with colloquial English or, more to the point, twentieth-century colloquial English. It was the most delightfully expressive and, maybe more important, least understood language in the universe. I could literally insult someone's parentage, and my enemy would be none the wiser.

I answered the man standing in front of me with a nod and a smile, and the color in his face drained away. I nearly laughed as he silently mouthed "oh craz" when he finally realized who I was.

He stepped back, but it was too late. My fist was already in motion, and it connected with his jaw in a sickening thud that sent him to the floor out cold. "Is that quick enough for you, Errol?" I said to the bartender.

Another wave of laughter rolled around the room as people stepped over the prostrate body of my victim.

"Nice one!" The bartender gave me one of his toothless grins, amusing all those around me. I brushed myself off and turned back to my guest. Yes, it was a nice weapon to have a second language to fall back upon to confuse my enemies, and I had ten years' worth of study to perfect it. Even today I had a few of the old stories and historical recordings stored in my computer's memory banks for reading on those lonely trips out to the Carbine Trough or the Malleus Nebula to pick up cargo. If I was going to insult anyone, I wanted to make sure I said it right.

"This happens to you often?" Andrissa asked.

"Sometimes. Most of them back down when they find out who I am. Only a couple of them are stupid enough to try anything," I said, with a little brash confidence.

"You think very highly of yourself, then."

I heard disdain in her voice. "No, not really. They just know what I'm capable of." I was glad our dinner had arrived, because I had worked up an appetite with the fight.

"How long have you been in the delivery business, Miss Laren?" Andrissa asked in between bites of her meal.

"Call me Jordana, please, or J if you like." But I had sensed the change in her. It was the fight. I knew it. Her attitude had changed once I sat down for dinner.

"All right, Jordana. How long have you been flying?"

"Since I was able to walk. My dad used to be one of the best until he got hurt in an accident. Someone needed to take over the family business, and since I was the only kid, it fell to me."

"Your father?" Andrissa asked politely.

"Gareth Laren," I replied.

Her eyes widened at his name. "*The* Gareth Laren?" She looked impressed.

"The very one."

"Everyone has heard of Gareth Laren. He was the hero of Riker's Moon."

"He was certainly my hero when I was growing up." But eventually, even I came to realize that he was just an old, worn-out fighter pilot lost in his glory days until he died. "Sometimes, it's a pain in the ass to live up to that rep."

"You seemed to be coping all right just a while ago."

"That's my reputation, not his." I gave her my best charming smile, looking for an elusive one back, but I didn't get one. "We'd better get going," I said as the meal came to a close. "No point hanging around this piece of crap."

7

We stood and I threw a few credits on the table for the meal. "See you around, Errol," I said as I passed the bar. He gave me a wink, silently wishing me good luck. As I followed Andrissa toward the exit, I watched the gentle sway of her hips, knowing the ship was now a hands-free zone. What a waste.

"So, is it just you, or is there someone else we have to pick up?"

"Just me, and I'd like to get started as quickly as possible," she said. Three days alone with her was going to be torture, because I realized now it was a matter of look-but-don't-touch with her. I only hoped the journey would be free of Consortium interference.

"When are we leaving?" she asked.

I looked at the chronometer on my wrist. "Refueling should be about done. Would you be ready in, say, twenty minutes?"

"I'm ready now."

"Well then, let's go." I extended my hand in the direction of the doorway. I escorted her from the front of the building toward the bustling spaceport and my ship.

But something wasn't right. I could feel it. I hadn't survived as long as I had by ignoring the churning in my stomach. Then again, it could have been the food.

Chapter Two

Up into the Wild Black Yonder

I directed my companion from the dim light of the space bar out into the brightness of the false day. When I first came here, those damned hovering lights were the most ridiculous thing I had ever seen, but since then, I had learned my lesson. Aldronicus VII was a hole like hell itself. Its two suns could burn the skin right off an unprotected man or woman in a matter of hours. Only raving idiots or the certifiably insane would go outside the protection of the electromagnetic domes.

Maybe that's why the Consortium left this place alone. There was nothing here but dust, heat, and the odd assortment of pathetic souls who had nowhere else to go. To this day, I still question my sanity for using this planet as a meeting place for my clients. I suppose if they're prepared to come here they must be desperate enough to pay what I ask. Maybe I should raise my price.

Currently, we were on the lunar cycle, which was stupid because there was no moon. Two suns—not enough room for a moon, as I thought about it. Screwed up, like the rest of us.

I guided Andrissa along the pathway to the spaceport. If we didn't hyperjump soon, we'd have to wait till the next lunar cycle fifty-eight hours away. That should be enough time to get in a couple of fights and rot away the rest of my stomach lining with booze, assuming that I could lose Andrissa along the way. In my book, it wasn't considered polite to get drunk in front of a lady, at least not on purpose.

Vendors were shoving their wares in my face and seriously pissing me off. "Get the hell out of my way," I growled. I looked over at Andrissa. She seemed unfazed by the unwanted attention.

"Hello there, J, darling," said a familiar voice.

Oh, craz. I turned around to face someone I hadn't seen for a while and had hoped I wouldn't again for a while more. "Kat. Hey." My words sounded less than enthusiastic, even to my own ears.

"Where have you been, honey?"

"You know... here and there," I said nonchalantly.

"More there than here, lately."

"Been busy. You know how it is." I tried to brush past her, but she grabbed my arm.

"Hang on. How about a bit of fun?"

"Not tonight, Kat. I've got a job." Kat studied Andrissa. The contrasts between them couldn't have been more evident. Kat was a blocky mountain next to the elegant, petite Andrissa.

"Your tastes have changed," Kat said.

Nah, just gotten better. Kat had come into my life at a time when I wanted to experience everything, and the more dangerous the better. Kat liked her sex rough, and plenty of it, and I was more than a willing participant. After a couple of broken bones, I thought better of it and found my appetites had tempered with age and common sense. And now? Well, sweet and tender was just as important as amorous and demanding. All I needed to do was find someone who fit the bill.

"You're not in that much of a hurry, are you?" Kat said. "I'm sure your little friend here wouldn't mind waiting. Hell, if she wants, she can join in."

If I didn't think I'd break my hand on Kat's jaw, I was tempted to smack her into next week. "No, thanks." I grabbed Andrissa's elbow and steered her around Kat in the direction of the hangar.

"Hey, J, wait a minute. I haven't seen you in months, and you're trying to skip past me? You've got time for an old friend, haven't you?" Kat was, if nothing else, persistent.

I'd had enough of Kat's sniping. I released my new client and stepped up to Kat, invading her personal space and then some. "If you don't back off, everyone here is going to see me kick your butt from one end of the port to the other. You got me? I'm going to kick you so goddammed hard you'll be opening your mouth to get my boot out."

With that final remark, I walked away and grabbed Andrissa's hand in passing. What in the wide galaxy possessed me to ever get myself hitched to Krazy Kat? Oh, yeah. Sex.

While I guided Andrissa in the direction I wanted to go with one hand, I rested my other on my blaster, though it was more to protect it from being stolen than to actually use it. The closeness of the crowd pressed in on all sides, irritating my last nerve.

What was it about the lunar cycle that brought out all the crazies? Or maybe it was the crazies looking for an extreme suntan. Whatever it was, the inhabitants were on edge, nitpicking over wares, pushing and shoving and using a liberal vocabulary that would have made my daddy's hair stand up on end, if he ever had any. If the crowd didn't part soon, someone was going to get hurt.

As if my thoughts had been read, a path cleared in front of me and allowed us to make up some time to the hangars. Maybe one of the numerous life forms calling this place home picked up my vibes. I looked up to see my image on one of the enforcement screens floating above the crowd. Staring back at me from the mass of bodies on the screen was a woman whose anger was written in every line of her body.

I continued to stride toward the hangar, but I couldn't help but look at the screen, observing every imperfection I possessed. I hadn't realized that I had run myself down so much, so I swore off the alcohol again. That was the fifth time this solar week.

It was a little game I played. I looked at myself, got disgusted, swore off the alcohol, then broke that promise as soon as I could find another bar. This time, however, it was going to have to wait until my return. How was I ever going to last that long? I wanted a drink already.

"There she is." I pointed at the small craft tucked away in the corner of the large area loosely called a hangar. It was more a large expanse of dust where they parked the ships not in use during the lunar cycle. Of course, the ships were towed under cover before sunrise otherwise the controls melted into place.

"That?" Andrissa asked, incredulity in her voice.

"Yes, that," I said indignantly. The ship wasn't that bad. Sure it had a few million miles on the clock, but she was reliable... most of the time.

Andrissa's nose wrinkled as if she sniffed something that had turned bad. "Will we fit in it?"

"Of course we'll fit. Did you think I was going to strap you to the underside? It's one of those 'it's bigger on the inside' things."

From her expression, she seriously doubted the space-worthiness of my little "Bessie," but I knew the craft well. The mechanics often laughed that I had given my ship a name, but as soon as someone said the name in one of those archive tapes from that planet, you know, *3rd Rock from the Sun,* I knew it was the name for my gal here. It was a friendly name, a name that would encourage conversations between her and me. It was lonely out in the cosmos, and a gal had to keep herself busy or go crazy in the process.

"Come on. Time's a wastin'." I nearly pushed Andrissa toward Bessie as she resisted. I had to get into the air before she changed her mind. Andrissa had surprising strength in her slim body, and her resistance slowed my progress to a crawl. "You're not having second thoughts are you?"

"Well..." Her gaze roamed over the hull, taking in the scorch marks and the crack in the antenna. "She seems a little..."

"'She seems a little' nothing. She's fine. More than fine. She's a great little ship, and I seem to remember you were in a hurry." I had to get her on board and in the sky before she spotted another spaceworthy ship nearby. So, I lifted her in my arms and boarded my vessel. She glared at me, and I just muttered, "You were taking too long."

I lowered her into the copilot's chair and strapped her in. I backed away and strapped myself in, then fired up the engines before she could react. The sooner we were off this rock, the better.

"Hey!" The single word echoed down my earphone. "Wait up." Standing in front of the ship was one very angry head technician.

"I owe ya, Rales. Pay you next lunar." I tried to sound nonchalant, but we both knew it was a plea for credit.

"Yeah, yeah, and I know Corath Blane," he said.

I knew he didn't. Did anyone know the most powerful creature in the known universe? I suspected very few did, and they were living in constant fear of being found and terminated.

"Sure you do, pal."

"Jordana, you know better than to ask for credit." He stood there refusing to budge.

"Aww, please Rales. I'm in a hurry here. Can't I pay you when I get back?"

"Honey, I'd have the Port Authority on my case for letting you go—again—without paying for the fuel. I've already bailed you out twice."

"Dammit!"

"Don't you swear at me, young lady." His rebuke came down my tiny earpiece, and I immediately felt guilty.

"Sorry, Dad," I said a little sarcastically but with affection nonetheless. I stood up and removed the earpiece and reached into an overhead compartment to remove my emergency stash of credits. "Back in a minute." I trudged to the hatch and waited while the ramp lowered to the ground. Sheepishly I stepped on the soil and stood in front of Rales.

After I handed over the cash, he kissed me quickly on the cheek. "That's better. Have a safe trip."

"Was that really necessary?" I looked around to see if we had been caught.

"No, but I do it because I can. If you come across Sasha in your travels, tell her her old dad is missing her."

"Will do. I'll be back in a few days."

"Where are you heading?" Rales's foot scuffed the ground as he asked the question. I knew he desperately wanted to know, but he didn't want to appear too eager

"Covaris."

"Covaris? I've heard there's Consortium activity in that sector. Stay out of trouble."

"I'll be home before you know it." I slapped my hand on his shoulder and patted it a few times. That was as much of a public display of affection he was going to get from me.

Once I had settled back into the pilot's seat and the hatch was securely locked, I waved Rales off and he reluctantly stepped aside so Bessie could spread her wings, metaphorically speaking, and fly. Well, it was more like she had a solar flare up her ass, but the wings image was much nicer.

Bessie rose smoothly from the planet, barely disturbing the dusty field she had been parked on, and as she accelerated up into the darkness I caught a glimpse of the larger of the two suns slowly maneuvering its way around the planet to scorch it once more. The planet was rather pretty, looking down on it while it was dark. The twinkling of lights from the city seemed like a star field on a black blanket of deep space. In a matter of hours that scenery would change to a battle-scarred dustbowl where nothing lived, the ground heated to beyond human tolerance.

"That was your father?"

I nearly missed the question as I concentrated on getting through the stratosphere and clear into deep space.

"Hmm?"

"That man you talked to is your father? You don't look very much like him."

"Rales? Oh, no no no. He's not my father."

"But you called—"

"It's kind of a joke, kind of not. He and I found each other at a time when we both needed family. He already has a daughter, and I suppose I fill in for her from time to time." I really didn't want to talk about my personal relationships. That's why they call them personal. Right?

Since she was curious about me, I felt it was time to ask my own questions. While I didn't consider my personal life any business of Andrissa's, that didn't stop me from sticking my nose into hers. "So what do you do, Miss Mandoorva?"

"What makes you think that I do anything, Miss Laren?"

So now she wanted to play games. "All right. Who are you? Why is the Consortium so interested in you?"

"No questions asked, remember?" she replied firmly.

"What else is there to talk about? The weather? Who'll win cornerball? Oh, come on, we have nothing in common and a long way to go." Our small talk barely lasted an hour into the trip. The conversation cut short when she reached for her bag.

The only luggage Andrissa brought with her was the small bag she came to dinner with. If I had been thinking with anything else except my brain, that piece of information alone should have issued an alert signal. Maybe she was going home to Covaris, but as she wouldn't answer any questions, I had no idea what she was up to.

To wile away the hours, she pulled out one of the new interactive readers on the market and attached the tiny magnetic button behind her ear. I had tried one of those once but never really enjoyed the experience of reading by osmus... mussis... osmies... absorbing it.

For the next three hours, Andrissa meditated while her book read to her, and I plotted the quickest course to Covaris. The next two hours and fifty-eight minutes of those three hours I muttered, whistled, and sang to myself.

When it looked like I finally had her attention, I spoke. "So what do you think of her?" I was showing off, I knew, thinking that Andrissa would appreciate the comfy little vehicle she was traveling in.

"It's quaint."

"Quaint?" She was insulting my girl. "It's the fastest thing this side of Barracker's Reef," I said.

"Nevertheless, it's what? Fifty years old?"

"Fifty? She's twenty if she's a day." I patted the panel in front of me, trying to make the hunk of junk feel better.

15

"She's nearly an antique," Andrissa said. "And you still have that thing." Her finger rose and pointed at the steering wheel.

"I'll have you know that's cutting edge technology." I was insulted.

"That hasn't been used for at least half a millennia."

Which was true, but I wanted to be different. "I retroed her. Don't you like it?"

Andrissa didn't reply, but her expression said it all.

"It makes the trip a little more interesting." And a little more dangerous. Deep space travel had become boring, to the point that I really wasn't needed anymore. If I didn't have something to do on board, I might as well send Bessie off without me. "I wanted to be a more 'hands-on' flyer."

"Do you want something to drink?" She changed the subject.

"Sure. The replicator's out in the corridor."

The replicator had been programmed for nonalcoholic drink only. I had to stay sober while driving, or I might run the old gal into a piece of space junk.

Andrissa returned with a hot caffeine synth for me to help clear the fuzzies from my head. "Thanks," I said.

"Where are we now?" she asked.

I activated a three-dimensional map on a small metal plate situated between the two seats. My finger pointed to Aldronicus VII. "We started here and we'll end here." I moved my finger to the other side of the holomap and neatly poked a hole into Covaris. "By my calculations we are about here." I moved my finger back across the imaginary star field to just over halfway.

"Is there any way we can get there sooner?"

"Not unless you have a spare engine tucked away in your back pocket," I joked, but she wasn't amused. Andrissa was killing all the life out of this trip. I took a large mouthful of caffeine and let it slide down my throat. There was nothing like hot caffeine, unless it was hot caffeine with alcohol synth in it.

"What jobs have you done?" she asked.

"Jobs? Just the usual, I suppose."

"Have you ever failed to deliver?"

"There was one job years ago when I was just starting out. The Consortium was all over my ass on that one, and I had to do some fancy flying to avoid getting caught. I missed the delivery deadline by a couple of hours, but he wasn't happy. Geez, I gave him back his cargo and the credits and he was still fuming."

Andrissa stood up abruptly and grabbed my mug. "I'll just get us refills."

What a mess that job was. While Andrissa was gone, I thought about that particular event in my life, remembering even the words we exchanged.

I was tired, I was hungry, and I was pissed. The Consortium had been on my tail for the last two days, and it was only by good luck that I lost them at all. I was beginning to wonder whether my client deliberately tagged his cargo to let me get caught.

The flying junker I recently acquired got knocked around in the Gravel Pit because of it. The ship wasn't new when I got her, but now it had dents and scrapes from the dust field I flew through to avoid getting caught. The antique antenna dish also sustained damage by laser fire, and I was going to make sure that the next time I saw my client he would pay for it.

Unfortunately, all the detours and hiding had cost me time and I missed the rendezvous by a couple of hours. I hailed my client, Grimm, but it didn't matter what I said, he kept yelling at me.

"Do you have any idea what you have done?"

"Hey, Mr. Grimm, it's not my fault. I can only do so much against the Consortium."

"We had a deal and you broke it!"

I looked at the worried man on the other end of the communication. He was sweating profusely and looked disheveled. Whatever was in the shipment, its nondelivery was important, at least to him.

"If you wanted someone to blast the entire Consortium fleet out of the sky, you should have paid for it!" I was losing this battle of words.

"They're going to kill me," he muttered to himself. "I'm a dead man."

"Look, if it'll help, I'll just tell them—"

"You've done enough!"

The screen went blank. I had been tempted to just keep the cargo and pocket the cash, but my daddy would have put me over his knee for doing such a thing, so I dumped Grimm's possessions and credits on his own doorstep. I suppose I was glad I didn't have to test that choice too often, because I completed all my deliveries after that.

There was a nudge on my shoulder. I hadn't even noticed Andrissa's return. "Thanks." My hand wrapped around the familiar cup, and I sipped the hot beverage without much thought. It was a familiar taste, but there was something else in it. Maybe she added some sucarine to it. Andrissa sat in the copilot's seat, a smile appearing then disappearing behind the heated mug in her hand.

"What's so funny?"

"You are so funny." The liquid in her throat accentuated the slight hiss in her voice.

"Me? I know I can be the life of the party with my jokes, but... but..." My words faltered as my head spun and my vision suddenly went black.

Chapter Three

Betrayal Is Worth Twelve Hundred Credits

I felt like shit when I woke up. I was lying facedown in dirt, and the heat rising up from it was immense. Had we parked in a nearby sun?

I opened my eyes and instantly regretted it. Bright, heated whiteness streaked across my irises in a flash that blinded me. "Carn," I swore. "Miss Mandoorva?" It was deathly silent around me. "Andrissa?"

At last I could see. My surroundings were empty. Flat and empty, with a heat haze shimmering over it. There was no Andrissa. And no Bessie. I turned my head sideways from my position on the ground. It didn't matter which direction I looked, my ship was gone. What the hell happened to my ship?

"You son of a—" I shouted. "No, scratch that. You bitch!"

Deathly stillness surrounded me, and orange dust for as far as the eye could see while lying down. There was the occasional rock here and there, but that was it. That—that—*serpent* stole my Bessie and marooned me here on whatever this hellhole passing for a planet was.

"You could have at least left me a drink!" Why was I hollering? No one could hear me. "Uh... water, I mean water." I really had to get hold of my drinking problem.

I sat up and immediately regretted it. My head spun like an imploding black hole that sucked in what common sense I had. I was left to die on this miserable piece of rock, and all I could think about was my Bessie and where my next drink was coming from. Off in the distance I saw a small puff of swirling dust. I stood up, set off toward the disturbance, and hoped it would actually lead to something other than more dust.

The heat was sapping what energy I had. The dust cloud I was trying to catch rippled and swirled as the air shimmered just above the earth, making me wonder whether there was anything there at all. But I knew I couldn't think like that. While I believed I was walking toward something, I had hope.

I forced myself to put one foot in front of the other in the direction of an orange mirage that was slowly getting closer. My mouth was so dry it had gone past thirst and was now looking at survival. The air got hotter and hotter, and it burned the back of my throat before coating it with a fine layer of dust.

Whatever was on the horizon was slowly growing in size. I wasn't moving that fast, so I figured it must have also been coming at me. Some sort of contraption that approached at a speed that was barely above mine. Okay, now I was worried. If this was the best this planet had to offer, I was in real trouble. But I couldn't be choosy about what came to meet me. Either I used this thing, or my feet, and I knew my feet weren't up to the challenge.

Finally, the thing came close enough that I could get a good look at it. It was unlike anything I had ever seen, and believe me, I had seen a lot in this particular cosmos. The engine sounded more like a squeak than a hum or even a rumble, and I wondered if there was an engine at all. The vehicle, if it could be called that, was a small rectangular platform that sat on two sets of wheels, one set at the front and one at the back. On the platform were six women. Four of them were standing, while the remaining two were seated and seemed to be using their legs to power it. I knew they were women; the rags they were in covered very little. I wasn't that demented to not know a woman when I see one or, in this case, six.

The vehicle stopped in front of me, and the women stared at me with some wariness.

"Hey, I seem to be lost—" My words were cut short by a rock thrown at my head. "Ow. What was that for?" A second rock followed, and I was ducking and weaving the hail of rubble. "Will you quit?"

"How did you get here?" A big-boned, dark-haired woman glared down from her lofty height of a foot and a half off the ground.

"Some bitch kicked me off my Bessie and took off." I knew what I was talking about, but it soon became apparent that they didn't.

"Someone took your woman?" the dark-haired woman asked. This particular activity must have been frowned upon in their society, because the women looked at one another and muttered amongst themselves.

"Yeah, she did," I answered innocently. Since the statement got them on my side, who was I to argue?

"Which way did she travel?" The dark-haired woman looked in all directions until I pointed skyward. She sighed and stared out over the desert before waving me onto the contraption. It seemed I was saved from a stoning, at least for now, but if they ever found out that Bessie was a spaceship, a stoning would be the least of my troubles.

"Where am I?"

"Rigeus," she said. That was it, nothing more, just one word. Rigeus.

"*The* Rigeus? As in the 'Planet of the Amazon Women' Rigeus?"

"Rigeus," she repeated. This woman needed to seriously expand her vocabulary, but my question really only needed one word.

How did I end up on a penal planet? I know Bessie wasn't the best ride in the universe, but did I deserve to be judged and sentenced to life on Rigeus for having a lousy ship? Maybe I should have taken the offer of that stoning when I had the chance, especially now there would be no bar in sight.

Trying to get someone on this machine to talk to me was like getting credits out of my pocket, which was empty. I had a better chance of a decent conversation with Bessie than I did with these women, whose hyper-vigilant observance of the surrounding land was beginning to annoy me as much as the squeaky wheels moving us along at a ferrel's pace.

It looked like any sort of conversation taking place would be left to me. "Where are we going in such a hurry?"

The woman who seemed to be in charge just glared at me. Her attention returned to the horizon, her head constantly turning from one side to another. "There." Her finger pointed at a small puff of dust in the distance, and the other women tried to turn the vehicle around and head in the opposite direction.

I could see that whoever it was would be upon us soon. Maybe these women should ask for mechanical tips from their enemy, because it didn't take long for them to catch up. While the foreign vehicle looked vaguely similar to the contraption I was on now, the glaring difference was that it had an engine. Rudimentary, of course, but it was still an engine and it pushed their vehicle along at a much faster pace.

I reached for the holster at my side and cursed. That bitch of a woman had taken my sidearm, something nearly as unforgivable as taking Bessie. Andrissa's list of crimes against me was growing long and varied and when I caught up with her—well, let's just say I'll be finding out if she can shed her skin.

The air was filled with the sounds of "putt, putt, putt" from what I assumed was their engine. Small puffs of black smoke, released in time to the sounds, created a nearly musical scenario. But the passengers on board that mechanical beast were anything but peaceful. They stared at us with hostility.

"Don't even bother trying to escape," the woman who appeared to be their leader said. It was a warning that my fellow travelers took seriously, and they slowed their vehicle to a stop.

"What are you doing?" I asked the leader of my group, quietly.

"Nothing," she muttered.

"Great," I said with a sigh.

We were escorted across the desert to a tangled heap of twisted metal that could be loosely called a compound. There were maybe twenty women training in an open space of dirt. They held makeshift metal poles in their hands as they practiced moves of war. Other women were cooking, washing, or on guard duty. It looked like a pretty disciplined tribe that knew how to subdue its enemies.

My fellow travelers nervously looked around. Obviously whatever tribe they came from had no such rituals, which explained a lot about their surrender. To them it must seem easier to surrender first, before getting the crap kicked out of them and then having to surrender.

Now me, I liked a good fight, and I was not one to make it easy for anyone. But I liked good odds as well, and at the moment, thirty-plus to one was just a little too one-sided for my liking. I would have to bide my time. Before I had a chance to think of a way out of this mess, we were violently nudged in the back toward a large hut in the middle of the open courtyard. The door of the hut opened.

"Well, well, well. It seems my luck has changed."

I knew that voice, and it was one I had hoped never to hear again. I groaned to myself. "Hey, Vel. How's it hanging?" I taunted her. I always wondered if she had been a man in a previous life.

"Much better, now that you're here," she said, right before she grinned at me.

I finally got the nerve to look her straight in the eye, and what I saw was not good. We hadn't separated on the best of terms, if you could call a broken jaw on her part good. She was a nasty bitch who made Kat look like some tiny tot playing in zero gravity. Vel liked inflicting pain during sex. It was not to my particular taste, but she was a friend of Kat's. It was during one of Kat's playful sessions that Vel crossed the line, giving some poor young thing they had picked up in a bar a severe beating that Vel had no intention of stopping. I had to step in before she killed the girl, and I broke her jaw, and my hand, in the process.

Kat suggested that I take a long, long holiday somewhere far, far away. Hence, my current address at Canaris Minor. I couldn't go any farther out without leaving the universe. By the look of the feral smile on Vel's lips, maybe I should have left my last job well enough alone and stayed put.

Erica Lawson

"Sit down a spell. You're going to be here for a while," Vel said.

Knowing Vel as I did, I suspected that my life right now was worth shit. I had heard from Kat that she was a woman who never forgot an indiscretion against her.

"You six—" Vel addressed the captured women as if she were their queen—"you should have known better than to get involved with this one."

"Yeah, right, Vel. I told them my life story after I fell from the sky," I said sarcastically, and it earned me a smack across the mouth. "Well, that accomplished a lot." Another smack. The taste of blood in my mouth was familiar, but I ignored it. I knew I was giving Vel exactly what she wanted, but I couldn't help myself.

"Take them away," Vel said to the guards. "I'll decide their fate later." Vel watched the prisoners leave. She was in her element as the leader of a group of women who would do her bidding. She'd always struck me as a megalomaniac in the making. Now it looked like she had her wish.

"But you, my dear J—I think we have something to settle up right now." The gleam in her eye told me I was in serious trouble. That stoning was looking better and better by the minute.

"Do you think it's really fair?" I said. "One, two, three, four, fi—" I whispered as I counted the guards surrounding me. "Six against one?"

"One thing I learned about you, Jordana, was to never listen to your crap because you were always figuring the angles. I'll just keep my six-to-one odds, thank you very much," Vel said calmly, right before she grinned wickedly at me. "Besides, those sorts of odds never worried you before."

"But those times I could defend myself." I made my point by wriggling in the rope wrapped around me that held me captive.

"I can't let you have it all your own way," she said smugly.

"You're not letting me have it any way," I shot back.

"Exactly. This is supposed to be punishment, not entertainment." She waved her hand, and the guards moved in toward me, closing in from all sides.

"This is going to hurt," I said.

24

"It sure is," one of the guards answered.

†

"You don't look so good," the big-boned woman said as I was dragged into a tiny hut filled with my fellow prisoners.

"Tell me something I don't know," I said, wheezing. Vel had finished with me, at least for now. My mind had taken a holiday for a while as Vel proceeded to show me her bad side.

"You know her?" the woman asked as she obliged me by removing the ropes around my body. The guards had left me tied up and used me as a human punching bag, and there wasn't a damned thing I could do about it. I was boiling mad that not only was life treating me bad at the moment, but that it was also playing dirty.

"Yeah, you could say that, but she's no friend of mine."

"I can see that," she replied with a smirk. She was obviously enjoying my discomfort. Probably because while Vel was torturing me she wasn't turning her attention on them.

"Is there any chance of escaping this hellhole?" I asked. Even the desert seemed preferable to sitting here waiting for lesson number two.

"Nope." The word she uttered was short, sharp, and precise.

"No? That's it? Aren't there more of you out there?" I was hoping against hope that a rescue was in the cards.

"Yep. And yep," she answered matter-of-factly.

"Well, what are they waiting for?"

"Not for us." She sat down next to me and leaned against the wall of the hut.

"You just abandon your women?"

"Once captured by the Velkren, no one returns."

"Velkren? Figures." Looks like I was right about Vel's megalomania. "Well, I don't know about you, but I'm not waiting around to find out what comes next. I'm out of here."

"That is not wise."

One of the younger women hugging the wall of the makeshift hut said, "They will catch you, and you will die."

"I think that's a foregone conclusion now, blondie. I'm dead either way." I stared at the looks of defeat. "So that's it, huh? You're going to sit here and let her kill you?"

"That is our way," the first woman explained.

"You had me fooled. You threw rocks at me."

"It was to scare you off." She sounded apologetic.

"To where? There's nothing out there but dust and more dust. You're sending me mixed signals."

"We are a peaceful race," she said, "but sometimes there is a need for that fact to be hidden."

"So it's okay for Vel to know you're cowards, but you have to beat the crap out of me? I think you've got it the wrong way 'round."

"Vel already knows us. You could have been sent to spy on us."

"A spy?" I stopped for a moment. "All right, I'll give you that one. But to set the record straight, I'm not a spy. Some snake in a snazzy dress left me here for dead. End of story."

"If you say so, stranger. It does not matter now," she said, defeated.

No, it didn't matter. We were in Vel's hands and at her mercy, me even more so. I moved, cursing internally every so often as I tried to bring myself to an upright position. What a bunch of losers. Vel had it all over these women. Well, not me. She can rot in hell. I made my way to the door of the hut and listened.

"There are a couple of guards outside," one of the younger captives spoke loudly across the hut.

As expected, the door opened, and I was the first in line to get a punch in on the guard. "I could use a hand here," I said, but I knew my fellow prisoners wouldn't help me. If I wanted to get out of here, I would have to do it alone.

The two guards finally fell, and I was eager to get as far away as possible. "Let's go find this contraption of yours and get out of here." I led the escape party around the outside of the compound, hugging the walls and shadows to reach our goal. It took some direction on my part to get the other prisoners to conform to a single line policy, as every now and then one of them stepped out of line and wanted to make her own escape. After much hissing and threatening, they got the message that it was my escape and, ergo, my rules.

Their contraption was sitting right where it had been left as if it had been discarded as junk. While the other women prepared to leave, I armed myself with a piece of titanium pipe and went looking for Vel's own vehicle to do a bit of creative tinkering. If they were going to catch us, they'd have to run.

As we left, I looked back at Vel's kingdom. It was built out of scrap metal and junk from eons ago that had either fallen from space or been abandoned in one of many explorations.

"Some of it is from the outpost," the brunette leader said.

I gave her a look. Had she read my mind?

"Epi."

"If you say so," I said absently.

"That's my name. Epi."

I decided I'd better keep my thoughts to myself. "Did you say an outpost?"

"Sure. The guards at the outpost," the younger blonde woman from the hut piped in.

"Where's the outpost?"

"That way." Epi pointed in a specific direction, not that it meant anything to me.

I looked at the vast expanse of dirt and wondered how she could distinguish between one rock and another. "And where do you come from?"

Her finger changed direction to the front of their vehicle, and pointed at the purple sunset. "Twelve clicks that way."

At that point, I gave up. The air was slowly getting cooler with the setting of the sun, and my body was really starting to hurt. My head ached, my muscles had stiffened up, and my swollen eye was pissing me off. A number of times I had to stop myself from punching someone into next week because they came up on my blind side.

Mile after mindless mile passed by in relative silence, and while there was no sign of Vel's minions, it was still after dark by the time we reached wherever we were going. Now I just had to hope that I hadn't traded in one crazy woman for another.

"You're late," a voice in the dark said.

I couldn't see who owned that voice, but it was deep and melodic. Sexy, even. Despite my variety of aches and pains, I might have been in love.

"Vel," Epi answered.

"I see. Come on." The voice faded, and it seemed the speaker had left our presence.

Two guards steered me toward a cave entrance. They led me carefully inside and down a tunnel until we reached an underground cavern. The space was large, well lit, and surprisingly comfortable, except for a slight chill in the air. There were numerous hydroponic gardens scattered around that had been lovingly cared for, while a small mineral spring flowed from the rock face. Makeshift beds and cooking facilities filled the leftover space. Not one square foot of floor hadn't been used. Even the crevices were packed with metal boxes.

"Take me to your leader," I said, and then winced. Why did I say such a corny, outdated line when I could have said, "Hi, how are ya?" or "Whew! That's better," or even, "Where's the bathroom?" No, I had to settle for the most inane statement since time began.

As if in answer to my stupid statement, a space blanket was shoved in my face and a finger pointed to an available corner. After that I was left alone to find a suitable sleeping place.

I suppose I could have complained about not having any food, but as I was finally left alone, I decided not to push my luck. Suddenly a plate of hot something that I could only assume was food was placed in front of me. There goes that mind-reading shit again. I sniffed it suspiciously, trying to decide whether to take my life in my hands and eat it. Then again, the only other option meant I could be dead either way.

Whatever I was eating really did look awful, but I'd eaten worse. My stomach was only interested in filling up, not the actual contents it was trying to digest. I had barely finished my dinner when an urge to sleep overwhelmed me. Not one to ignore such a strong demand, I closed my one good eye to sleep. But what would tomorrow bring? Would this tribe kick me out or would Vel track me down and make me pay for denying her her fun?

Chapter Four

A Brand New Day

I woke up to what I assumed was morning. It was a bit hard to tell, since I was in a cave and one of my eyes was swollen closed, but there seemed to be a lot of activity.

"Up." The voice belonged to a woman standing in the shadows.

My good eye focused on the worn boots in front of me. I slowly drew my gaze up the body to the face hovering over me. Her visage was half-shadowed, but I could see that she had short-cropped blonde hair. Now I could see where Epi got her conversation skills.

"Up," she repeated impatiently.

"This is how you treat all your guests?"

"Never any guests. Only prisoners." Her gaze shifted to the two women beside her, and she signaled them to assist me. They each grabbed an arm and hauled me upright.

"Thanks," I said sarcastically. I never took too kindly to being manhandled, especially first thing in the morning. Obviously they were still treating me as a spy. I had no idea what it would take to convince them otherwise.

"Come." The woman walked off and fully expected me to follow.

We stopped at the entrance to the cave and daylight. At this point, I was glad for my swollen eye so that only one eyeball was cooking in its own juices. It looked like the day was going to be nasty, an intense heat already palpable so early in the sunrise.

"So, what's on the agenda for today?" I asked.

The blonde woman, who seemed to be the leader of this ragtag group, just glared at me from pale eyes. I could now see her clearly—well, as clearly as I could from a serious case of flashover. My vision was awash in white spots from the severe brightness.

The woman was shorter than I was, but her physique spoke of a hard life. Clearly defined muscle was on display under the skimpy outfit she wore. She was a pretty little thing, and I took my time to look her over carefully.

"What's your name, cutie?" A broad hand clipped me over the back of the head. "Ma'am," I amended.

"Beri."

"Tasty." There was a snicker behind me, but I ignored it. My attention was focused on Beri's shoulder or, more to the point, past her shoulder.

"Beri." The woman who spoke that name came to join us. It was the voice from the night before, the voice that made me want to give up my evil ways. She took up a position behind Beri's left shoulder.

My gaze connected with her clear hazel eyes that studied me with both amusement and interest. Her pale brown hair sat atop her head in a riot of curls, tied together with a cord on top and sprouting like some sort of massive bush.

"And who might you be?" I asked as I put on my best "courting" voice.

Beri glared at me. Maybe I was moving in on her girl. I don't know, but something had certainly deflated her cordiality. She had it in for me, I could tell. "Fen," Beri replied abruptly.

"Hi. I'm Jordana, but my friends call me 'J.'" I smiled, ignoring the pull on my split lip and Beri's hostile stare. "I'm sorry. I must look a mess." My hands swiftly tried to push everything on my head back in place, but by the looks on their faces, I wasn't successful. This was all Vel's fault. Not only did she do a number on me, now she was messing with my potential love life.

Fen leaned in and whispered in Beri's ear, her hands resting familiarly on her. So, I was right. I tried to close the distance between us. My move toward the luscious, fawn-haired woman was blocked by Beri. Her stance made it very clear what she thought about me moving in on her territory. As much as I wanted to give Beri some competition as far as Fen was concerned, I decided it was best left to another day when my life didn't depend on their generosity.

Beri was about to turn her back on me when I asked, "What about me?"

"What about you?" Beri's words were dripping with condescension.

"What am I supposed to do?" She wasn't going to leave me out in the desert alone, was she?

"Whatever you want to. I don't care."

Yes, she was. My hand shot out and grabbed her arm. The muscle bulged, and I took a step back. Damn. She could probably arm wrestle me into the dirt. "You're just going to abandon me out here?"

"You have probably brought down the Velkren on top of us."

"Listen, sweetie, that's not my fault. Vel's been pissed off with you long before I arrived." But we both knew better. By now Beri had the whole story. Vel would dig up the whole planet inch by inch to find me because she was a vengeful bitch.

"Besides, I think you need my help," I said arrogantly.

"Oh, really?" Those two words were dripping with so much sarcasm that there was enough left over for a few more sentences.

"I suppose your friend there neglected to tell you it was me who got your girls out of there." Now I was getting angry.

"They did what they were ordered to do."

"You told them not to escape?"

"No, I told them to offer no resistance."

"And that's different how?" Did she really know what she was doing?

"Resistance would only end in suffering. We have learned that lesson," Beri said.

"In that case, why don't you just turn up on her doorstep and put yourselves out of your misery?" If I stayed here much longer, I'd be dead as well. "I'm assuming you girls are able to fight. After all, to get here in the first place you must have done some nasty things, right?" I didn't wait for an answer. Instead, I put my arms around their shoulders and guided them back into the cave. "We have some planning to do."

Beri stopped in her tracks. "Wait. We will do nothing."

I had a bad habit of butting in where I wasn't wanted. I knew it was a failing of mine, but this time it was warranted. "And what did that accomplish?"

"This is my tribe!" Beri shrugged off my arm and stepped as close to me as she could. Her face came level with my shoulders, but her demeanor meant business. "I make the decisions here, outsider."

"I think you've been living here too long, blondie."

"I agree. We all have. A lifetime's worth." Beri let go of her anger and stepped back.

"You can change it, you know. Vel has you living in fear."

"And what do we do?"

I think Fen meant it as a hypothetical question, but I answered it anyway. "You—*we* fight back."

"But she has the weapons," Fen said.

"Then take them back. Have you forgotten everything so soon?"

"Soon? We barely survive from day to day, intruder. All of us have been on this planet for many years. We no longer know anything outside our world here." As Beri spoke, Fen rested her hand on Beri's shoulder.

"Then maybe it's time to step back into the universe."

Without a word, Beri and Fen turned and walked down the path to the cave. I don't think I convinced them of anything. While Fen seemed a little more agreeable than Beri, in the long run it was Beri who would make the final decision.

I sat in the shade of the small cave entrance, watching life, or the lack of it, pass by. I searched my memory for any recollection of Rigeus. The name had been used in idle threats and intimidation, but there had been a useful piece of information here and there. The outpost. What was it about the outpost? Being a penal planet there would be armed guards. I had forgotten about it until Epi mentioned it. The outpost was the only habitable piece of earth on the entire planet, but it was also the place to make an escape from.

Still, I had to wonder at the fact that two tribes had found a way to survive on a planet where survival was considered impossible. Now I knew Beri's story, what about Vel's? Her tribe seemed to exist above the surface. How was that possible? What about food? Any food crops would have withered away under the intense heat. Unless Vel also had an underground crop, where did their food come from? The only possible answer sent a shiver down my spine.

The sun baked the earth as I studied the landscape, and the heat finally reached into the cave entrance and down my throat. I had to give these women some credit for their tenacity to survive in such a desolate climate. I heard steps echoing from the cave, and I knew someone was coming up the tunnel. Moments later, Beri stood beside me and looked down.

"What's the verdict?" I asked.

"We are divided."

"And there's your problem. You need someone to take charge."

"We are a democracy."

"A democracy doesn't cut it in war, sweetheart. In battle you can't stop every so often to convene a meeting. You need a general to make those split-second decisions for you." I had made my point. Now all I wanted to do was find the nearest bar to deaden my aching body. I had been without a drink for two days now, and I didn't like it.

"War? We don't want war," Beri said. "We're quite happy with the way things are."

"Really? You mean you don't want to get off this rock? Go back to families, friends, and loved ones that have probably forgotten your names?" I admit I was shamelessly using everything in the hope of stirring up a positive response from this woman.

"We're not talking about—"

"But we are, darlin'. The first step is to get Vel before she finds you, and after that, the outpost. Then after that? Well, the universe is the limit."

"We can never leave," Beri said, but she sounded a little uncertain.

"Where do you think the guards come from, huh? Sprout up out of the ground? I don't think so. They would have to rotate them every so often, and they would do that by ship." This woman was really out of touch. I was starting to wonder whether maybe she was the one who sprouted out of the ground. Something needed to be done, and soon.

"We should be preparing, not standing around arguing about it," I said. Time was running short. "Does Vel know where this place is?" There was an imperceptible shake of the head. "Well, thank goodness for small mercies."

"There will be no fight," Beri said.

"But—"

"No. There will be no fight."

"Whether you like it or not, Beri, the fight will come to you, and unless you're ready, Vel will swallow you up." I had hoped my words would have some effect, but they didn't. Beri walked away, and that seemed the end of it. I continued to stare out across the hardened landscape, and I nearly missed the scuff of boots on stone.

"You been out there?" the voice of a young woman asked. I couldn't see her clearly, because she stood in the shadows.

"Where? Out there in the heat? Yeah."

"No," she said quietly, "up there."

"Do you mean space? Yeah I was up there until yesterday." The girl shifted in the darkness. "Come here and sit down." I patted a patch of dirt next to me. She slowly emerged into the light and tentatively sat down. "What's your name?"

"Rice," she said shyly.

"My name's Jordana, but you can call me J if you like." I spoke in low tones. I didn't want to scare the kid off by yelling at her.

"What are you doing here? Did you do something bad?" she asked.

How could I answer that? I had done a lot of bad things in my life, but I wasn't here because of them. Or was I? "Not that I know of. Someone drugged me and dumped me here."

"That person is not very nice."

"No." I didn't say more because I knew I would get angry and start using words that would make my dear old dad blush. "But the only way to get off this planet is through the Velkren."

"Why do we have to destroy them? Can't we all live our own lives?"

"You've been doing that now. Is that good enough?"

"But it's all we know."

"But what you know is so limited. There is so much more here—out there—for you." The girl seemed fascinated with what was beyond this planet, but was it fair to pique her curiosity about something she would probably never see?

There was movement in the shadows, and Rice stood. "I have to go now." She was already out of sight when I replied to her statement. I was alone once more to contemplate my next move. These women were stubborn, but despite my dire circumstances, I liked them.

✝

For the next few days, Rice was the only one who paid me any attention. Together we sat in the same spot, usually early morning before the heat of the day was at full strength, talking about life on Rigeus and life off it. I could tell she wanted to see it all, but I knew she wouldn't go without her sisters.

Rice turned out to be quite a character with a slightly warped sense of humor. I really liked this kid. She reminded me of, well, me, asking thousands of questions and not bothering to wait for an explanation before asking one more.

It was while Rice was monologuing one morning that I saw it. "Do you see that?" My finger went up automatically, pointing at a distant spot on the horizon.

"What?"

"There's something moving out there." I squinted in the hope of making the object bigger. Huh, as if. That only worked in Bessie.

Rice stared long and hard, her conversation long forgotten. Moments later she stood, brushed herself off and trotted down the tunnel.

"Okay, don't believe me," I mumbled. At this point I didn't know what it was. It could've been anything from one of Beri's tribe to Vel's vehicle or even those guards that no one ever saw. Hell, it could even be Rales coming to scold me for not seeing Andrissa's deception sooner. Sadly, I was sure it wasn't Bessie.

I must have been daydreaming because the next moment I was conscious of being surrounded. Beri stood in the position of authority at the front of the group, with Fen standing by her shoulder. Beri drew a cylinder up to her face and peered through it. "Gan," she muttered, setting off a wave of murmurs through the assembled women.

I stood and trotted to the front of the group. "Can I take a look?" Beri handed me the cylinder, and I examined it. "Ah, it's a set of maculars. How is it powered?" I flipped it over in my hands, but there were no obvious activation pads. "How does it work?"

By the way Fen sighed, I just knew she thought I was an imbecile. Her hand snatched the cylinder back, and she shoved one end up to my eye. Her other hand grabbed my own and placed it on the barrel, moving my fingers to rotate the cylinder.

"Ah." At that moment I agreed with her. I was an imbecile because it was all so ridiculously simple. Sometimes technology wasn't all it was cracked up to be. After all, that was why I equipped Bessie with the steering wheel. I wanted to feel in control of my ship and my life.

As I focused on the blurry image, Fen moved the barrel until the picture came into focus. The woman in the distance didn't look in good shape. Even from where I stood, I could see that Vel had really roughed her up. "This could be a trap."

"She is one of our sisters." Beri turned her head and murmured over her shoulder. "Go."

The rescue was going to take some time, with both the vehicle and the victim traveling at sub-light speed, so I retired to the cave for a cool drink and a light nap. A meal wasn't coming anytime soon with all the tribe outside watching the proceedings. To me it was like watching water evaporate on a cloudy day. Not like today. It was burning hot out there, and I was tempted to strip down to my skin, but such a maneuver would probably be frowned upon despite their own scant clothing.

So I leaned against the cavern wall and sipped cool water from an ancient metallic cup. Just like everything of use in this cave, it was worn and had been discarded by someone else. Kind of like me.

I sifted through a number of scenarios, none of which seemed particularly good. What if it was, indeed, a trap? What were my—our options? I stood and surveyed the enclosed area. If we were cornered in here, was there any way out? I owed it to myself to find out. Oh, and of course, these women. So I proceeded to check everything, from those pesky nooks and crannies to the sparsely scattered metal trunks hidden away in said nooks and crannies. I didn't find another way out, but I did find some useful stuff that obviously the tribe didn't think they would need. At least they had the good sense to store it away and not throw it out. I extracted a few little items and pocketed them. As for the rest, I let them be for now. As time wore on, I grew bored. How could these women take so long to do anything? No wonder Vel felt they were easy prey.

I don't know how much time had passed as it meant little here. It wasn't until the sound of voices echoed down the passageway that I suspected it had been quite a while. Did I fall asleep?

A quiet murmur accompanied the arrival of the injured woman, as if they were enacting some ancient ritual. She looked in bad shape. Her left arm hung uselessly from its socket. Vel really did a number on this poor soul. I was no sertech, but even I could see that the damage was extensive. The most advanced medical droids in the universe would have been tested to repair the blatant carnage. Maybe this would be the catalyst to make these women see their enemy for what she truly was.

I left the cavern to allow Beri and her tribe to do whatever it was that they did in such circumstances and took a seat on the dusty ground at the top of the ramp. As I looked out over the horizon, nothing had changed, and from what I had seen so far, nothing ever changed. There was a scuff of boots on the ground.

"How is she?" I asked as Fen took a seat beside me.

"Not good. She'll probably lose the use of her arm."

"Did she say why Vel did this?"

"She was to deliver a message."

"I see. And you're here to deliver me the bad news?" Maybe Vel wanted a trade. If I turned myself in, she'd stop roughing up these women. But why did Fen have to be the bearer of the bad news? I wondered if she knew the timbre of her damned voice made my stomach do flip-flops.

"Yeah. Something like that." Fen's gaze held mine, and for a moment I thought she knew.

"Well, at least you're straightforward. So now what?"

"That depends on you."

"On whether I put up a fight or not?"

She sighed. "Yes. Something like that."

"Of course, there is another option." Not that I believed for one minute they would accept. "Surrender first." Wasn't that their motto?

"Not as far as we can see." I think Fen was trying to stop the argument before it began.

I looked into her hazel eyes and saw sympathy. "So you can look me in the eye and still send me off to my death?"

"Yeah..." Fen began to say.

"Something like that." I filled the words in for her. "You need to expand your vocabulary."

"Don't need it. Not here."

"Vel won't stop at just me, you know."

"I know." She sounded sad.

"Then why don't you fight?" Even at the end, I was still trying to sway them.

She stood and looked down at me. "We were told that fighting is what got us here in the first place, stranger."

39

"Jordana," I whispered.

"Jordana." She smiled. "This is our punishment. We accept that."

"Do you all think of yourselves as past redemption? That your punishment includes whatever Vel can think of to do to you?" They were making me so mad.

"Maybe. Maybe not."

After she left, I sobered. I couldn't just sit here and wait for my death. I had to do something to change this, and I really needed a shot of liquid courage to get to that point.

Chapter Five

Looking Death in the Eye

"So this is the place, huh?" I looked around where we had stopped. Miles and miles of nothing spread in every direction, so how could they pinpoint an exact spot without any visible markers? It had me stumped. Still, there was no point in wasting my time wondering about such things. My life was worth—what was it? Ah, yes, twelve hundred credits and, I suspected, some interest.

"That was the arrangement." Beri's gaze constantly scanned the horizon. She turned her attention to me for a moment. "You surprised me. After all that talk of resisting, here you are submitting to the exchange."

"Yeah, it kind of surprised me as well. I usually look out for number one."

"Then why?"

"Let's just say I'm doing you a favor." I hoped I was. I really didn't want to explain myself. "And what are you doing here? You could have easily sent along a couple of your girls to escort me."

"I suppose I wanted to see Vel."

"That could be a risky wish, my friend, and it would probably be safer not to be here." I looked closer at Beri as I spoke. "She'd like you."

"I'm not scared of her."

"Could've fooled me." Despite her bravado, I could nearly smell her fear. I studied the young face in front of me. Beri had lived so much in such a short life. I noticed then that she had very expressive eyes, and I liked that. What Fen could do with her

41

voice, Beri could do with her eyes. "You don't have to prove anything to me. And Rice doesn't need to be here, either."

"I can look after myself." Rice shifted, a little uncomfortable.

"I don't doubt it, but it's a risk you don't need to take." Now was not the time to argue about her lack of fighting ability.

"Don't treat me like a child."

"Rice," Beri said harshly, and Rice shut up.

"I'll be out of your life soon enough," I said to Beri. "Or did you want to size up your enemy?"

"She's not my enemy."

"She keeps killing your girls, and you still won't admit she's your enemy. Why?" I moved to her side and whispered, "What is stopping you from taking action?"

Beri's lips tightened.

"Something you don't want your enemy to know about? Am I right?"

Beri stared at me, and I knew I had hit the mark.

"I'll make a deal with you. If we ever meet up again, you tell me why. Deal?"

Beri hesitated, perhaps sizing up my ability to keep a secret. "Deal."

"Now get out of here," I said.

"There," Rice called out as she spotted a tiny speck of disturbed dust.

"There's still some time to get away." I didn't want any more blood on my hands than there already was. Besides, I sort of liked these two. "You don't need to be here."

"Why do you keep trying to get rid of us?" Rice sounded like a petulant child.

"This is not one big adventure, okay?" I stepped in front of her and grabbed her shoulders. "This woman is crazy, and she is likely to kill you just for the fun of it."

"I'm not afraid of her."

"Well, you should be. You saw what she did to me and to your friend. If I were you, I'd be long gone."

"Then why aren't you? What's stopping you?" Rice demanded.

In my peripheral vision I could see the group getting closer—too close. "All of you are stopping me." My gaze moved to Beri. "I don't want your blood on my hands." My fingers tightened on Rice's bronzed skin. "Don't you understand? I don't want you to die, not because of me and not if I can help it." My voice dropped to a whisper, "Please, Rice, leave before it's too late." But even as I said the words, I knew it was already too late, the sound of the engine-powered vehicle just touching the range of my hearing. To run now would have only provided sport for Vel's soldiers.

"Stand your ground, Rice," Beri ordered.

In a matter of minutes the three of us were surrounded, makeshift spears pointed at our chests. The circle broke with the arrival of Vel.

"So, you decided to come yourself," I said.

"For you, J, I would have crawled here." Vel moved closer, and the ring of spears separated to allow her in.

"Then why didn't you?" I retorted and got a jab for my trouble, opening up a nick in my skin.

Vel just smiled. I could see all the limitless possibilities for my suffering in her eyes. "Take them all," she muttered before turning around and walking away in dismissal.

"We brought you the woman, now leave us be," Beri said.

"Did you honestly expect me to let you go?" Vel laughed, and her eyes blazed with a dark fire.

"That was the agreement."

"And what did J tell you?"

Beri said nothing, but she glanced over at me.

"You should have listened to her."

"Now just one minute." Rice took one step forward.

"Rice," I warned. "Shut up."

"No, I won't shut up," she practically shouted. "She broke her word." Rice pointed at Vel, whose attention was now on her.

"Just ignore her, Vel. She's only a kid."

"I am not a kid. She promised," Rice said.

"Rice," I yelled a second before Vel attacked, her hand swiftly jabbing toward the girl's abdomen. In disbelief I watched Rice drop to the ground. Beri rushed to her side and gently cradled the girl's limp head in her lap. I joined the two of them on the ground, my hands sweeping over the fallen girl as if trying to incant some magic spell to make it all right.

"Damn it, Rice, why did you have to go and do that?" I whispered.

"Be... because I want... ed to be like you." Rice exhaled on the last word, her life leaving with her last breath. Her eyes stared vacantly into my eyes, death already claiming her soul.

I didn't want to look, but my eyes were drawn to the cut Vel had made. It was brutal, forceful, and uncaring in its delivery, and it showed on Rice's skin. My eyes came up to Vel, who was hovering behind Beri. "She was a kid, Vel," I said.

"She was a troublemaker, J," Vel said soberly but the madness in her eyes told me that Rice would've died whether she had spoken or not. No, Rice was a warning to those who would come looking for us.

I looked at Beri for her reaction and saw a mixture of emotion swirling in her eyes. Anger was foremost in her, at war with her passive nature. Whatever belief she held true, she was fighting hard to keep.

Beri looked at me, and I shook my head. Now was not the time for rash actions. My thumb stroked Rice's cheek. "She was a good kid."

"Yes, she was." Beri inhaled deeply and let go the anger, once more finding that plane of passivity that she existed on. "She moves to a better place."

"Do you really believe that?" I asked.

"Yes, I do." She smiled benevolently at me as if bestowing on me some kind of absolution for the young woman's death. I think she knew I wanted—no, needed— that. Guilt weighed heavily on my shoulders, and knowing that Beri did not blame me for it helped a little. Not a lot, but a little.

"Get up." Vel had enough, and she was going to make the separation uncomfortable.

"Come on." I sympathized with Beri's pain. "There's time for mourning later." I came around Rice's body and helped Beri up, giving her the support that she so sorely needed. In a way, I saw a bit of myself in Beri. Not the pacifist part, because I loved to fight, but the stoic part. She would not give Vel the satisfaction of a response, but both of us knew Rice deserved better than what she got.

Two guards manhandled Beri onto the platform and forced her against the front railing. Vel stepped up to me and stared right into my eyes. "You should have left well enough alone, J."

I didn't know that I had stuck my nose into anything, so whatever the cryptic message was, it was lost on me. "I have no idea what you're talking about Vel."

"I'm sure it will come to you sooner or later." Her guards shoved me. "Then again," she said, "it would probably be better sooner. You may not be up to any serious thinking later." She chuckled and continued on to the vehicle, where she sidled up to Beri and pressed herself against the smaller woman. Vel was making her very uncomfortable, and everyone knew it. She chuckled louder as Beri squirmed around trying to put space between them.

Meanwhile, I was barely on the platform at the back and shackled to the handrail. Only my tentative grip held me to the contraption, otherwise I'd be dragging along behind in the dirt. I'm not exactly sure what happened, but suddenly I was doing just that, my back taking the brunt of the contact with the ground. The vehicle picked up speed, scraping even harder against my clothed back. The cloth soon disintegrated, leaving my bare skin exposed to the abrasive dust.

I tried to find somewhere inside myself to get lost, but the pain slowly increased until I couldn't stand it any longer. Layers of skin were disappearing quickly under the constant scraping, leaving my nerve endings exposed and inflamed. This was just the start, and I was ready to throw in the towel. Hell, I would find religion if it would stop the pain.

But that was not meant to be. Mile after mile of endless agony was all I knew for the next hour or so, as time and distance lost all meaning to me. At some point I must have passed out, because the next thing I knew, I was lying facedown in the dirt. I looked around as I tried to take in my surroundings before the pain overwhelmed me.

"Lie still," Beri said. A slow drizzle of water ran over my back, and I struggled to hold in the anguished cry that wanted to come out. "I'm washing off the dust," Beri said soothingly.

"Fine. Just don't... take... too long." I was barely hanging onto my brash façade. "Check my pockets." The water stopped, pooling in the small of my back. It slowly evaporated in the warm room. Beri jostled me as her hand fished around in my pants pockets. On any other day I would have encouraged her, but right now I couldn't wait for her searching to end.

"What're these?" She held up the half a dozen small packages nestled in her palm. She picked up one of the items in question.

"That thing in your left hand is medispray. Push the button on top and spray it over my back," I said with a strained voice. I could barely think straight with the intense pain.

"And what will it do?" Beri asked as she proceeded to use the spray.

"It's medispray. It'll... put a thin film of artificial skin over my back while it heals." My body slowly relaxed as the anaesthetic took effect, and despite our dire situation, I smiled. I was just happy I was lying down and the stinging had subsided because I knew the circumstances would change soon enough.

"So what did I miss?" I struggled to whisper.

Beri shrugged. "Not much."

"Huh." It was all I could manage to say. As far as Beri was concerned, it was a matter of I don't ask and she wouldn't tell, which meant that Vel, being Vel, probably played a game of touchy-feely with her prisoner. Beri tried to hide her discomfort, but I knew better.

"Sorry. You okay?" I asked. I wanted to know more, but I could see Beri didn't want to discuss it.

"What are these?" Beri changed the subject, and I let her.

"The long cylinder is a laser, so don't point it at anything you don't want to put a hole in." The "long cylinder" as I called it was really not more than a palm's width in length and about half an inch in diameter.

"How does it work?" Beri waved it around.

"Will you stop?" I gasped as my jostling sent a spike of pain through my back nerves. It seemed the medispray was still trying to work. I tried to relax, allowing muscle, sinew, and skin surface, or lack thereof, to loosen. I was in serious trouble.

"There's a small depression on the barrel near one end. That's the end you hold." I saw another tube in her hand. "The other small tube that rattles has water tablets in it." Actually, they were rehydration tablets, but the more common expression was water tablets. We were in the desert, so I figured I would need them sooner or later. It looked like it was going to be sooner.

"Water tablets?"

"They're rehydration tablets." When Beri's expression didn't change, I elaborated. "When you're out in the desert, you get thirsty. If you don't drink, you dehydrate. You lose moisture from your body. These tablets help to slow down that moisture loss. It doesn't replace water, but it helps to keep you going." I knew a little more about it but trying to explain things like electrolytes and such would be just a waste of time for both of us. "You'd better give me a couple of those."

"Do you need water?" Beri made a move toward the water bucket near the door then stopped.

"Yes, but that's not the reason. I want to keep them handy for tomorrow."

"Are you going somewhere?"

"Hopefully only a few feet away, but who knows what Vel has in mind." One thing about Vel, she was very inventive when she wanted to be. When Beri stood to make her way to the water bucket, I said, "Find hiding spots for those things. Don't let Vel get them."

I watched carefully where she put them in case something happened. I was hoping that it wouldn't come to that, but I might only have one opportunity and I needed to know where they were.

Beri came back to me with a tin cup, and she eased herself down to the dusty floor to help me with the water. I struggled to my elbows, my back stinging every now and then, but most of the pain had receded. "Thanks," I said between sips. I watched her carefully as she fed me the water. Her gaze met mine for a moment before returning to the cup and my lips.

"So what's the other stuff?"

"Rations, mostly." I was hoping she wouldn't ask, especially with her aversion to violence. I didn't know how old or stable the explosives were, but if it came down to a last resort, Beri would be far away from here before that happened.

We heard a rustle, the door opened, and Vel stepped in. "I see you've made yourselves comfortable."

"What do you want now?" Even to me my voice sounded weary.

"I've come to tuck you in, J. Tomorrow's going to be a long day." I didn't like the way she said "long," because it probably meant trouble for me.

"I'll set the alarm for seven, then. Tell room service I want a large breakfast."

One of the guards kicked me in the side, and Vel laughed. "Good. Very good. Let's just see if you have that same sense of humor by tomorrow night."

As she turned away, I couldn't help but call out, "What? No dinner? That's bad manners on the part of the hostess."

She hesitated but continued out the door without uttering another word.

"Why do you do that?" Beri asked.

"What?"

"Make her mad like that?"

"Yeah, I know, it's a failing of mine. I just can't help myself." I thought about it. "I suppose it's so Vel doesn't think she's beaten me."

"And because of that, she might not feed us. I'm not sure that's an effective strategy."

I glared at her, but only for a second. She was right. "Sorry." I lowered myself back down to the dirt, inhaling sand up my nose. I sneezed and instantly regretted it, because it jarred my back.

Despite my smart mouth, dinner arrived soon afterward, and it gave me a fairly good idea that I was going to need all the strength I could get for whatever Vel had in mind. While not in the class of Augur's Emporium on Alterius Proximus, the food was palatable. At least it was better than the glop Beri's tribe survived on, which again made me wonder where Vel got all this stuff. The adrenaline in my body was wearing off, leaving me weak and tired. "Let's get some sleep. Vel promises tomorrow will be a big day." At least for me.

✝

The day had barely begun when I was kicked awake. "No thanks, Mom. Just one more hour," I said. I was soon reminded why I was sleeping on my stomach by a whack across my back that had me standing up pretty quickly. I was on my feet before the woman had even deposited the end of her weapon on the ground. The heavenly skies behind my eyelids were splashed with flashes of white exploding on a black backdrop.

No sound came from me, but my eyes watered from the contact. I was glad I had the medispray on my back. I didn't want to think about what it would have been like on unprotected skin. "Where's breakfast?" My words nearly exploded from my mouth as the adrenaline once more flowed through me. One plate arrived and was quickly handed to Beri.

"None for you. Come." One of the guards gave me an evil grin.

My gaze met Beri's, and I smiled in an effort to allay her fears. "Be back soon, honey. Have dinner waiting on the table, will you?"

"You have a smart mouth," the older of the two guards snapped.

"I've been told that." And it was my smart mouth that was probably holding me together right now.

"We'll see how long it lasts," the guard said, almost as a promise.

I was marched out to the edge of the compound to where Vel and a handful of her supporters stood. A structure had been built overnight, effectively a large upright X. I could imagine all sorts of things they could do to me on that X, none of them pretty, and I

49

was hoping it didn't involve my back. Vel's smirk didn't give me much hope of that happening.

"Strip." Vel's voice carried the few feet she stood away from me.

"Now? Shouldn't we go back to your place?" A metal pipe hit me across the back of my knees, and my legs collapsed.

"Don't make it any worse for yourself. Strip," Vel repeated.

"Any worse? Sooner of later I'm done for, so what's the point?"

"But how you get there is up to me. You can make this easy, or you can make this hard." Vel delivered the words with casual disregard.

I sighed. "All right, but no complaints if they start giggling." My head nodded toward the audience. The metal pipe struck my ass, stinging the muscle with the contact.

"Next one is across your back," Vel said.

"Been there, done that," I muttered. Normally, I didn't worry too much about undressing in front of people, but having such a large audience while I did so was a little unsettling. I stumbled over removing my shirt to hide the movement of the water tablets from my hand to my mouth. I pushed them into my cheek, not breaking them until the time warranted it. My instincts told me I would need them later on.

Finally, I was down to my skin, trying to stand negligently at ease as I was inspected from head to toe. I was strapped to the cross to face a day in the hot sun.

Vel stood in front of me and stared into my eyes. "Have a nice day," she gleefully murmured.

"You go to hell," I said with a snarl.

"I probably will. Oh, by the way, your little friend will have a nice day, too. She will have my personal attention." She knew she had hit the mark when I struggled against my bonds. "By the time I've finished with her, she'll be begging me."

"Begging, Vel? Yeah, begging for a real woman." I saw the fist coming in slow motion and was unable to stop it. First, the pain, and then warmth dribbled down over my lips to my chin. Glaring back at her, I tried to look unaffected. Vel's eyes narrowed, and she turned away, striding off across the compound to what looked like her hut. Had I made things worse for Beri? I sure hoped not.

The first part of the day was easy, just a matter of staying upright. I kept my wits about me and studied the Velkren. These women were as diametrically opposite as they could be from Beri's people. Aggressive, angry, violent, and eager to be off this planet. So why were they here?

Obviously they had been sentenced to spend the rest of their days here, but I thought I knew Vel. She and I were not great pals by any means, but I had had enough contact with her to know how she thought. She wouldn't be on this speck of space dust without a reason. Vel was too clever to be somewhere she didn't want to be.

I feigned discomfort early; I didn't want Vel thinking this kind of torture was too easy for me. The last thing I needed was her to think up something more devious. But as the hours passed, my arms started to lose feeling, and pins and needles tingled in my fingers. My legs ached from the constant standing, and the dehydration sent my muscles into cramps. I bit down on the first capsule in my mouth, wishing in some way that it was actually water. I was a bit disappointed that I didn't feel any different. I knew what the capsule was, but I almost wondered if I had taken anything at all.

The thing that really got on my nerves was the constant jeering and fondling. Being tied up like I was, arms and legs spread-eagled on that X, seemed to be a passport for fondling me. Some of these women overstepped even my bounds of propriety. Now if I had been in their shoes I would have probably caressed a bit of skin or two, maybe even steal a kiss, but some of them—hoo wee! I could see why they ended up on this piece of shit called a prison. The way I was tied seemed to be an invitation to push and probe wherever they liked. All I could do was memorize faces and take names. If I survived this, I was going to enjoy revenge.

By the end of the day, every inch of my skin was bone dry, and I mean every inch. Anyone hoping for a response from me was out of luck. I was tired, I was dehydrated, I was burned to a crisp, and I was very, very pissed.

The sun hung low in the sky, which had taken on a lovely violet hue, not that I cared by then. My ordeal had been long, hot, and tiring, and I just wanted it to end. I watched Vel stroll toward me, a canteen of what I assumed was water in her hand.

"Hello, J, darling. How was your day? Mine was very"—she paused and slyly smiled at me—"enjoyable." Vel deliberately took a sip of water and watched my reaction as she let it dribble from her mouth and onto the dry ground. Her eyes rested on my crotch, and her lips widened. "I hear you've got a fan or two."

"Yeah, we're going out on a date tomorrow night." My voice was dry and raspy. But I stared at her to show she hadn't broken me.

Vel moved close and slapped her hand down hard on my shoulder, aggravating the sunburn and causing me pain with the sting. "My, my, you should have worn some protection," she said with obvious enjoyment.

"Nah, I was trying for an all-over tan. What do you think?" I suspected I looked like one of those crusty clampers from Ro whose bright red shells make them a favorite for hunters.

"Just like you. Overdone." Vel nodded to the two guards. She must have seen confusion on my face as my bonds were untied. "Get some rest. Tomorrow is another day. Wouldn't want you to catch a chill and die on me before then."

So it was for her benefit and not mine that I was being taken inside. Still, I couldn't care less if it was for the benefit of someone I didn't know two light years away. I'd take the relief where I could get it.

Just when I thought the humiliation would end, Vel lifted her hand and waved a piece of leather dangling from her fingers back and forth. "Just one more thing," she added. Vel was taking too much perverse pleasure in my suffering. Her entourage laughed as she buckled the collar around my neck. "There. Now everyone knows whose bitch you are."

My muscles flexed in reaction to the insult, and I barely held them in check.

"Before you do something stupid, just remember whatever you do to me will happen to that lovely blonde of yours." Vel was making damned sure that I knew she held all the cards. Well, she could play cards all day with herself for all I cared. All I needed to know was that I held the Joker and was just waiting for the right opportunity to play it.

"Enjoy it while you can," I growled.

"Or what? We both know it's a hollow threat."

"Do we?" I didn't elaborate but just smiled. Her grin dropped to become a thoughtful pursing of lips. I hoped I had her worried.

"Take her back," she said.

I looked at the pile of material on the ground that was my clothes. "What about those?"

"You won't need them, you being a big tough girl and all."

"Suit yourself." It made me realize just how petty Vel could be. She was a mean-spirited bitch, and I just couldn't give a craz about her anymore. I didn't wait for her dismissal, instead I walked away from her to the shed classified as the holding cell. Wolf whistles and lewd remarks were thrown at me as I walked, but I ignored them.

As I neared the row of metal sheds, I grabbed a bucket of water that was lying around for the guards' consumption and dumped it over my head. A deep sigh escaped my lips as the cool liquid ran down my burnt skin. I could nearly imagine the steam rising off my body from the contact. A smack upside my head followed, but I didn't care.

"Are you all right?" Beri asked with concern as I stepped through the door of the hut.

"Sure, nothing to worry about." I leaned against the wall of the hut until the guards left. Once out of their sight I slumped, allowing Beri to see me falter.

"Come. Sit down." She deliberately ignored my nakedness and the spiked collar around my neck. As soon as my ass reached the floor she rushed over to the bowl and filled the cup to the brim with water.

"How was your day?" My voice wavered as the cool liquid hit my vocal cords.

"Fine," Beri said tightly. My hand touched her cheek, and she flinched.

I studied her closely and saw a bruise here and there, but looking into her eyes told me more than she would ever say. Vel had used her and used her well. If I could change places with her I would, but my place was not much better than hers.

Beri grabbed her blanket and draped it over my shoulders, the rough texture acting like gravel on my abused back. I hissed as it touched my skin, drawing a look of concern from her. "Sorry," she said.

"Don't be. I've had enough of being naked for today." What I really needed was a day or two of sleep.

"Eat." She handed over her plate to me, pushing the food in my direction.

I could see she hadn't eaten, and I was worried about taking the food out of her mouth. "What about you?"

"I'm not hungry."

"How about we share?" Maybe I could encourage her to have something. "You need to keep your strength up." Reluctantly, Beri took a piece and nibbled on it. When I scowled in her direction, she pushed the food into her mouth. She made a show of eating it, and I smiled.

And so we ate until the plate was clean and finished it off with a cup of water to wash it all down. At least we had that.

"We have to get out of here." I could see that Beri was not handling the situation well, but I wondered if I was in any shape to effect an escape.

"We do," Beri said. "What do you suggest?"

"Was that affirmative action I heard come from your mouth?" I smiled at her discomfort, trying to take the sting out of my words. "I'm joking, Beri. Don't take it so seriously." But Vel's words came back to haunt me. She had said I might not be up to any serious thinking later on. I guessed she was right. "I can't think straight at the moment. How about we rest for a bit?"

I was worried. Beri and I were in the clutches of an insane woman with no hint of rescue. I had been used and abused, but I was more worried about how Beri was coping. It wouldn't take much more prodding from Vel for her to break, so it was up to me to be the hero and rescue the girl. Now that I had a plan, sort of, two seconds later I was asleep.

Chapter Six

Help Is but a Heartbeat Away

"Wha—?" Something prodded my side, and I tried to swat it away. There was another touch, this time on my arm. The sting sent a shock along my nervous system to my brain, forcing my eyelids open with a rush. "What?" I asked angrily.

"J. Wake up," the voice commanded.

"Go away and come back tomorrow." I was too exhausted to face the universe just yet.

"J!" The letter came out as a whispered bark, and the prodding increased in strength to become a heavy pat. The stinging pain animated the star field behind my eyelids and added a sun going supernova. "It's me, Fen."

"Fen. Sweet, sweet Fen," I murmured, smiling. "I like this dream." I said a few more words, and I think I might have licked my lips.

She cleared her throat.

My eyes opened, and I looked around. Some sort of dim light shone in the otherwise dark room. "What?" A shadowed face hovered over me, and I knew I could feel the blush forming. Had I said what I thought I had said? "You didn't hear anything," I said, embarrassed.

"Fine," she said, amused.

"So are you here to rescue me?"

"Sort of. I'm here to free you so you can rescue *us*." But Fen couldn't wipe the grin off her face. She was enjoying my slip of the tongue.

"How did you find us?"

"I just followed Vel's tracks." There was a hint of pride in her voice.

"Good job. How many of you are there?" I was imagining a small force of warriors ready to storm the compound and take on Vel.

"Me."

"And? Who else?" I looked around the hut to see who else was there.

"Me," she said again.

"You? That's it?" Oh, no. I went from hope to despair in a split second.

"Epi came with me, but she returned to the village."

"And hopefully she's bringing more help?" I tried to sound optimistic, but a fact was a fact. There were three of us to fight thirty bloodthirsty women. Not three. Me. I was to fight thirty bloodthirsty women. The only thing going in my favor was they wouldn't expect me to do something so stupid. Well, they should have known better. I was that stupid.

"They'll return in the morning," Fen said.

"The morning is too late. We need to do something now while the Velkren are asleep." Then the obvious question occurred to me. "How did you get in here?" I knew very well there were at least two guards outside. Fen held up a large, lethal-looking thorn.

"Poison?" I asked. Had Fen killed them?

"Sleeping tincture. It's almost instantaneous."

"Good. Very good. Can you two help me up?" Fen and Beri managed to get an arm under each of my armpits and brought me to my feet with little trouble.

Being it was so early in the day, the compound was quiet. After I retrieved my clothes and got rid of that disgusting collar, we went on a mission of disabling the opposing army. I took Fen's thorn and began jabbing the sleeping bodies. At least they didn't have too far to fall, since most of them were still asleep. When the tincture ran out, I resorted to my usual method of disabling someone—with my fist. I enjoyed this part more, because I recognized a face or two from yesterday, and it gave me a chance to thank them for their personal attention to my body. I felt a lot better about doing the disabling and left Beri and Fen to tie them up.

It didn't take long to run out of rope, which forced us to improvise with whatever was handy. Wire, cord, cable, strips of metal, belts, anything that could be used to incapacitate them. Some women we tied together in compromising positions just to save on what supplies we had.

There was only one hut left, the one that contained the woman I was eager to subdue. I slid easily inside to stand against the hut wall. Fen stood outside holding the light, which cast a muted glow over the interior. Approaching slowly and quietly, I could feel the thorn between my sweaty fingers. I wanted this woman with a vengeance. She was a boil on the backside of the universe.

I pounced quickly and held my arm across the naked neck available to me. I was about to touch her skin with the thorn when her head moved to face me. It wasn't Vel but her second-in-command, and by the looks of her state of undress they had been having a good time earlier in the night.

"Where is she?" I growled. I was in no mood for chitchat.

"Gone." She glared at me with a mixture of fear and surprise.

"Obviously." I pressed down on her windpipe. "Where?"

"Outpost," she gasped. I studied the woman under my arm and wondered what on earth Vel saw in her. To me she was an ugly bitch, so she must have been good in bed. Maybe she enjoyed Vel's games. I couldn't tell, but Vel would only keep her around if she served Vel's purpose.

"Why?"

The woman didn't answer but just smiled.

"She knows them that well, huh?" That answered my suspicions about where the food came from. And yet even Vel's skills weren't worth that much. There must have been something else. "Come on. What's she up to?"

When nothing came, I insinuated my knee between her legs and lifted my leg slightly so I could put pressure on her crotch. I leaned in and shoved, drawing a yelp of pain from her. A smile spread across her dark lips. Oops, wrong move.

"Uh-uh. Naughty, naughty. What is she up to?" I closed off her windpipe until she was clawing at my arm. "What is she doing?" I spat out the words in contempt.

"A... mine..."

"Where?"

"That—" She inhaled as she tried to fill her lungs. "That way." Her head flicked upwards.

"How far?" I moved my head a little closer to hers.

"Two... clicks." The two words came out between gasps for air.

"And where's the outpost?" I pressed harder as I asked the question.

She hesitated, still holding onto the loyalty she had for her leader.

"She'd sacrifice you in a split second, honey, so don't think you hold some place in her heart." I eased off her throat for a moment. "The outpost. Where is it?"

She seemed to think about it before relenting. Her head pointed in the same direction. "Four clicks." As she muttered the last word I sent her into oblivion.

"So now what?" Fen asked from her position at the door.

"Unless you want to go stumbling around in the dark, I would suggest we wait until dawn." However, I did think it prudent to mark the direction Vel's woman had pointed because in the light of day it all looked the same. The outpost? A mine? What was Vel up to?

I was running out of energy, so after a quick check of the camp to make sure all the women were tucked away, I commandeered Vel's hut and slept in a bed for the first time in what seemed like years. Beri and Fen took turns staying awake while I slept, and I was forever grateful for that. Despite having been with the tribe for a while now, I never really got used to roughing it. Okay, I admit it. I was a tough bitch who liked her creature comforts.

The sunburn was irritating me, but I was so damned tired I ignored the sting running over the surface of my much-abused skin and fell asleep almost immediately. I was content to leave my troubles to the light of day.

†

I don't know how long I slept, but it must have been awhile, because I could feel the heat of the day already and I was still in bed.

"Time to rise," Fen said cheerfully.

"Yeah, yeah, I hear you." My response was less than enthusiastic.

"Our sisters are here."

"Why didn't you say so?" I threw off the blanket and made a move to jump out of bed, but my skin screamed in protest and forced me to slow down. There weren't as many women as I could have hoped for, so I would have to make do. I left a handful of sisters behind to keep the Velkren in line, having my blessing to knock them out with the tincture again if the need arose.

The rest of us headed off in the direction of the outpost, stopping halfway to find the mine Vel's second-in-command had mentioned. Apart from the vehicle stopped outside, it was well hidden. The entrance was barely more that a shallow indentation in the ground that led down a tunnel to the mine itself. With the possibility of an attack, I led the assault while Beri and her sisters followed behind.

The sound of voices and crying from below reached our ears before we actually saw anything, and it took all my willpower to stop myself running the rest of the way down the tunnel. A hand came to rest on my arm and squeezed gently. I looked over my shoulder to see the silhouetted shape of Beri. While her eyes were in darkness, her hand continued to massage my arm. I knew she was advising caution.

This was all so new to all of us. I had to learn some restraint, and Beri and her sisters were about to get a taste of firsthand violence. They were going to see the ugly side of me.

The deeper we went down the passage, the lighter it got. When we reached the edge of the cavern, it was lit up with an

60

orange glow. Small light-packs, buried in the clay-like walls, illuminated the work area effectively.

Beri reacted to the sight. Her gaze swept over the disheveled women covered in ochre slime, digging with makeshift shovels. She had obviously recognized some of the prisoners and wanted to rush to their aid. My hand rose and grabbed her arm, and I shook my head.

I studied the layout of the mine, taking in the placement of the guards and prisoners. By my reckoning there were perhaps ten guards and thirty workers, and despite being outnumbered, the guards were in total control. They hit and shoved the near-exhausted women to work beyond their capacity.

I tended to jump into a fight before thinking of the consequences, but this time finesse was needed in order to save casualties. What the hell had happened to me? In my book I was a loner, not a leader. Maybe I should just leave them all behind and go and do what I do best—knock some heads together.

I was about to say so when I turned around and looked at the expectant faces. Somehow I just couldn't do it. This was as much their fight as it was mine. With a series of hand signals, I directed some of the sisters to the right and others to the left, indicating to use their thorns to subdue the guards. That was something they seemed prepared to do, so who was I to spoil their fun? They could do it their way, and I could do it mine.

When everyone was in place, I signaled and dove into the fray with my usual enthusiasm. There was nothing like a good fight, especially when I was fueled by some anger and righteous indignation. I started with fists, slugging the first jaw that came into the path of my hand, but soon I had a rod of titanium and was swinging it with abandon. Heads were bouncing around like balls as I smacked left and right.

I felt sorry for them, really. They were taking the brunt of my fury, so they really didn't stand much of a chance. It took a few seconds for me to realize the fight was over, I was so wrapped up in the excitement. When the cheering broke through the haze surrounding me, I was finally able to let my guard down. To see the joy flowing between these women made it all worthwhile. It was the reunion of a nation, old and young finding each other.

Fen came up to me and reached for my hand. "Thank you." Nothing more, just "thank you." It was a sentiment that I felt down to my soul. "Now," she said, "let's take our sisters home."

"Hold on just one minute." As far as I was concerned, the mission wasn't finished. We had set out to get to the outpost, not storm the mine, but all the women wanted was to go home with their injured colleagues. "We haven't finished yet."

"Yes, we have." Beri ushered the women to the ramp before approaching me.

"If we stop here, we've accomplished nothing."

"No, we have accomplished everything." In Beri's eyes, her sisters were all that mattered, and I certainly couldn't argue with that sentiment.

But after what we did in Vel's compound, our lives weren't worth shit. It was of prime importance to get off this planet and as far away from it as we could before Vel got back. "Vel is not going to be pleased. If you think she was nasty before, just wait until she sees this."

"And that is your fault," Beri said.

"So it's my fault you have your sisters back?" I took a step forward until she was about a foot away from me. I tilted my head down to look at her, showing her my displeasure.

"You forced us into a confrontation, Jordana, and it's one we are not prepared to engage in again."

"But you took on Vel's women—"

"No." Beri prodded my chest with her finger. "You took on Vel's women. We were left to clean up your mess."

"Of all the..."

"Say it. You obviously want to curse me."

"Beri..."

"You know what your problem is? You want everything without the sacrifice."

I glared at her. Beri was irritating me like a bad rash, or what my sunburn would be like in a week if I left it unattended.

"Beri. Jordana."

"What?" I yelled, then realized who I was yelling at. "Sorry, Epi. What's wrong?"

"Nothing, but if you two don't stop arguing, you'll be able to ask Vel yourself what she thinks of the mess."

Epi had a point. Whether it was to the outpost or back to Beri's home, we had to move.

Beri turned abruptly and walked up the ramp. Epi waited for me to move and fell in step beside me. I looked at her warily. "Are you going to get the drop on me or something?"

"The drop?"

"Prick me with that thorn of yours."

"Of course not," she said indignantly. "How would we get out of here?"

"We can put the elderly on one of the vehicles above ground. You girls can trot alongside. We should be back at the base by nightfall."

"No." Epi moved closer to me. "Leave this planet."

"Leave?" I stopped in my tracks. "You want to leave?"

"Of course. We all do." I could barely see Epi's face, and she seemed amused by my words.

"Beri could have fooled me."

"She is in a difficult position, Jordana."

"Call me J, please."

"She is our leader, J, so she must be the voice of reason." Epi started forward. "Do we have a chance?"

"Of course we have a chance. Not a good chance, but it might be the only chance we have." I would have to approach this carefully. "Things are in disarray at the moment, and while Vel's not here, we can move around a little more freely."

"What do you have in mind?"

The darkness faded away as we approached the top of the ramp and walked out onto the surface. It took several moments before the blinding flash of sunlight dissipated and I could see again. I scanned the area around the mine and saw a large flatbed vehicle. Sitting on top of it were a dozen canisters that I assumed were filled with mud from the mine.

From what I could see, Vel was mining the mud. If I needed any indisputable proof of her insanity, this was it. The woman was mining mud. It looked like the canisters were going to be delivered somewhere, and that only reinforced my suspicion that Vel had a connection to the outpost. It explained a lot of things in my mind.

"Are you up to a little trip to the outpost?"

✝

"This is not going to work." Epi's muffled voice came from between canisters of ochre.

"Of course it'll work. They won't know what hit them," I said confidently.

Beri had stood there stone-faced for a while, but between Epi and myself, we talked her into a compromise. She spared her five best women for this expedition while the rest escorted the sick and elderly back to the cave. I wished there were more, but any arguing from me could have changed her mind. Damn, the woman was stubborn!

One of the younger women, Gan, dressed as a guard, drove the vehicle a little erratically. The rest of us were hidden behind the canisters on top of the flatbed.

I had scanned the landscape with Beri's maculars and discovered no other way to get close to the outpost. The three-story building and compound sat in the middle of nowhere. No one could sneak up on them without them knowing about it, which is probably why they chose that location.

"If she keeps driving like that, they'll know something's wrong," Epi whispered.

"You worry too much." But I had to admit the thought had crossed my mind, as well. I scanned the compound once more with the maculars and spotted the top part of a spaceship sitting behind the building. We were in luck. But if the ship was still here, where was Vel? Did that mean we were going to catch up with Vel at the outpost? Oh, craz.

"Gan, you're doing great," I said, trying to bolster her confidence. I finally figured out why she was driving the way she was. Her hands were shaking so badly, she could barely keep the vehicle straight. But she was the only one who sort of looked like one of Vel's women and fitted into the clothes, so I couldn't leave her behind.

"What do I do now?" Gan's voice rose to a high squeak. She was terrified. The only reason I wasn't driving was that I was still bright red from my sunburn. The dress code for this planet seemed to be skin, and lots of it.

"Drive up to the gate. Keep your head down and give them a wave," I said. She did what I told her, and we breathed a collective sigh of relief when the gate opened.

"Now, drive up to the door and stop," I said.

Gan did as she was asked and sat there with the motor running.

The door opened, and a guard stepped up to the truck. "We weren't expecting a delivery today," he said.

"That's okay," I answered as I leaped from my hiding place and vaulted over the side, "we're not delivering." My fist was already in motion as the guard tried to bring his weapon to bear. I beat him to the draw and felled him with one blow. "One down," I muttered.

"Do we know how many are here?" Epi asked. It must have suddenly occurred to her that we could be walking into real trouble, but I had that thought the moment we left the mine.

"Nope," I said with an evil grin.

"Are you crazy?" She stared at me in consternation.

"I've been told that on occasion. Lighten up, girl. Enjoy the mayhem."

"I'm the one who hates violence, remember?" Epi pointed out.

"You could have fooled me. Don't worry. I'll protect you from the big bad guards." As if they had read my mind, two guards emerged from the lift to the second floor and the guard tower. I looked on the upcoming fights as therapeutic, imagining Vel's face on each and every one of them as I knocked them out.

I systematically worked my way through the building until I had one conscious guard left. I wrapped my fist tightly in his shirt and twisted the material until it cut off his windpipe. "Where is she?"

"Who?" His voice was a wet gurgle, accompanied by drool running down his chin.

"Vel. Come on, where is she?"

"He could probably answer you if you loosen your grip," Epi said with a slight smirk on her face, belying the fact that she didn't believe in violence. It seemed she harbored a secret desire for him to suffer, at least just a little.

"Oh, yeah." I was so intent on getting an answer that I was hindering my own questioning. "For the last time." I still had his shirt in my hand, but it wasn't cutting off his air. I had unconsciously balled my other hand into a fist, cocked and ready to hit him.

"She's off-world," he croaked.

"She left?" I couldn't believe it. "She can come and go as she likes?"

He nodded his head frantically as my fist shifted restlessly.

"Just what the hell is going on here?" Surely he must have some idea, otherwise he would question Vel's apparent freedom of the planet. "And I'm sure you can fill me in." I pulled him closer until he could see the anger in my eyes, but I could see a mixture of emotion in his. "You'd better get rid of that thought, or I'll rip it out of your head."

"Jordana," Beri said, "that is not the way."

"No, it's not your way. My way gets results." I shook him violently, my strength fed by the anger inside me. Again my hand tightened on his shirt. This time I lifted him up onto his toes.

He gurgled again. If he was trying to answer, I wasn't letting him.

I suddenly let go, and he stumbled. I used his loss of balance in my favor, pushed him against the wall, and pinned him with an arm across his windpipe. "Tell me."

"I'm trying to. She left about an hour ago."

"She didn't use your ship." What did Vel do? Sprout wings and fly off or something?

"Someone picked her up in some little old junker," he said.

"Junker?" I had a bad feeling about this. "What did it look like?"

"One of the 'D' classes. A tiny thing with a laser burn on the underside and a split in the antenna dish."

"Bessie? That bitch is in my Bessie? I'll... I'll..." Words momentarily failed me.

"Bessie is a ship?" Epi asked.

Uh-oh. Epi now knew the truth, and I would be in for a tongue-lashing. "Uh, yeah. I'd been meaning to tell you."

Beri walked up to me and looked me straight in the eye. "So what does all this mean?"

"It means that I was abandoned here on purpose. The person I was working for at the time drugged me and left me for dead on Rigeus. Now she's using my ship to transport Vel. That is so not right."

My anger was growing rapidly. "I hope she got her twelve hundred plus interest, because when I find her, she's going to pay big time." I lashed out with my fist and slammed it against the wall next to the guard's head. Acting as a drug, the pain swirled with my anger and indignation into a cocktail of adrenaline.

"Don't hit me." The guard looked scared enough to pee in his pants.

"When is she coming back?" I didn't like the thought of having to wait for my chance to give Vel some payback.

"I don't think she is," he replied nervously.

"You mean to tell me she's disappeared, and she's keeping Bessie?" Now that was crossing the line, even for Vel. "My Bessie?"

"J, will you drop it?" Epi said.

"Oh no, no, no, no. This is not the end of it. Not by a long shot."

"It's just a ship." Epi watched me as she spoke.

"She is not just a ship. She's my best buddy, my pride and joy, my—"

"Wife?" Epi joked.

"Are you asking for a smack in the mouth?"

"No, but everything comes to those who wait."

"Well, Epi dear, I'm not known for my patience." I suppose it was stating the obvious, but I felt it needed to be said.

"I can see that."

"Ahem." A masculine voice cut through the argument.

"You know—" The guard should have been happy for the diversion, but he broke the cardinal rule by interrupting a conversation.

"I would be keeping my mouth shut if I were you." I glared at him, and he ducked his head.

Before I had a chance to say anything more, Epi pricked his skin with the thorn and sent him into an enforced sleep.

"What did you do that for?"

"He wasn't going to tell you anything more," Epi said with finality.

"You don't know that."

"Too late now." She smiled.

I didn't know what was the matter with her, but she was getting too much fun out of my misery. My fingers let go of the unconscious guard. He fell with a thud, a tangled heap on the floor. I brushed my hands off, with a flourish.

"Don't you have somewhere to be?" I asked Epi.

"Not right this minute, no."

"How about checking out the ship?"

"What ship?"

"Well, if you'd been paying attention when we arrived, you'd know there's one sitting behind this building. The one that will get us off this planet." I hoped. I hadn't checked it out yet and prayed it was big enough to take everyone. I didn't want to have to make that particular decision if it wasn't.

"I don't know anything about ships, and you know it."

"Then it's time to learn."

"Don't be silly," she said with some humor.

"Then I'll go and check it out."

"Okay. I'll come, then."

"No. You stay here and supervise." The crestfallen look was nearly my undoing. "Look, tie the guards up tightly. Can you do that?"

"Of course." She sounded insulted.

"I'm sorry, but you being smart-mouthed about it isn't helping any." Epi just smirked at me.

"What? What is your problem?"

"Are you listening to yourself?"

"What did I say?" I was clueless.

She shook her head. "You're really not good with other people, are you?"

"It's not that," I said. "I'm just used to looking out for myself, that's all."

"Isn't that what I just said? Aren't you just a little bit sick of getting hit every time you open your mouth?"

"I thought it was their problem, not mine."

"Well, J," Epi said soothingly, "I hate to tell you. It's you."

"Really?" I was perplexed. "And you're telling me the people I insulted didn't deserve it?"

"I didn't say that. I'm just explaining why you telling me I have a smart mouth is a reflection on you," she said with devastating logic.

"You know what? This is the most I've heard you speak since I've known you. Who are you?"

She chuckled and pushed me away. "Go and see to your ship, troublemaker."

"Hey, you were the one losing this argument."

"Fine. If it'll make you happy, I was losing the argument."

"See," I mumbled as I turned away, "told you so." What was so enjoyable about having the last word? Oh, yes. Being right.

I enjoyed a certain amount of satisfaction striding through the outpost as if I owned it. It was an acknowledgement by the world around me that I had conquered the odds, and that I was one more step toward getting off this piece of rock. I stopped at a blank wall. There was supposed to be an exit, or so I surmised. The ship was on the other side of the wall I was facing, so how was I supposed to get to it? Maybe it was on the second floor.

I backtracked to the turbo-lift and took it one floor up. Confident I had solved my problem, I walked swiftly to another wall. I was beginning to wonder whether the ship I had seen was in fact nothing more than a fake left there to tease the prisoners with. No, there had to be a way to get to it. I just had to find it.

I started at the beginning of this puzzle and went outside to look. As soon as I stepped out into the heat and glare, I regretted doing so. The temperature inside the building beckoned to me, and if I weren't so intent on claiming the ship, I might have stayed put. I trudged around the inside of the perimeter fence until I reached the end of it, or a least as far as it would let me go before I reached another fence. This was ridiculous. How was I supposed to get to the ship or, maybe more important, how did the guards get to it?

I took Beri's maculars from my back pocket and took a look. High up on the second floor of the building was what looked like some sort of gantry attached to the wall. It seemed that access was only possible via the guard tower. But I had just been up there and didn't see an exit.

"Carn Almighty," I grumbled to no one in particular. Was it me or did everything on this planet seemed harder to do? Couldn't one thing be easy?

As I stepped back inside the outpost, Epi called to me, "Back already?"

"I wish..." I didn't wait for her and quickly stepped into the lift for the trip to the second floor. If I didn't get access soon, someone was going to get hurt.

I roused one of the semi-conscious guards and dragged him to the window, pointing at the ship just out of my reach. The scowl on my face must have been enough to convince him to find the hidden release, because a wall panel slid aside and the gantry dropped into place. I was about to return him to his sleep when he slumped out of my hands to the floor.

"You've done enough damage for one day," Epi said as she held up her thorn, her smile annoying me no end. "Go." She nearly pushed me onto the scaffold then left me alone to play with my new toy.

I did a cursory inspection of the ship. It was too big for the half a dozen guards on duty at the outpost. So why would they need something so big? My curiosity was piqued, and so I did the only thing I could do. I snooped around and was so glad I did. The ship had a very large cargo hold, and it was already full of metal boxes. Dozens and dozens of them.

Of course my nosy nature wouldn't let me stop at that. I just had to find out what was inside. My smile widened as I saw what the cargo was. Credits, thousands and thousands of credits. "I'm rich!" I giggled. I had to check every box I could access and found more of the same, changing my estimate to hundreds of thousands of credits. "Almighty Carn!" I blew my breath through pursed lips, and it came out as a whistle. What the hell had Vel been up to?

Tucked in one corner of the hold were more cylindrical barrels. I popped the lid on one to find the ochre mud from the mine. What was so important about this mud? I supposed only Vel could answer that one. I knew she would be back despite what the guard said. She wouldn't leave all this behind without a reason. I suspected she would be returning with a large force to collect what she thought was hers, or maybe she was planning to tie up all the loose ends before she left for good.

Now here was a dilemma. I really wanted a piece of Vel, and I was prepared to wait for her return. However, some of Beri's tribe could get hurt or, worse, killed. On the other hand, we could all leave this rock with her money. Could I wait awhile longer for my revenge? I admit I rather liked the idea of stealing her ship and her money. Of course, I didn't give the idea of all that money being mine a second thought.

As I sat in the cockpit with my feet resting on the control panel, I contemplated various scenarios that could be my future. There wasn't much of an internal judicial drama for me to make up my mind about what to do, even though the only sticking point was my lack of morals in stealing what was obviously crime money. I justified it to myself as getting back at Vel, and that seemed to make it all right. All I had to do was convince Beri of my plan. Just as I was about to go looking for her, she stood in the doorway.

"We need to get out of here, and now," I said.

"Why? Where are we going?" Beri walked into the cabin and sat down in the copilot's seat.

"Off this dustbowl for one thing. Come on, Beri, get your girls on board."

"What's the hurry? Didn't that guard say—"

Why was Beri being such a pain in the ass? "Yeah, I know what he said. Now I'm saying let's go."

"What's going on?" She sounded suspicious.

"Nothing's going on."

"And you're a terrible liar. What are you not telling us?"

"I think Vel's going to come back." I only hoped she didn't ask anything more.

"And? I thought you'd jump at the chance to get some revenge."

"Now that surprises me. You, of all people, have preached nonviolence and yet here you are, encouraging me."

"Not at all. I just know how you think. And there's something else you're not telling us." She held up her hand before I could answer. "But to save time, we'll discuss this later."

Somehow, I knew the discussion would be an argument. "Get the guards on board."

"We're taking them with us?"

"Just as far as the cave. We'll pick up the Velkren on the way."

"What do you have in mind?"

Now this was the part of my plan that might cause a stir, but I said it anyway. "We're going to put them all in your cave and seal it off."

"Seal it off? Are you mad?" Beri's hands began to move. "You'll kill them."

"It won't kill them. We just seal the cave mouth to hold them for a while, that's all. We need to be long gone from here before they surface."

"And why do we need to do that?"

"Can't you just take my word for it?" I was hoping I could avoid an argument, but I knew Beri well enough by now to know she wouldn't accept that.

"We'll talk later." It wasn't a threat. It was a promise.

Chapter Seven

Just One of the Girls

We took a busy few hours to make sure Vel's little empire was unusable. With all the prisoners in tow, we emptied the cave of anything useful, leaving behind food and water for their survival. After much deliberation on Beri's part and stubborn refusal on mine, I reluctantly punched a hole in the roof of the underground cavern because Beri thought the prisoners deserved to breathe fresh air. I was still arguing that point as I sat in the pilot's chair muttering while doing what she asked.

So everyone who wasn't part of Beri's tribe was tucked away in the sealed cave, happily sleeping through the ordeal. By her reckoning, they still had some hours yet before they woke up to their new surroundings. It was more than enough time to finish what I had in mind and be off this rock.

Any vehicles were driven to the mine and cut into pieces with the handy little lasers I had found in one of Beri's metal boxes. Her women then stuffed the pieces into the cavern, filling every possible pocket of empty space, right before I used the explosives I had. I was playing my match-winning Joker to end the game. If Vel ever tried to reopen the mine, she had all that twisted metal to contend with.

There was one final thing to do, and I had been looking forward to it, practically salivating at the thought. It was a bit of overkill, but I wanted Vel to know she was not welcome back here on this rock. Besides, I wanted to blow something up.

The ship was full, with perhaps a seat or two to spare, and I was ready to leave this hellhole. I circled the ship around the outpost, looking at this beacon of authority with some disdain. Beri didn't want to watch the wanton destruction, but Epi was in the copilot's seat studying the landscape with some interest.

My thumb pressed the button, and I felt the discharge as if it had passed through me. The deadly ray streaked toward its destination and exploded on impact as it reached fuel supplies. I continued to fire until the whole complex was in flames, making sure landing was impossible.

Without looking back, I guided the ship to Vel's camp. I made damned sure nothing was left standing. Everything was leveled, leaving a junkyard of twisted metal and flame. I had left my personal signature on the damage so Vel knew exactly who was responsible so she would come after me, not them. "That's for you, Rice," I said.

My thoughts rested on the one lost innocent soul who needed to find rest. "Now let's take Rice home." I flipped an overhead switch. "Everyone, buckle up," I announced over the com. There was a clacking noise beside me, and I glanced at Epi. She struggled with the belt, and I chuckled. An image of a hundred women trying to figure out how to secure themselves was just too much to handle.

"Ladies," I announced over the intercom, "on the left-hand side of your seat is a metal tag. Pull it out and wrap the belt over your lap. To secure it, tap the red square on the right-hand side of your seat with the tag." A rising tide of clicks echoed down the corridor and bounced around the walls of the cabin interior. The sound must have gone on for a full minute and a half before it slowly died away. Obviously, some of these women were smarter than others.

The departure from Rigeus went smoothly, and before too long, we were well on the way out of the system and heading toward the unknown. With the autopilot on, I went in search of Beri. "Time's up. What was so important that you had to hide it? Remember, we had a deal."

"I could say it's none of your business."

"Uh-uh. A deal's a deal. What's so important that you risked everything for it?"

She sighed and looked at the floor, like she was weighing her options. Then she squared her shoulders and looked at me again. "We are the Noorthi," she said in a soft voice.

That stopped me. I stared at her. I didn't know a whole heap about the Noorthi. They were a closed order shrouded in mystery, at least to most of the galaxy, so what I had heard about them was probably myth rather than actual fact. It was an order of women, a sisterhood of sorts. As far as I was aware, they weren't religious, but the lack of knowledge about them encouraged the thought that they were. If they were, I certainly didn't see any of that in my time with them. Sure, they had strange rituals but nothing I would have openly claimed to be religious. Still, for Beri to keep this secret was not worth my life.

"And?" There had to be more to their story.

She looked at me like I was an idiot. "We are the Noorthi," she repeated.

"I got that part. And what was so important that you had to hide it?"

"We are known for our pacifism, so Vel would eventually have come for us."

"Beri, honey," I said, "she already knew that, even without your label. You didn't fight back, at least not until now. Vel just picked you off one by one. It was more fun for her that way."

The crestfallen look on Beri's face was nearly my undoing. Past her, I saw Fen approach until she stood behind her leader and rested her hand on Beri's shoulder.

"What were you doing there? Setting up a new base of operations?" I tried to be jovial as I spoke to take the sting out of Beri's disappointment.

"No," Fen said. "We were kidnapped and abandoned on Rigeus."

"Kidnapped? Why in the stars would anyone want to kidnap the Noorthi?" My brain asked the same question a split second behind my mouth.

"We don't know." Fen had taken up the conversation.

"How long had you been there?"

"Time does not have meaning on Rigeus. You know that. We were but mere children when we first arrived."

"So where are the Elders?"

Beri responded. "Gone, like so many of our sisters. Or so we thought. A few survived the mine, but they are old and frail. We are all that remains. The Children of the Noorthi."

"How many of you were there?"

"We numbered well over a hundred but time, and the Velkren, took its toll until we are all that are left." Beri's expression was solemn and pained.

I knew Vel hadn't been on that rock for that long. My own contact with her four years ago confirmed that, so these women must have been there all alone for many years before that. How had they survived? Suddenly the myths and legends reared up in my memory, whispering of mysterious rituals and forgotten magic that possessed the Noorthi. Could any of it be true? Were the Noorthi as mystical as all the rumors?

I had seen how they lived with my own eyes, and yet apparently, they had started with nothing. Subconsciously, I took a step back, not unnoticed by the two women facing me. I looked into their eyes to see disappointment there. Had this been the galaxy's reaction to them all their lives? I smiled in an effort to bridge that gap once more.

"So is any of it true? The myths? The legends?" I could see they knew what I was talking about.

"Some," Fen answered.

"Some?" I waited for Fen to elaborate but she didn't.

"And some you do not know," Beri said.

"And you were afraid if Vel knew she would use that?"

Beri nodded. "It was bad enough that she used our sisters as labor in her mine. Not that we knew that at the time."

"At least they're still alive," I said.

"True. And we owe you great thanks for that."

"You're welcome. Now let's go and find your home." That seemed the logical thing to do for them, after all of this.

"Or we could have just stayed on Rigeus and remained unknown," Beri said thoughtfully, like she might be going over options.

"But what about your sisters in the other star systems?" I couldn't understand why she didn't want to leave the planet.

"You could deliver the message that we are alive." Beri almost sounded defeated.

"But you have so much good that you can do out there. Besides, don't you want to know why you were taken? Why somebody dumped you on Rigeus?"

Fen and Beri looked at one another. I could see they wanted to know why they had been left to die. I know I would. "All right, sister," Beri said.

Sister? Had I earned enough trust for that title? I supposed I had, considering they had told me their secret. I grinned from ear to ear, and they responded in kind.

"Come," Fen said as she moved from behind Beri to stand in front of me. She grasped my hand and led me to the common room. There stood the tribe, murmuring in low tones at my approach. The circle of women broke to allow the three of us to stand in the middle.

"What's going on?"

"This is part of your indoctrination," Beri said to me in hushed tones.

"In-doctor-what? Oh, no, no, no. I'm not joining you. I wanted to get off Rigeus, and you just happened to be along for the ride. Don't go making this into something it isn't." I tried to leave, but the circle remained strong.

"This is your path," Fen said, her voice low and sweet.

"Fen, you stop this right now." Why did I have the feeling I was losing this battle?

Beri came up behind me and rested her hands gently on my sunburned shoulders. "We sense your desire to be part of something bigger. You need this."

"I don't need this. Stop trying to confuse me." I made the mistake of looking over my shoulder at Beri and into her eyes. In this light, I could sense everything. The flip-flops I had felt for

Fen's voice had turned into a light tickling sensation, tenderly caressing my sensitized insides over and over.

One of the older women stepped forward and beckoned me to sit. She unrolled a small parcel wrapped in cloth. Laid out on the floor was a primitive set of tools. "Your wrist, sister." The deep tone was intoxicating, and before I even knew I had done it, my wrist was in her palm.

A very sharp needle punctured my skin rapidly, and tiny drops of blood spread out in a small ornate pattern. The other women chanted softly, and the air above them shifted as tiny orbs of light danced in the recirculated air. The pain seemed more like a friend, like it was not pain at all, but a warm inviting sensation. I watched fascinated as the ritual unfolded, dimly aware that I was probably the one person in the known universe, outside the Noorthi, to see such a mysterious ceremony, let alone participate in it.

The pain receded, and it drew my attention back to the tattooing. The woman wiped away the tiny drops of blood and smeared into the marks what looked like the ochre dust mixed into a paste. She rubbed gently, massaging in the orange mixture thoroughly. When she was satisfied, she left the paste to sit over the punctures and bandaged my wrist. She put her hands together and bowed, murmuring some words that seemed to be just out of my understanding.

The tiny orbs of light burst into pieces and showered all of us with tiny sparkles that seemed to stick to our skin. Slowly the lights faded, their blessing given and received with reverence. Beri and Fen helped me up and smiled benevolently. "Welcome to the sisterhood, J."

"I'm a Noorthi?" I was so numb with astonishment I didn't even realize what I was saying. I knew it was a big deal, but I can be a real dimwit sometimes.

"Yes, you are, sister." Beri pointed to the bandage. "Leave that on until Grit removes it. It is most important."

I just nodded. "What is that stuff?"

"It is the ochre from the mine."

The mud? "You know what it is?"

"Yes." But Beri said no more. Was I supposed to just accept the fact without an explanation?

"And? Why is it so important that they would go to these lengths to keep it hidden from the Consortium?" Maybe I had partially answered the question myself.

"Because they did not want the Consortium to get it."

"Even I figured that out. Tell me something I don't know." I hated these word games they played. "Obviously, it's special. How special is it?"

"We were barely out of childhood when we arrived here. Our instruction was incomplete."

"So you're telling me you don't know but it's really, really important?"

"Yeah..." Fen said as she grinned at me.

"Something like that." I completed her sentence for her. I sighed. "You women think you can get around me with a vague answer and a smile?"

"Yeah." Fen continued to grin at me.

"Stop it. I want the truth."

"That is the truth. Instruction in our Order is ongoing through childhood into adulthood. When we were abandoned here, the instruction continued for a while but as our teachers were captured one by one, it fell away. Soon there was no one left to teach, so we had to adapt what we already knew."

"I hope you're not expecting me to follow in your footsteps. Passivity is not my strong suit," I said.

"True. You are definitely one in a billion." Fen was still smiling. "I wouldn't even try to change you, though."

"Then why all this ceremony? Why me?"

"You may not feel it yet, but you are one of us, at least in spirit." Beri looked deep into my eyes, and I started to squirm under her intense stare. "You were passive in your own way, J. You tried to warn us about Vel, tried to keep us out of trouble, but you took action when the situation called for it. You were our protector."

"You mean I'm now the Noorthi's enforcer?" I had a bad feeling about this.

79

"That is such a harsh word. But in effect you are."

Wait a minute. This was not a good idea. "The sisterhood won't like that."

"Maybe they won't, but I'm sure you will talk them around to your way of thinking." Beri winked then laughed at my shocked expression.

"Sure, I'll just sweet-talk them to a standstill." What had I gotten myself into?

"Now let us introduce you to your fellow sisters, Ratha," Beri said.

"What was that? Ras-Res—"

"Ratha. It's means 'defender.'"

I looked at Fen like she'd gone crazy. "Does this mean that I don't get any sleep anymore? Are you going to have me flying all over the universe being your personal messenger girl?" I was skeptical with this arrangement. To me it sounded like they were getting a girl with a ship for nothing. How much was this appointment going to impinge on my profession as a space bum?

"You can go back to being a 'space bum' as you call it," Beri said.

Had she read my mind?

"Yes, Ratha, your mind is an open book."

Was this a trick or something?

"No trick. You just give yourself away." Beri continued to answer questions I hadn't asked, at least not out loud.

Stop that.

Only if you agree to be our Ratha.

Now just one minute.

Beri was in my head. Now that was out of line, because it was my turf and no one else's. "Isn't that against the law somewhere in the known universes?" I asked aloud.

"It is outlawed in many systems. I was just, how did you say, 'making a point'?" Beri smiled at me, the picture of innocence.

"I suppose it's too late to back out now, especially with this tattoo on my wrist." I looked at the bandage and just knew the tattoo would be permanent.

"You can still change your mind." Beri sounded sad about that, if I chose not to be a sister.

"What about the tattoo?"

"If you do not wish to be our Ratha, simply remove the bandage." But I saw the sadness there. Beri had hoped I would jump at the chance to be one of them. "Do not decide right now. Think about it, and let us know your decision tomorrow morning. If the bandage remains, then we know your answer."

I couldn't ask for more than that, except I now had to make a life-altering decision. Did I want all this grief from a band of defenseless women? They were the Noorthi, sure, and it would be a great tale to regale others in my old age, but did I want the aggravation? I grabbed my space blanket and went in search of a nice quiet part of the ship. It was going to be a long night.

†

I woke with a start. Despite the prediction last night, I had slept like a baby. Had my mind made a decision that I wasn't aware of yet? I suppose it must have, otherwise I would have been complaining about the lack of sleep. As the bandage was still around my wrist, I knew my answer. Now all I had to do was tell everyone else.

The door slid open, and I was face-to-face with the one person who wanted my answer. Beri. Maybe she could see the confusion on my face, I don't know, but she ushered me back along the hallway. "Come with me."

I followed along after her, catching up with her smaller steps in a stride or two. "So, what do you want?"

"More to the point, what do you want?" She stopped and faced me. "You do not need to fear this. If you say 'no' there will be no repercussion."

But I felt she needed me, needed my acceptance of both the situation and the belief. "It's not that, B." She smiled at my slip of the tongue. "It's..." I hesitated. How could I put into words what I didn't understand myself? There was something there, and it was

81

just out of my reach, something that would make everything crystal clear.

"I know you have doubts. We were born into this life. Born and raised. We have our own fears about returning to the Order. While on Rigeus, our beliefs strayed, mutated. Changed. We're no longer what we were when we first arrived on that planet, and it's something we all have to come to terms with. That's probably why we're hesitant to return to the fold. Our sisters wouldn't understand our new lifestyle, and especially our acceptance of you, my friend. But my belief in you is keeping me strong."

It was a pretty speech and one that was drawing me in. "I don't know. I'm so used to being on my own I don't know if I can get used to caring for you women."

"Caring?" She chuckled. "You?"

"Yeah, I know. Strange, huh? But you had a way of getting under my skin, or maybe I should say under my new skin, eh?"

"I would give you more time if I could, but the tattoo will become permanent if you take much longer."

I looked at my wrapped wrist, staring at it as if it contained all the secrets of the universe. Maybe it did, at least as far as my own life was concerned. "I'm probably going to regret this but..." My gaze connected with Beri's. "On one condition."

"What?" She must have expected me to ask for something impossible; there was apprehension in her eyes.

"No more sneaking a peek inside my head, okay? And that goes for everyone else. It's the only place I've got that's my own, you know?"

"Rest assured we do not make a practice of doing such a thing. You were..." Beri searched for an appropriate word.

"An easy target?"

"Yes, a very easy target. Your mind was filled with such..." Beri hesitated again.

"Depraved thoughts? Yeah, I can't help it. Bad influences."

"No, not that. Bursting with life. It was refreshing and an education." Beri smiled at my blush.

"My brain really thinks of only one thing. Sorry."

"Don't be. It's part of what makes you so unique," Beri said with some fondness.

Unique? Me?

"Yes, you." Beri replied to the unasked question.

"Hey!" Was I going to be the rest of my life having my thoughts read?

"I didn't have to read your mind. Your face told me." Beri moved up beside me and gently placed her hand on my shoulder, ever mindful of the burn. "Come and meet your sisters now."

I stepped through the common room door to a familiar scene. The tribe was once again assembled in a circle, as they had been the night before. Grit was on the floor in the same position awaiting my arrival. Well, this was it. I was moving into unfamiliar territory for me, and I wasn't sure I liked it. One thing I had always known about myself was that I was confident of my abilities to handle any situation, but this... I felt like a human out of oxygen, struggling to understand and breathe in the foreign atmosphere.

"Sit, sister," Grit said, her deep voice rising above the faint chanting of the tribe.

When I was settled, with my legs crossed, the older woman held my wrist in her palm. She murmured something that again set my nerves on edge, something that was just out of my reach to comprehend. The wrap was removed, and I studied the crusted tattoo. It didn't look or feel any different to when the wrap had been first applied, so what was all the fuss?

She removed a small vial of viscous liquid, popped the lid, and spilled a few drops on the ochre. She muttered reverently. It almost seemed like a prayer but unlike any prayer I had ever heard. Beri stepped in and took the vial out of her hand, allowing Grit to continue the ceremony. Her thumbs massaged the oil into the ochre, once again making it a mud-like consistency. Warmth entered my wrist and traveled up my arm, spreading out from there to fill my body. But it was a friendly warmth, a mysterious warmth, a warmth that seemed to come from everyone around me.

Suddenly Grit's words came into focus. "Sordi ka une junto na." Our sister is now one with us. I knew Grit had spoken the words, but my mind had translated them. It was both strange and frightening.

My face must have shown my turmoil, because the next thing I knew, Beri and Fen were on either side of me seated on the floor, their hands resting on my shoulders. Grit wiped away the ochre to reveal the tattoo, blazing with a mystical fire before fading to its orange shape. It was a pretty pattern, looking something like a flower.

"It's the *lokaleen* from our home planet. The oil that you were anointed with comes from the plant," Beri said quietly.

Anointed? Now there was a word I hadn't heard for many a year. Beri's use of it lent an age-old flavor to the ceremony. And it probably was. The Noorthi had been around for centuries, and yet as little was known about them today as it had been centuries ago. Those who lived the cloistered lifestyle jealously guarded their secret. Now I was one of them.

When the ceremony was over, the Noorthi sisters surrounded me, slapping me on the back and shoulders. I had just about reached my limit of stinging contact when Beri intervened and placed herself between the overzealous women and my sunburn.

Grit rose from the floor and left the room. She returned a few moments later with a bowl. Her fingers were stirring something in it, and it wasn't until I felt my shirt move that I realized that she was applying a thin layer of the mud to my red skin. Immediately, I felt the coolness and it was a welcome relief. The sting slowly faded as Grit continued to spread the mixture.

"Come," Beri said. She and Fen guided me out of the room, down a tiny corridor, and into a smaller storage room toward the back of the vessel. "Remove your clothes."

That was the last thing I expected Beri to say. Maybe I misunderstood her. "What?"

"Remove your clothes, so Grit can finish her work."

I glanced sideways and saw the woman standing there, her fingers swirling in the muddy concoction in the bowl. The ochre felt so good that I didn't argue. If Grit could take away the sting from the rest of my body, I'd be in heaven.

While I stood there naked and Grit's muddy hands slid over my heated skin, a thought occurred to me. I don't know whether it was because I was naked or because a woman's hands were touching me that I asked the question, but I did. "Why didn't any of you have sex while I was with you?"

"We are a chaste order," Grit said.

"Then I'm out of here." I reached for my clothes, but two hands clamped down on my arms to halt me.

"We seek the emotional connection rather than the physical," she said.

"But you said you were 'The Children of the Noorthi.' How can... why...?" Okay, I admit they had me stumped.

"Only if the body remains pure can we have children," Grit said as though reciting from an old scripture.

"Children *without* sex? Is that what you're saying?" Now I was really confused.

"Beri told you that you would not understand," Grit said almost condescendingly.

"Ah, so it's one of those 'I don't want to know' situations, huh?"

"In time you will learn." Grit was starting to get on my nerves as she talked to me like I was a child.

"Oh, no. I like my sex, thank you very much."

I had noticed that Beri had been silent through the conversation, and I snatched a glance at her face. There was a deep sadness there, and I knew why. Vel had destroyed something else with her interference.

"I don't have to give that up, do I?" I sure hoped not.

"You hold a special place in the sisterhood, Ratha." Beri finally spoke, her voice wavering on the words. "You are one of us, but you are not bound by the restrictions of our vocation. You can come and go as you please."

"But when you yell 'help' I come running, right?"

"Yeah..." Fen grinned.

"Something like that." I just knew Fen was a troublemaker. "So where are we headed?"

Beri hesitated. "Parnus Helix in the Braxus system."

"Can you narrow that down a bit? Braxus is a pretty big place."

Beri's eyes shifted to Fen for help. "Juno," Fen said.

"There, that wasn't so hard, was it? Now let's take Rice home."

Chapter Eight

A Noorthi in the Head Is Worth Two Sitting in Economy

There was little to do on the trip to Juno. The ship was on autopilot, and I had an unopened bottle of synth alcohol in my hand. I had been begging for a drink day after day on Rigeus, and now that I had it literally in the palm of my hand, it was still unopened.

"Fuck this," I muttered and unscrewed the lid. I took a decent swig of the drink and swallowed it before my taste buds had a chance to analyze it. "Oh, craz! What is this piss?" Suddenly a thought came to me, and I jumped out of my seat. It took me a minute or two to negotiate the passageways to the common room, but I found who I was looking for.

"Did you fuck around with this?" I held up the item in question and looked pointedly at Beri.

"No. Was I supposed to?" There was genuine confusion on Beri's face.

"Well, someone has. This is awful." It was hard enough not to drink when there wasn't a bar in sight, but now I had my salvation in my hand and I still couldn't touch it.

Grit stood up and approached me. "It's probably the tattoo."

"A tattoo did this?"

"The ochre is in your bloodstream. Your body will remain pure."

"You mean I joined this outfit and now I have to give up alcohol?" The consequences of being a Noorthi suddenly dawned on me.

"It looks like it." Beri grinned at me.

I was ready to forcibly remove that smile from her face. "If it fucks up my love life, I may just have to kill someone." I turned around, walked away, and left the now useless bottle on the table.

This was not turning out as I had hoped. Joining the sisterhood was becoming one giant pain in the ass, and I couldn't wait to get to Juno to drop them off and be on my way. I suppose I was lucky I still had the urge to spend some of those stolen credits tucked away in the hold. Now that would be depressing, to lose that urge.

I went back to the cockpit and resumed my previous lounging in the captain's chair while contemplating the universe. I wondered where Bessie was. The thought of her in the hands of my sworn enemy just burned me. They were probably treating her with disrespect. Bessie needed to be gently nudged, or more precisely, caressed, into doing what I wanted her to do. She was a grand old lady of the cosmos, and as such, she needed some soft handling to get her to fly right.

I could see it now. That snake Andrissa slamming the power to the floor like she was drag racing in the Tresellis 500,000. Bessie and me had been through a lot together, and I had promised her there would be plenty more adventures to come. If Andrissa did anything to her, getting skinned would be the least of her problems.

And as for Vel... I couldn't wait to meet up with her again. The scales were tipped in her favor, and I felt a need to even the score.

Can I come, too?

"Yeah, sure." Now I was talking to myself. Maybe the loss of Bessie had pushed me over the edge. No, that wasn't it. I had long conversations with myself all the time. After all, that's what got me into this all-girl club in the first place.

Vel is not a nice woman.

"Tell me something I don't know," I said absently. I stopped for a moment. "Okay, now this is getting scary."

"It is? We haven't even arrived there yet." The voice belonged to Fen. Now that I found out she was a Noorthi, my chances with her were about the same as Bessie ever winning Tresellis. Don't even go there.

"What are you doing here?" I asked. "No, let me guess. You lost the coin toss, and now you've come to make nice."

"Yeah..." She graced me with a shy smile. "Something—"

"Like that. Yeah, yeah." I pointed to the copilot's chair. "Sit."

"So what's scary?" Fen said as she made herself comfortable.

"I'm hearing a voice," I said calmly.

"And that's not normal?"

"Well, this particular one isn't. My other voices at least sounded like me. This one is different." I suppose it should have scared me, but it didn't.

"Does it have a name?" Fen asked.

"I didn't have the chance to ask before you arrived."

"Well, I'm not going anywhere. Take your time." Fen settled back in the seat, mimicking my position by placing her feet on the panel in front of her.

"Okay." I tried to focus inward. *Who are you and what do you want?* This time I wasn't going to play around. I wanted answers and I wanted them now.

Hey, Jordana, it's me.

That didn't help me much. *You'll have to be a little more specific.*

Rice.

"Crap," I said out loud. Rice was the last person I expected.

"What?" My expletive caught Fen's attention.

"It's Rice." It was bad enough that these women had me at their beck and call, now I would have one in my head for every minute of every solar day.

"Interesting." Fen looked at me, clearly intrigued.

"Interesting? Oh, no, not interesting. Anything but interesting. Disastrous? Maybe. Inconvenient? Certainly. Going to happen? Uh-uh, no way."

Aww, J.

No, Rice. You're just going to have to find someone else. "You report back to your buddies, and you solve this, you hear me?" I was getting angry now. How far was it to Juno?

Fen left me in the same position she had found me in. In their usual fashion, they held a meeting, leaving me to bide my time. Awhile later, Beri and Fen arrived in the cockpit to find me dozing in the captain's chair. Or so they thought.

"Did you come to a decision yet?" I murmured.

"We're not sure what to do. This hasn't happened before."

I must have really pissed off someone in this lifetime, and I wasn't counting Vel in that question. She was an exception, and as such, there was a special place in hell for me for whatever that particular indiscretion was. "You better come up with something soon."

Hey!

Sorry, Rice. Nothing personal.

You're trying to move the universe to get rid of me. I think that's personal, she said indignantly.

"What's she saying?"

My face must have delivered the message loud and clear to Beri for her to ask the question. "We're just having a slight disagreement."

Slight disagreement? I should be insulted.

"I like Rice, you all know that, but having her wandering around in my head is not what I signed on for." I turned my attention to Beri. "So what went wrong?"

Wrong? There you go again.

Shut up.

I don't think I could get used to someone monologuing in my mind, at least someone that wasn't me.

"We're not sure but we think it was because of the violence of her death. She had not been prepared for her next plane of existence," Beri said.

"Next plane of existence? You make is sound so... so..." I stumbled around for an appropriate word.

"Spiritual?" Fen laughed at my stunned look.

"That doesn't solve my problem now, does it?"

It's not a problem for me.

Rice.

"But others would have died violently by Vel's hand," I said.

"True, but they were older than her and had been instructed in the Way," Beri noted.

"This is one of those 'I don't want to know' moments, isn't it?"

"Yeah..." Fen started. She just couldn't help herself.

"Okay, I get it, but it doesn't solve my problem."

"Maybe you should look on this as a positive thing, *Ratha*." Beri emphasized the name, most likely in an effort to guilt me into accepting what had happened. It was a low blow, and we both knew it.

I think it's positive.

Don't you start.

I pointed my finger directly at Beri. "By the time we reach Juno, I expect some answers and a solution."

"I seem to recall that Rice said as she died that she wanted to be like you. Looks like she got her wish."

I didn't appreciate Beri's parting remark. It was a solemn reminder of that heartbreaking moment of the young woman's demise. I had felt a deep sorrow and a certain amount of guilt for my part in the circumstances leading to Rice's death.

The following day, the Noorthi kept to themselves, content to endlessly chat among themselves about returning to their home, and as long as they didn't discuss it with me, that was fine. I had enough to contend with while Rice was doing exactly the same thing in my head. At this point, I was praying that returning to the Great House would be the panacea to cure the problem of Rice's place of residence, preferably anywhere else but in me.

We made the hyperjump to Juno successfully and came out on the far side of the planet. I slowed down to blend in with the local craft, and I felt like we were dawdling. Beri entered the cockpit as I was maneuvering the ship in and out of space debris loosely called traffic. It seemed Juno was the hub of trade in this area, and it must have been market day.

"Why don't you just fly in?" she asked.

"You know, for someone who was suspicious of anything that breathed on Rigeus you sure are eager to get caught."

"But this is our home."

I sighed. Beri was being naïve about the danger. "And you got kicked out of it, B. What makes you think whoever did that isn't still here?"

"It's been a long time."

"And it's been a long time for that same person to get settled in, sweetie. Just trust me on this one, okay?"

Beri looked disappointed.

"I thought you weren't eager to face the sisters. What's the hurry?" But I could see she didn't know. "I know there isn't much privacy on this ship. Is that it? Looking for a room where you can just close the door and step away from the universe for a while?" Beri had been through a lot, even though she would never tell me.

"Yeah, something like that." Beri said it with the same intonation as Fen. That phrase was like some virulent disease, infecting everyone on this ship, and I was well and truly sick of it.

"What about Rice? Have you managed to come up with a plan yet?"

"If you don't want her, there is only one option we can see."

"And?" I asked. Here's the bad part. I could see Beri was hedging.

"We could exorcise her." Beri's face expressed her distaste at such an option.

"Exercise? I have her in my head, and now she wants to exercise?" I was confused.

Beri's brow crinkled up for a moment before she finally understood what I had said. "Not exercise, J, ex-or-cise. Cast her out of your body."

"And where does she go?" I had a bad feeling about this.

"Out into the cosmos to roam forever."

I couldn't let that happen to Rice. "You play dirty, Noorthi lady." My eyes narrowed to show her my displeasure. "All right, she can stay, for now, but you're just going to have to find someone else willing to carry her." I felt a need to regain some control over my life. "Tell the girls to strap themselves in. I'm going to take the ship in low and find some quiet spot outside the city. Look, leave this up to me. We don't want to announce ourselves just yet."

I barely gave the sisters time to secure themselves before I moved out of the flow of traffic to look for a suitable landing spot. An open patch of ground outside Juno's capital that would take the ship's size was the only option open to me. It was a tight squeeze, but I'd fitted Bessie in much less. As the engines ran down, I waited patiently for Beri and Fen to arrive. I hadn't called them, but I knew they would come anyway, trying to press their case for inclusion in the landing party. Yep. Here they were.

Beri began. "Ratha—"

"No," I interrupted.

"But—"

"No. I'm going alone."

"We have a more pressing claim than you to go," Beri said.

"True, but they're not looking for me." I hope. "If I run into trouble, I have a better chance of getting away if I don't have you along to worry about."

"We can take care of ourselves," Beri said, but she was convincing no one.

"What's the point of making me Ratha if you're not going to let me do my job?" I stood up and moved to stand in front of her. "Everything will be fine. Just let me check it out first, okay?"

She simply nodded. I knew she was disappointed, and I watched Fen come up behind her and place her hands on Beri's shoulders. I wasn't sure why that little move was starting to annoy me, but it felt like I was watching something so intimate that it made me feel uncomfortable.

"What am I looking for?"

"It's a large building."

"That helps a lot," I said sarcastically. "How many floors?"

"Three."

"Anything else?" Beri was giving me a description one word at a time. "And how about everything in one go, please?"

"We haven't been here for over ten years, Jordana. It's all a little fuzzy."

I resisted looking into Beri's eyes, because I knew I would give in if I did. I would just have to hope that a large building with three floors was enough for me to find it. "Where was it in the city?"

"In the middle," Fen muttered.

"The middle," I muttered back. "Well, all right." I left the ship and moved around the poorer sections and the busier parts of the city, slowly making my way toward the city center. There were scattered remnants of an ancient culture around, either knocked down or defaced in the intervening years. It was sad, really, especially if all that was left of Beri's culture was in ruin. So many centuries of history wiped away in the flick of a signature on a decree.

The Noorthi house was my priority, but I made a detour first. I knew I risked the chance of discovery, but I just had to see if Bessie was at the spaceport. My sweep of the bay with Beri's maculars looked to be futile, and I had all but given up hope when I caught a glimpse of a familiar broken antenna dish. My discovery sent my pulse racing. She was still in one piece. I couldn't see her clearly, but she was here and within my reach. Before I could stop myself, I was sneaking closer to get a better look.

Who was I kidding? It wasn't for a closer look but to touch her. I had to touch her. She was a part of me, and it just broke my heart that she was being abused. Somehow I managed to get to her without being discovered. When I reached out, I noticed my hand was shaking. She meant a lot to me, my Bessie, and I didn't really feel at home unless I was sitting in my seat inside her.

My hand caressed the cool metal and felt the familiar lines and bumps on her hull. I allowed myself a moment to reacquaint myself with her form before looking for any new dents that snake might have inflicted on her.

Okay, I gave it to Andrissa. Bessie looked in pretty good shape considering she had been driven by someone who didn't know her like I did. But that didn't stop my plan to find Andrissa and make her pay.

I tentatively went inside and breathed in the familiar smell of ozone and lubricant. I was this close to jumping into the saddle and riding off into the sunset with my gal until I remembered that I had another ship waiting for me out in the badlands. It angered me that

I had to leave Bessie behind in the hands of Andrissa and Vel, but there was nothing I could do about it, at least not without raising the alarm. This time, however, I made sure that I knew Bessie's whereabouts by installing a well-hidden tracker button. I was not going to lose her twice.

It took more willpower than I thought possible to pull myself away from the spaceport and go in search of the Noorthi's home. It wasn't that hard to find. All I had to do was to look for the biggest building in the heart of the city. I managed to find a convenient rooftop that overlooked the compound. The maculars allowed me to study the layout and what forces, if any, were present. Any chance of a surprise attack on the hall was dashed when I observed guards liberally spread about inside the facility. I had easily counted at least twenty, and that was those I could see. All heavily armed.

I lay there for some time to watch the activity coming and going. A large square building outside the compound seemed to house the guards, and constant traffic flowed to and from there as shifts came and went. Besides the men, there were a number of electromagnetic fences to hurdle as well and I was just not equipped to tackle them. I was one woman—a resourceful, athletic woman, sure—but one woman just the same. Returning home was not an option for the Noorthi, at least not yet.

I waited a while longer in the hope of seeing someone in authority, but I was disappointed. Today was obviously one of those days where the leader didn't come out to play.

There was no point waiting around any longer. I'd been away for several hours, and I knew Beri would be ready to chew me out for taking so long. Just wait until she heard the news. I left the roof with a heavy heart. I didn't want to go back to the ship to deliver the bad news.

I was making my way through the city to the ship when I spotted a run-down mechanic's shop. In the pile of junk outside was a second-hand antenna dish that reminded me of Bessie's cracked dish. While I stood there contemplating buying the dish, a loud angry voice came from inside the shop.

"What did you do, you piece of crap?" There was a smacking noise after the words, and it made me move a little faster into the building. A rotund man was standing over a slightly built kid—more like a teenager—his hand raised for another strike. He looked up to see my angry face. "Can I help you?"

"For one thing, you can leave the kid alone."

"She's none of your business," he said. He pushed the kid away as she lay on the floor too scared to move.

She? I looked again, this time more closely, and I still couldn't see it. Then again, it was hard to see anything underneath all that grime and dirt. I would just have to take his word for it.

You can't leave her here, J.

I know that, Rice. Please be quiet.

"What if I make it my business?"

"Then I'll call the troopers," he said angrily.

I didn't need that. I don't know if he could sense that or not, but getting the troopers involved was not a good idea. "What's she worth to you?"

What are you doing?

Trying to find his weakness.

"Now why would I be interested in selling her?" he said warily, but his eyes glistened with the thought of extra credits.

By the way he was treating the girl, I knew he didn't really care about her, so paying him to take her off his hands was a good option. "Because you're not interested in looking after her," I said. "Again, what's she worth to you?"

He settled a hand on his chin and rubbed it thoughtfully as he tried to come up with a figure. He wanted it all; I could see that. "What are you willing to pay?"

I glanced at the kid on the ground and could see sadness, resignation, and hope in those eyes. While she wished to get away from the abuse, it was heartbreaking to know that she wasn't wanted.

"One hundred credits," I said.

"One hundred? That barely feeds and clothes her." He tried to sound insulted by the offer, but I knew different.

"Yeah, I can see you spend that much on her," I said sarcastically. My gaze raked distastefully over the poor girl's state of dress. "All right, one-fifty."

"Two hundred." He tried to squeeze a little more out of me.

"One-fifty. That's my last offer."

"Two hundred," he repeated.

"No deal," I said before turning on my heel and walking out. I didn't look at him or the kid as I left.

Why didn't you pay him the two hundred? I could hear the panic in Rice's voice.

I don't have that sort of money, I lied.

What about all that stuff in the hold?

Where did you hear that?

Your mind leaks secrets.

I suppose it was hard to keep secrets from her, considering she was in my head. *Just don't tell Beri,* I said to her.

But—

No, Rice. Keep it to yourself.

"Stranger, wait up," the man from the shop called behind me. I smiled. I had him. *Told you,* I thought smugly.

I wiped the smile off my face as I turned around. "Yes?" I asked nonchalantly. From the moment I had walked into that store, I knew I had a deal.

I left the shop well satisfied with the transaction. The owner had his one hundred and fifty credits, and I had gotten a kid out of an abusive home. She trotted next to me as I moved swiftly to get out of the city.

"So, kid, what's your name?" I asked brightly. If I had to guess, she must have been in her adolescence, maybe fourteen or fifteen, but there was a steely strength to that wiry frame.

"Malt," she mumbled into her shirt.

"Well, Malt, say goodbye to home. You're not coming back."

Despite the news she smiled. Not that it surprised me. I had been studying her for a few minutes now, and I could see she was quite happy to leave behind her roots.

"Where are we going?"

I had absolutely no idea. My thoughts hadn't gone past the fact that the Noorthi had no home here now and I had to find somewhere they could live without being hunted down. Suddenly the reason for stealing those credits became crystal clear.

"Don't know. I suppose I'll find out once we get out there." My head nodded toward the sky.

After a couple of wrong turns, I found the passage that led back to the forgotten path behind the city. It took a bit of time to negotiate the boulders and debris one more time, but I was finally blessed with the sight of the stolen ship in the distance.

"That's a trooper ship," Malt said.

"Really?" I had already seen a number of them at the nearby spaceport, but I was interested to hear what truths the girl would tell me.

"Yep. Ships like that visit the Count all the time."

"Who's the Count?" I asked.

"That's what we call him." Suddenly Malt became very chatty, filling in some gaps in my vague knowledge. "He lives in the Big House."

The Big House. I figured she meant the Noorthi compound. So someone named the Count had banished the sisterhood to Rigeus and was obviously Vel's boss.

I thought about that. It had been a random thought, but was Vel connected to the Count? There had to be a connection. The Noorthi, Vel, and the Count all shared one thing in common. Mud. Rigeus mud.

I smiled. I would love to see his face when he found out Vel had his ship and his money stolen from under her nose. He would not be pleased. I could only hope that he would take his anger out on her. Death was too good for Vel after what she had done, so I welcomed any discomfort the Count could inflict on her.

As we boarded the ship, Malt stopped.

"What?" I asked.

She just stared at the gathered Noorthi.

"You've seen someone like them before?"

She just nodded.

"Where?" But I knew where. I assumed she had never been off this planet, so that left only one other place.

"The Big House."

"A Noorthi?" Beri asked hopefully.

Malt nodded again then replied, "Saw her in the courtyard a few times."

"Was she alone?" Beri said.

"Nope. Troopers all around. Like she was a prisoner."

"Maybe that's why Vel was on Rigeus mining the mud. Then again, there's also this Count guy Malt mentioned. Who is he and where does he fit into this picture?"

"A sister would never divulge the secret," Grit snapped.

"Well, can you explain why they're mining the ochre?"

"Now is not the time for discussion," Beri said.

"Beri's right. We need to get out of here before we're discovered." I was already heading forward to the cockpit.

Beri stood in the door and moved restlessly.

"Will you sit down? You're making me jumpy." When she didn't move, I said it again. "Sit."

"Well?" Beri's eyebrow rose.

"You're not going home." I held up my hand before Beri could answer. "At least not yet. I checked things out, and it doesn't look good. This guy they call the Count has moved into your—your—what do you call it? A Great Hall?"

"It's as good a word as any."

"Okay, he's moved in and it doesn't look like he's going to move out anytime soon. There are armed guards everywhere, and before you ask, I am not going to take on a pack of armed guards by myself. From what Malt has told us, he and Vel are working together so it's likely that whatever is here is just the tip of the meteor."

"What about our sister?" Beri asked anxiously.

"Malt said it didn't look like she was in any immediate danger. She's just going to have to wait."

"You seem to have decided our fate for us," Beri muttered.

"You asked me to do this and now you're complaining? You can't have it both ways." What did they want from me? The impossible, obviously.

"But our sister—"

"Is alive. My priority is to find you a safe place to hide."

"Maybe we should have stayed."

"Well, maybe you should have." I got up and stomped away before we both said things we couldn't take back.

I stood outside the cockpit and leaned against the ship's hull, inhaling deeply to get my anger under control. Sometimes Beri could be the most infuriating woman this side of the Lamnus Moon.

"Let me guess. You and Beri fight again?" Epi walked up to me and steered me toward the replicator. "How about something to drink?"

"Caffeine synth?" I suggested.

"What's that?"

"It's something hot with a bit of a kick. Guaranteed to keep you awake for the next two days."

"Really?" When the replicator delivered the caffeine synth, I offered it to her. She took one sniff and pushed it away. "Water, thanks," she said.

Beri emerged from the cockpit and passed us while we were sipping our drinks. She said nothing to me, but she did acknowledge Epi.

"Come on," I said to Epi, "I can't leave the cockpit unattended for long. Come in and sit down."

Epi made herself comfortable in the copilot's seat. "What do you want to know?"

"What makes you think I want to know something?"

Epi said nothing but took a sip of her water to fill the silence.

"What's up with Beri?"

"She seems fine to me."

"Not to me. She's being a pain in the ass." I realized what I had said and added, "Sorry."

"I know what 'pain in the ass' means." Epi turned her head and smiled at me. "Beri is still young, and she has a great responsibility."

"How young?" The question escaped my lips before I could censor it.

"She was fifteen when we left Juno."

"And that's an excuse for her crankiness?"

"She's only cranky with you, from what I can see. Maybe you should be asking yourself what you are doing to make her that way."

"So what do you girls do when you get the urge?" I blurted out. I'm not really sure where that question came from. I was worried about Beri, and I knew the reason why. She was getting angry and lashing out because of Vel's abuse, and that wasn't a good thing, especially in a society that based its beliefs on peace and harmony.

"The urge? What urge?" Epi turned her head sideways and looked at me with amusement.

"You know, have thoughts about someone else. Let's say someone in the sisterhood." I asked the question as a personal one to divert any suspicion from Beri.

"We don't, at least not for what you have in mind."

"And what do you know about what I have in mind?"

You're not fooling anyone.

Rice, this is probably a conversation you don't want to hear. I didn't know how much I could shelter her from my jaded mind.

And how am I supposed to ignore that?

Sing in my head? I hoped she would come up with something a little less distracting than making noises in my brain.

"We're not as cloistered as you think we are," Epi said.

"You could have fooled me."

"We do not go into this life blindfolded. When we are older and more mature, we are given the opportunity to study life outside the sisterhood."

"How old?" I suspected I knew the answer even before Epi said it.

"Between fifteen and eighteen. The time is decided by the Elders."

"And Beri missed out on that," I said.

"She didn't have the opportunity to be exposed to life. Her mother was missing, and she had to step into the position of Ashaltea. It's not easy for her. She's young, inexperienced, and was left on a barren planet with no help from her mother or the Elders."

"And she's done a great job, Epi. I'm not disputing that. The Elders allow you to wander the streets of Juno?"

Epi laughed at me. "Of course not. We have holographic discs that supply all the information we need to make a rational choice."

"And that choice is the sisterhood."

"Of course. The discs only reinforce our belief that our path is true."

"What if you decide that you don't want to stay?"

"That has never happened."

"Never?" I found that hard to believe. "And how do you get into the sisterhood? Walk in off the street?"

"One is born into the sisterhood."

"No wonder the Noorthi are mysterious. Unless you're a Noorthi, you can't join." It wasn't surprising that with such a closed society the universe knew nothing about them.

"Except you," Epi said quietly.

She was right. "Except me." Suddenly the enormity of the gift they had granted me sunk in. I changed the subject. "So that's my love life, huh?" I didn't want to readily give up my chances with Fen.

"Probably." Epi stood and took my mug from me. "Where do I put these?"

"Back on the replicating shelf. Don't leave your hands there, though," I warned.

"Why?" she asked.

"You'll see." I decided to let Epi discover the truth herself.

"I'll talk to you later." Epi's voice faded as she left the cockpit. A few moments later I heard a squeal of delight. Yep, that replicating machine could be a barrel of laughs.

About twenty minutes later, Fen found me in my usual position, but this time my feet weren't up on the instrument panel. I had the starfield map up on the holoboard.

"She can't come and talk to me herself?" I asked, not that I wasn't pleased to see Fen whatever the reason.

"She is as stubborn as you are." Fen flopped down into the copilot's seat.

"While I disagree, because I'm more stubborn than she is, doesn't it go against your rules or something to be argumentative?" I couldn't help it. I was still arguing.

"I suppose it does. I think Beri is just nervous about facing her fellow sisters." Fen shifted in the chair to a different position.

"But there aren't any sisters back on Juno."

"Not those, the other Noorthi sisterhoods throughout the cosmos," Fen said.

"That's not going to happen just yet, so tell her to lose the attitude. That's my department." I took the opportunity to do a little prying. "Can I ask you something?"

I saw Fen stiffen at my question.

"Don't worry it's nothing you can't handle." I smiled as her body relaxed. "Why is it so important that we rescue your sister on Juno?"

"Beri lost her mother on Juno. Maybe that has something to do with it."

"Does she think it's her mother?" That would put a whole new complexion on the situation.

"She doesn't know. But it's a matter of not leaving one of us behind." Did Fen really understand her leader or was she second-guessing her?

"Look..." I started to say.

"Before you explain, I understand. I really do. You will do what needs to be done when the time is right." It seemed that Fen was on my side, at least for now.

"I wish you would tell your leader that." And since we were talking, there had been something that had been bugging me since our escape from Rigeus. Beri had been very upset about not being able to get pregnant. "Why is it so important for Beri to have a child?"

"Beri's mother, Gerasthamée, was Ashaltea, head sister. And it was handed down to her daughter, just as Beristhamée will do when her daughter reaches adulthood."

Damn. Beri's pain came into sharp focus. Vel had taken away a hell of a lot more than her dignity. Suddenly I wanted to turn this bucket of bolts around and go in search of Vel and beat the crap out of her.

"Is this Ashaltea the leader of all the sisters in the cosmos?"

"No, an Ashaltea is assigned to each House."

"I see."

What's the matter? What are all these new words you're thinking? Suddenly Rice made herself known.

Better not to know. I didn't want to be responsible for the spiritual corruption of a minor, but I applied to Vel every colorful, venomous epithet I could think of.

"Jordana, are you there?" Epi's voice came over the intercom. I reached for the switch. "Yeah?"

"The young girl you brought on board?"

"Yeah. Is there a problem?" Of course there was, otherwise Epi wouldn't be calling me.

"We're trying to get her cleaned up but she's—"

"Pissing you off. I get the picture. I'll be there in a minute." I turned to Fen. "Anything else you need me for before I go and see to the kid's bath?"

"You're taking your duties seriously." Fen seemed amused by my constant mothering.

"I figure if I don't, things are going to get out of hand. Now, if you'll excuse me, I've got to go clean the kid's ears. You can stay if you want and make sure we don't run into anything." The autopilot would take care of that, but if Fen wanted to watch the stars go by, who was I to stop her?

In the meantime, my head was filled to the brim with problems. Was Rice going to slowly drive me insane? Would Beri finally snap? Would I be free long enough to find out what Vel was really up to? Who was the Count, and where did I figure into the scheme of things? Would Malt try to escape and get herself into even more trouble? Or would I wake up from all of this and find I had experienced a truly horrible nightmare? I sighed deeply as I went off in search of a cleanser.

Chapter Nine

An Unexpected Surprise

When I arrived at the rear storage room that had been converted into a bathing chamber, it was mayhem. The kid was backed into a corner, trying to shrink away from the many hands attempting to strip off her rags.

"What is going on?" I roared. Everything stopped. Heh, there was nothing like making an entrance. "Hey, kid." What was the kid's name again? Ah, yes. "Hey, Malt, get over here."

She looked nervously from face to face, trying to decide whether she could get to me without being mobbed.

"They're not going to hurt you. Come here." I was stern but trying not to sound angry. Finally she came over and hurried the last few steps to hide behind me. I looked down at the head peeking around my waist. "They're not going to hurt you. They just want to clean you up a bit." With the girl this close to me, I figured she could use a clean. She stank. "Now go on." I nodded my head in the sisters' direction, hoping Malt would take the hint. The kid shook her head at me. "What's wrong? I said they're not going to hurt you." Again, she shook her head.

I looked up at my sisters. "Give us a moment, please."

Once the room was empty, I turned to face Malt. "Okay, they're all gone. Now why won't you let them touch you?" I had a sudden disturbing thought. "Did he... you know?"

Malt's brow wrinkled in confusion for a moment. She shook her head. Lucky she did, because I would have gone back and rearranged his manhood.

"Okay, then what's the problem? We're all women here." I looked her in the eye. "You are female, aren't you?" Was that her secret?

She nodded but her head dropped at the end. Something was definitely bothering her.

I grabbed her arms and pulled her with me as I backed up to find a seat. Sitting down, I was finally at her eye level. "Come on. Let's get this sorted out now." I knew I wouldn't have time later. What was I doing? I've been called a "mother" many times in my life, but I'm sure those that called me that didn't mean the nurturing kind. I had gone from barroom brawler to maternal figure in a few short weeks. "What are you trying so hard to hide?"

Malt backed away from me and began to remove her clothes. Piece by piece the material fell away until she revealed what she had tried so hard to cover.

Now if I had made a bet with myself as to what she was hiding, I wouldn't have even come close. "You're a Davorian," I said.

Whoa! That girl's got—

I know, Rice. "How long were you a slave, Malt?" I asked gently.

"Three years."

"And I figure slavery is illegal on Juno. Is that why you're strapped like that? So he could hide the fact that you were an illegal alien?" The girl just nodded, but a single tear slid down her dirt-laden cheek. "Come here, kid." I pulled Malt back and hugged her gently. "Everything will be okay." The last binding came free, and Malt was able to move as nature had intended her to. "Where are your parents? Back on Davor?"

"They're dead," she said with finality.

"So where do you want to go?" After the sisters had attended to her, I would take Malt home.

She thought about it for a moment before answering, "I have nowhere to go. Can I stay with you?"

Oh, poor kid, J.

You got that right. "On one condition. You let the others clean you up."

Reluctantly she agreed.

"Hey, Epi, you can come in now," I hollered.

The sisters stepped through the door and stopped, their mouths dropping open in shock.

"Oh." Epi managed to find her voice. "She's got four arms."

"No kidding? I must have missed that." I gave Malt a wink, and it earned me a smile. I had a feeling I would be doing lots of things unfamiliar to me to see more of those smiles. I waited in the corridor while Epi and the sisters washed Malt. I took the time to do a little research at a terminal in the hallway and found out an interesting thing or two about Davorians. The day was looking up.

I could hear an occasional tear being shed, but on the whole, the washing was quiet. Epi came and went, finding something fresh for Malt to put on. When it was all done, the door slid open and there stood a girl or, more precisely, a young woman who I had never seen before. If she hadn't had four arms, she could have been one of the many young women on this ship. "You clean up good." I was impressed.

Malt didn't say anything, but she did smile. It lit up her face and changed her whole visage. Was this the same girl I bought in a mechanic's shop? I don't know where Epi found the clothes, but she had enlarged the armholes to take in Malt's second set of arms, which originated in the armpits of her first set. Her bottom set of arms looked fractionally longer than the top set, probably making the use of both sets in unison easier. But to the average observer, like me, her second set of arms wasn't obvious.

You did a good thing, Rice's gentle voice said in my head.

You think so? I suppose I was feeling a little humbled by the whole thing. For the first time in my life, I had changed someone else's life for the better.

Of course I do. What do you want, a medal or something? I could hear the chuckle in Rice's voice.

Don't push your luck.

Sometimes you suck all the life out of death.

I hesitated in case Rice had something more to say, but she remained quiet, so I wrapped my arm around Malt's shoulder and walked with her forward to the cockpit. Maybe I could find something for the girl to do. I really wanted to know what she was capable of, but I wasn't going to push it.

"So, kid, is there anything you're interested in?" Her head tilted in question. "You know. Anything you're good at?"

"I like tinkering with stuff," she murmured. I guessed she had been told rather forcefully not to raise her voice.

"What sort of tinkering?" My senses were tingling. I had a feeling Malt was going to come in handy.

"With, you know, stuff."

I sighed. Malt was turning out to be as vague as Beri. "Malt," I said seriously, "what stuff?"

"Anything I can find. I like stuff like... that." She pointed to the instrument panel as we reached the cockpit. Her second set of arms remained by her sides, probably from being restrained there for so long.

"Do you invent—er, make up stuff?"

"Sometimes," she replied absently, but her eyes were fixed on the electronics in front of her.

She was, as they used to say in the ancient days, a geek, her mind already mentally taking the panel apart and building something more to her liking. I really liked this kid because she was me. Not the geek part, no. I was hopeless at fixing things—at that age, anyway. Necessity made me a crude mechanic. But I had a feeling she was smart and inventive. I could see that in the depths of her eyes. She just needed someone to encourage her.

When I was her age, I was single-minded in my pursuit of reaching for the stars, forever hot-wiring my dad's speeder to go in search of adventure. I always said it was his fault for getting me into trouble. If he hadn't reminisced so much, I probably wouldn't have tried to follow in his footsteps.

Ha ha. Sure, J. Keep believing that.

Well, that's my excuse and I'm sticking to it. "I've got nothing really for you to do at the moment. Everything's here that we need to fly the ship." But I was curious as to how inventive Malt was. A familiar tingle ran down my spine, and that was always a good sign. Something was telling me I had gotten a real bargain for my money.

I could see Malt was nervous about what was expected of her, so I tried to allay her fears. "Come here." I sat down in the captain's chair and dragged her with me until she stood in the cradle of my legs. "You are not a slave. Do you understand me?"

"But... you bought me."

"I know that, but it was to get you away from him. You're free. You can leave anytime you want." But I hoped she wouldn't. The kid had struck a nerve with me. Maybe it was not so much a mothering instinct as a fierce sisterly protection.

"Really?" she asked the question in disbelief.

"Sure. Just tell me where you want to go, and I'll take you there." I knew the other question sat on her lips, but she didn't want to ask. "You don't have to hide anymore, Malt." She watched me, and I let my gaze drop to her arms. "How about you go find something to eat?" There was no point in pushing her. She obviously was still processing my words. No, Malt, you don't need to hide anymore.

†

A short while later, Beri joined me in the cockpit and we lounged around while the autopilot had the ship hovering on the far side of a nearby moon. We were close enough to Juno to make a return trip if need be, but we were also out of sight of any random scanning of near space. Currently I was trying to explain about Malt... for the fourth time.

"Malt comes from Davor. I looked it up on the computer. It was colonized about four hundred years ago. Not long after the colony was established, the planet was hit by a radiation storm called a cosmic splinter. Got that so far?"

"Of course." Beri looked nearly insulted.

Okay, I was being condescending. I knew that, but if I could figure it out, I couldn't see why she couldn't. "The population was affected at a genetic level by the passing storm. The generations that followed were littered with mutations. Two heads, extra legs, ESP, telekinesis—you name it, they had it. Malt has four arms, but

I suspect she also has an intelligence the likes of which we haven't seen before."

"If she was that smart, how come she ended up a slave to some worm selling junk?"

"Her planet was raided and her family killed. Did she have a choice?"

"Well, she could have opened her mouth and ended up somewhere better."

"Somewhere better? I doubt it. No, B, just somewhere else. Maybe she'd still be in that compound you call home." I looked directly into Beri's eyes. "If she's as smart as my smart-o-meter is telling me, she could be the advantage we need. Believe me, I can smell a smart-ass a light year away."

"We need an advantage?"

"If we want to stay alive, yeah."

Beri gave me a look and left. Malt joined me in the cockpit, passing a disgruntled Beri on her way in. She looked hesitantly at me.

"Don't worry about her. She's still upset about leaving the Noorthi on Juno." A little white lie was needed in this instance, because I didn't want Malt retreating into her shell.

This kid is good.

You're telling me. Maybe too good.

I like her.

Yeah, I see a lot of you in her.

Thanks.

"Who were you talking to?" I must have looked stunned because she giggled. "Your face does that little scrunching thing..." Her finger rose and doodled in the air in imitation of her description.

"Um, her name's Rice. She's one of the Noorthi. She was killed a little while back, and her spirit ended up in me. The woman who killed her took my ship."

"And you want her and the ship back, huh? It doesn't take much to figure that one out."

"Well, I want the ship back. And the woman? I'd like to strap her to the back of my ship and incinerate her as I jet off to the stars."

"That's not very charitable."

"She doesn't deserve charity, Malt. She's an evil woman."

"This girl in your head? Would I like her?" It was an almost wistful question.

"Yeah, actually. You two would be great friends." And then it hit me. "Maybe you should get together."

"Why would I want her in my head?" Malt asked curiously.

"Well, then you'd have a friend with you always, and you'd never be alone."

"But what about you?"

"I'm not alone, Malt. I have you."

That was an extremely mushy thing to say, J.

It was a moment of weakness. It won't happen again.

Heh, she saw you.

Rice, if you don't shut up...

You'll what? Shoot yourself in the head?

Damn. Rice had figured it out. All my threats were useless. She was inside my head, and there was nothing I could do to control her. Then it was probably wise that I didn't have a blaster in my holster. Andrissa had that, damn it. Of course, a few rooms away, I could lay my hands on as many as I could carry.

But it suddenly dawned on me that if I was injured, or worse, killed, who could pilot the ship? I had one hundred celibate women, who barely knew what a spaceship was, and a girl who could probably speed-read the manual and fly it by day's end. No, I needed someone who could not only competently fly this bucket of bolts but who could also make split-second decisions when they were needed.

There was only one person I could turn to in this universe who could help me. If Rales didn't know the answer, then he knew someone who knew someone who knew someone. I had no qualms about calling him. I would trust him with my life, and with Bessie.

I moved to the rear wall of the cockpit and ran my fingers over the touch screen. I tapped the earpiece resting in my right ear. "Hey, Rales? It's J."

"What have you got yourself into?" he whispered.

"Why are you whispering?"

"Keep it down, will ya?"

"What's going on?" I found myself whispering in response.

"This place is crawling with guards, and they're all looking for you. Vel's really pissed. She's got a reward out on your head."

"I need a favor."

"Why am I not surprised?" Despite the circumstances, Rales managed a laugh.

"Vel's in with bad company, with someone the locals call the Count." I tried to keep the story as short as possible.

"And how did you get caught up in it? Sticking your nose in it again, huh?" He knew me too well.

"We haven't got time for this. Will you just listen? I need a good pilot. Someone who can be trusted implicitly." I was rather proud of myself for using such a big word.

"Implicitly, huh?" he said right before he laughed at my expense.

"Yeah, yeah, I need a name." I returned to the subject because I was never very good at being the butt of a joke.

"There's only one who would turn down that reward in the blink of an eye. Sasha," Rales said.

"No. Definitely not. Not her. Pick someone else. It's too dangerous."

"Do you think I could stop her? Once she's got something in her head, nothing will change it."

"Then don't tell her. I don't want her involved in this." But I had a feeling my words were falling on deaf ears.

"She already is, just like I am. Like father, like daughter. Could you use a rusty old mechanic?" he asked.

His question was a surprise to me. "And why have you become so interested in trouble?"

113

"Because things are changing here, and not for the better." He sounded scared. "These guards look like they've moved in for the duration, and I don't want to be around if they stay."

I sighed as I rubbed my forehead. This was getting more and more complicated by the minute, and it was drawing in friends who I didn't want to see get hurt. Still, if Vel had taken over the spaceport, then no one was safe. "All right, I could always use a great mechanic, Rales."

He chuckled and I knew I had said the right thing. Not that it was a lie. He had kept Bessie going long after others had given up on her. For that alone I would have him, but I knew by reputation he was one of the best. "I'm on the lookout for a couple of ships— one about the size of my Bessie and one slightly larger that can take about twenty. Both will need to be armed. This has got to be done quietly, my friend."

"You don't have to tell me twice."

"Good, 'cause I'm not going to. Look, got to go in case you're being monitored. I'll be in touch."

"Hey, hon?" I could hear the concern in his voice. "Be careful."

"You, too. I want you both in one piece." I cut the transmission and took a couple of steps to my chair. What was I doing? Vel was bringing a war to me that I suspected I wouldn't be able to avoid without someone getting hurt. I had already lost Rice, and I was damn well going to try not to lose anybody else.

You can't be responsible for everyone, J.

I'm the Ratha, remember? That's my job.

We all expect too much of you.

Maybe. I may be a bitch, but I'm not a foolish one. If I don't start taking precautions, this is going to end badly. I looked over at the kid in the copilot's seat. She smiled at me knowingly. "Yeah, well, she's become my conscience," I said to her. My attention turned to the holomap I had called up. We were trying to find a suitable planet to hide on. "You got any ideas?" I asked Malt.

"I don't know much about out there." Malt stared out the cockpit window toward the vastness of space.

I exhaled. "This isn't my territory, and Aldronicus is now in the hands of the Count. It looks like wherever we choose, neither of us will know much about it."

"What about the archives?"

"It came up with a few possibles, but I have reservations about using them. If we choose one of those, what's to say they won't do the same thing? Consult the archives then visit them one by one until they find us. No, we have to come up with somewhere on our own." God, sometimes I hated this job.

"What about fuel?"

"It's getting low, so there's another problem."

"There's a fuel dump behind the spaceport on Juno," she said.

"And what are we going to do, huh? Just fly right in and say 'fill her up'?"

"Why not? It's a trooper ship."

"For one, Vel would have filled them in about us, and they'll be on the lookout for a trooper ship."

"But they wouldn't be expecting you to do something that bold."

"Bold? Try stupid, insane, balls the size of..."

"What are balls?"

I was not going to sully Malt's innocence with vulgar references. "Never mind." Could I do it? Malt had a point. They wouldn't be expecting it. Besides, our options were practically nil. This was going to take balls, all right. Big brass ones the size of Juno.

Chapter Ten

Bold as Brass

"This is not going to work," Epi said for the tenth time.

"Haven't we been through this before? Why do you have to be so negative?" I muttered from the pilot's seat.

"Because if something goes wrong, then I'm never disappointed." Epi was turning out to be a pessimist.

"Okay, we're coming up on the fuel dump. Everyone to their places." Everyone? What a laugh. There were only four uniforms. I commandeered one, and Malt took another one. As much as I wanted to leave her out of it, she was the only one who knew the layout. That left two uniforms for my two remaining "soldiers." One fitted Beri like a glove while the last one sat on Epi like an overstuffed sack. The bottom half of the suit blossomed out over her backside loosely, but the top half of the uniform lay taut over her breasts.

"Can't you put those somewhere?" I asked as I waved my finger at her breasts.

"And where do you suggest? My back pocket?" Epi glared at me.

"That would be preferable to where they are now. They're sticking out too much."

"I can't help that. It's the way I'm built."

"I can fix that." I made a move to stand up. "Now where did I put that laser?"

"Ha ha. The woman thinks she's funny." Epi looked out the window with concern at the rapidly approaching depot.

"Where to, Malt?" I could see where to go, but I wanted the kid to feel she was contributing something to this fiasco.

"Right over there, see?"

"Yep." I nudged the control and gradually descended until a gentle shake told me we had landed. "Now no one talk unless you have to." I cleared my throat and prepared to speak. "Trooper ship requesting refueling," I ground out in my deepest voice.

"State your clearance code, trooper ship." The monotone voice over the intercom sounded bored.

"Clearance?" Epi's voice rose to a high squeak. I barely managed to cut off transmission before her squeal could be heard.

Malt was already on the terminal searching for information.

"One mo... shhhh... tran... shhh..." I feigned static to buy a bit of time. "Come on, come on." I knew Malt was working as fast as she could.

"I repeat, state your clearance code," the spaceport operator ordered.

Malt brought out her other two hands and four sets of fingers flew over the keyboard. Man, she was so fast it was nearly a blur. Suddenly she stopped, smiled, and turned the monitor in my direction.

"One six nine zero five alpha Michael beta." My heart beat heavily in my chest. This was it. Had those balls proved to be lucky, or had I signed our death warrant? The silence over the intercom felt like an eternity.

"Move your vehicle into the bay, trooper."

"That's affirmative, control." I had no idea what I was saying because of the harsh whispers bouncing around the cabin. I gave the rest of my "crew" my best scowl, and they stopped their chattering.

All I can say is I was glad I had some time in this ship because she didn't want to go quietly. I had to adjust and readjust as she overflew her mark. It must have made me look like a right idiot to the guards standing around waiting to fuel us. Finally I got her where I wanted to and killed the engines.

The section head made a series of hand signals indicating he wanted me out of the ship. Damn. I had hoped to get away without having any contact with them. While I certainly wasn't built like Epi, I had my long hair to contend with. I took a deep breath and stood up. Somehow I would have to talk my way out of this. If not, then... I patted the newly acquired firearm strapped to my thigh. "Stay put." I thought it was a waste of time saying that, but knowing the Noorthi as I did, if you didn't spell it out, they had a tendency to interpret what you didn't say any way they liked.

The ramp lowered to the ground. "Here goes," I muttered to the ship, not that it did me any good. Each step I took down the ramp was like one more step toward my death. It was agonizing and nerve-wracking.

Just as my eyesight was about to get the full view of the field, a woman's voice cut through the background noise. My eyes widened as I recognized who it was. *Oh, craz!* I reached for my cap, pulled it lower over my face, and relaxed my posture in an effort to look shorter.

"You there. Captain. Why isn't Grimm's ship fueled and ready to go?"

I peeked out from under the brim at Andrissa. In the light of day, she looked completed different. The scales were clearly visible on her mottled skin. Her tongue flicked out in irritation. Eww. What had I been thinking?

"This ship can wait." She gestured at mine. Get your men busy. Now." She yelled the last word, and her skin turned an angry red.

"Yes, ma'am," I said, trying to make myself sound gravelly. A number of other titles came to mind that I would call Andrissa, and "ma'am" wasn't one of them, but I had to keep up appearances. She slithered away over the ground to the rather ostentatious ship on the far side of the field.

Wait a second. Had she said Grimm? Could this be the same Grimm from all those years ago? He didn't strike me as the universal domination type. Besides, Vel would eat him for breakfast. No, surely it had to be someone else. But if it was, how did he get mixed up in something like this? If he found out I was here, he'd be just as happy to see me as Vel would. Which meant, not at all.

"You," the foreman said to one of the lowly helpers, "stay here and give them what they want. The rest of you follow me." The group left at a trot to catch up to Andrissa. From here I could see her venting, her arms waving in the direction of the ship and then the stockpile of rods.

"So," the young guard said brightly, "let's get you on your way, eh?"

"Sure." This made things a little easier. If I had to fight my way out, I only had one guard to contend with. I had no idea where the fuel went, so I walked to the pile of fuel rods. "Can you get the hatch?"

Craz! I lifted one of the rods and nearly gave myself a hernia. Suddenly the weight lessened as the young man grabbed the other end. "Keep doing that and you'll be in the infirmary," he joked.

"Don't you guys get hurt?"

"We have robots for that, but as you can see they're tied up." He nodded in the direction of the hive of activity. "You've got long hair."

This was it. Could I get to my blaster quick enough before he sounded the alarm? "Yeah, it's for religious reasons." I always found that if something was strange, claim it was for religious reasons.

"Fair enough. Just don't let the boss catch you."

"The boss?" Which boss were we talking about?

"You know. Him."

"The Count?" Could I find out more?

"Yeah, him."

"Doesn't he ever get tired of being called that? You know, what with his other name and all." I had to know for sure. Was Grimm the man they called the Count?

"From what I've seen, he seems to enjoy it."

"I've never had the pleasure of seeing him. I'm stuck on outpost duty." And the farther away the better. "Maybe it was the hair that sent me there."

"Maybe," he said with a chuckle. He guided the rod into the slot, and we went back for another. I looked around. Maybe we could get away with grabbing more fuel than we were entitled to.

All the activity was on the far side of the tarmac, leaving the two of us alone. I looked over my shoulder and sensed my shipmates were watching. I hoped my hasty hand signals would convey what I wanted them to do. We were about to steal some rods, and I only hoped Beri would forgive me in time. Meanwhile, I kept my coworker occupied. "So what does he look like? Back at our base we always wonder that."

"Well..." He looked around to see if he would get caught gossiping. "He seems a bit snobby."

Oh, no. It was him. It seemed that Grimm had delusions of grandeur. It must have been catching. First Vel and now Grimm. "Really?" I tried to sound casual. "But—" I caught movement out of the corner of my eye and shifted the guard so he couldn't see what was going on behind him. "I dunno, this guy as the next leader of the universe?"

"Leader of the universe? Where did you hear that?"

Okay, now I was confused. "Then what's he doing here?" I lifted my end of another rod casually. This conversation was proving most enlightening.

"What, you think they're going to tell us? All I know is that some big, fancy ship comes in once or twice and all hell breaks loose. You think that was something?" He pointed to the ship at the end of the field. "This other ship draws out the entire city. I heard a rumor, though, that the boss is gunning for somebody. Heard somebody did him wrong a while back—caused him some big problems—and he's all twisted up about it." The guard shrugged. "Glad it's not me. He's got some crazy bitch with him, now, and from what I've heard, she's one sick lady." He looked around, worried, but nobody else could've heard him.

"Damn. I'll definitely keep to my outpost." So, I finally had my answer. Obviously, Grimm never got over the failed delivery all those years ago. He wanted me dead, plain and simple, and he'd used Andrissa's obvious wiles to lure me into the trap. But did he have any idea that in marooning me on Rigeus he was putting me on a collision course with him? Or did he expect Vel to solve his problem for him? That seemed more likely. He threw a piece of meat to the carnivore and expected there to be nothing left.

Well, I showed him. The loading of the rods was slow work, and I made sure that I kept this guy busy because I certainly didn't want him discovering the pilfering that was going on behind his back. We talked about mundane things, and my storytelling prowess was on show as I described life at a trooper outpost. I'm sure he would quit the force before he accepted a posting out in the spiral arm.

The activity had finished, and the fueling garrison was returning to duty.

"Well, that's about it," I said. "Anything I need to sign or what?" Signatures were a thing of the past, but the meaning was the same.

"Nope. That's it. Just your name and number."

Luckily I found that before I left the ship. "Garmen, one nine seven two two."

"Thanks," he said, and his finger swept over his hand-held recorder. "Have a good trip." He turned and walked back to the hangar, his hand raised over his shoulder in farewell.

"As if," I hollered back, in keeping with the story I'd told him of an outpost that survived on the edge of an exanol swamp, the horrifying smell from the gases filtering through every orifice in the place. He now knew that I wanted to be anywhere but there.

I hurried on board and jumped into the pilot's chair in an attempt to get the ship off the ground before the theft was discovered. "Strap in." I had barely said the words before the craft lifted off and headed toward the stratosphere.

"Whoa!" Malt was hanging onto her belt as I accelerated at a dangerous rate. "Slow down."

"Not until we're safe." Here, "safe" was a relative word. I suppose it depended on whether we wanted to risk incineration escaping so fast or dawdle and get caught for theft, right before they discovered who they had and then the real trouble would start. Now me, I'd take my chances with a risky escape, and as I didn't want a lengthy discussion on the matter, my choice was the only one that mattered.

I had the computer do the calculations for a hyperjump, so I could activate it as soon as we were out of gravitational range. This was just one more thing I would have to teach Malt. With her four hands, she could do it in half the time it took me with my two fingers.

The jump went smoothly, and we exited just past Ix, the farthest planet in the system from Juno. I parked the vehicle on the other side the planet, out of scanner range.

One angry Noorthi stood in the doorway. "What the blazes are you doing?" Beri asked. "That was reckless. None of us was ready. The common room is a shambles."

"Sorry, B, but I couldn't take the chance of being caught."

"Was it that bad?" Beri's anger faded.

"Andrissa was there." I said the name as if it would explain everything.

"And who's Andrissa?"

"She's the one who abandoned me on Rigeus." Every time I thought of that snake, I got angry. She had duped me so easily.

"Oh. Well, please try not to do it again." Beri looked at Malt, who was sitting in the copilot's seat. "Could you give me a hand to help clean up?" she asked her.

"Sure." Malt jumped out of her seat and disappeared through the doorway.

It took only a few moments before Fen appeared in the doorway. Obviously Beri had sent her to talk to me.

"Oh, great. What did I do now?" Whenever Fen was around, I was in trouble, and usually with Beri.

"What makes you think you've done something wrong?" She made herself comfortable in the spare chair.

"You're here and B isn't. What more is there to say?"

Fen just sat there silently.

"All right, what do you want to know?" These were battles I wasn't going to win. Fen was way more patient than I ever was.

"What's got you so all fired up that you're leaving the planet like you have a fuel rod up your... ass." She hesitated on the last word.

"Ass, Fen?" I smiled. The Noorthi were not known for their cussing, so it came as a bit of a surprise. It looked like I was having a bigger effect on them than I thought, so maybe I should clean up my act. I couldn't have holy women cussing out the universe. "Besides running into the one person on that planet who knew who I was, you mean?" Did I want to know the truth myself? Probably not.

"Does sound like a reason to leave in a hurry." Fen sounded sympathetic.

"This thing is getting bigger and bigger, Fen, and I don't know where it will all end. When I took on this job, it was a matter of getting you girls home. With all this other stuff, I don't know if I'm up to it." I had been looking out the window at the huge visible crescent of Ix. Their sun was on the other side of the planet, so we were sitting on their dark side.

Fen reached over and placed her hand on top of mine, and it was warm and soft and took me a little by surprise. "You'll do just fine."

Was it just that simple? Four words and everything was all right? I doubted it. "Maybe we should have just stayed put on Rigeus." Even to my ears, that sounded defeatist. I glanced at Fen. "What?"

"This is not like you. What's wrong?" She looked concerned.

"Hell, I don't know." I was too confused to think straight with Fen's hand on mine.

"We all have our doubts, J," Fen said soothingly.

"Yeah, yeah. You don't have to give me the pep talk. I know all that. I'm tired, I guess. My mind is mush, and I don't have the answers." And then it finally hit me. "I'm scared."

"You're scared of the Count?"

"I suppose I'd be stupid to say no. But I'm more scared of making the wrong decision. I don't want anyone else to get hurt or worse. Maybe it comes down to that I'm scared of failing. I've been used to being on my own where my decisions have only affected me."

"Don't you think Beri feels the same? Or that I feel the same?" Fen looked at me. "We can only do what we can do, and I, for one, only expect that of you." She patted my hand and pulled her own away, much to my vast disappointment.

"Is this part of your Noorthi training?" I asked suspiciously.

"More like Fen training, I think."

"No wonder Beri sends you to do the sensitive talks. You're good at it." I gave her a smile.

"Are you feeling better, then?"

"A little. I just wish we had somewhere to go. I think being cooped up in here with no end in sight is getting on my nerves."

Fen was about to leave me when I thought I should make something clear. "Look, about that stuff with the Count," I said cryptically. "It's between you and me. The others don't need to know about it."

"Oh, you mean you being scared and all?" she teased.

"Yes," I growled, giving her my best glare.

"Your secret is safe with me, Ratha."

"Yeah, yeah," I grumbled as she left, chuckling to herself. My secrets were piling up like the waste of the Misturn of Bateen IV. Now that's a monstrously huge creature so you can imagine its poop. The only difference between its poop and my secrets was that its poop glowed in the dark. Maybe if I worked at it hard enough, my secrets would do the same thing.

†

Two solar days had passed, and we were still parked on the dark side of Ix, awaiting Rales's arrival. Malt spent the time using the computer. I had looked once or twice to see what was holding her interest, but I have to admit it looked like the kid had gone berserk with a writing stick. She tried to explain it to me, but she lost me after the first cosmic theory reference. If it made sense to her, fine, but it did prove my theory about her. She was a smart-ass.

"Are they here yet?" Beri asked.

"Nope." I kept my eyes closed as she settled herself in the chair next to me. "What's for lunch?"

"Do you really want to know?"

"Probably not." The Noorthi cooking, to say the least, was a little boring. It was always the same, and my taste buds were ready to surrender.

"Maybe we could drop down to Ix," Beri said.

"After we meet up with Rales."

"I could go." It seemed that Beri was as eager to get off this ship as I was.

"I'm not letting anyone go down without me, and I have to wait for Rales, so everyone is just going to have to wait." As if uttering those words announced the arrival of the second ship, I was hailed. "Hey, there" I answered. "Have trouble finding us?"

"I'll be glad to get my feet on solid ground, J." Rales sounded relieved. I suppose he was, considering the circumstances under which he left Aldronicus VII. "And find somewhere to relieve myself."

I chuckled. I knew I liked this guy for a reason. "So what did Sasha say?"

"She said, 'Why didn't you ask me yourself'?" The female voice was instantly recognizable.

"Sasha. Hi. I didn't want to drag you into this."

"This was right up my alley, and you wanted to leave me out of all the action? That's not very nice."

"Maybe so, but at least you wouldn't be hunted down."

"Ah, but that makes life a bit more exciting, my friend. Dad said you needed a hideout."

"Hideout is a bit strong. Maybe more a place to settle." When I explained it that way, it didn't sound so much like a life-and-death situation.

"Hideout... place to settle. Mish mash, J. But you're in luck. I think I have the ideal place for you."

"Yeah. And where is this mythical land? In your mind?"

"Do you want my help or not?"

"Put your dad on." I waited while the transmission went quiet.

"Yeah?" Rales answered.

"I thought I told you not to tell her."

"She beat it out of me."

"But I didn't want her—"

"Look, if things are going to get as bad as you think they will, I'll be a lot happier if she's with us. I don't want to be worrying about my little girl out there in the big nasty universe."

I chuckled. "Your little girl? Did you hear that, Sash?" She may have been little in stature, but she was larger than life in spirit.

"Yeah, and he's the only one to get away with it. You get my drift?"

"Yeah, yeah, you midget." I heard her disgruntled sigh from where I was sitting. "Okay, are you going to tell me what I'm in store for?"

"Huh?"

"The hideout, Sash. You haven't told me where the hideout is yet."

"Oh yeah, that. It's an old smugglers' settlement."

Why was I not surprised? Considering the circles she moved in these days, I should have expected the suggestion. Still, it was worth serious consideration. "Been there lately?"

"No, of course not."

I caught a tinge of panic in her voice. So Daddy didn't know about Sash's current lifestyle, huh? I wouldn't be the one to break the news. After all, I was no angel, either.

"Do you know Telgan?" she asked, clearly in a hurry to change the subject.

"Yeah, sure. I've used Arcus once or twice on my way through to the Galleus system."

"It doesn't get used much these days, not with the new generation of hyperdrive."

"As if I'd know about that." I laughed. "What do you think I'm made of? Credits?"

"Well, the settlement is sitting there practically abandoned. I've heard of the odd smugglers using Telgan for refueling, but it should be safe enough for what you have in mind."

"Then I suppose it depends where on Telgan this settlement is." Did I want to put the sisters in danger with the occasional smuggler dropping by?

"It's not on Telgan itself. It's on one of the moons."

"Uh-huh."

126

"No, really."

"Has it got air?" I knew that would be a big hurdle if it didn't. Day-to-day living was going to be hard enough without worrying about environmental conditions.

"Yeah, no problem. Good vegetation and some desert at the northern axis. Temperatures are okay. Pretty good, in fact. Or so I believe."

"Sounds good. When we get back, we'll need to stop at Ix to resupply." Finally, I could go down to Ix. I had been locked up in this metal coffin for way too long, and I was about two inches short of losing my mind. Even though I hated shopping, I'd take the opportunity presented to me. I had one problem. Where would I store the stuff on the ship?

†

Rales took my place on the trooper ship while Sasha and I took her ship to check out the hideout. I was a little disappointed. It turned out to be not much more than a hole in the wall of an escarpment. While I had some reservations about exchanging the hole on Rigeus for a hole on this moon, it did have some improvements over the previous home, like sarcon generators for light and heat and some bedding, but only enough for about twenty people. If we settled here, huts would need to be built on the valley floor.

The heavy vegetation made it impossible to land the ships any closer than a flat hilltop nearby which was ideal for easily landing our spacecraft. However, it left us with a small walk down the hill, across the valley floor, and up a winding path carved out of the rock. I suspected that smugglers used the plateau for the same thing. The moon's location in the star system was what tipped the scales in favor of settling on it.

We finally entered the orbit of Ix after our little expedition, gently coasting along its outer stratosphere until the Noorthi ship came into sight. We were hailed as soon as we were within visual range.

"How did everything go?" The familiar gruff voice said over the intercom.

"Hey, Rales." I tried to sound chipper as I spoke. "It's not perfect, but I didn't expect it to be. It seems good enough."

"Hey, darlin'. How was the trip?" Rales asked.

I nearly answered him until I remembered who was sitting next to me. I snapped my mouth shut and allowed Sasha to maneuver her ship alongside the trooper ship.

"Hey, Dad," Sasha said affectionately. "Uneventful, and it looks like we've found somewhere."

I left Sasha alone to talk with her dad and headed to the hatch. When it opened, it revealed Malt standing at the door of the other ship waiting for me. I hugged her. "How are you doing, kid?" I let go and lifted my hand to ruffle her dark hair. By the stars, the look in her eye had a way of making me feel all mushy inside. Even if she wasn't such a whiz with making stuff, I'd still keep her with me. Maybe I was going all hormonal. Me, care about a kid? I muttered to the tattoo on my wrist, "You have a lot to answer for, buster."

Beri and Fen joined me in the cockpit of the larger ship as I sat down and put my boots up on the dashboard.

"So how did it go?" Fen asked.

"It was... interesting."

"Interesting good or interesting bad?" Beri asked carefully.

"A bit of both, I suppose. It's got food, water, vegetation. The cave has beds and is pretty roomy."

"So what's wrong with that?"

"B, I didn't want you to go from one cave to another. I guess I wanted your lives to be better."

"Is it in a desert?" she asked.

"No."

"Then it's better."

At least she was satisfied. "Don't you wish for something more comfortable than just a cave?" I knew I did.

"J, we lived in that cave on Rigeus since we were kids. A lot of us don't remember much of the compound anymore. If you think it's an improvement on Rigeus, then it's fine. I, for one, will be happy to have a bed and not sleep on the ground."

"If you say so."

Beri patted my arm in an attempt to comfort me, so maybe it was just me who was disappointed in my performance so far. I wanted everything to be perfect. "Let me go tell the sisters," Beri said as she and Fen left.

Rales moved out of the way and let the two women go past before taking his place in the copilot's chair. "So..." he said.

"It looks good, except it's going to take some work. We're going to need some serious manpower. Any suggestions?"

He gave the matter some thought. "We could count on maybe six or seven guys, but it will depend on what we can offer them."

"They'll have to live here. The conditions aren't comfortable, but if we can make it worth their while they might overlook the hard beds and bad food. There won't be any liquor or women. We have to keep the peace, so that might narrow the field even more." I suddenly realized what I was offering was nothing. It was time to put my credits on the table. "How about we offer them five thousand credits each for six months' work?"

"Five thousand? Where do I sign up?"

"All you have to do is ask, you know that."

"I have asked and you keep telling me your pockets are empty."

That was true. Wasn't it only a few months ago I was trying to get by him to skip paying for fuel? "Things have changed."

"Do I ask where the money came from?"

"No, but I know you want to. When I liberated the trooper ship on Rigeus I found it was loaded with credits in the hold."

"Ah." He nodded his head.

"What was I supposed to do? Throw them out?" I could feel his disapproval. "I see it as compensation for the Noorthi and myself for what happened on that planet."

"You don't have to justify yourself to me."

"I feel like I have to, Dad. Your opinion matters to me. This was a workable solution to a dire situation. We need the money to survive."

Erica Lawson

"I know that, honey. I just wish there was another solution. Or, better yet, we weren't in this situation in the first place."

"Me too."

"Back to business," he said.

"Yeah. Five thousand for a six-month contract. It might also be a good idea to find a cook. I don't know how much longer I can stand Noorthi cooking."

"I'll see what I can do," Rales said.

"And that's good enough for me, my friend. Now before we get much older, we have some supplies to get from Ix."

As I guided the trooper ship down to Ix, I had a feeling that picking up supplies was going to be my easiest task of the whole affair.

130

Chapter Eleven

To Wash Away the Hurt

I sat on the hilltop that overlooked the valley we now called home and sipped my hot beverage. We had been here for about two months, and life was progressing well. Not as well as I would have liked, but progressing nonetheless.

The cave had been cleaned up and was now in daily use. Malt and Rales had worked some minor miracles in delivering power to our lives, but our main problem was we still didn't have satisfactory camouflage. We resorted to ancient methods and hid the ships with vegetation. Though it was primitive, it was effective. The cave was another matter. We had no choice but to abandon the front part so that from the air the cave looked unoccupied.

I relaxed and watched the early morning rise of the star system's sun, enjoying the slowly warming air as it slid over my body. I found I had come to appreciate the small things in life. There were no more bars, no more fights, and no more distractions. I now saw the magic in a flower or the contentment in the rising of a sun. Who would have thought?

Beri came up the hill and sat down on the grass-covered ground next to me. "Hi there, stranger," I said cheerily.

"You're awfully happy this morning."

"I suppose I am." It was a surprising comment from me, considering the overwhelming amount of work that still needed to be done.

"Something happen that I don't know about?"

"Nope. Just pleased to see you. We haven't had much chance to talk lately."

"That's true."

I watched her reaction to the scenery, and she seemed strangely calm and content. I suppose that was how I felt. Suddenly the name of this speck of dust finally came to me. It was Heaven. Yeah. That was it. Heaven.

"What are you thinking about so hard that you have to hide yourself away from the rest of us?" Beri sounded almost hurt.

"Nothing, really. I was just enjoying a bit of quiet time with my caffeine synth." I held up my cup as if trying to prove the truth of my words. "It's beautiful up here, isn't it?"

Beri glanced at me sideways. "Yeah."

"I'm not hiding or anything. Really." I tried to explain, but I was probably not doing a very good job. "It's just that every now and then, I like the solitude up here. It clears my mind."

"Are we getting too much for you?"

"No. Not at all. Keep in mind that I've spent most of my life alone. I just need to step back every now and then and allow life, and time, to pass me by."

"Maybe I should have sent Fen." Beri sounded despondent. "You don't think you can do the sensitive talks? I think you're doing okay." There had been a burning question sitting on my tongue for quite a while now, but I didn't know how to bring it up. "How are you?"

"Me? Okay. Why?" But she couldn't look me in the eye.

I reached over and tapped her temple. "How are you here?"

"My head?"

All right, either she was pretending to be ignorant or she didn't understand what I was asking. I was trying to be delicate, but it seemed I had to ask the hard question. "How are you coping after... um... Vel?" I still couldn't bring myself to say the word. It took a lot for me to accept that I had been violated on Rigeus, and I had regularly indulged in sex. For someone like Beri, who had never experienced sex, it would have been devastating.

"Fine," Beri said, but I could read the tension in her voice and in her face. She was anything but fine.

"Why do I get the feeling that you're not?"

"I said I'm fine," she said with a clear warning in her tone.

"Look—"

"No." Beri stood and glared down at me. "This is none of your business."

"Yes, it is," I replied. "You put me in charge, and your problem is my problem. You're my friend, Beri. I don't want to see you hurting. Besides, I was there. I went through it, too."

Beri's eyes brimmed with tears, barely held in check by her considerable will. "She... I..."

I suspected Beri was trying to justify her anger and despair by saying I wouldn't know what she was going through. In a way, I didn't. I didn't have a daughter at stake. "Does anyone else know about what happened to you on Rigeus?" I asked.

"No," she said as I watched a tear slide down her cheek.

"Not even Fen?"

"No."

"Trust me. Holding it inside is not good." I said the words, and yet I wasn't taking my own advice.

"And what should I do?" she said despairingly.

"Let it out. Yell, scream—hit me if it'll make you feel better. Do whatever it takes to come to terms with it."

"You do realize we are pacifists." There was a hint of sarcasm in Beri's voice.

"But I'm sure not one of you has been in this situation before." Beri didn't answer me.

"No one else, right, B?" She looked at her feet.

"Oh. Um, so how did she cope?"

"She didn't," Beri said flatly.

"Didn't your sisters help her?" I was surprised.

"How? None of us had the knowledge of what she was feeling. She didn't want our help." Beri paced a little, her nervous energy forcing her to move.

"She may not have asked, but she certainly needed it. All you had to do was be there. Let her know she wasn't alone. Let her know you empathized with her." Geez, I was getting good at giving advice. "And in my case, let her know I knew exactly what she was going through."

"I can't." Beri stopped and looked down at me. I could see it in her eyes. She wanted help but didn't know how to ask.

"Yes, you can. You're withdrawing from your sisters, and you're withdrawing from life." Was I helping or making things worse?

"I can't help it," she cried out. "I've lost everything."

"Lost everything? I don't understand."

"I can't do this anymore."

I grabbed Beri's hands and pulled her down to sit next to me. "From what I can see, you're doing just fine." Those damned eyes of hers were still swimming with tears, and it made me want to fix everything. "Does this have something to do with being Ashaltea?"

"How—"

"They're worried about you." That wasn't technically true, but I felt a little white lie would help Beri. She needed to know she had support, even if it was phantom support for now. "So what's the problem?"

"No problem."

Beri had dismissed me. That was one thing that annoyed me immensely. Okay, my IQ wasn't all that great, but that was no reason to be treated like that.

"Beri." She tried to look elsewhere, so I yelled at her. "Beri! Talk to me." She struggled to rise, and I tightened my hold on her wrist. "No. Not until you tell me what the problem is."

"I can't have children. There, will you leave it alone now?"

"With that news? No. I need to hear more." I gave a tug on her wrist indicating that I wanted her to stay put. She wriggled around to sit on the grass in a huff. "Talk to me, B." I placed my hands on the ground behind me, using them to support my body. I kept my contact with her to a minimum. While she needed my support, she didn't want my comfort.

"An Ashaltea is supposed to have a child to pass on her right of caste to."

"Where do you get this idea that you can't have children?"

"Vel—she... she... A Noorthi's body has to remain pure."

"Vel did something to stop you from having children?" My body tensed in anger. I was ready to spring into action, head back to Juno, and walk to the front door of the Noorthi Great House to pound on that door until I saw Vel's ugly face again.

"Yes. No. I don't know. I think so."

"You're not sure? Then how do you know?"

"What?"

"How do you know that your chance at motherhood is gone?" I was probably clutching at straws, but I needed to give her something to hold on to.

"I just know." Beri was confused, I knew, but if this was the first step on the road back to life, then she could remain confused.

"But has anyone seen it? Been there for it to happen? You believe you can't have children because your mother said so?"

"It's our culture. Don't go talking about things you know nothing about." Beri glared at me, her face contorted in anger.

"That's true, but I'm looking at it from a fresh perspective. You have no proof it's true, but your belief is driving you to give up."

"My belief is all I have."

I shifted my weight to one side and put a hand on her arm. "Surely you know that in this universe, not everything is controlled by belief."

"Why can't you leave me alone?" She stood up and turned around to face me.

"Because you're hurting." I stood, too.

"It's all your fault." Her words cut through me.

There. It was said. It hurt that she said it, but it was something that had been eating away at me. I had been responsible for a lot of things regarding these women, and some of them weren't pleasant. Beri's violation. Rice's death. Both weighed heavily on me.

"Yes, it's true. And I would undo everything if I could, but I can't." I grabbed her hand and felt the instinctive withdrawal, but I held on tight. "I'm truly sorry, B, for everything."

Beri took a deep breath and reined in her escalating emotions. "No." Her voice broke as she spoke. "No, you warned us and we ignored it."

"I shouldn't have interfered." And I was right.

"What's done is done." Beri sighed, and she slumped against me. "I just don't know what to do."

"Talk to me. Let me in, Beri."

She looked at me for quite a while. I could see there was a struggle within her. "She..." Her eyes closed for a moment before they reopened and focused on me. "She touched me. I didn't like it, and she wouldn't stop."

"I know. The same thing happened to me." I didn't want to drag this all up, but I thought it was necessary for her to face it head-on so she could live again. "Over twenty women pushed, prodded, and felt me up."

"Felt you...up?"

"Yeah, what Vel did to you. You know, she touched you intimately."

"I don't understand. Intimately?"

I felt embarrassed talking about this to her, maybe more embarrassed for her than for me, so I thought a visual demonstration would be more precise. "Yeah, she touched you...here." My hand slid down to my crotch and stayed there.

"No," she said.

"No?" Now I didn't understand.

"She didn't touch me there."

"She didn't?" I was starting to wonder what actually did happen. "Where did she touch you?"

"Do I have to? It... wasn't nice." Beri was struggling, but I had to know.

"For me, please. Just show me." Her hand rose to cover her breasts and then moved down to her ass. So it seemed that Vel was content to just make Beri uncomfortable, and for that I was grateful. Was Beri so naïve that she didn't know the difference between being touched and being violated?

"Because of her I can't have children."

Yes, she was that naïve. I wanted to laugh out loud, but I knew doing that would hurt Beri beyond comprehension. It took all my concentration to keep a serious face. "Listen to me. What Vel did to you was awful, I know that, but rest assured you will have your daughter."

"No. She took that away from me."

"Beri, your body is still pure." Maybe her definition and my definition of pure were different. If I were her, I'd be accepting my definition as the right one. "She did not violate you."

"She did. She took my innocence, and for that I will never forgive her."

"And she will pay. I'll make sure of that. But it's important to me that you find yourself. Only when you are whole will I be whole." What the hell was I saying?

"What do you want from me?"

"I want the old Beri back. She's in there." I reached out and touched Beri's arm. "Vel was messing with you, but she didn't violate your body. Trust me, I know." I leaned over, grabbed her hand, and brought the back of it gently to my lips. "You will have your daughter. I promise." Maybe I had gone too far. How could I make a promise like that? Beri had one thing missing from her life, and I wondered if I had given it to her. Hope.

"That is a promise you can't keep."

"Why can't you at least keep an open mind, huh? Can you do that for me?"

"What's the point?" Defeat laced Beri's words.

"The point? The point is that you still have faith. Faith in the impossible, faith in me, and most important, faith in you. Your whole life is based on faith, so it should come easy to you."

"Not this faith, Jordana. I don't know if I can."

"Fine." I was hitting my head against Bessie's outer shell and getting nowhere. "Then Vel has won." I hung my head in defeat. "Go back to the Noorthi. Can you organize some planting of crops or something?"

Beri nodded her head and walked away, following the well-worn path from the plateau to the cave. Damn, she was stubborn. But bringing up her problem also raised the question of my own pain. Up until now, I had put it in a compartment in my mind and locked it away, but now it was open and needed addressing.

I looked over the valley covered in lush vegetation. Using the beautiful landscape as a cushion for my emotions, I gazed into that box in my mind. Logically I accepted that what had happened on Rigeus was beyond my control. Those Velkren took advantage of me, finding every square inch of skin on me and abusing it. But that didn't lessen the shame I felt and the guilt that I couldn't stop them.

I at least had the benefit of experiencing sex in most of its forms, so I was a bit numbed to what they did, but it still bothered me. Not that I would show it to anyone. But it raised a serious question for me. The Noorthi had taken drinking away from me. Had sex become distasteful as well? Would I ever find out?

Suddenly it became necessary for me to find out. Okay, so maybe it was a matter of "climbing back in the saddle," as they used to say. I wanted to know if I could do it and whether I would enjoy it. Like most things in my life, I would tackle the problem head-on. And, as I said to Beri, I didn't want that bitch Vel to win. She had taken too much from me already.

I brought the mug to my lips, but it was empty. My time off had run out, and I had to return to real life. I sighed. Unless I actively went looking for it, I was going to remain as celibate as the women who surrounded me.

A familiar figure intercepted me on my way back to the cave. "Have you become my shadow now, Malt?"

"I'm bored."

"Have you done your chores?"

"Ages ago." Malt said it in such a way that she made me feel silly for even asking the question.

"What about the shield for the cave?"

"I can see it in my head, but I don't know how to do it." A crease appeared on her forehead as she frowned.

"And the computer can teach you only so much, huh?"

"Yeah, something like that." Had Malt been talking to Fen?

"Maybe you need a mentor."

"A what?" Malt glanced at me with something akin to apprehension.

"A mentor. A teacher."

"A teacher? I'm not going back to lessons." Malt backed away quickly. "And you can't make me."

"Whoa, hang on a minute. This mentor will help you figure out how to move your ideas from here"—I tapped Malt's temple—"to reality. You could achieve so much more, kid. I have faith in you." I used the term affectionately, and I saw her eyes glisten. Of course, I still had to find someone who would accept the job as her mentor

"I want to know more, but I don't want to do the boring stuff, Jordana. I want it to be fun."

"And it will be. This is a way for you to learn." I put my arm over her shoulder, and we walked back to the cave together.

†

"Are you sure about this guy, Rales?"

"It was the best I could do on short notice."

He had organized a meeting with someone named Floric on the planet Locar. I suppose the only way to make a decision on Malt's prospective mentor was to go and meet the guy.

"What have you heard about him?" I tore off a piece of flatbread and popped it in my mouth.

"Ex-Consortium fallen on hard times. I was told he needed a job." He bit into a carrabee, spilling the juice down his chin. "Things seem to be going well here." He gazed out over the valley from our picnic on the ridge. "You've done a great job."

"Hmm. I was thinking…"

"Oh, please." He held up his hand to stop me. "When you say 'I was thinking,' it usually means more work for me."

"How did you know?" I laughed at his grumpy face.

"Honey, I've known you long enough to know when you're trying to tell me something I don't want to know about." He took a swig of his caffeine-synth. "Malt and I have the sarcons

139

working well, and the huts are all but finished. What on Carn can you possibly need now?"

"I checked out the top of the cliff the other day and discovered a second side to this wall about half a mile away." I paused and took a sip of my drink. "You have no idea how grateful I am that you found those skippers, by the way. I was really getting tired of all that walking to the second landing field."

"You're an easy girl to satisfy."

I spat my drink across my trousers after he spoke, coughing as the remnants slithered down my throat. I glared at him.

"Buy you a ship or two, and you're a happy woman. What did you think I meant?" But he smiled cheekily at me anyway.

"The reason I mentioned the wall..." I gave him my best intimidating stare. Rales just laughed at me. "I was wondering if it would be possible to hollow out the wall on the other side to make a landing bay."

"What's wrong with what we've got now?"

"Nothing, I suppose."

"And we don't have enough to do?"

"I didn't say that."

"J, honey, couldn't you find a project a little smaller? There's only a handful of us here."

"Can you at least think about it? There's always the chance of the ships being spotted from the air, especially now that we've expanded the fleet to four ships and two new terrain skippers. That's an awful lot to hide. Talk to the boys and see what they think. We can always buy the equipment to make the job easier. I'm not expecting you to pull out the rock with your bare hands."

"All right, I'll at least consider it."

It was the best I could hope for. I had big plans, but without Rales and the boys, they would be nothing more than that—plans. "Thanks."

"I never had the chance to say how proud I am of you," he said after a pause.

"Really?"

140

"Yes. All this." His hand swept over the valley. "The Noorthi. Malt. That was a very commendable thing you did for that poor girl."

I could feel the heat of a blush rising on my face. "Yeah, well. Anyone would have done the same."

"No, they wouldn't. They would have ignored her pleas and walked away. Not you. It was a good thing, and she's proving your faith in her." His hand landed on my knee and patted it. "I'm very proud of you, kiddo."

I smiled at his words. It was always nice to be praised by a parent, even if he's a substitute one.

Disappointingly, no decision had been made on the excavation by the time I was due to leave for Locar, but we decided since I was visiting the largest commercial planet in the system, I might as well pick up a couple of mining lasers if I could. Just in case, of course. Rales came up with a name and managed to arrange the exchange and a time. Everything was coming together, and I was a happy woman. Now, if Vel would die, I'd be an ecstatic woman.

Chapter Twelve

A Walk on the Wild Side

We took one of the new ships for our trip to Locar so I could get a feel for the vehicle. The flight didn't take too long with the hyperdrive, but Malt and I still had time for conversation.

"I don't like this."

"Malt, for the last time, this is a good thing."

"And what do we know about him, huh? He could be a cold-blooded killer or something."

I laughed out loud. "Sure, kid, we're going to meet your future teacher and he's the universe's biggest serial killer."

"You never know."

"All right. Let me ask you this. You're bored stupid, and you've read everything that's available in the archive banks. What are you going to do now?"

"I'm doing just fine." Malt folded her arms—all of them— and huffed.

"Maybe," I said as I glanced at her, "but you could learn so much more. And this guy could help you develop strategical techniques." As soon as I said the words, I stopped. "Where in Carn did that come from?"

Malt stared at me. "I don't know. Maybe from that kid inside you?"

"Rice? I don't think so." Rice never struck me as the sort of kid with an extensive vocabulary. I glanced at my wrist. Could it be? As illogical as it sounded, had the ochre improved my language skills?

"Why are we going to Locar?"

"For one thing, if we get spotted, it's on the far side of Juno and as far away from Telgan as is humanly possible. That is, without leaving the system. Besides, I promised Rales I'd pick up a couple of mining lasers." Okay, that was a little white lie of sorts. It was true, but it wasn't the primary reason for Locar. I had wanted to pick up a present of sorts for Malt. If I decided Floric was the man for Malt, she was going to need a present to make the decision a bit more palatable. Damn! I was doing it again. A big word!

We were directed to land near the perimeter of the spaceport at the city of Corwel, forcing me to walk the entire length of the field. Damn autocrats. I had a meeting with Rales's friend of a friend of a friend concerning the mining lasers, but Malt wasn't too happy about being left behind. I would be sending the lasers to the ship once the deal was made, and she would have to pay the courier when they were safely on board. One rule I learned early in my career was to never pay up front. I lost a lot of money that way, and it made me very wary of deals made with people I didn't know.

While we were here, I also had to organize supplies. I checked my chronometer to see how much time I had before I had to rendezvous with Malt for the lunch meeting. There was still plenty of time, and the lasers were already on their way to the ship, so it was safe to move about without stumbling on the kid.

"Hey, there," a female voice yelled.

I ignored the call because I didn't know anyone here.

"Tall, dark, and dangerous."

I didn't know why I looked around. Did I think that description fit me? The fact that I did look made me realize that I probably did. I was tall, and had long black hair, so I supposed her description fit. Dangerous? My memory went back to where this adventure began: in a bar and the fight that ensued. Just the mention of my first initial was enough to make my opponent blanch. So, yeah, I suppose I was dangerous. That seemed ages ago, though.

"You talking to me?" I finally turned to face the caller. I stopped short. Wow. She was stunning. I glanced around in case she really was talking to someone else, but no, she was looking directly at me. My finger came up and pointed at my chest.

"Yes, you, gorgeous," the woman said silkily as she walked toward me.

Okay, what was going on? I normally didn't get compliments in the middle of the street from a total stranger, so I looked around in case there were troopers ready to jump me.

"I'm sorry. Do I know you?"

"Not yet," she purred.

I tried to focus on her to gauge her sincerity, but I couldn't get past how stunning she was. Easily as tall as I was, she had fine porcelain-like features and long blonde hair. She made me think of that ancient Earth word "Amazon." Athletic and slightly muscular in build, she didn't have an ounce of fat on her. The pit of my stomach growled. I felt something, all right. Pure lust.

Which probably had something to do with my not having had sex since... oh, Almighty Carn. I hadn't done anything since this whole fiasco began. Seeing this woman, and the response from her, made me realize how empty that part of my life had been. Were my memories of conquest slowly fading with time or quickly fading with the ochre tattoo? Please, oh, please. Anything but that. The only thing that kept me sane among the Noorthi was I still had my memories. If not for those, I was residing in hell.

But something held me back from the obvious offer. Every voice in my head was screaming at me to walk away from the woman, but my libido wasn't going to give up without a fight. Just once. That was all I needed to carry me through a little while longer. One unemotional session of sex.

The stranger sauntered up to me and ran a long fingernail down my tattered shirt. My eyes followed the path that finger took, and I suddenly noticed how shabby my clothes looked. Maybe I could invest in a new set while I was planet-bound. My mind gave up its mental shopping list when her finger dipped into my cleavage. I began to sweat as she inched closer. My heart was really thumping, either from her proximity or the thought about what it might lead to.

"So, is it a done deal?" she said seductively.

A done deal. Ah, now I understood.

"I don't think so." I stepped back to break the contact and looked her straight in the eye. "Thanks, but no thanks."

"What happened?" She looked genuinely confused.

"I may be desperate, but not that desperate."

"Hey!" She sounded nearly insulted. "What's going on? I thought you were interested."

"Just like you're interested in credits?"

"Credits? What credits?"

"Like a business transaction?" Did she really want me to spell it out?

"Bus— Oh no. Nothing like that. I just thought we might have some fun, that's all. There's no money involved." She tried to make contact again, but my brain had regained control. Her spell was broken, and I was ready to move on.

"Try it on someone else, honey," I said. "I thought my clothes would have been a dead giveaway that my pockets are empty."

"But I thought we had something here." Her fingers spread out in entreaty.

"We did, until you tried to seal the deal. Better luck with the next sucker." I walked off knowing I was leaving her standing there looking like the Sporian fish of Weemod Minor. Yeah, she would be standing there with her mouth opening and closing in confusion. I sure showed her.

I continued with my shopping trip and put the mystery woman out of my mind. I had a few things to pick up before I met with Malt to greet her new mentor. Well, I hoped this guy would be her mentor. The kid was way ahead of me in the brains department, and she was in need of some guidance in her life.

I really hated doing this stuff, especially now. Who did I trust? Every time I brought someone new into our little community, I worried that this was one more person who could betray us to the Count.

Actually, now that I thought about it, I was surprised I hadn't gone crazy from all the stress and anxiety I was carrying on my shoulders. I suppose all that was holding me together right now was spit and wishful thinking.

The shop I had been looking for finally came into view, and I hoped to find Malt's present here. The second-hand technology shop was certainly nothing to look at, but for what I wanted and no questions asked, it was probably what I should have expected. The door slid aside automatically, and I entered. The dark store was crowded with broken-down pieces of machinery and junk.

"May I help you?" The reedy voice came from someone behind a desk at the far wall of the building. One never knew what could happen in these sorts of establishments. There were plenty of places for someone to hide and jump you, whether to capture you or to simply rob you, so I always went in with a certain amount of caution. I walked down the aisle, and my gaze shifted from one side to the other.

"I was looking for a tool set."

"I see. Anything in particular?"

"I have a child who is particularly gifted in constructing machines from scratch, and I wanted to get her a set of tools."

The middle-aged owner of the shop studied me. I think he was trying to see what amount of money I wanted to spend. "How large?"

"Just your basic set," I said, so he was in no doubt as to how many credits I was offering. I wanted a small gift, not the keys to Bessie.

"I don't have anything at present..."

I turned around and prepared to leave the shop.

"But I can put something together for you by tomorrow." I stopped but didn't turn around. "I'll even give you a discount for the inconvenience."

I smiled. Those were the sort of deals I liked. After leaving a credit or two in good faith, I left the shop, pleased that I could cross off one item from my mental shopping list. I grinned even wider. Of course, I had to return tomorrow, and that guaranteed I would be planet-bound tonight.

I still had a little spare time before my rendezvous with Malt. The incident with the woman in the street brought the state of my clothes to my attention, so I went in search of some sort of tailor, clothier, or outfitter, whatever they called a clothes shop these days. I wanted sturdy, practical clothes. It wasn't like I was on the prowl for a girlfriend or anything, so as long as I wasn't in tattered rags, I was fine. However, it seemed that I had reached that magical line between clothes and rags, and it was time for an update.

I browsed the stalls as I wandered, and I finally asked directions. I hated when I had to do it, but I wasn't finding anything on my own.

A shiver traveled down my spine as I sifted through the wares in the street. Was someone watching me? My peripheral vision scanned the area without finding the source of my concern. I risked looking, but everything seemed normal.

I got to the side street in question and tried to decide whether the walk down it was worth the prize at the end. There was still human-like traffic using the alley, and it seemed to be bustling enough to guarantee a modicum of safety, but my paranoia reared its ugly head again. Still, I needed clothes.

The uneasy feeling didn't leave me as I sought out the shop I was looking for. A local passed by with his toorak, which was large enough to block me from view for a moment. I sidestepped into a doorway and waited a few moments in case someone passed by. When there was no suspicious activity, I risked a glance around the corner. Nothing jumped out at me. I decided I was being paranoid.

About two-thirds of the way down the alley stood the doorway to the clothing store. Above the door was its name written in Scyrian: Shamar's Portal of Pulchritude. It was more like Shamar's Basement of Bullshit, if you asked me. I hated shopping, so if it had anything near what I wanted, I would be satisfied.

I stepped into the artificial light and nearly missed the step down to the shop floor. It had been so bright outside that I was temporarily blinded. I bumped into something soft and made my apology. "Excuse me," I muttered.

"You're excused." The voice had a similar timbre to Fen's. Low and melodic, and it hit a chord within me.

She was about to pass me when my hand shot out and wrapped gently around her arm. "My apologies, ma'am. It was so

147

bright outside my eyes hadn't adjusted to the low light." In a moment I was glad for the low lighting, so she didn't see my reaction. I stepped to the side to allow her to exit from the shop. As she passed by, I inhaled a sickly sweet smell that, I assumed, was a perfume of some kind. My gaze followed her out and caught a glimpse of her enormous silhouette as she hesitated in the doorway. Had I managed to strike up more than a friendship with her, I could have suffered a broken hip or two.

"You were lucky," a female voice said from the semidarkness.

"I wouldn't go so far as to say that." I didn't want to sound rude. I was sure the creature was considered very beautiful by whatever species she was from.

"I would." The owner of the voice moved closer and into the semi-light.

Now she was more like it. At least she only had two nostrils that I could count. I took the misadventure with Miss Three-Nostrils as a sign and decided not to strike up a friendship. Instead, I moved farther into the establishment to solve the dilemma of my ragged clothes. But the woman followed me and stood close to my elbow as I inspected the wares.

Finally I couldn't stand the silence any longer. "Can I help you?"

"Maybe," she said mysteriously.

"What's your problem?" I probably said it a little too harshly, but I wasn't up for twenty questions.

"You," she said softly.

"Me?" What had I done?

"You are quite a distraction."

"Me?" I repeated. What was it about this planet? Every woman on it wanted me. Maybe there was some sort of cosmic vibe coming off me saying "desperate female here, up for anything."

"Would you like to join me for a meal?" she said.

"I'm sorry, ma'am, but I have an appointment and it's one that I can't miss." Which was true. Malt's teacher was a higher priority than me having sex.

"Then how about a coffee synth back at my home?" She seemed awfully eager to have me in her house.

My eyes slowly perused her up and down, and I could see she was looking for a casual fling. That usually meant there was someone else in her home who was off world, so she was ideal for my experiment. There would be no problem with messy breakups or attachments. I could live with that. "Sure."

We left the shop without buying anything. She sauntered along the street in front of me and constantly looked over her shoulder to make sure I hadn't taken a wrong turn or changed my mind. The seductive sway of her hips had my interest all the way to her home, so she had no worries that I wouldn't follow.

Should you be doing this? Rice again. Damn.

Probably not, but I'm doing it anyway. I smiled because I knew what was coming and Rice didn't.

Doing what?

Doing something that you girls have no idea about. This was certainly going to be different. I was going to have sex while there was a virgin in my head.

We arrived at a low building in a well-to-do neighborhood. Well, it looked well-to-do to me. From the outside, the home was solid and practical. She allowed the security opticon to scan her.

"Aren't you coming in?" she asked as the front door slid open.

I hesitated on the doorstep. Why? It was just sex. All my life, that's all it has been. Sex. Nothing more. I had never met anyone I wanted more than that from. This woman was beautiful, charming, and willing, and most of all looking only for a casual meeting. It was perfect. "Sure. Why not?" I answered, taking that final step across her portal.

J, what are you doing? Suddenly Rice realized what I was up to.

Seeing if I still have a life.

But... but... but... Rice sounded like Vel's vehicle on Rigeus.

I'll explain it all later. Now was not the time for lengthy discussion. I entered the building and immediately felt the cooler air. It must have been the mud walls.

"So, where's your partner?" I asked casually.

She turned and looked at me, her eyebrow raised in amusement.

"Girlfriend?" I amended.

"Both are off-world, thankfully."

I wasn't sure whether she was kidding or meant it. At this point, it really didn't matter much to me. One quick roll in the sack and I was off. "So... er..." I didn't even know her name. Was that a good idea? Maybe it would be safer just to remain anonymous.

"Deson," she said.

"Well, hello there." I gave her a bow, and she seemed amused by my actions. "Something funny?" I was trying to be polite, and she thought it was funny.

"Not at all. I thought it was just... quaint." Her rich, elegant voice spoke almost condescendingly. Not quite, but almost. "Would you like a drink?"

"Sure." Maybe a drink was what I needed to calm myself. Normally I would have her halfway to the bed by now, but I figured this one needed the control. I would have to work at her pace.

Deson disappeared for a number of minutes, and I had already finished my inspection of the room. She had money, there was no doubt about that, so seducing me was a diversion for her. Hey, I didn't mind being someone's diversion. She was being mine.

I was about to go looking for her when she emerged. She had changed, if you could call it that, because what she was wearing was very little. Deson handed me the drink, but the "come hither" look told me not to take long finishing that drink. Carefully I took a sip, and as I expected, I got that horribly bitter taste in my mouth. Damn. I hid my grimace. What if...? I couldn't bring myself to say the sentence in my head, because if I got the same result with sex, I might just shoot myself.

Where are her clothes? Rice asked nervously.

Shut up. Go and look at my brain cells or something. I was anxious to get started. I wanted to be put out of my misery one way or the other. Either I was going to be enjoying myself or crying into my pillow. I put the drink down, moved quickly over to my intended target, and grabbed Deson roughly before I planted my lips on hers.

Jordana! I felt Rice's jolt of fear as she called my name.

Deson pulled back. "What's the hurry?"

"Do you really want to waste time with small talk?"

"I'm free all day." She smiled.

"I'm not," I said.

Her smile dropped. "You won't change your mind?"

"I'm afraid I can't. I have an appointment I have to keep." Which was true. This little experiment was not the main reason for the visit to this planet.

Then why are we here? Rice decided she was going to be my voice of reason.

I moved in again, and this time Deson didn't fight it. Her fingers slid into my hair and grasped it.

Why is she hurting you?

I really didn't need Rice's incessant questions at that moment, so I tried to ignore her. There was desperation to our kisses as our tongues slid around one another, fed by the urgency of the meeting. "Where do you want to go?" I muttered between kisses.

"I don't care."

Eww... I do.

I started to have images of the peaceful valley on Heaven. If Rice persisted, my ardor would not only cool it would be snuffed out.

For Carn's sake, Rice! I have to do this. Would she understand?

And what do I do?

I don't care. As long as you do it quietly... and without pictures, I added, in case she got any ideas about getting around my order.

So I lifted Deson and backed her against the wall of the lounge room, prepared to take her there and then. I continued to kiss her, sliding my lips from hers to her neck, so I could nip the soft flesh there. Once her back was against the cool brick, my hands wandered and found the hem of the material she was wearing. I was pleasantly surprised that she had nothing on underneath. Despite her words to the contrary, she was prepared for my frantic lovemaking.

One hand kneaded Deson's breast while the other sought a baser response. I felt her soft skin under my fingertips as I slid them down her body, seeking out her heat instinctively. It had been so long that I almost felt like a virgin all over again. Well, if I was truthful, my last sex was just before my contact with the Noorthi, but being with those women made me think it was an eternity.

All I can say is I'm glad I don't have to do this. It's a disgusting habit.

Rice, so help me... What was the point? I couldn't threaten her with anything. There was no doubt that Deson was excited and that thrilled me. Even after everything that had happened to me, I still had the magic touch. Maybe there was some hope for me yet.

Wha... what's going on? I feel kind of hot. Rice's voice sounded a little shaky.

That's arousal, Rice. Now let me continue. All this talking in my head was not helping me. Deson's slickness was stirring my blood, and my fingers reveled in her enjoyment. At this point my mind was still holding back, allowing me to please the woman under my fingers but not to seek pleasure myself. That was terribly bad form on my part to do that, but for the sake of the exercise, my question had been answered.

Deson squirmed under my knowing touch, her ragged breathing as restless as her body. "Oh..." It seemed I had left her speechless. A smile touched my lips as my ego preened under her praise. I can be an egotistical ass sometimes.

One of her hands slid down my arm to my hand buried between her thighs, her fingers entwining with mine. She didn't guide, but just wanted to feel what I was doing. I didn't mind, and I found the action sort of, well, erotic. There was a twinge in my crotch in answer to the fondling we were both doing to hers.

"Come on, Deson, honey," I whispered into her ear as my fingers moved with purpose. Nothing like bringing out the winning one-liners to seal the deal. My mind flitted back to the woman in the street. Was I doing the same thing she did? Well, at least I wasn't going to charge Deson for the fun.

Call the sertechs! She's convulsing! Rice's panicked words reverberated through my head. This time I ignored her, but she was being insistent. *She's going to die, J! Don't just stand there!*

It's called an orgasm, Rice. It's part of making love.

But you keep calling it sex.

Same thing. I knew it wasn't, but I wanted to end the conversation. *Later, okay?* But I felt guilty. It was my damned scruples, or maybe it was Rice whispering in my ear. I didn't want meaningless sex. I wanted love, but I wasn't getting love, so meaningless sex was all that was left to me. I was going to go crazy going around in circles with the ethics of what I was doing, not to mention the fact that it was terribly rude to be thinking of other things while having sex and not paying attention to the woman in my arms.

I needed to get away and think for a while, and being in Deson's arms was not the right place to be while I sorted this out. "I've got to go." I stepped back from a disheveled Deson, leaving her leaning against the wall.

"Now?"

When I had accepted the offer, I knew I would be cutting it fine. I was already late for the meeting, and Malt would be worrying. While I myself didn't get relief, I was greatly pleased that Deson did. Despite the ethical dilemma, the damned ochre hadn't taken it away and I still felt like a red-blooded woman.

"Sorry."

"Can you come back? Tonight?" She sounded nearly desperate.

"Well..." I said, despite my concerns. Depending on when the supplies were delivered, planet curfew could keep us on Locar overnight, so maybe I could sneak out when Malt was asleep. After all, I still wanted to feel the thrill of an orgasm. "It would be late." Then I had a thought. "What about your partner?"

"He's off-world for another week, and late is not a problem."

It is for me, Rice piped in.

I had obviously impressed Deson, otherwise she wouldn't be asking me to come back. My chest puffed up with the compliment. It was always nice to know I could give a woman what she wanted.

That was, of course, if she wasn't a Noorthi. Then I realized that I had answered my own question. Whether I liked it or not, I wasn't leaving Locar until I felt the rush.

"It would be really late."

"That's fine," she said, almost too eagerly.

I looked at her chronometer on the wall and did a swift calculation. "Okay, about one a.m." I made my way to the door as she answered me. "Until then."

I stepped out into the bright sunlight, my libido uplifted in the knowledge that I still had one vice left. Tonight, I would find out if that vice was fully intact.

And that's sex, is it?

I could hear the disdain in Rice's voice.

In a nutshell, yeah.

And sweating over it is also pleasurable?

Anything worthwhile is worth sweating for.

Rest assured the Noorthi won't be losing any sleep over sex.

I already figured that out. Why do you think I'm here?

That shut her up.

†

I made my way back to the tavern where we were going to meet this guy. Vendors were pushing their wares in my face, and I didn't even care. Normally if they got too close, I would shove whatever they were selling up their asses, but I was in a good mood and ignored their impassioned pleas. Hell, I even asked for directions twice without batting an eye. I just felt too damned good to care.

I was about a hundred feet away from the meeting place when I spotted Malt. She was leaning against the wall in the shade talking to some other girl. So, it looked like she had been busy, as well. I noticed she made no effort to hide her extra arms, which didn't seem to worry who she was talking to, and she positively beamed at the response.

"Hey, there," I called a few feet away from her. Malt started and looked at me like she had been caught doing something bad.

She finished her conversation with the girl and turned her attention to me.

"Who's your friend?"

"No one," she said and shrugged her shoulders as I led the way to the restaurant where we would meet the mysterious teacher. I found a booth for us and ordered something to eat. "Did the lasers arrive okay?"

"Yeah, but they tried to up the price when they saw me," Malt answered. "That changed when I told them the deal."

"You talked them down?" I was impressed.

"Yeah, that and the pistol I had in my hand."

"That's my girl." I patted her available hand that rested on the table.

The waiting went on and on, and I was on my second drink, whatever it was. Since alcohol no longer held a fascination for me I settled for something more sedate. So here I was sipping something loaded with sweetener and not much else. Malt and I were giggling like idiots with all the sugar in our systems.

Suddenly a stick figure stopped in front of our table. His eyes would have barely reached my chest if I had been standing up, and he was so thin I could have snapped him in two if I felt the inclination to do so.

"You Jeshua... Jeremy Julia...?"

"Jordana," I answered, annoyed. I really, really hated it when someone got my name wrong.

He squinted at me as if trying to get me into focus. "Whatever."

I couldn't believe it. He dismissed me. "You must be the doc."

"Palmenter Floric," he said.

"So, Palmenter—"

"Palmenter is my title. Floric is my name," he said huffily.

"Whatever." However, I was intrigued. "What's a palmenter?"

"A scientist of the Royal House," he said with pride in his voice.

"Royal House? I didn't know there was royalty around anymore."

"The Consortium thought it sounded good." He looked me up and down as much as he could with me seated in the booth. "Let's just say I'm far smarter than you are."

Now I understood why he was no longer with the Consortium. He was an asshole. More than that, he was a narcissistic asshole. Did I need the aggravation? I looked at Malt and saw her dislike. Was I that mean? "Sit down, Floric." Yes, I was.

"What is this offer you have?" he asked. Floric wasn't going to waste time, which was probably a good idea before I spent money buying him a meal.

"I'm in need of an inventor of sorts."

"What sort of inventing?" His eyes narrowed behind his rather ancient-looking eyewear. Not that he would have needed it. These days no one had bad eyesight, unless they wanted it.

I looked at Floric and thought he would be just stubborn enough to refuse any scientific help for his sight, despite his supposed history in the field. Maybe that's why he refused. He knew something the rest of us didn't.

"Nothing explosive, Floric. It's more defensive." I was being deliberately vague in case he decided not to accept.

"Hmm." He looked at Malt and curtly asked, "And what are you doing here? Shouldn't you be in lessons?" He then glared at me like I was deliberately encouraging her delinquency.

I looked at Malt, and her eyes pleaded with me.

"She's the reason you're here, Floric. I'm in need of someone to mentor her. Malt here has an aptitude for tinkering. She needs someone to guide her."

"Tinkering? You mean inventing?"

"Precisely." I knew my options were very narrow indeed, so it was either him or no one. "However, you will be required to move for the position."

"Move? Leave here?" He sounded nervous.

"Yes." Maybe this was going to decide the outcome for us all.

"To where, exactly?"

"I can't tell you that."

"Does that mean I'm going to be a prisoner?" His suspicion rose once more, and he studied me carefully. "Just what is going on here?"

"It's for our safety that your destination remains a secret."

"Who are you in trouble with, because I don't—" He was trying to back out, and I couldn't afford for him to do that.

"You listen to me." I leaned across the table toward him. "I'm not going to allow you or anyone else to get your grubby little hands on knowledge that could be dangerous for us all. You understand me?" I stared at him menacingly.

He looked at the two of us in turn. "Are you on the run?" he whispered.

"Did I say that?" But I could see the twinkle in his eye behind the clear titanium. Was he excited by the thought of being a wanted man?

"But you said—"

"I didn't say anything. This is just a teaching position." I leaned back as I spoke and tried to give an air of unconcern.

"I do not teach." He was vainly trying to hold on to his dignity, I could see that, but I suspected he had very little of that dignity left. I had heard bits and pieces about his unceremonious dumping from the Consortium's employment. There had been some clouding of the story as to why, but looking at the man today, I could see that age and his fractured mind had caught up with him. I was the end of his line.

"From what I hear, that's about all you're good for now." I realize it was harsh, but he needed to know he wasn't fooling me. "If you take it, you'll need to sever all ties, at least for now. I don't want you to think this is an easy job. It won't be. But, on the other hand, you're not going into a war zone. It's just necessary for all of us to remain anonymous for the moment."

"From whom?"

"I give you that, and you go looking for a reward. No. It's a once-only offer. You decide now, because I leave with or without you."

"I have to decide this minute?"

"Well, the length of the meal." I waved my hand over the electronic eye on the table. A moment later a squat service droid arrived.

"May I help you." The monotone voice of the machine took away the intimacy of the meal. It was just a little bit too clinical for me. Sure, I had a replicator on old Bessie but that was from necessity, not by choice. For one, I was usually too busy avoiding getting caught to worry about cooking, and probably more important, I couldn't cook. That was not to say I didn't appreciate a properly cooked meal every now and then.

Once Floric knew I was paying the bill, he ordered like it was his last meal. Despite whatever image he was trying to present to me, he was desperate and would accept the offer.

I looked at Malt and saw her furrowed brow. She noted his desperation, too, and didn't like it. Her eyes met mine, and I could see the unspoken question. *Why?* I reached over and patted the back of her hand. *Because it's good for you.* She sighed in resignation. I had won for once.

We didn't talk much over the meal, but I watched in amazement as Floric steadily ate everything that had been put in front of him. Maybe he had a second stomach to handle the volume, I don't know, but for someone whose lean figure wouldn't have cast a shadow, he sure ate a lot.

I had been sipping my caffeine synth while he was finishing his dessert. When the final morsel passed his lips, I asked, "Have you made up your mind?"

He seemed to take his time to answer, but he wasn't fooling me. We both knew it was a show, but that didn't mean I had to like it. "Yes. When?"

"Before curfew," I said.

"Until then." He stood to leave, but I stopped him.

"You're not leaving alone. Malt?" The young girl looked at me. "Would you escort Palmenter Floric to his house and watch him while he packs his things?"

"You don't trust me?" His voice was filled with incredulity.

"No." To Malt, I said, "Once he's packed, show him back to the ship and you all wait there for the delivery of our supplies. They couldn't promise delivery before curfew."

I watched Malt leave, Floric leading. In a way, I felt sorry for the poor old guy. Little did he know he was entering female hell and hot on his heels was one of the meanest hounds in the universe.

I spared a smile at the sight of the two of them heading to his home, wherever that was, before I turned to finish the shopping. I had gotten waylaid from my clothes hunting, and now I was forced to return to the melee.

After a couple of wrong turns, I reached my destination. The door swept aside at my arrival, and I entered the dimness with a certain amount of familiarity. This time I managed to find two sets of suitable clothing. As I was leaving, I thought better of departing without at least getting something for the Noorthi. After all, they had been living in those same clothes for longer than I had known them. Still, with all the washing, their clothes were shredding in some very interesting places.

I beat Malt back to the ship, so I awaited the delivery of food, clothing, and some second-hand junk that I was hoping Malt, Rales, and this professor guy could mend. The hold had to be repacked to allow for the extra baggage, and that filled in the waiting time nicely.

"Hey." A familiar voice broke the silence as I sat on the ramp to the ship. I looked up and saw the scrawny doc walking ahead of Malt. Even with her four arms, Malt was struggling under the weight of his luggage.

"Where's the food replicator?" I asked jokingly.

"Do I need one?" Floric asked.

"Are you sure it's not there in all that junk?"

"Junk?" Floric was most offended at my offhand remark. "I'll have you know that in there is my most delicate equipment." He scowled.

"And that's not all of it," Malt said with slight disdain.

"There's more?" I blanched at the thought.

"You did say I wouldn't be back for quite a while. Well, I need all this." Apparently, Floric wasn't leaving without the contents of his entire house going along as well.

"Malt, how much more?"

"More than one trip." She shook her head.

My ship had more than enough space to take everything he had, but it was a matter of principle that I was objecting. Still, he did say "equipment." Maybe collecting Floric's belongings would push our departure back safely into the curfew hours, and me into Deson's arms. I admit I have a selfish streak in me, and this particular streak was telling me I had the time for that. "All right. Let's bring it."

Chapter Thirteen

Love and Other Bruises

I found myself standing on Deson's doorstep with a few minutes to spare. It took some work to get all of Floric's belongings to the ship then settle my passengers down to sleep. I had debated with myself and Rice about this rather impulsive act all the way to Deson's house. Maybe I should have stayed put and slept the night away, but despite two against one in my head, I just knew if I didn't take this opportunity I might never have this chance again.

I did, however, lock Floric in his room as a precaution, leaving a sleeping Malt safely tucked into bed without the worry of him escaping. I chuckled. He wouldn't stand a chance.

So here I was ready to take that step that would satisfy one of my basic needs. I knew I shouldn't feel guilty about it, but somehow I did.

It's not too late to go back to the ship. Rice was still vainly trying to change my mind. She thought the whole sex act was just too awful to repeat.

My hand rose and passed over the electronic eye, announcing my arrival.

Too late now, I said smugly.

"Hey." Deson looked surprised.

"Didn't think I'd come back?" Maybe she wasn't expecting me.

"The thought did cross my mind, but I hoped you would." She smiled and stepped aside to allow me to enter.

Erica Lawson

I walked into the familiar living room and looked around. It's funny how humans are creatures of habit. I already knew what was in the room and yet I looked. Maybe something was different. But the question was "why did I care?" After tonight, I would never see Deson again, so if she had a giant phallic statue to the deity Ornus on a pedestal surrounded by six dancing naked women, I shouldn't care less.

Well, this was awkward. I stood there with my hands in my pockets, wondering what I was supposed to do next. Do I have the unnecessary pre-orgasmic drink, or do I just grab her and get this show on the road?

Take the drink, Rice muttered.

Why? You know I don't drink.

Maybe it will make me numb.

Maybe Deson read my mind because she pulled one of my hands out of my pocket and led me toward what I assumed would be the bedroom. Now she was talking.

"I won't bite. Really," Deson joked.

Are we eating?

What could I say to that? *In a manner of speaking.* "Sorry. I wasn't sure what was expected of me." Suddenly I was nervous.

"Lots of things, J, but I won't waste them on formalities." Her seductive lines were really wasted on me.

I suppose I should have twigged that something was wrong when Deson called me J, since I had never said my name, but stupid old me wasn't listening to my brain at this point because Rice was still talking. I let regions farther south dictate my actions.

We arrived at the bed, and she began to reach for my clothes. Deson certainly was in a hurry. Maybe she had a ship to catch, but she was undressing me faster than I could undo the clasps. I glanced at the bed, and it was enormous.

"That's a big bed," I said huskily.

"Yeah, my husband is a little on the large side," Deson answered between nips of my skin. Large? The guy must have been monstrously huge. "He's Vendan." Ah, that explained it.

"So he's loaded."

162

"That goes without saying. He's one of the richest of his species."

I'd only seen a couple of Vendans in my lifetime, and I have to say that no amount of money would encourage me to climb into the same bed with them, so unless this particular guy had some hidden talent, Deson was obviously in it for the money.

Eww, Rice commented.

Now what? I was losing patience.

I just saw your mental image. You know I'm going to have nightmares about this.

All I can say is Deson was a fast worker. In the time it took for me to think about what her husband looked like, she had me naked. The air was cool enough to brush my nipples erect. Or was it the fact that Deson stepped back, and with two swift hand movements, dropped her attire to the floor, leaving her as naked as I was? Why did I get the feeling she was well practiced at this?

What is a harlot? Rice asked.

Why do you ask?

Because you're saying it over and over in your head.

Suddenly the moment didn't seem so special. I was one in a long line of somebodies passing through Deson's life. And yet wasn't I doing the same thing? I was trying to make some emotional attachment to a moment I had gone into as a diversion.

A gentle shove had me on my back on the bed. I was about to move myself more to the center when Deson stopped me. "It's easier here," she whispered. I sat up to see what she was doing, and my breath caught in my throat as her tongue found the heat of me. Her hands gripped my thighs and eased them apart, and she settled herself on her knees on the floor. Was she on the clock or something? Was I supposed to leave the cash on the table afterward?

Is this going to hurt? Rice asked timidly.

Of course not. Why? I amended my previous thought. Rice wasn't only a virgin, she was an ignorant virgin.

Well, she cried this morning. I just want to be prepared. It seemed that Rice had given this some thought.

I chuckled inwardly. Rice was in for the surprise of her life.

Deson's tongue teased me, and all thought left my brain. With every lick of her tongue, my body responded as it twitched to her rhythm. Even as I cried out in passion, Deson continued her assault, her fingers adding to her delightfully agile tongue. It went on and on, and just when I thought my body would collapse, she stopped.

Praise Almighty Carn! I couldn't say how happy I was that I was still able to feel that particular vice. A lot had been riding on tonight's performance, including my sanity.

Rice was surprisingly quiet, and I wondered whether she had fainted. Maybe she was overcome by what had happened. The pleasure rolled around in my head, bouncing off the walls like a ball. *Rice?*

Uh? Rice's answer sounded more like an agonized groan.

Are you all right?

All... right? It sounded like Rice was dazed. *Er...*

"Just lie still," Deson whispered to me. Her hands rose up my body to my breasts and began tracing a path around them.

"Wha..." My mouth and my body felt numb. "What about you?" I felt guilty that I was getting all the attention.

"This is your night," she said.

Who was I to argue? "All right. If you say so."

"I do say so," Deson muttered, right before her lips kissed my skin, sliding up slowly to join her roving hands.

Oh, Carn! I recognized Rice's panic in my mind, and I suspected she had had enough.

Calm down, Rice.

But she's... I don't think Rice could say the words.

Yes, she is. I didn't think Deson could cause another orgasm in me so soon, but she somehow managed to do just that. Whatever the woman had, she should market it as an all-purpose aphrodisiac. Then she wouldn't need to be married to that husband of hers. Unless, of course, she was into that sort of kinky sex. Maybe I should introduce her to Vel. Then again, maybe not. One Vel in this universe was one Vel too many.

J, stop with the images already! I felt Rice's shiver.

Sorry. No one should ever see Vel at her worst, not even me.

164

Deson's hands slid slowly over my stomach, lightly massaging my skin as they went. It was an unhurried and thorough seduction, designed to relax me even further. Any more relaxed, and I'd be asleep. Her index finger slid through my pubic hair to the small bundle of nerves. Slowly her finger circled it, neither hard nor soft in its touch but more a firm determination to see me at that idyllic place once more.

But all the stimulation was slowly turning to pain. The saying "the agony and the ecstasy" came to mind, and at that point, I knew exactly what it meant. I wanted her to stop and to continue, but was it worth the pain for that one final orgasm? I must have debated in my head for too long, because that familiar swell was gathering momentum in my loins.

I barely heard Deson's words over the din in my ears. "Come on, one more time." One more time, and I wouldn't have to worry about Fen, Beri, or Vel. I'd be dead. But I couldn't stop that tidal wave from crashing over me as my body heaved to its own selfish desires. All I could do was hold on and hope I didn't drown.

Buh... jar... der... Rice was a babbling mess, and I wasn't too far behind her.

It took quite a few moments before I was aware of my surroundings, just barely acknowledging someone clapping.

"I've got to give it to you, J. You always knew how to enjoy yourself." I recognized that voice.

Uh-oh. Rice's comment wasn't really needed, because I knew I was an idiot. My hand rose and covered my eyes. I had just done the most foolish thing of my life. Lifting my hand away I sought out Deson, who now stood next to my mortal enemy. I had been so concerned about betrayal from within that I let my suspicion skip a total stranger. I had no one to blame but myself for this one.

Do I have to say I told you so? Rice said.

You had no idea, so don't be so smug, missy.

Nothing good ever comes from sex. You are living proof of that.

Suddenly Rice was being a real pain the ass. When did she grow up?

"Hello, Vel." What was it about Vel and me being naked?

"Long time, no see. You've caused me a lot of trouble," Vel said, almost amused.

"Good." I swung my legs over the edge of the bed and sat up. Every eye in the room was on me, from my crotch to my breasts, and let me tell you, it was uncomfortable. I had a horrible flashback to Rigeus and my day in the sun.

Jordana! Rice spat out my name so hard that it hurt my head. I had done it again and given the poor girl an image that would go down in the annals of depravity.

Vel grabbed my clothes off the floor and handed them to a trooper standing behind her. "Search them." He did as she asked, taking the credits that were in my pockets.

"Hey," I complained, not that it would have done any good. The dozen troopers watching me shoved their laser rifles forward in threat. There was little I could do, so I held up my hands in surrender.

"Get dressed," Vel said as she nodded to the guard with my clothes. He threw them at me, and I caught them. But nobody moved.

"Don't I get some privacy?" Not that I expected any. I buttoned my mouth shut to stop any smart-ass remark escaping my lips. I didn't want Vel to change her mind about my state of dress, or undress as the case could be. Being naked outside on Rigeus was one thing, but being paraded through a city of this size in my birthday suit was not on my to-do list.

Praise the goddess for that, Rice said.

"It's a bit late for that. Everyone's seen everything you have." Vel chuckled at my obvious annoyance, and it was one more thing to get under my skin.

Why don't you just hit her? I could feel Rice's ire.

My, my Rice, is that violence you're suggesting? Despite my dire position, I was amused.

For her, I'll make an exception.

I slipped my legs into my trousers and leaned over to stand up. Something cold landed on my skin at the base of my spine and trickled down to my ass crack.

What was that?

Rice, do you have to question everything?

Well, what was it? Rice persisted.

How the hell do I know? Do I have eyes in the back of my head? Maybe it was a drop of water. I was losing patience with her. I took a deep breath and tried to relax. *Sorry.*

No, I shouldn't—

Rice, stop it. We're in this together, all right? There was no answer. *Right, Rice?*

Right, came the sullen reply.

I wanted to check it out, but any sudden movement from me could set off a firefight that would probably put a dozen holes in me. So I let it pass, even though I felt my nose crinkle and my eyes squeeze shut as I stood and the cold traveled farther down my ass. By the time I did up my trousers, the cold had warmed and I couldn't feel it anymore. It was just going to have to stay put until later. Then again, considering where it seemed to be, I didn't think I wanted to know what it was anyway. I just hoped that whatever it was, it was sitting in my pants and staying put.

Just as I slipped my arms into the sleeves of my shirt, my boots came flying at me and hit me in the chest. I had to move fast to catch them before they fell to the floor.

"Nice catch," Vel said. "You have thirty seconds to get dressed. Otherwise you go out as is."

J, Rice warned, *don't let her rile you.*

I said nothing as I scrambled to get my boots on and button up my shirt. I fell short of the allotted time by two buttons, but at least I'd covered all the essentials. For the moment, Vel was calling the shots and there was nothing I could do about it.

"What? No smart comment?" She chuckled softly as I glared at her. "You disappoint me."

My words wanted to come out, and I was hard-pressed to hold them in, because Vel had the knack of bringing out the insults in me.

"Okay, be boring then. Take her to the ship."

Two troopers approached me with magnetic manacles in their hands. Before they manhandled me, or in this case woman-handled me, I held out my arms to await the shackles. They clipped them on around my wrists, not too tightly but firm enough that I felt them constantly. The guards took a few steps back before Vel touched her belt and the two bracelets clamped together, holding my wrists in place with a strong magnetic field. There was no point in struggling. I knew the manacles were escape proof.

As I was being escorted out of the house, I stopped in front of Deson. "I hope it was worth it."

"Twenty thousand credits," she exclaimed gleefully. The bitch wasn't even repentant.

"But your partner's wealthy." I couldn't understand why she would need the money.

"It's his money, not mine."

Why that... that... Rice stammered.

Bitch, Rice? You can say it. You know I'm thinking much worse.

But still it was nice to know my value had gone up so dramatically. I snickered at the thought, but it came out as nothing more than a quick exhale out my nose.

"What's so funny?" Vel asked.

"Nothing." I wouldn't give her the satisfaction of an explanation. I got pushed in the back, and I stepped out of the house and into the sunlight of the extended day. We gathered out in the street awaiting Vel's arrival.

She stopped for a moment and nodded to her captain of the guard. He walked back into the building, his hand reaching for his weapon. A moment later I heard the telltale sound of a blast from a pistol and then silence.

What was that?

Vel's justice. Deson's life wasn't even worth twenty thousand credits.

"Was that really necessary?" I asked.

"I suppose not," Vel replied blandly.

"Then why do it?" It was a bit of a rhetorical question, because I had a feeling I knew what the answer would be.

"Because I can."

And that was Vel in a nutshell. She had come a long way from her days as merely an enthusiast of rough bedroom games. She was now a full-fledged sociopath.

The captain emerged and handed over the chit to Vel who crumpled the document in her hand. She gave me a glance before looking in the direction of the spaceport. "Let's go."

I was in deep trouble, and nobody knew it except me, Rice, and Vel.

†

We made our way through the city quickly and quietly. I thought Vel would have had a parade for capturing me, but no, she was more intent on getting me to her ship. Was she afraid I would escape? Suddenly I felt happier, because she scared the shit out of me.

The ship at the spaceport was opulent, to say the least. It wasn't for practical purposes but more for lavish comfort. Why was I not surprised? Vel wanted the whole universe to know she was in charge. I followed the guards into the interior and whistled low. I hadn't seen anything like this. It was a palace, or so I imagined, since I'd never been invited into anything fancier than a local governor's office. In the center of the ship was one large room with six equally large chairs.

"Sit down." Vel pointed to a comfortable chair facing away from the cockpit. Who was I to argue? It was a hell of a lot better than hanging by my fingernails. Vel sat opposite me and reached for her seatbelt. "Buckle up."

I struggled to put the seatbelt on as my wrists were still bound together by the manacles. I just locked myself in as the ship took off. "The locals aren't going to like this."

"Like what?"

"You're breaking curfew."

"Screw 'em," she snarled.

"Tsk, tsk, Vel, breaking the law like that."

She laughed. "I was wondering where that smart mouth had gotten to." Vel touched her belt, and I felt the manacles fall away from one another. "Relax."

I suppose I had no choice. After all, where could I go? I was surrounded by guards on a ship I assumed was about to hyperjump to Juno. I relaxed about as much as a person going to their death could. And I knew there'd probably be a lot of pain and discomfort before that happened.

Death? Did you say death?

I could hear the fear in Rice's voice. *What did you expect? A slap on the wrist? Besides, you've already died once, what's once more?*

It's the pain leading up to the death that I'm worried about.

Me, too, Rice. Me, too.

I shifted my hands from my lap to rest them on the seat and rotated my shoulders as I did so. Before the manacles had even touched the seat's surface, they pulled my wrists down and magnetized them to the armrests.

"Can't have you wandering around free now, can we?" Vel grinned at me, clearly enjoying her manipulation of me.

"No, we can't," I said with a little hint of sarcasm.

Vel sat there expectantly. I think she was waiting for some pithy remark from me, so I decided not to oblige her. I just stared at her until her eyes turned away. "Aren't you the least bit curious about what's going on?"

"Nope." Of course I wanted to know what was going on, but my job here was to piss her off as much as I could. Not playing her game was a good start.

"Your loss." She turned her attention to activating a small screen attached to her chair. "I've got her." Vel was obviously talking to her boss.

"When will you arrive?" I recognized Grimm's voice. It had been awhile, but I knew that condescending tone anywhere.

"We're about to jump. Three hours," Vel said in clipped tones.

"Good. Contact me when you land." Before she even had a chance to answer, the screen went blank.

I tried very hard not to laugh at her expression. She obviously didn't like being hung up on like that. "You'd better get used to it."

"What?" Vel's brow wrinkled in annoyance.

"He's the boss. You'd better get used to being cut off like that."

"Screw you."

"I told you I wouldn't do that, so get it out of your mind right now." Despite my promise, I couldn't help a smart-ass remark passing my lips. I admit it. I didn't see it coming. Vel's hand balled into a fist and punched me right in the mouth before I even had a chance to inhale. My head snapped back with the force, and the copper taste in my mouth was familiar.

Ow! Rice whined.

Get used to it, kid.

Vel didn't even wait to see my reaction to the hit. She walked away and returned with a drink, which she consumed quickly, followed by another. When she was suitably mellow, I decided to gently probe her with questions.

"The Consortium's not going to like this, you know," I said.

"What are you talking about?" Vel blinked a few times as she tried to focus on me.

"They're not going to let you muscle in on their territory."

"They won't know what's hit them until it's all over." Vel took another swig of the synth.

"Yeah, right." Incredulity tinged my words. If I sounded skeptical, maybe she would reveal more.

"You don't believe me?"

"If you say so."

"Ah," she said, "you don't know what you're talking about."

So I had to give a little to get a little. "No? I've got one word for you: drugs." That one word made her sit up. "Drugs and mud. An unlikely combination, that's for sure."

She glared at me. "Lucky guess."

"Guess? You know very well I'd have to have an IQ of two hundred to make that sort of intuitive leap." Now where did that word come from? Maybe the ochre was improving my IQ as well. It was certainly improving my vocabulary.

"You've got a point," she said thoughtfully.

"But getting the universe hooked on drugs is nothing new. Many have tried and failed."

"But they don't have the secret ingredient." Vel took another mouthful of the alcohol, her face grimacing as it slid down her throat.

"But it's only mud, Vel. Everyone will soon discover that."

"That's only part of it." She winked conspiratorially at me. "It's what goes with the mud that makes it special."

I knew that as well. But what the sisters gave me wasn't habit-forming by any means, so maybe the bad guys were substituting something else instead of the oil.

"How special?"

"So special that once hooked, you can die without it." She giggled and it wasn't pretty. "But that's only the beginning."

"He's not happy being a drug lord?" I knew lots of people who would be.

"Shh." She sent a bit of spit my way and I cringed. I was so tempted to tell her to sober up, but while she was willing to share the information I ignored the glob on my shirt. "He wants to be Emperor of everything." Vel swigged some more alcohol. I couldn't tell whether the grimace on her face was for the drink or Grimm. "They wouldn't follow him unless he used mind control."

Mind control? My mind was running rampant with ideas. Was the ochre involved? "Using the ochre with a different additive, I suppose."

Her finger touched her nose. Was she scratching it or giving me a subtle signal? I couldn't tell.

I had an epiphany there and then. Was that why the Noorthi were so mysterious? Was this the secret they hid away from the universe? In the wrong hands, the ochre could be modified to be anything?

What are you talking about? We are a peaceful—

Later.

"Yeah, Vel. Special mud. You get high on it. Sure." I had my skepticism set on maximum in the hope of Vel telling me something I didn't know.

"That's one. Mind control is another." Vel giggled and put her hand over her mouth. "Oops." Her giggles sent chills up my spine, but finally I had gotten an answer. Mind control would be a good universe-conquering tool.

"He won't like you mouthing off like that."

No one should ever have to see that.

See what?

That woman giggling like a novice. She scares me.

And you should be scared, Rice. Right at this moment, she's the most dangerous thing in this universe.

The one question that had been driving me nuts was who the hell was in charge? On the one hand there was Grimm, who had been carrying this grudge for about fifteen years. On the other was Vel, who wanted me dead a hundred different ways. I figured either way I was screwed.

"What does he know, huh? The little piss-ant," she said.

"Now that's no way to talk about Grimm."

"I don't know what you did to piss him off, but he certainly remembers you."

"And yet he doesn't even take the time to stop in and say 'hello.'"

"You'll get your chance soon enough." Vel stood rather unsteadily. "Watch her," she said to the two guards watching my every move. She wandered across the room to the back of the ship.

I wasn't exactly sure where she had gotten to, but Vel didn't reappear until after the exit from the hyperjump.

"Just make sure you're there, Andrissa," Vel barked over her telelink as she reentered the room and took her seat opposite me. She had returned with a caffeine synth and a tablet. She popped the tablet in her mouth and washed it down with a mouthful of caffeine. In a matter of moments, she sobered.

"I hope you sent my love to her."

"And she said to drop dead."

"She did not."

I just smiled. I had successfully baited Vel, and she was clutching for a comeback.

"Besides you're not her type."

"I'm everybody's type," I said.

"She likes them dead." Vel grinned for a second before she frowned.

"Feel better?" I asked.

"No."

"But you need to be sober when you meet him, huh?" I knew I had guessed correctly when she stood, took a step or two toward me then slapped me across the cheek. "It just burns you that he's in charge." This time she grabbed my nipple and twisted it. "Ow. That hurt!"

I second that.

"That's the point. Get used to that feeling." Vel looked at her chronometer just as a voice came over the intercom.

"Coming up on Juno, ma'am."

"Ma'am?" I laughed loudly, which earned another brutal pinch. "Aww, come on Vel, where's your sense of humor?"

"It's waiting for you in a deep dark interrogation cell on Juno." She smiled wickedly at me. Maybe it was saying something to her that I was blissfully ignoring. It was probably better that way. "Now strap yourself in, it's going to be a bumpy ride."

"I'm sure it will be, but I seem to be at a disadvantage at the moment."

She touched her belt and the pressure on the manacles stopped. Her finger hovered over the button as I secured my seat belt properly. Maybe she was waiting for a wrong move from me. It would have been nice, but the escape options were nil. No, my best chance was on the ground before I reached the compound.

I held out my wrists awaiting the power to activate them. She looked almost disappointed at my meek surrender to her will. "I'll remember this moment, Vel."

"I'm sure you will, but I hope that in the next few days we will make some beautiful memories together."

"You are one sick woman, you know that?"

"Why thank you," she said brightly, as if I had given her a compliment. Her smile seemed genuine, so maybe I had. I mentally changed sick to certifiable. "So, do you want to know what's in store for you?"

174

"Not particularly, no. Unlike you, I like surprises."

"Where's your sense of humor?" she said back at me.

"Now let's see, I had it when I left Locar. Oh, your guard pocketed it along with my credits. Tell him I want them back after this is all over."

"Believe me, when we're finished, you won't need either of them."

"Promises, promises." But Vel confirmed what I suspected. It wasn't going to be pretty. As I said the words there was a gentle bump, signifying we had landed. My time had run out.

We had arrived during the solar cycle, and the sun was still shining brightly for the middle of the night. I looked through the window at the vaguely familiar spaceport, glancing at the hanger to see if Bessie was still here. There she was, her antenna sitting above the line of the ship parked in front of her. My thoughts wandered to fonder times when Bessie and me flew through the universe in search of adventure and our next paycheck. Would we ever see those days again?

Is that what one thinks about before their imminent death?

In my case. Fond memories to take away the pain.

"Come on. Your destiny awaits," Vel said as she stood.

"Really? You're going to die? Great!" I fumbled with the catch on the belt then stood up awkwardly.

Vel let the comments slip. I think she was too busy thinking about what she was going to do to me. Now me, I was trying to think of everything else but that. She extended her hand with a flourish. "After you."

"Yeah, yeah." I walked toward the two guards standing at the exit, unbowed and unbroken. Yeah, I know. Who was I fooling, right?

Not me. I can feel you shaking.

I'm trying to be brave and noble here. Don't destroy the image. At the bottom of the travelator, a hover vehicle waited for us. Apparently Vel was making sure I didn't have the chance to escape. Yep, I was right. I was in deep, deep trouble.

And you only realize that now?

If you weren't dead already...

You've got to catch me first. For the first time, Rice laughed inside my head. It was infectious. I laughed out loud, and the guards stared at me in astonishment. Let them think I was crazy. It didn't matter anymore. In a matter of hours, I'd be dead.

Chapter Fourteen

And the Winner Is...

After an uneventful and short trip from the spaceport to the compound, I found myself in an enormous foyer. "The guards will make sure you're comfortable," Vel said as she looked into my eyes.

"You're not joining me?" False bravado tendered the offer.

"My, my. You're in a hurry."

When she walked away, I couldn't help a parting shot. "Off to report to your master, huh?" I made a move before she could think about hitting me again, but I knew I had found her weakness. On any other solar day, I would have exploited that weakness, but considering the situation I was in, it was probably prudent to shut the hell up. "Let's go," I said to my jailers.

I lost count of the stairs as we descended, but the outside light slowly faded away the farther down we went. Finally we reached the detention cell, lit by portable lighting jammed into wall crevices. It was cool, it was damp, it was dark, and it probably suited Vel's mood perfectly. In one corner was a small room, if it could have been called that. It was a space of floor surrounded on two sides by rock and the other two by an invisible force field, evident from the mechanism on the wall. At least there was a bed in it.

"Turn around," a guard said and I obliged. Two guards stood back and focused their weapons on me while the third disconnected the magnetic bracelets. He stepped back and placed his palm on the scanner on the wall. "Step back three paces." I did as he asked and then watched as he waved his hand over an electronic eye to reengage the force field.

"I could use some food." I hadn't eaten since my lunch with Floric, and my stomach was starting to grumble.

Two guards left while one stayed on duty. Did that mean I would eat? I looked around the small space that was now my home and finally decided to lie down on the makeshift bed. Time passed and nothing happened. "Hey," I called to the guard, "Are you going to feed me or what?"

He glared at me for a moment before standing and going to the intercom.

"What?" I barely recognized Vel's voice as she barked out the word. It looked like her meeting with the boss didn't go too well.

"She wants food," the guard said curtly.

"Fine."

I could hear the click from where I was. She was really pissed, and I was her outlet for that anger. I just hoped my last meal was first class. Then again, the way my luck had been for the last twenty-four hours, I wasn't holding out much hope.

What are we going to do?

Not much.

You don't have an escape plan? Rice sounded surprised. I guessed she had expected more of me.

No, no escape plan. This is the end of the line.

But—

No buts, Rice. If you have any way of escaping, now is the time to do so.

I don't think I can. This has never happened before.

Or so you say. Maybe, in another universe, you girls are popping in and out of people's heads on a daily basis, playing with people's minds.

We would never do that! We are a peaceful—

A peaceful race. Yeah, yeah, you keep saying that. Then why are you here?

Because you brought me. I have to go where you go.

I sighed. The girl was right. *Sorry. I'm sorry that what will happen is not going to be pleasant for either of us. Maybe we should both get a little rest before that.*

More time passed without my guard stirring. Either he was giving great thought to what he was going to bring me or I wasn't eating anytime soon. "Any news from the cook?" I asked politely. I didn't feel polite, and I didn't want to be polite, but here I was, being polite. He glanced over at me and went back to his contemplation of his navel fuzz or whatever he was doing.

Just when I had decided that Vel was going to starve me to death, a woman came down the staircase and glided across the room. And when I said glided, I meant it. She moved smoothly like she was floating on air. I recognized her as Noorthi. There wasn't any distinguishing physical feature that labeled someone as Noorthi, more an aura about them that defined them. Having lived with Beri and her tribe for a while now, I easily identified this woman by her poise. Of course, the tattoo on her wrist would help a little too, not that I could see it yet.

She placed the tray on the floor next to the force field and stepped back when the guard ordered her to do so. He deactivated the force field, his weapon ready in his hand as I reached for the food. I barely got the tray inside when the barrier came up, sending sparks off the metal in warning.

The woman was about to leave when I spoke up. "Can you stay awhile?" She looked uncertainly at the trooper. "Just to talk, that's all." To my surprise he nodded, and she pulled up a chair to sit against the wall.

I sat cross-legged on the bed and picked at my food, eating a pinch of food at a time. "What's your name?"

Again she showed a guarded look. I could only guess why, but I suspected that it was a reaction born from years of internment.

"My name is Jordana. Nice to meet you, Noorthi lady." Her eyes now took an interest in me. "You have an air about you," I said.

"You have met my sisters?" she asked almost wistfully.

"Some of them." I showed her my tattoo.

"Do... do you..." she hesitated as if afraid to ask. "Do you know Beristhamée?" It was a look of hopefulness.

"I'll tell you what. You tell me your name, and I'll answer your question." I had my suspicions as to who this woman was now, but a name would be helpful if I ever escaped from here.

"Tarsthancus." She looked around as if saying her name would strike her down.

"And who are you in the scheme of things?"

"No one. I am no one."

Well that's torn it, I grumbled.

What's wrong?

Beri was hoping to find her mother.

I'm glad you're going to be the one to tell her that this woman isn't. I could hear the smugness in Rice's voice. But she was right. I was the unlucky one who would have to deliver the sad news. That is, if I ever got out of here.

And how do you know it isn't? Rice asked.

Her mother's name is Gerasthamée. Who is this woman, Rice?

I don't know. I was only a child when we left Juno. Maybe Beri can tell you.

But she's not here right now, is she?

I wanted to tell this woman that everything was all right, but something was stopping me. Maybe it was the betrayal I had suffered only hours ago. "I knew Beristhamée."

"Knew?" she looked stricken, but I couldn't take any chances. I was in the belly of the beast, and I didn't want to bring any more death to this universe than I already had.

"Sorry, I was off-world when there was an explosion. It destroyed the entire settlement. They're all dead. You're all that's left." My heart thumped heavily in my chest as a lone tear slid down her pale cheek.

"Who was she to you?" I asked.

"A friend."

But "friend" held more meaning than she was saying. "Friend?"

"We shared a room. We were close—"

A different person spoke in a melodious and familiar voice. "You've made another friend, I see."

"Marius Grimm." I greeted him soberly.

"Leave us," he told Tarsthancus.

She stood and walked slowly to the stairs, her stoic façade firmly in place, but I could nearly feel the emotions rolling off her. If I was wrong about her, then she could curse me later.

"I've finally got you where I want you," Grimm said angrily.

"Got nothing better to do with your time?"

"As far as you're concerned, no." He moved the few steps to put himself right next to the force field. He studied me intently. What was he expecting to find?

"And you just happen to be here when I arrive?" Somehow I seriously doubted that.

"Vel signaled me when she first heard you were on Locar. I made it my business to be here."

"You're that eager to face me?" I couldn't help but smile at his desperation.

"I would have moved the entire universe, yes." There was an almost calm manner to him, and that was a bit unnerving.

"Why are you wasting so much time on me? Am I your only enemy? I find that hard to believe."

"You're the one who caused me to lose the most."

"Me? What did I do? Why don't you just get to the point?"

"I should have killed you myself when I had the chance."

"Why?"

"You don't remember?" he said with incredulity. "The day you ruined my life?"

"What the hell are you talking about? Of course I remember. I warned you then it wasn't going to be an easy delivery. Parscus Run is a universal improbability. How the hell was I supposed to track a series of habitable meteorites traveling in a pack across the various universes? They're impossible to find, let alone land on."

"And yet you took the job."

"Wave thirty-five-thousand credits under my nose, and I'll take on anything."

"Yes, you bitch," he said triumphantly.

"So I didn't deliver the packages. If I remember rightly, Consortium cruisers were on my tail for two days. I had to hide in the Gravel Pit for two more days before I shook them." Poor Bessie didn't take kindly to scratching around in that minefield loosely described as a cloud of space debris from a nearby supernova.

"You destroyed me!"

"I wasn't even there."

"Exactly. You didn't deliver the goods, and they came after me." He was panting wildly now, angered beyond reason. "They took my company, my reputation, and nearly my life."

"You got your packages back, and I didn't even charge you for it. If that wasn't enough, then I'm sorry—"

"Sorry isn't good enough for you. If Vel had been doing her job, I wouldn't have to face you now." He paced back and forth as his anger festered.

"Yeah, you should get rid of her."

"Enough." Grimm shook his fist. "I want retribution."

"You look like you're doing fine now, so what's the problem?" This guy was losing the plot quickly, and I was in his sights.

"They took something else."

"And what is that?" He was all but shouting at me to ask him, so it was probably something really spectacular.

"This." He reached up and twisted his left shoulder, allowing his left arm to fall away.

Wow!

You can say that again.

Wow!

Smart-ass.

"That's a bit dramatic." I studied the metallic hub that was his shoulder joint, wondering if it came with a series of attachments. Knowing how pissed off he was with me, I suspected he had the whole slice-and-dice set.

"You have no idea," he said almost too calmly. He reattached the arm with an audible click.

"So you want my head. I get it." I let a moment pass before I spoke again. "I'm sorry, I truly am, but it's in the past."

"There is no past. Not for me. The only thing that's kept me going all these years was looking forward to your death."

"And what's going to happen when that's done, huh? What motivation do you have after I'm terminated?"

Geez, J, all these big words.

Yeah, I amaze even myself.

"I'm sure being conqueror of this universe will be a good diversion," he replied.

He held my life in his hands, we both knew that, but keeping him talking was my best option. The guy was clearly nuts, anyway, for holding a grudge like this all these years. "And how long do you think the Consortium will let that happen?" I sat down on the bed and rested my back against the wall.

"They won't even know it's happened, the fools."

"Don't sell them short." I hoped I wasn't. I started making a "to-do" list for the afterlife. "If I know all about your drugs and mud, then rest assured they do, too."

He stared at me, as if trying to gauge if I was lying. I had no idea if I was, so I had nothing to hide from him.

How can you say that? You don't know.

This is what it's like in the outside universe. Lying, cheating, stealing, and sex are a top priority. Eating and breathing come a little lower on the list of importance. No one tells the truth, at least not all the time.

That's horrible. When do you know that someone is telling the truth?

You don't, and that's the fun part. "And what about the Noorthi woman, Grimm?"

"What about her?" His demeanor was one of disinterest.

"What is she to you?"

"Nothing, my dear Jordana. She's just a little insurance."

"Insurance? Against what?"

"Against someone doing something foolish like, oh, I don't know..." He contemplated his next words in a mock fashion. "Like trying to break into the compound."

"You've kept her prisoner for ten years? That's a little bit excessive, even for you."

"And why do you want to know?" He stopped pacing and stood facing me on the other side of the force field.

"She's more than insurance, isn't she? You're hoping to find out a few truths about the Noorthi." He looked thoughtful, as if trying to decide whether to tell me or not. "I know you're dying to tell someone how clever you are."

"She was a stubborn one, even with the Noorthi on Rigeus as collateral."

"Six years? You never struck me as someone that patient."

"Six years. That bitch strung me along for six years."

"It was time to end it," I said.

"Yes, and Vel was most eager to help."

"How did you find her, Grimm?" Knowing Vel, she would have made herself known to someone like Grimm, especially with the chance of advancement to a position of power.

"She just been sent to Rigeus and was eager to get off the planet. It seemed a simple enough deal. Hunt down the Noorthi, and I'd help her escape."

"Of course. After all, you couldn't have them running around knowing the truth about you. And the mine?"

"One of her scouts came back one day with mud on her shoes. Somehow Vel had heard about my search for the ochre and sent a sample. Un-freaking-believable!" he yelled. "I couldn't believe my luck. Six years I'd been trying to get information out of the Noorthi woman and Vel stumbles across it. Of course, it was nothing more than a fissure in the ground, so Vel put the Noorthi to work."

"That's not to say she didn't kill one or two along the way to sate her bloodlust." Wow! Did I just say that? I was really getting the hang of this new vocabulary.

"It was the least I could do." He smiled one of those smiles that sent a shiver down my spine.

"How you had to keep the Noorthi woman a little longer. You wanted it all."

"Of course I wanted it all. She cost me a lot."

"But you also got a lot in return." Despite what Grimm had said, there was only one reason I could think of why Tarsthancus would still be alive and, from the looks of her, unharmed after ten years. She wasn't a prisoner. "How many kids do you have?" I took a gamble with my question.

He watched me for a full minute before answering, as if waiting for me to flinch under his observation. "Three. Three boys to carry on my legacy."

"How nice for you," I answered sarcastically.

How can you say that? She has betrayed everything we are.

Calm down, Rice. It was probably the only way she kept herself alive.

But—

"And she's it? No more Noorthi?" I was asking for Beri's benefit.

"Except for those you've stolen from me." Grimm reached for his belt and pushed the intercom. "Bring him down," he said.

"Well, I don't have them." *Rice, before you say anything, yes I know I'm lying, and no, I'm not going to tell the truth anytime soon.*

"Of course you have them. And you will tell me." He seemed supremely confident he could make me talk.

"I've got nothing to tell." All right, I was fooling no one but myself, but at this moment, I needed to believe in someone. "Why don't you believe me?"

"Because you are a good-for-nothing, lying, cheating bitch who would turn in her own grandmother if there was a credit in it."

"Just what is your problem?" I moved to the very edge of the cell to within a hairsbreadth of touching the force field. "It's an arm, Grimm. Until you showed me, I wouldn't have known the difference. Why are you so hell-bent on destroying me? Destroying the universe?"

He moved closer. If the force field were shut down, I could have touched him without taking a step. I looked into his dark eyes and tried to see the truth. "They fed me to a neezak."

I shivered. I'd never actually seen one, but I'd heard the stories. Grimm was a lucky man to live.

"It tore off my arm at the shoulder and took my leg. I also lost a kidney." He stopped for a moment and let the information sink in. "Do you know how long I was in pain? Ten years, Laren. Ten long years. The only thing that kept me going was the thought of killing you."

"So it's because of me you're alive," I said. It was probably not a good thing to point out at this moment, but I had to hope that my part in his recovery was a bonus.

The sound of footsteps attracted Grimm's attention to the staircase. I caught Vel's movement in my peripheral vision as she glided across the room to stand behind him.

"True, but you're also the cause of my pain in the first place." He took a step back, as if distancing himself from the conversation. "And as for the universe, well that's just business."

Grimm seemed amused by my predicament. *Your time is coming, pal.*

"Are you staying?" Vel asked him casually.

"No. I want to have a word with Tarsthancus." He nodded toward the stairs and the building above them. "Call me when you're done." Grimm gave me one last look and walked across the basement to the stairs. "Goodbye, Jordana."

"You're going to miss all the fun."

"If I can see your lifeless body when it's all over, I'll be satisfied." He ascended the stairs and disappeared out of sight.

Why do you keep doing that?

Because I'm a masochist.

A massa-kissed?

Someone who likes being in pain.

You are a strange one.

Even now I was figuring all the angles, not that I would have much of a chance to tell anyone what I found out. Tarsthancus meant something to Grimm—that was obvious because they had three children together—but I suspected he would sacrifice her in a heartbeat if it suited him. Was Beri's Noorthi sister a traitor to the sisterhood? How far would she go to protect her family? I had no way of finding out, unless Vel wanted to oblige me and reveal everything, but looking at her expression, I doubted that would happen.

She stood in front of me on the other side of the force field. In spite of myself, I looked her over. Damn, she was an attractive woman. It was such a shame she was a nut case. Her almond-shaped eyes, dark brown pools of malice, simmered with unfulfilled retribution. But it was her mouth that had always taken my fancy—and I'm talking facial features here as the rest of her body was on a whole other level—because it was perfect. Her lower lip always had me salivating, wanting to nip at it in invitation. Too bad the curve of those beautiful lips was a lie. When I first saw them tilted upward at rest, I thought she was a sweet girl. It didn't take me long to realize that her face was a fraud, masking the sociopathic tendencies that burned inside her.

You're showing me images again, J. Stop it.

But just look at her.

I don't care about your love-hate relationship. Just stop with the undressing and other stuff. I want to throw up.

Well, if you lose it, you clean it up. In my peripheral vision, I caught movement. It was hard to break the visual contact Vel had made, and I had to force myself to look at the stairs. Two burly guards were hauling a rather large, solid-looking chair into the chamber. An elegant-looking older gentleman followed them, carrying a box. Oh, this was not good.

My eyes returned to Vel, and I looked her straight in the eye. A slow smile crossed her face. My heart started to race. All that was left to me was the hope that I didn't do something foolish like soiling myself.

If you lose it, you clean it up.

"Yes," Vel said with a hiss, "you should be afraid."

"Me? You must be joking."

"Your eyes don't lie."

"What do you want, Vel? What good is this going to do?"

"I want you to suffer, but before I can have my fun, we need some information."

"We, Vel?" I saw her bristle and knew I had struck a nerve. "You could have just asked, and these nice men wouldn't have to

187

injure themselves carrying down that chair." I looked over at the chair in question and the two men leaning on it who were breathing heavily.

"That chair will come in handy later."

Later. That was the part that worried me. "Well, let's see how this goes first, eh?" I said jokingly, but we both knew it didn't matter what I said. Nothing was going to save me short of a rupture in the time-space continuum or a fusion bomb. Maybe I should just do something foolish like try to escape and get shot for my trouble. Now that would piss off Vel no end.

Vel took two steps back, and the guards pointed their weapons at me as the shield came down. "Make yourself comfortable." She nodded at the chair. She was almost too happy when she said that. Vel enjoyed her torture just a little too much.

"What, no alcohol?" One of the guards slapped me on the back of the head. "Watch it. That's her job." I knew my jibes were going to be the death of me, but I was going down swinging.

"Thank you." Vel laughed, shortened the distance between us, and cuffed me over the head as well.

Will you stop that? They're hitting me in the head, too.

"That's better," I said softly as I sat down. The seat was uncomfortable, being bare metal and all, but it was probably designed with less comfort in mind. Nobody ever said torture was comfortable.

"Are you going to make this hard for us?" Vel cooed softly. By the look in her eye, I think she was hoping I would.

"I told you—" Vel raised her fist, and I held up my hand to stop her. "Okay, I'll stop."

Vel reached for her belt, and the manacles gripped the metallic armrests. "Happy now?" I said in a tone I hoped sounded sarcastic.

"Very. Now just relax. Fighting it will only hurt more."

But I knew she wanted me to resist, so if nothing else, she could see me in more pain. "Well, that depends on whether we get on well or not. I may ask 'it' out to dinner."

"I'm going to miss that razor wit of yours."

"Miss it? Is it going somewhere?"

"Possibly. Then again, if you lose your mind it won't matter." Vel chuckled.

My eyes moved to the old man with the box. She was manipulating me perfectly. I returned my gaze to my nemesis, but it was too late. She knew she had won this particular battle, because I had looked.

"And what makes you think I haven't already done that? After all, I'm here with you, aren't I?" It was all so pointless really. My mouth was not going to save me this time. While this conversation had been going on, the elderly gentleman had given the box to the guard standing by the chair and had opened it. From the corner of my eye, I saw him take out a piece of what looked like clear film; then he extracted a second, larger piece.

"I see the sertech is ready," Vel said. "I haven't seen this done before, so it will be an education."

"Well, I'm glad you're happy about it."

I'm not.

"And you're not?" Vel asked, smiling at me.

"And if I tell you what you want to know?" I already knew the answer to my question, but it was all part of the game.

"Don't disappoint me like that. Where's your spine?"

"Holding me up in this chair, you piece of craz." We both knew that swearing at her was the last act of a desperate woman.

Watch that tongue of yours.

And what is she going to do? Kill me? I hate to tell you, Rice, but she was going to do that no matter what I said. Now I was starting to get angry because I was partly responsible for the position I was in. I let this happen and did nothing to stop it. The sertech put the film on my forehead. I stared into Vel's eyes, and I could see the intense scrutiny she was giving me. It was almost like studying hummers scurrying about on the ground when I was a kid. Right before I stomped on them.

"What are you feeling?" Vel asked, like I was an experiment.

"I'm thinking of a lot of different scenarios about how I'm going to kill you."

Well, I'm peeing in my pants right now.

What a lovely image. Open the window when you leave.

"That'll pass once your mind is gone," Vel muttered gleefully.

"Don't write me off yet, Vel." I had to have some hope if I was to have any chance of surviving this.

She nodded to the old man, and his finger rose to the large strip of film resting on the box. "Bye, J. Can't say it hasn't been fun."

"I can, you sack of bones." The pressure on my forehead slowly built in intensity. I kept my face calm while this was going on. I didn't want to give Vel any satisfaction at my discomfort. Meanwhile, I could feel Rice's panic rise. There was little hope of allaying her fears. The pressure turned to pain that started as a pinpoint in the center of my forehead and radiated from there inside my head. Like a wave, it washed through my brain, sluiced over brain cells and synapses, and paralyzed them. My body jerked as the pain took hold of me. It heaved me to and fro as my control slowly shut down.

My mind screamed, drowning out Rice's tearful mutterings. Then I could no longer feel Rice in my head. Had she passed out or, worse, died? My thoughts were washing away. The harder I tried to hold on to them, the quicker they slipped away.

"How's it going? Are you still able to hear me?" I barely recognized the words as Vel spoke them.

I gurgled. My tongue just wouldn't work no matter how hard I tried. Drool slowly dripped from the corner of my mouth, but I was only barely aware of it. The jerking stopped.

"It works on nerve conduction," the sertech explained to Vel, "and covers the skull in a type of electrical neural net. Then, like a virus, it burrows into the brain and into the conscious and subconscious mind until it takes control."

I had heard it all but understood none of it. Vel hovered over me, and her distorted image swam in front of my eyes. "Whhaaa." The word was there but just wouldn't come out.

"J, listen carefully. J!" Vel barked at me to get my attention. "Where are the Noorthi?"

"No... aaccchhh..." I had a compulsion to tell her, but I resisted. That neural net he had spoken of tightened and buried into my pain center. If I screamed, I wasn't aware of it.

"What are you doing?" Vel snapped.

"I'm reducing the intensity," the man replied.

"Leave it where it is."

"But it could kill her." There was concern in the man's voice.

"Never mind that. We want that information."

My mind floated as the conversation took place, like a ship cast adrift in the vastness of space. Whatever they had said meant little to me. Any awareness I had was nearly gone.

"J?" Something hit my face. "J! Answer the question. Where are they?"

"Hee..." The word sat on my tongue and was trying to come out involuntarily.

"Helix Four?" Vel asked hopefully.

"Hee..." I repeated.

"Hesic Minor?" the torturer suggested.

"Hee... hee... heev... en." I barely felt the drool running down my chin as I stumbled over the word.

"Heaven? Did she say heaven?" he asked.

"Yes, you idiot. Make her more aware."

"I'll try."

"Don't try. Do it."

Suddenly the fuzziness lessened, and my awareness increased. I still had the urge to tell her everything, but at least the drooling had stopped. So much for trying to keep my dignity intact.

"J." Vel rapped on my head. "Are you in there?"

"Quuiiit iitt," I said and moaned.

"Where are the Noorthi, J?" she asked carefully.

The urge returned, and I didn't fight it this time. "Heeavvveeenn."

"Heaven? Did you mean heaven?"

"Heavveeennn."

"Does that mean they're all dead?" When I didn't reply, she grabbed me and shook hard. I felt numb to everything around me as my body flopped around with the shaking.

"Heeaavveeeenn." And that was the last thing I remembered.

Chapter Fifteen

Back from the Dead

There was black. The sort of black that one gets lost in. My mind was mush, and I couldn't put two thoughts together.

"Is she still out?"

"Yeah, been three days now."

The words together should mean something, but I could only grasp a word or two.

"She won't be happy."

"Probably not. This is the first one that survived."

The two male voices continued the conversation, but I lost concentration. I scarcely knew who I was, let alone what they were talking about. My body wanted sleep, so I didn't fight the urge. I dozed off in mid-conversation.

Over the next day or two, I woke for an occasional moment before going back to sleep. I was slowly gaining strength with each day. If Vel wanted me, she was going to have to wait.

Something was missing from my mind, and it took a bit of searching to realize what that was. Rice was gone. Whether she had died, fainted, or fled, I didn't know. All I knew was I called and she didn't answer. Then I remembered why Rice would have fled. Vel's interrogation had damn near killed me.

In one of my more lucid moments, Vel was standing a few feet away from me. My memory had been improving gradually over my recuperation period, so luckily, I knew the name of my enemy and I knew she was the enemy. The details were a little fuzzy, so I was hoping to pick up a few clues from her as we went.

"Whaaaa..." My voice sounded foreign. Had something happened?

"How are you feeling? Congratulations. You survived the interrogation."

"Int... eeee... rrr..." I felt like my jaw had been unhinged.

"Having trouble?" She seemed amused at my struggle. "Lucky for you, you told the truth. Grimm's bitch confirmed your story. Now all that's left is what I want."

Truth? Bitch? It was like my mind was a blank page, and she was scribbling all over it. To me it was the meaningless scrawl of a two-year-old child. All I knew was I didn't like this woman.

Vel crooked her finger over her shoulder. "Here's something to make you feel better." Some old guy came around from behind her and touched something cold to my neck. A warm sensation flowed through me, one limb at a time, that made me want to rise. Not that Vel helped me any in that department.

I sat on the edge of the bed and dropped my aching head into my hands. "Wha... aaa... tt." I cleared my throat and tried again. "What w–was that stuff?"

"Just a pick-me-up."

"This is dangerous," the old man whispered to her.

"Dangerous?" Now she had my interest.

"The dose was way too high," he said.

"She won't be alive long enough to be worried about the side effects."

"Does Grimm know about this?"

"You answer to me," she screamed.

"I shouldn't even be here. You knew the procedure was banned across the entire system."

"And yet you were quite happy to take the credits, Sertech, so don't go preaching to me about morals."

My brain was swimming with the drug the old man gave me, slowly reversing the numbness that had hold of it. The words started to come together, first as phrases and then as whole sentences. I still had a bit of trouble with the meanings, but I was getting there. Whatever he gave me was working wonders. The only concerns I had were the dire warnings of danger and death, and I was linked to both of them.

"This is the last thing I do for you." The old man picked up his small folder and left.

"Prick," Vel muttered to his back. "Pick her up and take her to the wall."

The two guards grabbed me roughly by the arms and dragged me the twenty feet to the far wall. Embedded in the rock were two metal squares about two feet apart and about six feet from the floor.

"Strip her," Vel ordered and the two guards jostled me. "Stop looking at one another and just do it."

Slowly the buttons came undone, and my shirt was taken off. One of them fumbled with the pants. "Come on, hurry it up." There was a sudden jerk as the guard yanked my belt violently. I just closed my eyes and let them do it.

"Back to the wall." They held up my hands above my head for a moment before the magnetic cuffs took over, securing me in an outstretched position.

"Now leave us," Vel said. The two guards looked uncertainly at one another. "Go."

Suddenly there was just her and me. As I hung there, memories came flooding back and I remembered just about everything, at least up to the moment that the old man put the film on my forehead. And now, whatever she had in mind was lethal and I wasn't in a position to stop her.

She grinned at me. "Stop worrying. You'll live past today. I promise."

I said nothing.

"Come on, J. No witty repartee?"

I barely had the energy to stand upright. What made her think I wanted to talk? My mind was still trying to boot up after being shut down, so any fancy conversation on my part was out of the question. I just stared at her.

"I have something special in mind for today." She walked to a cloth-covered table and wheeled it over next to me. "You always were too independent. There's only one alpha female here, and it's me." She grabbed the cloth and pulled it off to reveal two rings slightly smaller than my finger, a length of chain, and a rather nasty-looking spike. "I think you need to learn a little discipline." She paused as if waiting for a reaction from me. I had absolutely no idea what she was talking about, although I felt I should have. "As a slave."

"Now," she said as she reached for the spike, "lesson one. It's all about pleasure and pain." As if to illustrate, she held the spike in one hand, while her other hand ran over my breast. An instinctive reaction made me jump.

"Hello, what's this?" Vel's hand moved from my nipple to my wrist. "Where did you get this?" Her thumb brushed over my tattoo.

"It's a present," I said.

"Those bitches gave it to you, didn't they?" When I didn't answer, she screamed at me. "Didn't they?"

I closed my eyes. Vel was in no mood for idle play. Her hands left me, and I heard the scuffing of boots on the floor. She had walked away from me for a moment. A few seconds later, the scuffing returned and I could feel her heated breath on my skin. "You're mine, J. I can't have you marked by someone else." Her hand returned to my wrist, followed by an intense heat, searing pain, and the smell of burning flesh.

There was no escape. I frantically searched for some niche in my mind where I could hide while this was happening but found none. Oh, Almighty Carn! I swallowed the scream building in my throat and funneled it into a deep breath as I tried to get a grasp on the agonizing pain that now resided in my wrist.

It seemed that Rice had abandoned me, and for that I was forever grateful. No one deserved what Vel was doing to me... not even me.

"Let it out. You know you want to," Vel said. "Pleasure and pain. You can't have one without the other."

I had to admit the pain was cutting through the haze in my head like a laser scalpel. Or maybe it was the adrenaline running rampant. Just when I thought I couldn't take any more, the pain subsided. At first I thought Vel had burned away enough layers that I had no nerve endings left to destroy, but I dismissed it.

There seemed to be a cushion between my mind and my abused flesh. It was hard to describe, but it was like somebody else was helping me carry my burden so I could face the challenge head-on. I opened my eyes, looked at Vel, and showed no response to her torture preferences.

This only fueled her viciousness, and I could see she was hard-pressed to not kill me on the spot. She put down the small heat jet and picked up the spike, intent on continuing with her initial plan. I think she wanted to plant the spike deep into my heart, and the only thing stopping her was her need for torture. She pinched my nipple tightly, pulled it outward, and aimed the spike at it. As the muscles in her arm tightened for the swing, a masculine voice halted her.

"What the hell do you think you're doing?"

Vel jumped and whirled toward him.

Grimm? I would have thought my usefulness had run out, but I couldn't concentrate with the intense pain in my wrist, aggravated by the manacle sitting over it. Vel still had my nipple between her fingers, and it was starting to throb as well.

"Catching you torturing my prisoner, by the looks of it," he said firmly. He glared at Vel, who remained stock-still. "Let go of her."

Vel's hand backed away from my nipple as if it had burned her. "We got the information, you know that. And as she was of no further use to you—"

"That's my decision, not yours. Need I remind you who is in charge here?"

In my books, it took a brave man to dominate Vel. If I were him, I'd be watching my back very closely.

"But—"

"Let her down. Now," he yelled. While Vel hesitated, the two absent prison guards entered. "And where were you?" Grimm asked.

"My lord, we were ordered to leave." The older guard looked uncertainly at Vel.

197

"And why are you here now?"

"We heard raised voices—"

"At least you got that right. Let the prisoner down." The guards looked at Vel for some sort of confirmation. "I'm giving the orders here," Grimm shouted. "Get her down."

The manacles gave way, and I found myself on the ground. I curled up in a ball as I cradled my arm. The two guards picked me up and supported me so I was upright.

"Get her dressed."

The thought of material rubbing over my wrist made me resist. For me to get dressed took more strength than I knew I had. The copper taste was in my mouth again. I must have bitten down and drawn blood, but I pushed myself to continue. At least Vel wasn't touching me.

The troopers moved me quickly toward the staircase and out of Vel's way.

"What are you doing?" There was confusion in Vel's voice.

"I'm just removing the temptation, Vel."

"But—"

"In fact, I think you need some time to think. Take ten steps toward the back wall," Grimm said with authority. I couldn't see his face, but I did see Vel's. He must have been giving her a hard look. She had lost some of her aggressive posturing.

"But—but that will put me in the holding cell."

"I think you need some time to cool off. Do it."

She was reluctant to move.

"Guards, give her a hand."

Suddenly Vel was in my position, locked in a tiny room and looking out through a force field.

Grimm motioned for us to go up the stairs. When the two prison guards attempted to follow, he stopped. "You stay here." He looked at his chronometer. "Give her three hours then let her out." He turned to leave then stopped. "Oh, by the way, you might want to make yourselves scarce once she's free."

Every step up from the basement jostled my burn. I soon started dragging my feet as the pain became unbearable. It was at this moment that I was glad Rice was nowhere to be felt.

"Come on. Don't stop now," Grimm whispered.

"I don't understand."

"I'm always saving your butt."

"Huh?" At this point I was confused, but my mind wasn't up for riddles. It was too busy trying to get my legs to move and to cushion the pain.

Grimm reached up to a small ornate button on his left shoulder and tapped it. His image started to flicker until Sasha appeared in his place. "Holographic camouflage," she whispered before she disappeared under cover again, once more walking beside me as Marius Grimm. Considering she had done it in front of the guards made me realize she wasn't alone in this foolhardy rescue.

We stopped at the top of the stairs, and for that, I was eternally grateful. "There's a Noorthi in here."

"We haven't got time."

"We'll make time." One of the guards spoke, and I wondered which one of the sisters he was. If I had to guess, I'd say it was Beri. She was the one most eager to rescue Noorthi.

"Do you know where she is?"

"No."

"That settles it. We have to leave without her," Sasha decided.

As we stood debating our next move, the old man from the basement crossed the corridor toward the outer door.

"Get him," I said.

"Who? Him?" Sasha pointed at the figure trying to leave.

"Yeah," I winced as I moved. "Sertech. Doctor. Prisoner." Sasha just looked at me. "Trust me."

"Doctor," Sasha/Grimm called out, stopping the elderly gentleman in his tracks. "One moment."

"Sir? How may I be of assistance?"

"I have a job for you, but it's at the spaceport. Will you accompany us?"

"It will be my pleasure." He took his place beside Sasha/Grimm as we began to walk, his medical kit tucked firmly under his arm. The heavy wooden door was open, and we moved through it as a group. Just as we started to descend the few steps to the courtyard, a feminine voice called to Grimm.

"My lord? May I join you?"

Sasha looked at me and I shrugged. What could we do? Sasha mouthed "name" and I muttered back "Tars. . . something." She glared at me. Yeah, I knew it wasn't much help, but that was all I could remember at the time.

"Surely, my dear. We were just going to the spaceport. Would you like to go for a walk?"

She stopped suddenly and stared closely at Grimm.

"Is something wrong?"

"You've never let me out of the compound before."

"There are more than enough guards to make sure you don't run off. Just this once, I'd like your company on this walk." I silently congratulated Sasha on coming up with the explanation as Tars relaxed. Maybe this would be easier than I thought.

The party progressed at a leisurely pace, trying to look unconcerned about the crowd we were attracting. After all, Sasha was wearing the disguise of the man in charge of the garrison. I was able to walk on my own, but shock was settling into my body. I fought to keep the dizziness at bay, but that didn't stop me stumbling once or twice.

"Is she all right? Maybe I'd better take a look at her," the doctor said, but then noticed who I was. "She... she's alive."

"For now. We are in need of your services again, Sertech. Come." Sasha/Grimm didn't give the man a chance to say no. "Give her something for the pain now. You can attend to her at the spaceport."

The injection was a welcome relief and took the edge off the intense stinging and nausea that assailed me. I have to say I had never seen anything as good as that spaceport as it came into view. We still had some time before Vel was free, but there was always the chance someone would discover the ruse. I wouldn't breathe easy until we were far, far away in space.

The old man looked around at the field and asked, "Where do you need my services, sir?" He searched for some kind of emergency but there was none.

"That ship over there. There is a sick woman on board. You can attend to the prisoner there also." Sasha had brought one of the new ships in our fleet, so at least it looked like we had credits. The party walked across the expanse of ground to the ship, and the doctor was escorted inside by two of the guards. Tars stayed close to Grimm, seemingly content as he held her hand. That little detail didn't go unnoticed. This particular guard watched the Noorthi woman's every move very carefully, a frown crossing his features at the obvious show of affection by the woman toward her captor.

I muttered to the guard I assumed was Beri, "I'll explain everything later. What about Malt? Is she safe?"

"Yes. She contacted us, and one of the boys flew the ship back."

"Good."

Sasha/Grimm drew Tars into the ship and one of the guards signaled us to board quickly.

"Damn," I said.

"What?" Beri looked around for trouble.

"I'm leaving Bessie again."

"It's been taken care of."

My heart thumped quicker. "Yeah?" I wanted all the details, and I wanted them now, but Beri was pushing me up the ramp to the door. "What? Stop pushing."

"There's time to sort this out later, my friend," she said.

Her hand slapped the button to draw in the ramp and close the hatch. Before we had a chance to find a seat somewhere, the ship rumbled and took off, which shoved me back into Beri's chest. Her guard image flickered as she was hit, rippling until the image stabilized. She tapped her left shoulder, and the male image faded, leaving behind a disillusioned Noorthi. "You look awful," Beri said, with so much concern that I looked up at her.

"Yeah," I replied. It was stating the obvious, but I needed the attention so, good or bad, I'd take it. "I've had better days." She helped me to a seat, and I collapsed into it, grabbing for my wrist as I sat.

"Grit will see to that when we get home."

Home. I hadn't had a real home for a few years, at least not since Dad was alive. The Noorthi were now my family, and the family was growing. My thoughts went to the extra passenger with Malt.

The sertech knelt beside my seat and grabbed my wrist. I hadn't looked at the damage Vel had inflicted. I was scared to see what it looked like. He rifled around in his case, extracted an atomizer, and sprayed the burned flesh liberally with its contents.

It took a few moments for the liquid to solidify. In that time, he pulled out a small canister and slid it into his injector. He placed the instrument against my forearm and squeezed. A sense of cold swept through my arm, leaving a wave of faint tingles in its wake.

"What was that?"

"For infection." He glanced at Beri. "You. Water." He then wrapped a bandage around my burn.

Beri was about to answer when she closed her mouth and did as she was ordered. She returned with a flask of water.

The sertech popped the lid and poured in a few drops from a tiny vial. He handed the flask to me. "Drink."

"How about a 'please'?" All I wanted to do was find a bed and crawl into it. That was, if I could find a way to take the pain away.

Beri rolled her eyes. "Please, J. Not now."

I drank the flask and immediately got my wish, along with a drowsy lethargy that was quickly going to leave me sleeping sitting up. Beri's concerned face was the last thing in my line of vision.

✝

I woke up lying on a pile of blankets. When did I move?

"Trouble just follows you, doesn't it?"

My gaze wandered for a moment before latching onto the owner of the voice. B was smiling at me.

I cleared my throat. "It must be the tattoo across my forehead that says, 'Kick me.'"

She laughed gently, and I felt a tickle in my stomach in reaction to the sound, which was warm and comforting. "How do you feel?"

"Fine." But we both knew it was a lie.

"Jordana."

"What do you want me to say? I'm tired, my wrist stings like craz, and I feel like an idiot that Vel caught me."

"So nothing new, huh?" Her smile traveled up to her eyes, and I felt myself melting. Damn. How did she do that? Drugs. It had to be the drugs. Yeah, that was it.

"And how is Palmenter Floric?" Time to change the subject. Beri was the irritating one here, right? Wasn't she? But the more she looked at me, the more I wondered about that.

She frowned. "That self-righteous, egotistical—"

"My, my, my, B. I thought all Noorthi were pacifists and thought well of everyone."

"He doesn't count. What in this universe possessed you to enlist him, besides to annoy me?"

"Malt needs a mentor. We discussed this and you agreed. I know he's a pain in the ass, but he's got the credentials. And maybe I enjoy annoying you." I figured that since I used another big word my brain must be just about back to normal, at least normal for me.

"Yeah." She sighed, "I suppose he did save your ass. Why do you annoy me so?"

"Maybe I like how cute you look when you get that way," I teased, but somewhere in the back of my mind, I knew it wasn't teasing. She was cute, and even when she was irritated with me, it somehow got under my skin in a good way. She looked at me. Was that a blush? "Wait," I said. "Floric's here?"

"Nope, but the holographic camouflage is his invention. It was in amongst all the junk he kept telling us was his luggage."

Praise Almighty Carn that I let him take all that crap onto the ship, otherwise I'd be getting a nipple ring or two courtesy of Vel. And maybe some other nasty stuff as jewelry.

"Thank the stars." Rales stood in the doorway, his features etched with concern.

"Hey, buddy."

"How did that bitch sneak up on you?"

I glanced at Beri then at him. "Later, Rales. How's Bessie?"

"She's on her way home."

"Did you check for tags?"

He looked at me as if insulted. "As if I wouldn't."

"Yeah, stupid question." I looked from Beri to Rales and back again, and I could see they were waiting to hear the story. "Do you guys mind if I stay here for a while? I'm kind of tired and sore." At least it would give me a bit of time to decide what I was going to tell them. I don't know why I was agonizing over this. After all, I was a normal healthy female stuck in the middle of a group of celibate women. Where else was I supposed to go to get some action? And yet I didn't want to see their looks of disappointment, either. The conflict made my head hurt, so I put aside my decision for later.

Chapter Sixteen

The Grass Is Always Greener

"But why?" The sound of voices stirred me from my sleep. Two people.

"I thought you were all dead. I had been a prisoner for ten years. What was I supposed to do?"

"But you have strayed—"

"I had no choice. You left me and I was alone." Tars. I recognized her voice.

"Left you? That man that you hold so dear kidnapped all of us and abandoned us on Rigeus. He left us there with nothing, to scratch around in the dirt and to survive the terrible heat. We had no water, no food, and no shelter, but we kept to our beliefs. Even as Vel captured our Elders one by one, we kept to our beliefs. So don't go judging us by how we are dressed." That was Beri.

"You lie. It was Vel, not him."

"Do you think that woman would do something so drastic without him knowing?" Beri sounded angry.

Tars didn't answer.

"Exactly. Your sweet man is not so sweet."

"I want to be taken home."

"That's what we're doing."

"No, back to Juno. That is my home."

"Have you left something more than a man on Juno?" I asked, joining the discussion. Maybe I should have left well enough alone, knowing what I did about Tars.

"You are not one of us. Who are you?" Tars asked.

"You don't know? Doesn't your husband tell you everything?" I saw her bristle but continued. "I'm the woman who seems to have become an obsession with Marius Grimm."

"This is none of your business, outsider," Tars said imperiously.

"But it is, Tars," Beri said. "She is one of us."

"Her?" The incredulity in her voice sent me into action.

"I think I should be insulted," I said.

"Hold on, J. Let me handle this." Beri glared at me. As much as I wanted to respond, I decided Beri needed to take control. "Jordana is our Ratha."

"Ratha?"

"Vel was hunting us down like prey on Rigeus, and Jordana was the only one we could count on to help us." Beri smiled sweetly at me. She can be such a sentimental fool sometimes. But when she smiled at me like that, I'd let her be one.

To reinforce her words, I held up my bandaged wrist. "Unfortunately, Vel got to me first." I looked at my arm. I hoped the numbness was a temporary situation. It galled me that I would have to get a surgical correction for what Vel did to my flesh. "After ten years as a prisoner, why are you still alive?"

"Because he likes—loves me."

"No. There's something else, isn't there?" I picked up the slight twitch around Tars's eyes. "Are you going to make this hard for us?"

"Us or you, stranger?"

I chuckled gently, drawing Beri's attention. "That just took me back to when we first met, remember?" I said to her. "You called me 'stranger' as well."

"It seems like a lifetime ago."

"Indeed it does, my friend."

I turned my attention back to Tars. "Did you tell him anything about the ochre?"

"No, but he stopped asking about it a while ago."

"And that was about four years ago, wasn't it?"

"How did—" Tars looked from me to Beri and back again.

"That was when Vel came to Rigeus and the mine started. Do you have any idea what happened?"

When she said nothing, I continued. "He found the ochre and it's been turned into a drug, a very addictive drug. He has plans to use the ochre as a mind-control agent." I waited for a reaction and saw only confusion. "It's only a matter of time before he finds what's needed to mix with the ochre to give him the desired effect."

"He will not get that information from me," Tars said.

"You seem so sure about that. Are you?"

"I do not know."

"No?"

"No," Beri said. "No individual Noorthi knows everything."

"So your sisterhood understood the gravity of possessing that knowledge, and yet he asked you for six years. Did you encourage him?"

"No. He would not use me in that way."

"Lady, you've got to get those eyes checked, because you've already given him everything." I looked at Beri and she stared back. Did she realize what he had done? Did any of them? Did the Consortium need to know before it was too late? I left the two women facing one another and strode away before my head exploded.

I walked the few steps down the corridor to the common room where the rest of the rescue party and the prisoner were seated. The holographic camouflage had been removed, and I could see that most of the rescuers were Sasha and the boys, which would make sense considering the risk of running into trouble was high and the Noorthi were pacifists.

"I demand to know what is going on," the sertech cried.

"First, your name," I said.

"N-name?" he stuttered. I had command of the conversation, and he was taken aback.

"Name, unless you prefer me to call you 'old man.'" I let one eyebrow rise as a show of cocky confidence.

"Gorin. Sertech Gorin."

"You Consortium types certainly do love your titles."

"What do you want of me?" His demeanor had changed.

"I want you to help me kill Vel."

The look of surprise on his face couldn't have been more acute if I told him we were about to crash into a nearby sun. "You want me to what? Are you mad?"

"I know you hate her."

"Everyone hates her, woman."

"Jordana."

"If you think I'm going to help you kill someone, you must be joking."

"And yet you were quite willing to use that thing on my brain. What would the Consortium say if they found out you knowingly used a banned procedure? I'd hate to be in your boots, Gorin."

"Are you blackmailing me?"

My gaze scanned the room and touched on each of my rescuers. "What do you all think? Am I blackmailing him?"

My fellow outcasts offered their support: "No." "The stars forbid." "I didn't hear anything."

"But Vel could easily report you to the authorities. You will need my support to refute those claims." What was I supposed to do? I didn't have anything else to bargain with.

"And it comes at a price," he said wearily.

"I'm afraid so, yes." I felt rather pleased with myself for backing him into a corner. "Still, with Vel gone, your problem will be gone as well."

"And what's to stop you killing me afterwards?"

"Very little, in fact, but you did try to reduce the intensity of the device. For that I'll give you one reprieve. If you wish to earn another, tell me what's in store for me." He looked at me quizzically. "You told Vel there was danger in giving me the drug. What is it?"

"Normally the drug is given in a lower dose and the recovery is slow. Vel pushed me to bring you back immediately. The drug will accelerate your mind until your mind burns out." He told me this with a certain amount of clinical detachment.

"So it'll leave me in the same condition as if I didn't survive the procedure?" What a lovely thought.

"Generally, yes. The effects are slightly different, but the end result will be the same."

"Is it reversible?" I tried to sound nonchalant about my life, but my heart was pounding. Had I run out of miracles?

"Not here, no."

"Then where?" I think I knew the answer even before he told me.

"On a Consortium medical ship."

"That's out of the question." His solution to my problem was a no-win situation.

"Then you are left with only one option."

"And what's that?" At least the man had the sensitivity not to smile at my dilemma.

"You die."

"That's an option I refuse to accept." I wasn't going to give up without a fight. "How long do I have?"

"Not long."

"A number, Sertech."

"Two days, two weeks, two months. Who knows?" He shrugged as he spoke.

"Surely you must have some idea, otherwise you wouldn't know that it would kill me."

"Two weeks, perhaps."

"Then you'd better get busy, because you will find a way to stop this."

"And if I refuse?"

"Then I will find the first area commander's office and drop you off to face the consequences of your actions. You did this to me. Here's your chance to make amends for it." I walked away before I punched him.

I moved to the cockpit, still trying to get my equilibrium, and found Sasha driving and Rales in the copilot's seat. I leaned on the top of the pilot's chair with my good arm. "Hey, there," I said quietly. "Thanks for coming to my rescue."

"No problem. We couldn't let Vel have any fun now, could we?" Rales looked at me sympathetically. I wondered what I looked like to him. If it was anything like how I felt, I must have been a mess. "So, how did she catch you?" He was eager to know; it was the second time he had asked.

"I didn't want to say it in front of the girls," I said with shame.

"That bad, huh?"

"Yeah, worse." I hesitated and stared out into space for a moment or two.

"Worried we'll judge you?" Rales said.

"Yeah, something like that." I chuckled. How many times had I gritted my teeth when I heard that phrase? Now I was using it. "I—" I took a deep breath and just blurted it out, "I got caught screwing around." My eyes closed as I awaited the comments.

"And?" Rales said.

"Ha! Why am I not surprised?" Sasha said.

"I mean literally screwing around. I was in bed, in the middle of everything, when Vel was just there. The woman I was with was in on it, and I got caught naked. How embarrassing is that?"

"Very." Sasha seemed too amused by my situation, which only made me more uncomfortable.

"But what was I to do, huh? Surrounded by women I can't touch. Sasha, surely you understand how hard it is."

"Of course I do, but I'm not the one who got caught with her pants down." She chuckled and then laughed out loud.

"Stop it," Rales said. "J was tortured. Just remember that."

"Sorry." Sasha turned her attention back to space.

"Are you all right?" he asked with concern.

"You've got nothing to say?"

He sighed. "What could I say that you haven't already said to yourself?"

He was right. Maybe I felt I deserved a few harsh words for doing something so monumentally stupid. I was the leader, so wasn't I immune to stupid mistakes? Apparently not. What would Beri think? I puzzled over that for a moment. Why did I care? I pushed the thought away. "How did you find me?"

"Malt said she planted a tag on you."

"No, she didn't. Vel's men searched my clothes, and they found nothing."

"Not on your clothes. On you."

"Me? How?"

"She said when Vel gave you back your clothes, she dropped a tag from a small window in the ceiling."

So that was what that cold feeling was that slid down my back. My hand instinctively went to my backside as Sasha talked. I wondered if the thing was still there. If so, it had been there for a while now and it could wait a little longer until my next shower. Then it hit me. Malt had been there when I did it with Deson. I groaned. Now she'd want to know what I was doing. Wasn't that conversation something that came with motherhood? As if having a virgin in my head wasn't bad enough, now I would have to give the talk to Malt. That would certainly be contributing to the delinquency of a minor, and an innocent one at that.

"So..." I looked nervously at Sasha. I had a question to ask, but I didn't want to do it in front of her dad.

"Excuse me, I think I hear Beri calling," Rales said.

Beri did no such thing, but Rales always was a smart man. I took his polite leaving as a sign that the time was right. "So how are things working out between you and your dad? I know you're not one for domesticity." I was trying to gauge how long Sasha would stick around.

"I kind of like his attention, and things are working out okay. I was thinking that same thing the other day. Normally I would have been out of there in a few days, but it's different there."

"There? Heaven?"

"Heaven?" She laughed. "Yeah, I suppose it is. Heaven. There must be something in the air, because I kind of like it. Things are slower, more peaceful, relaxing. You know what I mean?"

"Yeah," I said, "I do." I slapped her on the shoulder, which was not a wise move on my part. The vibration traveled across my body and stopped abruptly at my wrist. I felt a headache coming on.

"Sash, you did a great job today."

"Yeah I did, didn't I? I hadn't really thought about it at the time, because I was busy trying to get you out. Did you see the look on her face when I told her to put herself into the cell? That made it all worthwhile." She smiled at the image then added quickly, "Oh, and rescuing you, too, of course."

"Of course," I replied then smiled. It seemed that there were many hidden bonuses in my incarceration. Unfortunately, I had the deficits but I would keep them to myself for now. Gossip about my conversation with Gorin would get around soon enough, so I would take what peace and quiet I could get before chaos erupted.

"Why don't you go and lie down?"

"Why?" Had my attempts to hide my lethargy been that bad?

"You look like hell. Go get some sleep. We've got a couple of hours before we land."

"Yeah, and before a hundred nosy women descend on us." What a terrifying thought.

"Heh." She chuckled. "Scary, isn't it?"

I patted her shoulder and left. Maybe another nap would help. It couldn't hurt. I walked back to the tiny room that had been my bedroom, tired beyond all reason. The room was now empty, and I hoped Beri and Tars had come to some mutual area of acceptance. I couldn't hear any arguing, so maybe they had.

My bladder began to ache, and I realized it had been quite awhile since I had relieved myself. I found the tiny room that was barely bigger than the toilet inside it. Carefully I lowered my pants in the hope of catching whatever had invaded the area of my ass earlier. There was nothing. Not in the pants, the underwear, the toilet bowl, or the ass crack. It had disappeared. There was only one other place it could be. After doing my business, I rushed to the cockpit and looked for the communicator.

"What's up?" Sasha looked over her shoulder at me as I made a mad scramble for the switch.

But I directed my question to Rales. "Can a tag be back-traced?"

"If it's still hooked up, yeah."

I reached for the switch and contacted the cave. "Get me Malt."

"Hello to you, too," Epi said.

"Yeah, hi. Now get me Malt."

It took a few seconds before I heard the familiar voice. "Jordana. It's so good to hear—"

"Later, kid. That tag you put on me, is it still viable?"

"Sure is."

"I want you to do a quick sweep to locate it then shut it down. You hear me? I want it dead."

"Why?"

"I think it fell out in the basement where Vel had me. If she gets her hands on it, she can trace it back to you."

"I'm on it." Then the line went dead.

"Bye," I said to empty air.

"Does she always do that?"

"I have no idea, Sash. She only came into my life just before you arrived." I smiled as I remembered the grubby-faced kid that stood silently in front of me that first time. Even then I think I sensed something special about her.

"She sure is pushy. Kind of like you."

"I'll take that as a compliment." Now that the emergency was over, the adrenaline rushing through me was crashing, as was my body. I staggered back to the tiny room that housed my bed and fell onto the pallet clumsily, foregoing the energy to lie down gently for a quick journey. At the moment it felt like home and would probably be home for the rest of my life. What was in store for me? A slow deterioration of my mind? A quick collapse of my body functions? An agonizing death? All were distinct possibilities, and none of them appealed to me.

Suddenly my thoughts went to Rice. Everything had been so chaotic I didn't even have time to think about her. I searched my mind for some sort of feeling from her, but there was nothing. Either she had left me or was hiding away so deep I couldn't sense her.

Rice?

I suspected it was a useless call. She would have made herself known to me before now.

Come on, Rice. I'm here. You can talk to me.

In a way, I hoped she had escaped. What I was going to face in the ensuing days was better faced alone. I couldn't even imagine what my slowly frying brain would do to her.

May your soul rest in peace.

The ceiling was bland and gray to my eyes as I lay on my back. Was there anything I could grasp onto to get me through this? My mind wandered aimlessly, and I let it. In the coming days, I wasn't going to get much chance to think about my life and the decisions I had made. I suppose my biggest regret was I hadn't found that special someone. Thinking there would be time for that, I had indulged in my shallower instinct for instant gratification. Now I was paying for it.

"Coming up on Telgan. Another ten minutes, J." Sash's voice blared over the intercom. I hadn't realized I had spent so much time thinking.

"Are you okay?" Beri stood in the doorway, watching me.

I looked over at her. "How long have you been there?"

"Long enough." Beri took a few steps inside the room and closed the door behind her. "We'll be home soon, and Grit will fix you up."

"What I've got, Beri, Grit can't fix." Saying it out loud sounded final, and I struggled to keep myself from falling apart.

"You once told me to have faith. Now I'm asking that of you."

"There's one difference. I'm not a Noorthi."

Beri came over to the pallet and crouched down. She grabbed my arm and looked at my bandaged wrist. "But you are. You have nothing to fear."

"I wish I believed that."

"Faith," Beri said with utter conviction. She leaned over and gently kissed the patch of material that covered my burned skin, and it seemed that warmth spread up my arm.

"If you say so, but I don't know if it'll help. The interrogation Vel put me through had a side effect that will burn up my brain in about two weeks. That's all I've got. Two weeks. Two weeks to organize everything that will go on after me."

She held my gaze, a mixture of worry and stubbornness in her eyes. "You can't do that. You've got too much to live for. Malt, I am sure, has lots of questions to ask you."

"I'm sure Sasha can handle that."

"I need you here."

"No, you don't. You never did. You all managed quite well before I showed up."

"No, J. I need you." She stared intently into my eyes. "I'm pregnant."

I stared back. "Well, that's great news, right? See? I told you everything would be okay—"

"And it's yours."

Chapter Seventeen

The Root of All E-Vel

I must have missed something. The next thing I knew, Beri was patting me on the cheek.

"What happened?"

"You fainted," Beri said with some amusement.

"I do not faint. I have never fainted in my life." I sounded almost indignant. I was trying to remember what Beri had said before my... blackout. Maybe it was the head trauma and not whatever Beri said that caused me to take a respite from the universe. I carefully avoided using that word. Fainting was for the weak-hearted, and I was anything but that.

"Now, what did you say?" I tried to focus my attention on her.

"I said you're the one who made me pregnant." I must have had a stunned look on my face, because Beri was grinning at me.

This was getting to be a habit. Beri was slapping my face again, this time a little harder. Damn it. My body had taken another holiday from reality.

"Calm down. We're not falling into a black hole. It's only a baby."

"How... who?" My finger was flying through the air pointing in all directions. It's not the sort of news you drop on a person without at least an explanation, especially if the person concerned had no idea how it happened.

"Let's see." Beri made a show of thinking about the answers. "When you kissed my hand. Because you asked me to open up to you. No one else has come within ten feet of me, so it had to be you."

"Kissing your hand? That's it?" If it were that simple, I'd have children all over the place.

"It seems so."

Was this piece of news going to be the final straw for me? As if I didn't have enough to worry about, now I had a woman claiming I had impregnated her. Beri looked at me with uncertainty as I absorbed the news. Maybe my face was telling her something different, so I had better set the record straight. "It's wonderful news." I reached out from my pallet and patted her arm. "You will make a great mother."

"And you? What about you?"

"Me? I'm not the one having a baby."

"But I sense that you are less than happy about the news." The sadness in her eyes went right to my heart.

"Of course I'm happy." I pulled her closer and gave her a hug then I quickly pushed her away. "Get away from me, or you might end up with twins or something."

She giggled.

"I'm sorry if it's not the reaction you want, Beri, but I'm still trying to get my mind around the fact that I'm going to be a father, so if I sound incredulous that's because that's how I feel." Now was not the time for fancy words but they had a habit of coming out when I least expected them. "Are you sure?"

"Of course I'm sure."

"Sorry." I looked sheepishly at her. Everything that was coming out of my mouth at the moment was trash, utter rubbish. No wonder she looked a little sad. Even to me, I sounded like I was trying to get out of it. That was not my intention, but my mouth had other ideas. It was spewing out everything I was thinking without editing out the negative bits. "Who else knows?"

"I haven't told anyone else, so you can keep it a secret if you want."

"Beri..." Oh crap. Now she was getting defensive.

"No, it's fine. I can see that it's a problem for you." She started to back away.

"Beri, come here," I said forcefully. I sat up slowly and met her halfway, both of us on our knees. "Now listen to me. This news is wonderful, and I am ecstatic. I know I'm not making much sense at the moment, but my head is sore and my wrist hurts. Believe me, my dear friend, I am very happy for you." And then I had a thought. "What about you? Are you happy about it?"

"Yes. And no."

"No? Why?"

"My life will no longer be my own. I have to take up the mantle of Ashaltea so my daughter can follow in my footsteps."

"What about your mother?"

"I think we both know the answer to that," she said sadly.

"But you don't know for sure." I was trying to keep her hopes high, but she was right. I just didn't want to be the one to tell her to face the truth.

"When the next generation is born, the Ashaltea stands down for her daughter to take over. When my daughter has a child, I will then step down for her to rule," Beri explained to me.

"So you're scared you're going to miss out on all the fun, huh?"

"Fun? We never have fun."

"Never?" I said impishly.

"Oh no. Get that thought out of your head. We are a holy order. We do not have fun."

"But everyone should have fun, even if it's just once." If I planned to do anything about that, I had two weeks to accomplish it.

"We're about to land. Everyone take their seats." The announcement over the intercom interrupted any further conversation, and for that, I was grateful. As if there wasn't enough going on in my life, now I was going to be a father. If someone so much as sneezed at me, I would collapse. I just couldn't take any more news right now.

"We'll talk about this later," Beri said.

"Sure." I smiled. Beri was going to make one hell of an Ashaltea.

†

"By the stars! What happened to you?"

"Good to see you, too, Epi." I stepped gingerly down the ramp to the plateau to meet up with Beri's third-in-charge. The trooper ship had been moved to the outer landing pad, so I didn't have too far to walk. My feet finally touched soil, and I breathed deeply. It was good to be home. A small group had congregated at the top of the path near the edge of the plateau to greet us. Beri walked next to me, her hand taking my elbow in support.

"Don't you think I can walk on my own?"

"Really? After all, you fainted."

"Fainted?" Epi asked.

"I did not faint," I said, but they were ignoring me.

"Yes. Twice." Beri was having too much fun at my expense.

"Twice? Impressive." Epi laughed. "Can you do it on demand?"

"If you two don't stop, I may have to exercise my right as Ratha and think up some fiendish punishment." I looked from one to the other as they turned and walked away. "Then again," I muttered, "you might enjoy that." I followed behind them, taking the familiar path to the plateau rim with care. I wouldn't say anything to them, but I was feeling a little woozy. Whether it was my head, my wrist, or the nap or two I took on board the ship, it was taking its toll on my stamina.

Malt was among the gathering on the rim of the plateau, and she shortened the few steps between her and me. "Are you all right?" I could hear the panic in her voice.

"Sure. A little sore and sorry for myself, but I'm in one piece."

"What happened?" she asked as she turned around to walk by my side.

"Vel caught me and took me to Juno. Sasha and the boys rescued me, and here I am." But Malt wasn't convinced. "I'm fine, kid, really." I reached over with my good hand and ruffled her hair affectionately.

"But... what was that lady doing to you? Was she torturing you? I heard you scream."

Oh, boy. She was talking about Deson. This would be the one final thing to send my sanity over the edge. "No, Malt, she wasn't torturing me." At least not the sort of torture Malt would understand. "Could we leave this conversation until later? It's going to take awhile to explain everything." I probably had one chance in a trillion that Malt would forget about it, so all I could hope for was that my two weeks were up before she asked again.

I looked over Malt's head to the lone figure now waiting for me. Fen. Malt went on ahead to follow the procession back to the cave, leaving me alone with her. I recalled the first time I heard her talk and the response I had. It was a shame that things didn't work out between us, but it was probably better that nothing happened before I found out she was a Noorthi.

She cleared her throat and took a few steps toward me. "Are you all right?" That sexy voice shot right through me.

I cleared my own throat. "Yeah, I'll live. Ran into Vel."

"So I hear and not in your best position, either."

"Who talked?" My heart picked up its pace, and I could feel the thumping in my throat. "It was Sasha, wasn't it?" If it wasn't her, there was only Rales left and he would be too embarrassed to pass that sort of information on. Still, it solved my problem as to how I was going to tell the Noorthi. Fen was the diplomat among them, so she could pass on the information.

"I promised not to tell."

We made our way along the path toward the cave. "I'm sorry. I—"

"What are you sorry for?" Fen seemed unconcerned about my indiscretion. "You did what you felt you needed to do, and I certainly couldn't help you."

"It meant nothing. Really. I just needed to know if I was still capable of having sex. That damned tattoo has taken away so much of me, I had to find out."

"Then why are you worried?" Fen glanced sideways at me.

"Because..." Could I say it?

"Because?"

"Because I was worried you would think less of me." I kept my eyes fixed to the ground.

"Not at all. Are you hurt?"

I held up my wrist. "It's not bad. I'll live." For about two weeks. I kept that piece of information to myself, at least for now.

We had reached the entrance of the cave by the time I finished my statement to her.

"There you are. I was wondering if you had fainted again," Epi joked.

"I don't faint," I said haughtily. I had had it up to here with their teasing, and I now had a headache. I grabbed my head in an effort to keep my brain from rolling around inside. I felt Fen's hand on my back, slowly rubbing in circles in comfort.

Grit stepped forward to cut the argument short. "Beri has told me of your injury. Come." She held out her hand to guide me to a spot she had set up as a healer's cot toward the back of the cave. Frankly, she was just what I needed right now. The headache was jumping ahead of my wrist, which now simmered with a low throbbing. I had taken only a few steps when I was intercepted.

"There you are. How long am I going to be in this infernal place?" Sertech Gorin had been here less than five minutes, and he was already being a pain in the ass.

"As long as it takes to find a cure and give me my retribution." I wasn't in the mood to debate the issue.

"You!" Floric appeared out of nowhere.

Gorin turned to face the man yelling at him. "What are you doing here?"

"Some real work for a change. I had hoped never to see you again." Floric looked at the medic with some disdain.

"The feeling is mutual. The best thing the Consortium ever did was to get rid of you."

"And what have you been up to, *Sertech*?" I suspected Floric emphasized the title to insult him.

"None of your damned business." Gorin lunged at Floric, forcing me to step in between them.

221

"Hold on." I placed a hand on each of their chests to push them apart and instantly regretted it. Suddenly this didn't seem a good idea. "What's going on?"

"This—this so-called sertech is a fraud."

"No more than you, you trumped up little upstart," Gorin shot back.

"A fraud? You mean you're not a doctor?" My heart sank.

"I am most certainly a sertech!" He insisted on using the correct title, which should have told me something.

"You'd better be able to fix up what you have done, otherwise the last thing I'll do is take you with me."

"What? What did he do?" Floric looked from Gorin to me and back again.

"He tortured me."

"What did he use?" he asked urgently.

"That is none of your concern," Gorin intervened, but I ignored him.

"I don't know what it's called, but it looked like two pieces of clear film."

"The neural net? You used the neural net on her?" Floric's tone was one of incredulity.

"Neural net?" Was that what it was called? No wonder I had a headache the size of the mountain we lived in.

"It's an insidious piece of technology that destroys whatever it touches." Floric looked at me with concern. "When activated, it emits thalium rays that spread over the brain like a net. It then burrows into the tissue to seek out the area occupied by the memory. It has a nasty side effect of destroying brain cells as it goes. If you survived, Jordana, then you are truly special. No one has ever survived the procedure before."

"And tell her why you know so much about this, Palmenter." Gorin sneered at his adversary.

I had a feeling I knew the answer before Floric even spoke. "Because I was one of the palmenters who invented it."

"You?" Suddenly I wanted Floric off Heaven and as far away as possible from Malt.

"I objected strenuously to its use." He spoke as if the excuse would make it all right.

"You still made a weapon," I said. "A really nasty, evil weapon."

"Yes, I did. But I also petitioned to have the procedure banned. That is why I am no longer in their employ."

"Thank Carn for small mercies," I said sarcastically. "So you two will have to work together to find a cure."

"There is no cure," Floric said sadly.

"And I'm not supposed to be here, either. Just do it." My voice hardened as I spoke. I was sick of their excuses and now wanted some action.

"I injected her with Flarisil to bring her out of her confused state. Vel made me give her an extremely large dose, and this woman's brain will burn out if we don't reverse the effects of the drug." Gorin spoke matter-of-factly, and it was rather disturbing to hear myself spoken of like that, like I wasn't even in the room with them.

"So we have to find a counteragent for the Flarisil?" Floric asked with scientific curiosity.

"Essentially, yes."

The two men suddenly became the best of friends, at least that was what it sounded like. Maybe the common scientific interest would put aside their feud for a while. Did I want Malt in their presence as they hurried to cure me? Both of them had dubious scruples and could inadvertently give Malt the wrong idea about cutting corners to achieve a positive result. I wanted her to know what was right and what was wrong.

"Since you two are best buddies now, go and find me a cure. After that, I want something to kill Vel." It was blunt and to the point I know, but they seemed to understand and I was in no mood to dance around the issue.

"What sort of something?" Floric narrowed his eyes as he looked at me.

"Something slow and extremely painful." Was I just as bad as them, asking them to create something to kill a woman? Perhaps. But I was doing it for the greater good. No, that was only partially true. I wanted the woman dead with a vengeance. Being able to justify her obliteration as a service to the known cosmos was just a beneficial side effect.

I had had enough and just wanted to find a corner to curl up and die.

"She needs rest." Grit pulled me toward the healer's cot, while her assistant ushered out Floric and Gorin. Maybe she had read my mind, but at this point I didn't care.

"What is the problem?" Grit said as I lowered myself gingerly to the bed. She looked at me without emotion and examined me with professional detachment. She switched on one of the portable lights, and her hands reached for my arm and gently raised my injured wrist. She removed the covering and examined the charred flesh.

"The sertech sprayed an artificial skin on it," I said.

"Hmm."

I wasn't sure whether her hum was good or bad, and it left me in a state of anxious limbo. "What's the verdict?"

Instead of answering me, she laid my arm down on the pallet and left me. She returned about a minute later with a bowl and a piece of cloth. "This may hurt a little."

Of course it would. My life at the moment was one big hurt, interspersed with fleeting bursts of joy, sadness, and utter confusion.

"Ka ne bajee si," Grit murmured as she sponged the burn with the liquid in her bowl. *There will be no pain.*

Her words became clear in my head.

"How does it look?" I was a little nervous when Grit swore. Was it worse than I imagined?

"It looks like a burn."

I was really not in the mood for Grit's rather dry humor. "I know it's a burn. How bad is it?"

"I cannot say, Ratha."

"Look, if it's—"

"You are in need of assistance. I will do what I can." While Beri, Fen, and Epi's dialogue had become lax, Grit still tended to speak the way I remembered when I first met the Noorthi. She left once more and returned with a mortar and pestle. There was something already in the mortar, which I assumed was ochre, since it seemed to be the base for everything they used. She added a leaf or two of some plant and a drop of liquid. She pounded the mixture into a paste and gently applied it to the inflamed area, covering it in a thick, brown coating of mud. It had a slightly anesthetic effect and left me floating above the harsh stinging as Grit covered the poultice with a material bandage.

"Ratha?"

"Hmm?"

"Is there anything else I can help you with?"

"A headache," I said. I told Grit of my torture. She nodded wisely from time to time, as if digesting what I told her. I wasn't expecting any help from Grit for this. I was pinning all my hopes on Floric and Gorin.

Grit scooped the paste out of the mortar and cast it aside. She reached for fresh ochre, a different liquid in a small vial, and a leaf she had wrapped in cloth. The concoction was mashed together with her pestle, and toward the end, she added some water and poured it into a cup. "Drink."

"You must be joking." I had seen her put the ochre in. "I'm not drinking dirt."

"Then put up with your headache." Grit was not going to take any craz from me, and I rather liked her for that. Not many people stood up to me.

I took the cup from her hand and sniffed the contents, which made me screw up my nose. There wasn't a smell as such, but the idea of drinking down the muck she had given me made me pause. The headache was still there and growing slowly in intensity. It wasn't going to go away on its own and left me with no choice but to pinch my nose and drink.

"All of it." Grit placed her finger on the bottom of the cup and pushed upward, forcing me to continue drinking.

"That was so..." I couldn't find a suitable word to describe the taste in my mouth. Suddenly a wave of lethargy rolled over me. "What was in that?" I looked into the cup to see the dregs.

"Ochre."

"I know that. It's making me feel groggy."

"It is just a little something to help you sleep." She found a blanket and draped it over my rapidly relaxing body.

"You don't play fair..." I was slipping away fast.

"Sleep well, friend."

Grit's face was the last thing I saw, fading to black as sleep took me.

Chapter Eighteen

Me and My Shadow

"It's about time you woke up." The cave faded in again, and Epi was standing over me.

"What do you want?" The words slurred. My mouth tasted of ochre, and I could barely talk through the weird sensation.

"I see Grit's given you one of her concoctions."

"Bleh!" I commented by sticking my tongue out. "She's dangerous."

"She sure is, but she knows her stuff."

I had to admit that the headache had gone and my wrist felt a lot better. Vel had defiled me once too often, and this time she had left her mark. "So it seems." The words started to come to me more easily now as my jaw became more flexible. "So what's going on?" I tried to get up, but Epi shoved me back on the bed.

"Grit's orders."

"Not to me, they're not." I tried again, pushing harder against Epi's hand. A twinge hit my bad wrist, and I withdrew it from Epi's chest. It was a sharp reminder that I was still injured. "Unless you want to break your precious vows, get out of my way."

"You are the most stubborn piece of—" She stopped there but must have been content to think the last few words.

"Can't say it? Or won't say it?"

"You have put impure thoughts in my head, Ratha."

Epi was not happy. I don't think I ever recall her calling me that. "Sorry. I'm fine, really. There's too much to do for me to hang around in bed all day." I had no idea if she knew how long I had to live. Since just about everybody on the ship heard, I figured it wouldn't be too long before it had spread to the rest of the colony.

"We are all here to help you. You just have to learn to delegate." She smiled sympathetically.

"Don't you start, too. None of this pity stuff, Epi."

"But it's so—"

"Yeah, yeah, but I'm not giving up yet. I've got Floric and Gorin working on it, okay? And if I catch you trying to do stuff for me, so help me..." My independent streak was glowing red. I would shoot myself before I became a burden to anyone, but my legs had other ideas about getting up. They collapsed underneath me every time I tried to bear my own weight. Epi extended her hand and looked amused as I glared up at her. "All right, just this once," I said, "but don't make a habit of it." She helped me up.

"So what's happened since I've been away?"

"I thought you didn't want the sympathy."

"Why? What did you do?" Damn the Noorthi. They were being independent again.

"We held a *Septil*, a vigil for you for safe health while you were asleep."

"Thanks."

"Oh? No resistance?"

"I could use all the help I can get on that front, so I'll let this one pass." I pulled her into a fierce hug and expelled some of the pent-up anxiety inside me. "Thanks, my friend," I whispered into her ear.

"You are most welcome." Epi's arms encircled me, and she returned the warmth in a hug. "You are not alone in this, my friend." She pulled away from me, once again putting a little distance between us.

"I don't think it's the dying that's worrying me," I said. "It's having to live through the anticipation of death."

"There are some things in this universe that are unexplainable. Some things that have to be taken on faith."

"Faith? I was never one to put my faith in faith."

"Then maybe you should start." Epi smiled.

My thoughts turned to Beri and her unborn child. Hadn't I asked Beri to do the same thing? And look at her now. Did I have anything to lose by letting go and accepting that all things were possible if I had enough faith? "Hmm. Maybe I should."

"Why are you not in bed?" Epi and I looked over our shoulders to find an irate healer standing there with her hands on her hips.

"Because Epi and I are going to skip through the valley naked and pick flowers." I put on my best straight face as I said it, and I was hard-pressed not to laugh when Grit's jaw dropped. I didn't even look at Epi, but I would imagine her face was a reflection of Grit's. "I'm joking."

Grit shook her head. "You are a strange woman indeed, Ratha."

"I've been told that a time or two." I smiled at her. "I can't lie around, Grit. There's too much to do."

"You need rest."

"I need time, something you can't give me, so excuse me but I have more important things to do than lie down." Trying to push past her, I heard the click of her tongue in disgust. For some reason I just couldn't help myself, and I leaned down and kissed her on the cheek. I stepped back for a moment and watched her blush. Sometimes I can be a real troublemaker, but as an afterthought I prayed that I hadn't just made her pregnant. With the Noorthi, you just never knew.

As I walked away from the healer's cave, I felt a presence behind me. "Where do you think you're going?"

I knew who it was even without looking, but I still glanced over my shoulder to see Epi there grinning at me. "Why are you following me?"

"The Council thought it prudent that I watch over you," she said with a certain amount of amusement.

"Watch over me? Are you implying that I can't take care of myself? Wait a minute. The Council? When did that happen?" I felt like a huge slice of time on this moon had been cut out of my memory. Then again, that particular piece of information may have been in the section where my brain cells were demolished.

"While you were taking your nap."

"That's a relief. I thought I might have missed an entire section of my life." I had an idea of who would be on the Council, but I wanted to hear it. "So who decided they would run my life?"

"Beri and Fen."

"That's it? That's the entire Council?"

"Of course not, but they were the... how do you say...?"

"Instigators," I said absently, letting my newly acquired vocabulary skills handle this one on their own.

"Yes. Instigators of the decree."

"Decree? You mean it's not just a suggestion? I'm now a decree?"

"As far as you were concerned, yes. You would ignore a suggestion, so they made it a decree."

Sighing deeply I started to walk away from her. I placed the back of my hand on my shoulder and curled my finger to signal Epi to follow. "Come along, then."

Like my shadow, Epi remained a step or two behind me as I went about my business. She stayed in the background, being there only if I happened to have a fall or two. I kind of liked the company, even if it was silent. But that was about to change. If Epi was going to follow me, then I would find out all about the Noorthi. With some luck, she'd feel sorry for me and surrender the knowledge that had been kept from the universe for hundreds of years.

We took the path toward the speeders parked near the plateau. I wanted to see how work was progressing on the other side of the escarpment, so we talked while we walked.

"How do the Noorthi have children?"

"Pardon?" Epi increased her pace until she was walking beside me.

"You know. Children. You reproduce without sex, without a male, and without the intervention of modern science. Neat trick for a human." Or maybe that was the trick. Were they wholly human? Would Epi even know?

"It's no trick. It's our sacred duty to the sisterhood to produce an heir to our name."

"When I met Tars in Vel's dungeon, Rice said Beri's mother was... damn, what was that name?"

"Gerasthamée," Epi said quietly.

"Is that it?" It worried me that I couldn't remember the name. I could remember everything around it but the name.

"It is a sacred name."

"And Beri's name has the same last part. So part of the name is handed down? Sort of like a surname?"

"In a way, but different. Our name is our identity, our soul." I could hear the awe in Epi's voice as she spoke about her sisterhood.

"And yet you don't use it fully."

"It's our Noorthi name, and we protect it from the outside. Only at the most solemn of rites is our Noorthi name ever revealed."

"And what's yours?" Now she had me interested. But Epi hesitated, and it was obvious she didn't want to say. "Don't worry about it. You can keep your soul." She gently smiled at my acceptance of her silent request. "But I'm curious about Noorthi pregnancies."

Epi seemed to weigh the pros and cons of answering. "What do you want to know?"

"How the hell do you get pregnant without any contact at all? Is there some sort of drug involved?"

"When one is ready, she informs the Ashaltea of her desire for a child. It is the most sacred of all our ceremonies, and it is shared by all."

"Shared? You mean you all watch?" Suddenly the idea lost its appeal.

"The child will be brought into the sisterhood. Is it not something she should share with her future sisters?"

"Well, I don't know. Doing it in front of someone."

"But did you not do the same?"

"That was an accident, not by design. When we make love, it's something for the two to share intimately. Not a public spectacle." There was no way I was going to elaborate on that and give her ammunition for her argument. "Okay, so let's see if I

231

understand this correctly. Let's say you and whoever you wish to be your partner in this go to the Ashaltea to ask for a baby. Then you all get in a circle, and the gathered watch you, and whoever is there meditates or something?"

"There is chanting." Epi sounded almost defensive.

I suppose I was not giving her beliefs their due so I decided to keep my comments to myself. But I knew there had to be more than this. For one thing, the Noorthi used ochre in just about everything they did. "No offering or ceremonial drink?"

"The Ashaltea presents a blessed drink to each participant. It is to cleanse the body and spirit so that a suitable receptacle is ready for the most holy of gifts."

I had noticed that Epi's casual dialogue had become more formal as she spoke about the Noorthi, sounding more like Grit than the woman I had come to know. It was obviously a response to long years of tradition and lifestyle and put into perspective the Noorthi way.

However, I suspected that the whole pregnancy ritual had the ochre at its heart, and it certainly raised a number of questions for me. Was the ochre solely responsible for the pregnancy, or even partly responsible? The thought that this dirt could reproduce life was just too incomprehensible to accept. Or maybe it was what was added to the dirt that produced the miracle. Still, the thought that one could become pregnant by drinking a liquid was a little far-fetched for me, irrespective of the spiritual aspect of it.

And if that were true, how did Beri get pregnant? Even by Noorthi standards, what happened between us was a miracle. But I said nothing, leaving Beri to tell them when she was ready. Did I really want to know the truth? Such a revelation might turn out to be too much for me to handle.

Still, I hadn't seen any Noorthi children since my contact with them. Beri led a group of young and middle-aged women when I first met her. Later, of course, when we found the mine, there were elderly Noorthi there. But no children. So was the reason for no children a conscious decision not to have them or that they were unable to conceive? Did location have a part to play in the ceremony? No. I suspected it was more a conscious decision to wait. Who would want to bring new life onto a planet such as Rigeus? Surviving was hard enough without trying to look after a baby as well.

"There weren't any children on Rigeus."

"No." I could hear the sadness in her voice. Something had happened that had halted their instinctive need to reproduce.

"What happened?" I asked quietly.

I thought she wasn't going to answer me, but after a short delay she spoke. "The conditions were not good. It was hot and dry, and we could hardly feed ourselves."

"You didn't try?"

"Yes, we did, but the babies were sickly and weak. We barely kept the mothers alive." Epi's voice wavered a little, as if she were reliving the time. "After that, we did not waste the gift given to us."

"But what if you had remained on Rigeus? Wouldn't there be a point where you would decide that your fate was on that planet and it would be necessary to try again?"

"We had faith that our destiny would not end on that planet," Epi said with conviction.

"You were expecting me?" Now that was a surprise.

"We did not know your name, but yes, we knew that someone would come to free us."

"Well, thanks for the 'hello.' You were far from friendly."

"If we had welcomed you with open arms, you would have run off."

"Me? Run off? You do know who you're talking to?" I thought about it for a second. "But I suppose if you had run up to me and said 'welcome, savior,' I would have thought you were all crazy."

"Exactly. You could have been one of Vel's minions."

"You have a point. You're excused then." Luckily it got a smile from Epi in response. "That's better." I didn't like seeing her sad. I thought she had a trait or two that I found in myself. Apart from her passivity, she had balls. The speeders came into sight, and I stopped in front of the nearest one. I logged into the onboard computer and put my leg over the seat. "Hop on."

"What?" I looked at Epi as she backed away. "I'm not getting on that thing."

"I hate to tell you this, but if you're going to stick with me, you'll have to climb on board."

"Do I have to?" She looked at the speeder uncertainly.

"Is this the same woman who flew into deep space in the trooper ship? Are you scared of one little speeder?"

"In space I didn't look outside the ship, but this is..."

"Smooth and fast?" And that was the best thing about it as far as I was concerned.

"So open. Oh, no."

"You are such a coward."

"There's not a lot that scares me, but that's one of them." Epi's dialogue relaxed, and I was pleased. That meant she was feeling comfortable around me again. Time was too short for me to be surrounded by sadness.

I extended my hand. "Please? For me?" I was playing the sympathy card, I knew, but I sort of liked her company.

"That is so unfair." She lifted her leg over the seat. "Don't ask for a favor again."

"You'll enjoy it, I promise."

"Let's get this over with."

"Hang on." I touched the screen, and the speeder sprang into life. "You might find it easier to wrap your arms around my waist." But there was hesitation from Epi, and I chuckled. "You won't get pregnant or anything." I really couldn't promise that after Beri's sudden pregnancy, but it was the only thing I could think of that would nudge Epi into touching me.

If I had been riding alone, I would have opened the throttle and driven at breakneck speed, but Epi was with me and decidedly nervous about the whole experience. I moved the speeder forward at a leisurely pace toward the cave and stopped short of the escarpment before pushing another button to ascend. The sudden squeeze around my waist told me what Epi thought about the idea.

"Hang on tight." It was a bit redundant to say that, because she had a death grip on me, but I felt she needed some verbal reassurance that everything would be okay. We ascended the wall smoothly, in a steady, even pace. I could feel the slight shake from my passenger's body as we reached the zenith. Epi was obviously a girl who liked her feet firmly planted on the ground.

"I've got something to show you," I shouted in an effort to get over the sound of the speeder.

"The ground?"

"Yeah. The ground," I said but it was probably not the same ground she was hoping for. I steered the speeder toward the point of the outcrop and landed gently on the plateau. "You can open your eyes now." There was silence behind me. Maybe she didn't believe me. "It's safe, Epi." I couldn't move until she moved. The speeder dipped, and I lifted my leg over the seat to get off.

She looked terrified. Epi kept her eyes on me, probably so she didn't have to look anywhere else.

"It's a beautiful view," I explained in the hope she would actually look.

"I'm sure it is," she said as she steadfastly stared at me.

"You're not afraid of heights, are you?"

"No, Of course not."

"You haven't convinced me."

"Can we please just get on with whatever it was you wanted to do?" Epi sounded like she was riding the edge of panic.

"What makes you think it wasn't this?" But Epi was breaking out in a sweat. "Look, we're quite safe here. I just wanted to show you the view. It's spectacular."

Timidly, Epi turned her attention to the edge and gazed out over the vast vegetation that covered the valley and beyond. She was safely a few feet away from the edge, but that didn't stop her apprehension. Her gaze dropped to what she was standing on, and she turned to glance back along the vast expanse of rock that was the plateau.

"I wanted you to know there was more beyond the valley. See?" My finger pointed toward the river that bisected our valley. "The river continues here then splits into two to go around that outcrop over there."

"Why are you showing me this?"

I really didn't want to bring it up, but it was something that needed to be done. "When I'm gone, you'll have to decide whether you want to stay and live here. I'm showing you there's a lot of land out there that still needs to be explored. If you don't want to stay, I'm sure Rales and the boys will take you wherever you want to go."

"Don't talk like that. I have faith—"

"I think we both know better, Epi. I'm not getting out of this one."

"You must have faith."

"I have faith, but I'm also realistic."

"If you had faith, my friend, you wouldn't be talking like this."

"Let's say it's just in case, then. I want someone to know what I was trying to accomplish. Of course when I'm gone, it won't matter one way or the other to me if you accept what's been done or abandon it."

"But—"

"Just indulge me, okay? I'd be foolish not to at least put my affairs in order."

Epi stared at me.

"What?"

"You've lost your fire."

"My fire?"

"You were all fists and cussing when we met you, but you've lost that."

"It's that damned ochre. It's taken away a lot of me, and I'm not sure I'm the same person anymore."

"Maybe you should rediscover that. Find your fire, Jordana Laren, and then maybe you'll fight a lot harder."

She was right, of course. I had let the ochre call the shots in my life, and now a moment of impulsivity and random insanity was needed. Some of the boys were heading off-world to the bars of Arcus on Telgan when it was dark, and maybe it was time I joined them. Getting drunk and finding a good bar fight would probably help me find myself. And if not, then I'd have one last good memory to take with me.

"Let's go." Once seated on the scooter, I shifted forward for Epi to sit behind me. "Now let's look at the hangar bay." Normally I would just open the throttle and let the scooter drop, but I had Epi on board... ah, screw it. The scooter dropped like a stone, and I pulled back on the stick before we hit bottom. A girlish scream nearly deafened me as Epi expressed her terror. "Is that fire enough for you?" I asked over my shoulder.

"You are a..."

I suppose Epi was trying to find a word that her mind didn't censor. "Idiot? Insane? Troublemaker?"

"Irresponsible," Epi finally said.

"Yeah, but that's what you love about me. Remember, you're the one who said go find my 'fire.'"

"I have no one to blame but myself. I should have said that after this inspection, when the scooter was safely back at the landing pad."

The scooter hovered next to the wall near where excavation had begun. There wasn't a lot to see; they only had the lasers for a couple of days, one of which was spent rescuing me. But there was an outline made, and the boys were using hover mats to cut away the stone.

"How's it going?" I hollered.

"You don't want it done already, do you?" Rales was standing on his own mat, supervising the work. I was glad he had taken a passive role in the cutting. He wasn't getting any younger, and he'd be sorely needed in the weeks to come.

"Nah, I was just hoping. I'm sure these guys already want it to be all over."

A chorus of approval sounded: "Yeah." "You got it, sister." "You can say that again."

"You guys still going to Aston's tonight?"

"Sure. Why? You coming?" Denneck asked with a huge grin planted on his massive face.

"Sure, why not?" There was silence for a moment as the comment was digested. They weren't expecting that, which told me in no uncertain terms I had indeed lost my fire. Oh, I had a

Erica Lawson

mouth on me, that was for sure, but the core of me had become a
little soft lately. Epi was right, damn her.

I was waiting for some kind of comment from behind me, but
there was silence. If Epi had an opinion, she was keeping it to
herself. "Don't work too hard," I yelled as I tapped the button to go
up. As the workers receded in the distance, I felt sort of guilty that
I wasn't lending a hand but I'm sure there would have been an
avalanche of complaints if I had so much as lifted a finger to do
some heavy work.

"You've got nothing to say?" I asked Epi.

"I'm sure you have your reasons." She sounded nearly
condescending when she said it.

"I do." That was all I said and left it at that. If she was
disappointed with me, I would just grin and bear it. The scooter
skimmed across the plateau to the other side, and we descended
rapidly to the valley floor. "Do you want me to drop you here?"

"But I'm supposed to—"

"Don't worry, I won't be far. I thought I'd spend some quality
time with my girl." I debated in my mind whether to tell Epi it was
just Bessie I was talking about or let her worry for a little while
longer. It was probably better to come clean now in case Fen heard
about it. "I finally got my ship back, and I thought I'd spend a little
time reacquainting myself with her."

Epi chuckled nervously. "You have no idea—"

"Oh yeah, I do." I grinned wickedly at her.

"But, J—"

"Please, Epi. I need some time to myself. Go on, get out of
here." I put the speeder into gear and set off to meet with my first
girl, leaving Epi to walk the short distance to the cave.

The speeder made quick work of the distance, and within
moments, I was landing the bike next to its mate. I didn't have far
to look to find Bessie. The broken antenna sat above the line of the
trooper ship. Bessie had been such a big part of my life, and I had
ignored her lately. I figured I needed to make up some lost time.

I strode across the field we used as a makeshift landing spot,
Bessie slowly being revealed to me as I moved around the trooper
ship. Carn, it was good to see her. Before I knew it, I was hugging

238

her hull and my hand wandered aimlessly over her outer skin. "Hey, girl," I whispered, "long time no see." My gaze followed her somewhat imperfect lines and scarred skin, but to me she was perfect. It was what was inside her that was important.

Slowly I moved along her hull toward the ramp. I let my hand drag along the skin as if to reassure myself she was really here. I was almost hesitant to step onto the ramp in case she was angry with me for abandoning her. "It wasn't my fault. She ambushed me and took you away."

The interior was cold, and maybe that was the reception I was expecting from her. All Bessie knew was that she was alone and I couldn't be found. At that moment, I realized I wasn't Jordana Laren, carrier pilot and adventurer anymore. My life had taken a different turn, and I was moving farther and farther away from my own identity.

Yeah, I admit all those mornings watching the sunrise were oddly soothing, but now that I took a seat in Bessie, I began to wonder whether it was the ochre that was enjoying the sunrise and I was just along for the ride.

My hands slid over the dashboard in an easy familiarity, finally resting on the stick in front of me. So many good memories existed in this ship, and I had promised her many more. But would I get that chance again? Less than two weeks left in my life were full of the Noorthi.

Maybe I was being selfish, but I had a sudden urge to spend that time by myself. I had given a lot of my time, and lost a lot as well, and I felt now was the time to step back and end my days enjoying what I had liked the most in my former life.

Knowing the Noorthi were in safe hands with Rales and Sasha, I kicked Bessie into gear and took off for the stars. There were a few credits hidden away on board, and I would need them soon to drown myself in mind-numbing anonymity.

Chapter Nineteen

A Bottle or Two and a Bar Brawl, Too

I found an establishment that was practically empty and walked up to the bar to order. "A bottle of your most potent." The square bottle slid across the tabletop to stop in front of me, followed by a glass. I tossed a handful of credits onto the counter, grabbed my poison, and took refuge in a quiet corner. This was probably way past foolish, but I was having a crisis, here.

The bottle called to me, and I unscrewed the top then poured it into the glass. Was this really the solution? Probably not, but it would give me instant gratification and that was all I could hope for. If I was going to die, I was going out as Jordana Laren— adventurer, boozer, womanizer—and not some Noorthi wannabe. I was being stupid, but Epi had planted the seed and it was sprouting at breakneck speed. I wanted—no, I needed—my identity back.

The glass sat in my palm, and I looked at it intently. Before I could think too hard about it, and the ochre had a chance to stop me, I threw the liquid down my throat. I ignored the bitter taste, the burn settling in my stomach and the nausea that followed. Beating the ochre at its own game was a victory of sorts, and it encouraged me to try again. Slowly and steadily I worked my way through the bottle, each swallow easier than the one before it.

"Don't you think you've had enough?"

I didn't look at the speaker. Instead, I took another swig of alcohol synth from the glass. "Nowhere near enough. Bartender!" I pointed to the empty bottle, and he nodded at me in understanding. Finally I looked up into the eyes of the person trying to spoil my fun.

Rales frowned. "And what are you hoping to accomplish?"

"To lose my memory for one. I'm trying to find myself."

"And you're at the bottom of a bottle?"

"Not this one, obviously." I held up the empty bottle and handed it to the bartender, who swapped it for a fresh one. "Maybe this one." My hand was on the top when Rales's hand came down on top of mine, effectively stopping me from opening it.

"You're being such an ass," he said.

"You're probably right."

"Come on, J. Come to Aston's with the guys."

I knew he said that so he could keep an eye on me. The room moved as I stood, but I didn't fall down, so I was not quite as stinking drunk as I wanted to be. "Why?"

"Come on." Rales grabbed my arm and slowly pulled. I think he was hoping I wouldn't resist and just go along with him. Did I want to drink alone or join the party? Drinking alone wasn't all it was cracked up to be, and at least I was still conscious enough to know that.

"Where did I put Bessie?"

"Not now. We'll get her later."

"But I can't remember..." My fingers rose to my temple and circled gently over the skin as another headache began. It was like the net thing that Gorin used, which started the same way right before it tried to fry my brain.

"J, there are only so many places you could park her. The boys will collect her later." His tugging got stronger as he wanted me to move. "Come on and have a drink with me."

"Why not have a drink here with me?"

Rales looked around the joint, then back at me. He let go and sat in the seat opposite where I had been seated. I flopped back into the booth and reached for the bottle, only to have it snatched away by Rales. He opened the bottle and poured a small quantity into my glass before signaling the bartender for another glass.

"That's it?" I held up the glass in question.

"Yep. You've had enough." The glass was delivered, and he poured himself an even smaller drink. He looked at me for a while without saying anything, as if sizing me up for a conversation.

"What in Carn Almighty do you think you're doing? Taking off in Bessie like that without telling anyone. You know, those women are anxiously awaiting your return."

"They'll live."

"What did they do to make you do this?"

All the words had been swirling around in my mind since I had taken off impulsively. Could I make some sense of them? Could Rales? "Who am I?"

"Ah, the hard stuff first." Rales smiled at me as if I had said something inane.

"Damn right it's hard. I don't know who I am anymore."

"You're still Jordana Laren."

I took a mouthful of the alcohol and swallowed hard. The liquid stung my throat all the way down to my stomach and left me gasping for air. "But which Jordana?"

"There's more than one?"

"Sure, there was carefree Jordana who loved to drink, fight, and love. Then there's the other Jordana. Responsible, caring, and almost a pacifist."

"And what's wrong with either of them?"

"I can't be both, Rales." I slouched in the booth.

"Sure you can. Each Jordana has her place, honey."

"But Jordana number two has ruled my life of late. What happened to Jordana number one? I feel like I've lost a bit of myself."

"She's there inside you. She always has been." He laughed quietly and shook his head. I suppose I appeared a fool to him, but he didn't seem to care. Rales had seen me in a lot of states over my life. Drunk, angry, injured, jovial, and serious. He knew me better than anyone alive, so I could let my guard down around him without judgment. "You've just recently found another side of you," he said.

"But I don't know if I like that side of me. It's that damned ochre."

"What ochre?"

Oops. He didn't know about that. "I sort of got dragged into the Noorthi culture. I'm their 'Ratha,' their defender."

"Well, that was... um..."

"Stupid? If I only knew then what I know now." I lifted my wrist and studied the bandage that sat over the tattoo. "They put a tattoo on me and used some sort of ochre as the ink. According to them, it has some special properties, including turning me off drink. Vel removed it with a blowtorch."

He looked at me and winced before he turned his attention to my glass.

"I'm forcing myself to get drunk." I was sobering a little with all the talk, and I wasn't sure I wanted to be in that state. Rales had his hand firmly on the bottle, so I couldn't grab it easily. "You don't know how much it's changed me. Suddenly I've developed scruples. Me!"

"And that's a bad thing?" As we talked, he sat there fingering his glass without actually drinking any of the alcohol.

"Bad? I'm not sure. Different, maybe. But I feel my life has been taken out of my hands and I'm no longer in control. The Noorthi did that to me."

"No, they didn't," Rales said firmly. "You listen to me, young lady. Vel did this, not the Noorthi. It's because of her and Grimm that you, and the Noorthi, were abandoned on Rigeus. She was the one hunting them down, forcing you to take action. She was the one torturing you. She was the one responsible here. She was at the root of it all."

"Yeah, but she's not here and she's not the one expecting me to solve all their problems for them. Vel's not trying to change me."

"True." I didn't expect that answer, but Rales continued to say, "But she put you in that position in the first place. These women didn't ask to be marooned on some hellhole like Rigeus. They're doing the best they can with what they've been given. To them, you're a gift."

"A gift," I mumbled. "Bah." I drained the glass of its last two drops of alcohol and held it out for a refill. "I want my life back."

"Then let's get rid of Vel and everything can return to normal."

"Oh, sure," I said sarcastically. "I have..." I mentally counted the days. "Ten days left to live. Unless Vel will accommodate me and drop dead at my feet in that time, it ain't gonna happen." I looked at the bottle, but Rales had his hand on it still. None was coming my way anytime soon.

"You don't know that."

"The doc said so."

"And you believe him?" Rales was beginning to piss me off. He had been brainwashed by those women and now believed I wasn't dying.

"Of course I believe him. He's a sertech."

"Maybe he said it so you would let him go."

"Yeah, yeah. And the Noorthi can fly."

"You don't know that," he said jokingly. "Maybe they can."

"If you don't stop this craz, I may just have to do something about it."

"What would Sasha say if you messed me up?"

"I don't know, but I would give her my condolences."

He sighed. "Are you finished?"

"I haven't even begun. Give me that bottle."

"No. Have you gotten it all out of your system with all this ranting and raving?"

"No." I sat there not amused.

"At least come to Aston's, okay? It looks lively there tonight. With some luck, you'll get knocked unconscious and give us all a rest." Rales stood and urged me to follow. I reached for the bottle, and he took it out of my hand and slammed it down on the table. "There's plenty at Aston's."

"You just opened that." I objected to paying for a full bottle when seven eighths of it was still there.

"Here." Rales tossed the coins on the table, grabbed my arm, and pulled me along with a surprising amount of strength. "Say goodnight."

"Goodnight," I yelled as we passed the bartender on the way out.

It was nice to step out into dark when it was supposed to be dark. In fact it was so dark that I stumbled all the way to Aston's. "Where's the lights?"

"They went out ages ago."

"Really? What time is it?" Not that I really cared. Just steer me toward another drink, and I was fine.

"Later than you think, young lady."

I was blissfully unaware of Rales's stern tone and just wanted to find sweet oblivion in the bottom of a glass. We found Aston's; its glittering lights sparkled like the askeran of Doogan.

"Come on." Rales steered me into the bar. The sights and sounds bombarded my aching brain and pushed my headache up to the next level. It took several moments for my eyes to focus on the hive of activity. Maybe it was pay week; the place was busy. Rales took the lead and dragged me along after him. "I found her," he called to the small party sitting in a corner booth.

"How?" Finally I could make some sense. So he'd actually been looking for me. That sneak.

"Malt tagged Bessie," he said as he pushed his way through the crowd.

"She tagged my girl?"

"Stop complaining. Don't forget she tagged you." Rales smiled as he spoke.

"Oh, please. She caught me off guard."

"That's not what I heard."

"She told you?"

"She was talking to Sasha. It seemed you didn't want to explain everything to her, so Sasha did."

"Almighty Carn," I muttered.

"It was quite an education." He laughed out loud before sobering. "Stop worrying. Anything is possible. I have confidence you'll get through this."

At least he didn't say "faith" like everyone else. I was beginning to wonder who between the two of us was more deluded, him or me. But he did have a point. A lot of weird things had happened since the Noorthi arrived in my life. I made Beri pregnant without any obvious help. I was still alive after a

245

procedure that should have killed me. So depending on how I looked at it, either I was due for my luck to run out or I was the luckiest bitch in the known universe.

Just as we reached the booth, someone shoved me in the back and sent me sprawling over the table and into the drinks. "Hey," I said. I drew the line at an alcohol bath.

"What's your problem?" a deep masculine voice asked.

I struggled to stand up from my position over the table, and I turned to face a behemoth of a man. "Was that really necessary?"

"Sorry," he said blandly.

"I don't think you mean it." I looked him straight in the eye. "I think you owe these men fresh drinks and a sincere apology to me."

"It ain't going to happen, sweetheart. On either account." He grinned crookedly at me as if I were some kind of joke. While I may not be known in these parts yet, I soon would be.

"Leave it, J," Rales said, sounding nervous.

"No. This guy owes me an apology."

"And you got it, sugar. Don't push your luck."

"I'm not asking for luck, pal, just an apology."

"Apology accepted." He grinned wickedly.

"You shoved me in the back, and I'm supposed to be sorry? I think you've got it wrong, asshole."

"Why, you—"

"What? Quit while you're ahead, baldy. You wouldn't want me thrashing your ass in front of your drinking buddies now, would you?" The alcohol had put a fire in my belly, and I was itching to hit something.

"You?" He laughed. He directed his comment to Rales and the boys. "I hope you have somewhere to bury her." His fist shot out with amazing speed for someone of his weight, and he hit my jaw with a loud crack. My head snapped back, and my headache jumped to life. I leaped to the side to get out of range of his left hook.

The floor cleared, and I was left alone to face him. "It's your last chance to walk away," I said, not that I expected him to do so. I could see he thought I was an easy target while I, on the other hand, would have preferred someone a little less weight challenged to take my frustration out on. However, it seemed I wasn't going to have a choice.

My usual fighting style wouldn't help me here, leaving me to dance around and throw a punch when the opportunity presented itself. Not enough space. His plan was to just come at me and crush me in his beefy arms, so he had an advantage. My first punch landed in his stomach and bounced back with all the fat he carried, leaving me no option but to go for his head.

"You call that a punch?" he taunted. He was trying to sound impressive to those watching, but even in my inebriated state, I could see he didn't have a lot of support.

Rales started yelling at me. "Is this a good idea? He might have a family." We both knew it was a game of strategy, especially when my opponent was the size of our intended hangar bay.

"He won't feel a thing," I yelled back.

"Too damned right," baldy said. "You won't even touch me." He turned around to his fellow drinkers and chuckled at his own smart comment.

But I was waiting for him, and my fist slammed into his jaw when he turned his head to face me. He staggered back and fell on a table, which collapsed under his weight.

"Damn." I shook my aching hand.

"No time to talk. He's back on his feet," Rales called, his finger pointing at my opponent now charging at me. He was going to slam into me with everything he had, and I prayed that the people behind me had the sense to get out of the way. I sidestepped his enormous bulk and looked for some clear space to move.

My headache pounded in my skull and made concentration nearly impossible. I would have to finish this fight fast. He let out a growl and charged again, his arms outstretched as if to pull me in. But I didn't wait for him to come to me. I launched my attack with a high kick to his head. He stumbled for a moment and dropped to his knees. I took a few steps back until I touched the crowd standing behind me.

Then everything happened so quickly I barely registered it. A hand grabbed my shoulder and turned me around to face one of my opponent's friends. He punched me in the face, high on my cheekbone. The force sent me backward. I fell over the kneeling giant and hit my head on one of the bar chairs as I went down.

It was all a blur after that. Voices sounded and images twisted and turned in front of my eyes. I heard Rales saying, "J? J, are you all right?"

And then I passed out.

†

You cannot use that!

I opened my eyes and I was back in the cave, but I wasn't exactly sure how I got there. The brightness from the lights was blinding, and it forced me to close my eyes. The throbbing in my head was constant, a slow steady beat out of sync with my heart. In a way it was indicative of my health, beating at a different rhythm to the rest of the universe.

We have no choice.

Grit and some of the elder women were discussing my treatment. I was really of no help to anybody because opening my eyes sent shards of white hot agony into my brain, so testing it by sitting up was not an option.

But it will kill her!

Should I speak up before they killed me?

Yes. It will either kill her or cure her.

"Ahem." I cleared my throat. "I can understand you." I have no idea why I could understand what they were saying, because what I heard and what my mind interpreted it as were two completely different things. My eyes were still closed, so I couldn't see which elders were involved.

"What is it, Ratha?" That was Grit.

"What is it you want to use that will kill me?"

"It is an old root that we have not used in centuries."

"And you managed to get hold of it how?"

"Before we left our Great House, Jama collected some of our most potent ingredients."

I still hadn't opened my eyes, so I couldn't see who Grit was talking about. "What is wrong with your eyes?" she asked.

"Headache. It hurts to open them." I stopped for a moment before continuing. "How... how long do I have?"

"We do not know," she said, sounding worried. "We are unfamiliar with the technology that damaged you." She tried to sound positive, but even without my eyesight, I could hear the uncertainty in her voice.

"Talk to Palmenter Floric. He invented it, so he should be able to answer any questions." There was silence and then I heard footsteps leaving us. "What is this root that will kill me?"

"It is a rare root from the Karis system, where our sisterhood sprang from. It has been passed down from generation to generation, awaiting the time when it will be used for a great purpose."

Now I was a "great purpose." All I wanted to do was live my life, and they were dragging me further into the sisterhood. "Don't waste it on me, okay? I'm not your great purpose, so stop trying to make me something I'm not."

"And what are we trying to make you, Ratha?"

"Nothing," I mumbled, "nothing."

"Then why do you complain?"

"Stop it." I forced my eyes open and tried to put the pain aside as I did so.

"What is wrong?"

"I don't want to be a hero."

"A hero?" Grit seemed amused.

"I'm no hero, all right? I like to drink, I like to fight, and I love to make love. I cheat, I steal, and I manipulate. I'm not a very nice person, but at least my life was my own. Now you've changed all of that."

"I see." She pondered for a moment. "And yet here you are protecting us. You can do what we cannot." Grit was not taking no for an answer. "What is worrying you?"

I wanted to say "nothing" but it was too late for that. "You're maneuvering me into a corner. Since I've met the Noorthi, I've been tortured and abused. I don't know how much longer I can take this."

"Ten days?" she said drolly.

"Oh, ha ha." Who knew Grit had a sense of humor? "If you're trying to make me feel better, you're failing miserably."

"Very well, Ratha. Then let me ask you this. Why is it so hard to accept your destiny?"

"This isn't my destiny. It's my sentence." Grit went silent, and I suddenly realized what I had said. "Oh, no. Wait. I didn't mean that."

"One does not say what one does not mean."

"Look—" I forced myself to sit up, and held one hand to the top of my head so it didn't pop off. "I didn't mean it, really. It's just that I'm at a—maybe *the*—crossroads of my life. There's so little time left, and I'm trying to find a place in me that can be content with how things have panned out."

"You give up so easily?"

"Of course not. But even I can see that time is running out."

"But you have indeed given up. Otherwise, you would not be thinking in such a way." She took a step toward me and pinched me. "Stop this nonsense."

"Ow." I rubbed my forearm and looked up at her. "What was that for?"

"Stop all this doubt and look forward."

"Am I the only one in this madhouse who has a handle on what's happening here?"

One of the elders came in and whispered to Grit. "One moment, Ratha." She held up a hand in the stop position and turned away to consult with her peers.

While they talked in hushed tones, I ran my hand through my hair. Was the thought of imminent death causing me to have this crisis? As they all said, I needed to get hold of my emotions and get on with what was left of my life, but something was blocking me. Something stopped me from taking that final step and accepting what the universe had deemed was in store for me.

There was frenetic movement around the bench that held the Noorthi herbs, leaves, and potions. Half a dozen of the elders crowded around the mortar as Grit placed various ingredients into the bowl. Each of them had some advice to give. Their voices scratched on my last nerve like the cackle of hyriads.

"Here."

My body twitched at the harsh word. I looked up at Grit, who stood before me. She handed me a wooden bowl. I studied the contents then looked at her again.

"Drink."

That was Grit. Always to the point. She was a no-nonsense woman who didn't suffer fools lightly, even though she seemed to be ignoring my past foolishness for now.

"Why?"

"Do not argue. Drink it if you want to live."

Of course I wanted to live. What sort of stupid comment was that? I didn't air my thoughts. Grit would argue, and my head was just not up to the task so I did what she asked. "Oh, stars. What is this craz?" And I thought the ochre that caused my headaches was horrible.

"This is not, as you say, craz." Grit must have known what the word was, because she blushed.

"Sorry." I have got to stop these women cursing, but stopping myself might well be impossible.

"Finish it."

"You're kidding, right?"

Her voice rose in volume and became stern. "Finish it." In no uncertain terms, she was telling me if I didn't drink it she would sit on top of me and pour it down my throat. I was tempted to refuse just to see her try.

"Yeah, you tell her, Grit." I recognized Sasha's voice, but I was unable to focus on her while my eyes were scrunched up. The concoction sat heavily on my tongue like sludge, and I couldn't stop myself from sticking my tongue out a number of times in an effort to get rid of it.

"Oh, now that's a pretty picture."

"What do you want?" I wasn't in the mood for games, at least not with Sasha.

251

"I came up to see how you were doing, but if you're going to be all snippy..." She made a show of turning away.

"What's going on?"

"I'm not too sure about that last Noorthi who came along for the ride. She's not too happy about being here, and there's been a bit of arguing going on."

"Her and Beri?" Maybe bringing back Tars was not such a good idea after all. I didn't want Beri upset, especially now.

"Yep, and those sertech fellows. They can't agree on anything."

"I had hoped they would put aside their differences in the name of science."

"Unless science involves a hairy rocah and a bulbous chetan, I don't think they found any common ground at all."

"I don't believe this." I took a few steps toward the cave entrance when Grit blocked my way.

"Where do you think you are going?"

"I've got things to do, and I can't do them here." I tried to sidestep her, but she moved with me. "Grit. Please?"

"You have no regard for our ways. You must stay here and rest."

"I have every respect for your... our ways, *memesh*." I had no idea where that word came from, and I suspected Grit was wondering the same thing. I was thinking of "healer," but I wanted to attach some affection to the word. Suddenly it was there in my head, and those damned vocabulary skills took it upon themselves to just say it.

"How do you know this term?"

"I have absolutely no idea. It just popped into my head." I moved again to get around her, this time shuffling left then right before she had a chance to change direction. "I'll be back, and then I'll rest."

"Yes, you will," she called as I left the cave with Sasha. Somehow it sounded more like an order than a prediction.

Sasha waited until we reached the valley floor before asking. "How did you know that word?"

"Like I said, it just popped into my head."

"You're getting really scary."

"Imagine how I feel." I slapped her on the back and pushed her along the path. "Come on, let's get this sorted out." I had ignored Malt for way too long, and I was feeling a little guilty about it. She had brought an innocence into my rather jaded life, and, well, I kind of liked to see her smile. She was seated outside the makeshift hut that had been designated for research. An argument could be heard from inside, and I looked at Malt.

"This is normal." She rolled her eyes.

"How long has this been going on?"

"Since they arrived."

"Son of a—sorry, Malt. How are you? Anything I should know about?" I was almost afraid to ask.

"Nope," she said innocently, but that spoken word said so much more.

"No? Okay. I'm sorry I've been so busy lately. I wanted to spend some time with you." I sat down next to her in the dirt, positioning myself so I could lean back against a log. Sasha leaned against a nearby rock.

"It's okay," Malt said, but I could hear the wistful sound in her voice.

"No, it's not okay." I glanced at Sasha. "You are just as important as anyone else here. You got me?" I said the words carefully. I wanted Malt to understand what I was trying to say.

"No, I'm not."

I was wondering if she was fishing for compliments, and maybe she was, or maybe it was more a matter of seeking reassurance that she hadn't been forgotten.

"If it weren't for you, I'd be dead by now," I said, "or at least be body pierced to within an inch of my life."

Sasha chuckled at my comment, but Malt just looked blankly at me. "Don't worry about it." I ran my hand through her thick hair. "If you need to hear it, you are important to all of us, isn't she, Sash?"

"Yeah." I had caught Sasha off guard, but at least she said yes.

Malt stared at her intently, and I kind of felt sorry for Sasha. Malt had a way of staring inside you and seeking the real truth. Sasha shifted her weight as Malt continued to stare. "You were a big help to us, Malt. You're one of us, just like J said."

"And you're one of us, Sash?" I asked cheekily. I thought it was amusing that Sasha had suddenly become one of the group, especially for one who said she valued her independence.

"As much as you are," she said back at me. Yeah, well, she had me there.

The argument between Floric and Gorin became heated. I would have to step in. "Hold that thought." I held up my finger in the air. "Sasha, keep Malt company," I said then stopped. "And no more advice, okay?"

"I don't know what you mean."

"Uh-huh. I heard about the talk."

"You've got no one to blame but yourself. If you had answered Malt's question in the first place—"

I waved my hand in dismissal. "I'll talk to you later." There was no point mentioning that Malt never got to ask me that particular question. It would open up a whole other discussion that I really didn't have time for.

I walked under the branch canopy to the cleared area designated for research. Gorin was bent over a bench looking at a sample through a crude magnification device, while Floric was seated at the other end of the table sorting out various plants that had been collected.

"You've got it all wrong," Floric snapped.

"As if you would know," Gorin said in snide tone.

"I'm the palmenter here, and don't you forget it."

"How can I? You won't shut up about it."

"Stop it," I bellowed. "If you two can't play together, I'm sure I could find some other job for you. Like helping with the excavation."

Floric looked like he was going to cry, and Gorin's jaw dropped. Obviously, they had thought they were immune from performing manual labor.

"Stop this bickering and get back to work."

They looked at one another for a moment before Gorin answered. "We can't."

"Can't? Or won't?"

"We've tried everything we can here. We can't reverse the process."

It was the worst possible news I could have heard. "What are the plants for?"

"In case we came up with another idea," Floric answered.

"What's the problem?" Not that I would have any idea what they were talking about, but I was hoping to prompt a new solution.

"We cannot break down the Flarisil."

"Break down?" I was lost already.

"Each molecule of the medication is impervious to any kind of modification," Gorin explained.

"Okay, so you can't get in. Is that right?"

"Exactly," Floric said.

"Well, if you can't get in, can you stop it from getting out?"

"What do you mean?" Floric straightened up in his seat. Had I said something right?

"Could you put something around these moles to isolate them?"

"Molecules." Gorin stroked his chin. "Interesting idea. Very interesting."

"Our supply of Flarisil is exhausted from the previous tests," Floric said. "Unless we could—"

"Would my blood do?" I asked.

"Of course it would," Gorin said excitedly. He looked at his coworker. "What do you think?"

"That might be the answer." Floric stood up and grabbed Gorin's shoulders. "So now what?" I asked.

Gorin grinned at me. "Now we take some blood."

Chapter Twenty

When the Impossible Becomes Common Practice

I left the research area rubbing my arm. Obviously, they had never taken blood that way before, probably relying on assistants to do it. A lot was riding on my blood, and I hoped they'd stop fighting long enough to actually cure me.

Malt and Sasha were in the same positions as when I had left them.

"Where's that girl inside you?" Malt surprised me with the question.

"Huh?" Sasha looked from Malt to me and back again. "What girl?"

"Rice? I don't know. After Vel tortured me, she disappeared."

"Is she dead again?" Malt asked.

"Dead? Again? What are you talking about?" Sasha looked at me, puzzled.

"A Noorthi girl died on Rigeus, and her soul somehow ended up in me. When Vel used that neural net thing on me, she just disappeared. I don't know whether she's still in there, moved somewhere else, or just passed out of existence." I thought about it. "It's a shame, really. She was a lot like you."

"Yeah?" Malt smiled.

"She was very smart and inquisitive as all hell." Malt's smile widened as I touched her nose.

There was a polite clearing of a throat. "Can we see you for a minute?" Floric stood at the entrance to the lab. Surely they couldn't have found the cure already. Inside the lab, two faces looked at me somberly. This was not good.

"We can't help you, Jordana." Gorin had taken it upon himself to break the news.

"That's it? My life is dismissed like that?" Now I was angry. "Have you tried hard enough? I only gave you my blood a few minutes ago. How could you come to that conclusion so quickly? Or is it that you wanted to get home to a nice comfortable bed. I should have—"

"Jordana." Floric held up his hands to stop me rambling. "We didn't say you were going to die. We only said we couldn't help you."

"That's one and the same in my book. Make some sense—"

"You're already cured," Floric said.

I stopped. "Sorry? Say that again?"

"I said you're already cured. We both looked at the blood sample we took from you, and there was no Flarisil in it."

"What? How is that possible?" Cured? After all the agonizing and fighting and drinking and stress, I was cured? Just like that? I stared first at Gorin and then at Floric.

"Either you are one remarkable woman, Jordana Laren, or some outside influence cured you." His amazement at the situation tinged Floric's words.

"Or you're just too stubborn to die," Gorin said with a shrug. "Either way, this is a truly remarkable situation. Do you suppose we could perhaps get a scan of your brain—"

"No. I'm tired of pokes and prods. Leave my poor brain alone."

"But you've made some kind of medical history, here," Floric said. "It won't take long."

"Let me think about it. Right now, I really need to sort some things out." I was going to live after all. Or was it simply a temporary situation?

"Can you remember if you've been subjected to something else that might have caused this astonishing turn of events?" Gorin leaned in close and stared into my eyes.

I didn't have to think too long or too hard to know what that was. Come to think of it, my headache had disappeared once I drank that craz Grit gave me. "Maybe. I'll need to think about it. In the meantime, work on something to kill Vel."

"You still want to do that? You've got your life back, and all you can think about is killing her?"

"Now more than ever, Floric. She is an evil stain on the universe, and I intend to remove her." I walked out before they had a chance to argue.

Once outside, I let my façade slip. Almighty Carn! Cured! I staggered over to a nearby tree and leaned heavily against it. Things were happening at light speed, and I wasn't sure I could keep up with it all. I needed somewhere to take a moment to collect myself, so I made my way to a place I had always found peaceful.

I walked up the valley pathway to the plateau to find my regular spot for reflection. Ah, what the hell! I let out a holler. "Whoo hoo!" My heart thumped heavily in my chest.

"What are you so excited about?" Beri had beaten me to my special spot on the plateau. She was already seated on the bare patch that gave the best view of the valley, her hands resting on the ground behind her and her legs stretched out in front of her.

"I just got some good... no, great... news!" I couldn't stifle the grin on my face.

"What?"

"I'm cured! I don't know how, but I'm not going to die anytime soon." I allowed my body to drop to the ground. "Unless, of course, I trip over my own stupid feet and fall down the hill and break my neck." I laid back so I could look up at the sky.

"I told you to have faith."

"Yeah. You, and Fen, and Epi, and Grit. If fact, just about everyone said to have faith."

"And?"

I looked at Beri. "All right, you win. Faith cured me. Happy?"

"That, and Grit's potion."

"Potion? When?"

"She gave you the remedy after you went to Telgan and got drunk," she responded. "You know, the mixture she made you drink for the headache."

"Ah." No wonder it tasted like crap. I'd finally got over the initial rush to notice that Beri looked worried and tired. "Something wrong?" I asked.

"No," she said at first then changed her mind. "Yes."

"What's up?" I lowered myself down to sit beside her.

"Nothing to bother you with."

"Is it about Tars?" I asked.

"How did you know?" She looked at me.

"It wasn't that hard to figure out. What's the dilemma? Um, problem. What's the problem?" I still wasn't sure where the better vocabulary was coming from.

"There's no problem, not really," Beri said, but she didn't sound convincing.

"B, come on. This is your Ratha speaking."

She smiled slightly. "She doesn't want to stay. She wishes to return to Juno."

"And that's why you're up here staring at the sky, looking like you lost your best friend? I'll take her back if she wants to go. She's not a prisoner." I was glad Sasha had the foresight to blindfold Tars before we left Juno. At least we had half a chance she couldn't identify the speck of dust we were living on. A thought came to me as I spoke. "B?" I waited for Beri to look at me. "Is it because she's not your mother?"

"What has my mother got to do with it?"

"Well, you were in charge of these women all these years, but you always had the belief that your mother was alive and it was only a matter of time before she took up her mantle of Ashaltea again." Beri watched me silently, and I knew I had hit the bull's-eye. "There's a chance she's still alive, you know."

"No, Tars has said she herself was the only one left." Beri used the shortened version of Tars's name, as well.

My hand rested on top of Beri's hand. "I'm so sorry." I pulled her into a heartfelt hug. My hand rose to her hair, and I gently stroked it as I felt her body heave. Her sobs echoed a sorrow that had been held in abeyance for many years. I held her firmly in my arms and let her cry, allowing her the time to grieve. I felt the pain in my heart as she let her pent-up emotion free. My arms tingled as I held her, and I allowed my heart to speak to hers.

"What are you afraid of?" I asked after a while.

"I don't want to go back to the Noorthi."

"Wait. I thought they were your sisters." Had Beri became so isolated that she had lost her way?

"Not that. It's about this place. I love it here."

"But you're worried about the sisterhood. Going out there"— I nodded at the sky— "and trying to assimilate back into the Order."

"Yes. I don't know if I can do that."

"Then don't do it." To me it was all so simple. "Live here. You have everything you need."

"We would be expected to return to the sisterhood. It is our duty. But we have strayed from the Way."

I grabbed Beri's chin and lifted it, so I could look into her eyes. "This is how I see it. The Noorthi were thrown into a harsh environment where you had to survive. All the basic principles of the sisterhood were adhered to, but some things had to change. You are still, in essence, the Noorthi, but you've discovered a freedom your sisters haven't yet found. You are a new generation of Noorthi, different but still the same. Am I making sense?"

"A little. But the Noorthi—"

"Is it the name that's bothering you? Don't you think you deserve that name?"

"Maybe."

"How about 'Children of the Noorthi'? *Noorthi-Cha.*"

Beri didn't say anything straight away, but I could see she was thinking about it. "How's the baby?" I'm not sure where that came from, but suddenly I needed to know.

"Fine." Beri's hand automatically went to her abdomen, and she rubbed it gently.

"Can I?" I looked at her hopefully. Beri removed her hand and leaned back. My hand hovered over the expanse of skin covering the tiny bump before I finally touched her. I watched Beri's reaction as I put my hand down, wondering what sort of sensation she was feeling. This was the first time I had touched her this way. Oh, I had woman-handled her from time to time, but that was from necessity. But this... this was done with both our full knowledge and anticipation. Surprisingly, her skin was soft. With the harsh conditions on Rigeus, I would have thought she would have dried up along with the planet, but no. It was soft, tanned, and taut. And under my palm, it felt extremely nice.

There was a nearly imperceptible movement inside, and my eyes widened in wonder. I glanced at Beri and grinned. "What name will you give her?"

"I haven't thought about it," she replied. Her stomach twitched as I must have touched a nerve. "That tickles," she whispered.

"Sorry." I removed my hand and leaned back on my palms. "How about Rice?"

Beri didn't answer. I put my head down close to her stomach and spoke to the unborn child. "Is Rice all right, little one?" I asked. I saw the skin buck with the slight kick from inside. "She wants to be called Rice," I told Beri.

"Speaking of Rice. How is she?" Beri's comment echoed my own thought.

"She's gone," I said flatly. Despite my objections to her, I kind of missed the girl inside my head.

Beri straightened up and faced me. "Gone?"

"Yeah. Gone. I don't know whether Vel's torture made her go quiet or..." I just couldn't say it. I didn't want to believe Vel had killed Rice twice.

Beri's face lifted to the breeze, and she closed her eyes as if she was scanning another plane for Rice's whereabouts. Maybe she was. Who knew? Her hand rose once more to rest on her stomach.

"You don't think..." My voice was tinged with wonder.

"Nothing in this universe is impossible." Beri looked down at the little bump that was the beginning of her child. "Maybe Rice will get a second chance at life after all."

"Let's hope so. She didn't deserve what she got. Look, let's call a meeting on the landing pad in the morning about the *Noorthi-Cha*." I offered this in the hope of giving Beri one less thing to worry about. She didn't speak, but just nodded in acceptance.

I stood and extended my hand to help her to her feet. "Come on. You can protect me from Grit while she removes this bandage."

"I won't need to when you tell her the good news about your immortality."

"Please! Don't even put that idea in her head."

†

The morning sun shone on the valley as the Noorthi gathered on the landing pad for this special meeting. I had gone over in my mind what I wanted to say but still hadn't formed any convincing arguments to sway my audience. Suddenly, this meeting didn't seem like a good idea.

One hundred-odd women stood waiting for me to say something, and I had no idea what to tell them. I just hoped my new and improved brain would jump in and do the talking for me.

"My sisters!" Now I had their attention. In fact, the Noorthi words that came out of my mouth surprised even me.

"I wish to petition you for an audience."

A wave of murmuring began. Even if I didn't know what they were saying, I could guess quite easily. I had impressed them with my use of the Noorthi language. Maybe at a later stage, I would tell them it wasn't me doing the talking; it was a side effect of Grit's inventive healing.

"Sisters." I took a deep breath and released it slowly, to buy me a few precious seconds to think. "I come to you with a dilemma. You are all well aware that the last ten years or so have been a great upheaval for the Noorthi. Many of you suffered at the hands of Vel, while the rest of you had to endure the harsh environment. You had been abandoned on Rigeus to die, and yet you lived." The murmurs became louder.

"Your faith survived and made you stronger." The random words turned to cries of joy. "Just as you had to adapt to the heat and the desolation, so did your faith. Your elders were taken away

262

from you one by one until you were left with no one to teach you the Noorthi way. You were left to survive as best you could." I allowed the noise to rise up and settle over the plateau. This was the first time they'd been given the chance to express themselves about this catastrophic event in their lives.

I extended my hand to indicate Tars standing next to me. "Now Tarsthancus will try to tell you that this life is not the Noorthi way. That you have all lost the true meaning of your sisterhood. But I say to you that your faith had been tested and you prevailed. Maybe the rituals are no longer practiced in the Great House, but you have something far better. Your faith resides within each of you, so to find the Great House all you have to do is to look within yourself."

I paused then continued. "Tarsthancus does not wish to reside here, instead petitioning to return to Juno. I am inclined to let her return. If any among you wish to return to Juno as well, seek me out later. But be warned. Juno will not welcome you. The Great House is still in the hands of the Count, Marius Grimm, the man who condemned you—and me—to Rigeus." The Noorthi were listening with rapt attention. "Before I come to the reason for this meeting, I feel you should all know the truth." My mind was formulating the sentences a microsecond before they left my mouth. "The truth about why we are being hunted and persecuted. Sisters, I think I finally know what is going on, and I think you deserve an explanation. This particular tale began about ten years ago, just before your incarceration."

I took another breath and exhaled slowly. "A man came to Juno with his small army and took over the Great House. He condemned the Noorthi who resided there to Rigeus and a slow death. But the Count, as he came to be known, kept one Noorthi— Tarsthancus—as a prisoner. He had heard things, mysterious things, about the Noorthi. Things that he hoped would give him everything he had ever wanted." I looked around the myriad of faces watching me as I spoke.

"And why didn't he just kill you all? Because he had promised to set you free if Tars cooperated with him. Why else would she not resist him? But sentencing you to Rigeus was a compromise on his promise to Tars. He couldn't have you interfering in his plans." I sneaked a glance at Tars, but she looked impassive.

"Finally, by sheer accident, four years ago he found an ochre mine on Rigeus. But the most important part still eluded him. The part that changed the ochre into a mind-control drug. His scientists discovered a way to turn the ochre into an addictive drug so powerful that once the body had accepted it, it had to be fed constantly, otherwise the user would die."

Murmurs circulated in the crowd.

"So the Count had nearly limitless customers addicted for as long as they lived. But he wanted more. He wanted the secret to mind control, and with that the whole cosmos would be his. He pressured Tars for the rest of her secret.

"But the Noorthi are good at keeping secrets. After all, they had been guardians of the greatest secret for hundreds of years. They knew only too well how to protect that secret. They had scattered parts of the information to the four quadrants of the cosmos. No one Noorthi knew it all, and it was safer that way."

I gazed out across the gathered women, and many nodded silently.

"And what about Vel? Her job was to eliminate you all. The Count wanted no witnesses to his crimes. That was why she was hunting you down. If you knew nothing, you were sent to the mine. She probably would have succeeded in eventually hunting down all of you except for one thing. Me.

"I was not part of this plan. I was merely marooned as revenge. The Count hired a woman to drug me and leave me in the desert with no food or water to slowly die of dehydration. If it weren't for all of you, he might have succeeded. But who would have known that putting us together on the same planet would change everything?

"You are all aware of what happened next, so I won't repeat it. I had known Vel before her arrival on Rigeus, but the woman I had reacquainted myself with on that planet had changed. Whether it was the power or the credits the Count gave her, I don't know, but she was out of control, taking as much pleasure from the pain and humiliation as she was from the hunt. My sisters, take heed. Vel is more dangerous than this man called the Count. Do not underestimate her."

"That is a lie. He is not evil. It is her, the woman you call Vel." The words slipped from Tars's mouth.

"Ah, yes. Tars, you had been Grimm's prisoner for ten years. Even the hardiest of prisoners wouldn't last that long, and I doubt that Grimm's patience was endless. So I asked myself 'why would Grimm keep you around for ten years'? At first it was for the secret, yes, but things changed between you two, didn't they? It was something that he felt for you that kept you alive." I looked Tars squarely in the eye. "Something that you felt also." There was a low hum through the crowd. "Do you want to tell them or will I?" I gave Tars the opportunity to talk, but she remained tight-lipped.

"Very well. The reason this Noorthi woman wants to return to Juno is to be reunited with her husband—Grimm—and three children." There were gasps. "So I put this to you, my sisters. Her request to be returned to Juno should be granted. She may be a Noorthi in flesh and blood, but no longer in spirit.

"Now I will explain my request for this meeting. Beristhamée fears that she may have contributed to the straying of the sisterhood, and it weighs heavily on her mind. She feels she is unworthy to be a Noorthi Ashaltea. I have tried to assure her that the sisterhood is alive and well on this moon, and that she has done an admirable job to uphold Noorthi beliefs.

"I offer a solution to this quandary. Some of you may feel you no longer should be called Noorthi, but I say to you, are you not the next generation of Noorthi? Can you not rightfully claim to be 'Children of the Noorthi'? Would this not be a more suitable name for us all?"

I'm not sure whether I expected an almighty hallelujah or what, but all I got was silence. "The only fair resolution to these questions is a vote. Fen and Epi will be available to accept your vote over the next solar day, and we will announce your decision soon. Is that acceptable?" There was a resounding "yes" from the assembled women. "Any questions?" They were silent, but I suspected it was probably more from confusion than anything else. "I know I have given you a lot to think about, but now you know it all. No more secrets. Thank you for your time, sisters," I said with finality and moved away as the women began to talk to each other. I relaxed and left the landing pad.

✝

Carn, that was exhausting. I knew I had talked for quite a while, but I had a lot I wanted to get off my chest. Come to think of it, I talked more in the last ten minutes than I had all last year. Talking was not really my strong point, or so I thought. I usually let my fists do the talking for me. However, I did have a rather colorful selection of epithets and smart-ass remarks to draw upon when the occasion called for it.

"And you said you weren't a talker," Epi said.

"I didn't mean to talk that long, but there were a few points I wanted to bring up and it seemed the right time." I looked at Beri, Fen, and Epi, each in turn. "Did anyone fall asleep?"

"I couldn't tell. My eyes were closed," Epi joked.

"Figures. So what do you think will happen?"

"The young ones might agree, but I don't know about the Elders," Beri said quietly.

"Fen, Epi, when you talk to each one over the next day, ask them where they want to live. Are they happy here? Do they wish to live somewhere else? Or do they wish to return to Juno and the cloistered life, once the Count has been removed?"

"That's going to make it difficult," Fen said.

"True, but it's better to know now. I think you could all live here quite comfortably, but that's my opinion. Some may wish to go back to the old ways and the Great Hall, and that will be their decision, but you have an opportunity here to break free of your guilt and pain. Here, you can live by your own beliefs without fear of trying to conform to rules imposed by your Noorthi sisters."

"She has a point." Grit moved slowly into the small ring of women. "Not all of us will be able to take up the mantle of Noorthi once more. It has been too long."

"And what about you, *memesh*?" I heard the quiet chuckles as I addressed Grit. "What's so funny?"

"Nothing." Epi held up her hands in surrender. "I just didn't know you and Grit had become so close."

"Don't start." I could see the conversation could get out of hand very quickly if I didn't stop it soon.

"Episthanamene," Grit said, "show some respect for your Ratha."

"Hah." I grinned at Epi as her Noorthi name was revealed. She looked suitably chastened, but I wouldn't have used it, even in jest. She seemed fearful of that name, so I caught her eye and nodded gently. Her smile slowly returned, for which I was grateful. While Beri was the serious one and Fen was an object of my love, Epi was the one I could joke with. Of the three of them, Epi was the one I could relate to best.

"Grit, what would you do?" Seeing how some of the Noorthi treated her, I knew Grit's decision would carry a lot of weight.

"It is not an easy decision, Ratha. I have known both worlds, and both have an appeal to me."

It looked like Grit was going to make the decision hard. "You want to return to the cold, lonely halls of the Great House?"

"I did not say that, child."

"Then you want to stay here?"

"I did not say that, either."

"Then say something." Carn, the woman could infuriate me.

"I thought she was perfectly clear," Epi said.

"Me, too," Beri added. She was a little more at ease now that the talking was done.

"And what about you?" I asked Fen. "Are you going to make fun of me, too?"

"No," she replied seriously. I looked for some sign that she was teasing, but she seemed sincere. "You seem to be doing an admirable job all by yourself."

"Well, thank you all so very much." They were all laughing at me, but I could handle it. These women didn't get to laugh often, so I could ignore my embarrassment for the experience. "Now can we get back to business?"

"Having trouble?" Epi said.

"Enough." Grit spoke with authority, and the three Noorthi stopped.

"What if you could combine the two cultures into one? Would you stay here?" It seemed like I was pushing them toward Heaven.

"And what's wrong with Juno?" Epi asked me.

"Nothing, I suppose." There wasn't any definite reason as such, but the place just gave me the creeps. "In my opinion, going back there is going back to the old ways."

"The old ways survived for hundreds of years," Grit said. "And they will survive for many more."

"So, that's it, then?" I was disappointed. Were they going to give up this paradise to live in a dusty mansion?

"You give up so easily, Ratha."

"Well, Grit, what you've told me so far seems to point to Juno."

"I am just not sure that we should dismiss the Great House so easily. After all, it was where we all came from. Can you give up all your memories so easily?"

"I'm not asking you to give up your memories, *memesh*. I just don't want you to go back there. Can't this be your home?"

"And why do you want us to stay here?"

"I don't know. I just do." I wasn't really making any sense to myself, so I probably confused them even more. "It'll make it easier for me to find you."

"You're not staying?" I heard desperation in Beri's voice.

"No. I still have things to do."

"But I thought—"

"Did I ever say I was staying?" Beri was backing me into a corner, and I was figuratively gnawing off my own foot to escape.

"No." Beri sounded defeated.

"I can't stay, and you know it. How can you be Ashaltea with me around? No, you must take charge, as you should."

"Then why are you against us returning to Juno if you will not be staying?" Grit asked an obvious question.

"Don't you think if I knew I'd tell you?" The words left my mouth tinged with impatience and frustration. Grit just stared at me patiently, making me wonder if she was imposing her will on me to answer. If it gave me an answer, then I'd let her do it.

"Maybe..." I stopped for a moment and let my mind settle. "Maybe I'm afraid if you go back there you'll become mysterious and unreachable again and I'll lose you all."

"You seem to forget one thing, Ratha." Grit reached for my wrist and took off the bandage. We all looked at my wrist. "How can you deny this?" I looked and blinked. When the material was removed, the burnt skin came with it, revealing new, healed skin underneath. "How?" The flower motif had become a raised scar, each line standing out in vivid relief against my pink skin. It was like I had been branded.

"Do you still doubt that the root wasn't used for a great purpose?"

"I'm not your savior."

"You have been given the gift of life, and you are going to throw it all away to go after Vel."

"I thought you would be glad to see the end of Vel."

"She will not find us here."

The argument between Grit and myself was getting heated. Why couldn't she just accept my decision?

"Of course she will. In time. Do you want to live with the knowledge that she could find you at any time and kill you all? I know I can't."

"And what of this Grimm person? Will he not control her?"

"He thinks he's in control, but he's not. Don't forget, I've looked into her eyes. I've seen the madness there. She is the most dangerous thing in this universe right now, and if I don't stop her, no one will. I'm sorry, I can't stay." It was best for all concerned. I was going on a one-way mission. "Maybe this was my destiny all along."

"Sa ki tantuu na."

I should have known what Grit said, but the words remained the same. She had invoked something, and I couldn't understand it. There was silence.

"Won't somebody say something?"

Grit turned and walked away, not uttering a word. Beri, Fen, and Epi did the same.

"Epi? What did I do? Won't you talk to me?"

I felt like a pariah. Had I just destroyed the best thing in my life? Besides my dad, Rales, and Bessie, these women were the closest thing I had to a family. And I had absolutely no idea what I said that so offended them.

Chapter Twenty-One

The Beginning of the End

For two days they ignored me, carrying on secret conversations and meetings that I was no longer privy to. Had I somehow insulted them by not wanting to stay? I didn't even hear the outcome of the vote.

No, they didn't accept whatever I had said with their normal stoic demeanor. In the long run, maybe it was all for the best. Now that I had made my decision to stop Vel, I wanted to be gone as quickly as possible. Long, drawn-out departures never turned out well, and this one would be particularly painful, at least for me.

I went to see Floric and Gorin to find out if they had some good news for me, because I could certainly use some. The floral canopy overhead was at odds with the work that was being carried out underneath it. The roof was just bursting with life, and yet the two men were working on death.

"Any news?" I asked.

"Right on time," Gorin replied from his bent position over the table.

"We think we have something," Floric added, "but I wish you would reconsider using it."

"If she wasn't going to use it, she wouldn't have asked for it, you stupid man," Gorin said.

"Please, stop it."

"There's no harm in asking, so stop being an ass." Floric spoke as if he hadn't heard a word I just said.

"Gentlemen, please." My voice was steadily getting louder.

"Look who's calling me an ass. You—"

271

"Stop it," I yelled. "You two are acting like children. Can't you talk to each other civilly?"

"What?" Gorin looked up from the magnifying device.

"What did we do?" Floric looked confused.

"You mean you like the fighting?"

"We're not fighting." Gorin just smiled at me.

"It's more a healthy discussion," Floric said.

I didn't get it. "Anyway, what have you got?"

Gorin raised his hand and waved me nearer. "Look at this." I peered over his shoulder. "This should do nicely," he said.

"Well, you don't have to be so happy about it." Floric sounded sullen.

"What is it?" All I saw was a dark red oily substance on a small dish. My finger instinctively reached out to touch it.

"Don't do that." Gorin smacked my finger out of the way. "It works by absorption through the skin."

"Oh." At least now I knew where Gorin stood. He could have easily said nothing, and I would be dead on the ground. "Okay, so how do I give it to her?"

"Don't you want to know what it'll do?"

To my mind, Gorin sounded just a little too enthusiastic about the damage the goo would inflict. "Sure." I might as well know what could happen to me.

"You are a sick man," Floric said as he backed away from the table. He was content to stand a few feet away, as if distancing himself from ever making it.

"As I said, it absorbs through the skin. Once in Vel's system, it should begin to break down her body. You'll know it's working when she begins to bleed from every orifice."

Now that was an unpleasant thought. I glanced from Gorin to Floric.

"We should destroy this." Floric was distressed by the whole thing, which made me wonder how he ever got involved with the neural net.

"Just ignore him," Gorin said. "From there—"

"Enough. I get the picture." Was this too much even for Vel? If I used this, did it make me any better than her? Granted, it would make sure once and for all that she was dead. There would be no coming back once the poison hit her system. "How long will it take?"

"I have absolutely no idea."

Considering they had accomplished this in a few days, I suppose I couldn't expect an answer to everything. "How do you know it works?"

"We experimented."

"On the Noorthi?" I was horrified.

"Of course not." The way that Gorin said those three words made me think he was adding mentally "you stupid woman." "We used fruit, mainly, and a rodent of some sort that we managed to catch. Even if it doesn't work exactly as we think it will, it will be sufficient for your purposes."

"So how do I stop myself from being poisoned?"

"Just keep it in a vial—"

"No, Vel will probably search me and find it. Knowing her as I do, she'd probably use it on me." That particular thought sent a shudder right through me. "No, I need to get it close to her without her knowing."

"You could try smearing it on a glove," Floric said.

"But wouldn't it get me, too?" I wanted to make sure that if I died it would be in one piece.

"Not if it were sealed. The weave in cloth would be no good so something more, ah..."

"Modern? Impervious?" I think I had an old metallic pair in Bessie, but I had to check. "But isn't this stuff like an acid?"

"Not really, no." Gorin shifted so he was perched on his butt on the table's edge. "It's normally dormant and only becomes viable when it touches living tissue."

"And it sounds like I run a pretty big risk of getting the stuff on myself."

"Isn't this a suicide mission?" Gorin sounded almost insulted.

"Yes, but I'd prefer to die in a less hideous way. Are you sure of this?"

"No," Floric said. "We're not sure of anything. This is a crazy idea."

"Have you got anything better?" Gorin snapped, but Floric didn't answer. "I didn't think so."

"Okay, let's do it," I said before I actually thought about it and changed my mind.

"Floric's right, you know. Are you sure you want to use this? It means you're walking into trouble."

"I want to be there when she realizes what's happened," I said.

"Is she that bad?" Gorin asked, puzzled.

"After all you saw her do to me, you still need to ask? I saw her kill a young girl because she spoke, Gorin. Gutted her right where she stood. Now, you tell me if this stuff isn't the right punishment for her."

"I could think of a more humane way to die," he said.

"Humane? She gave up her claim to that years ago. She's nothing more than an animal that needs to be put down. Believe me when I tell you she is already plotting to get rid of Grimm and take over his empire. No one will be safe if she succeeds."

"And sacrificing yourself is worth it?" Floric looked at me with some concern.

"Oh, yeah. I'd die ten times over if I could take her with me." Okay, that was a little bit of an exaggeration, but I wanted these men to know for sure how serious this was. If no one stopped Vel now, then it would be too late and her influence would spread across the universe like a plague.

"And how exactly are you going to get close enough to use it?" Gorin asked me.

"Well, I'm sure that Grimm would like his wife back."

"You do know they'll be waiting for you." Floric looked worried.

"Of course. In fact, I'm counting on it."

†

"Maybe I can get an answer out of you," I finally said to Fen. "Just what the Carn is going on?"

Fen looked around nervously. Was it that bad? "I'm not supposed to talk to you."

"Who did I insult this time?"

"You didn't insult anyone."

"Then why are you all acting like I'm not even here?" Now I was really confused.

"Grit called a *tantuu*."

I searched my mind for some translation, but I only had vague images. It seemed that Fen would need to explain this one. "Okay. What's that?"

"When a life-altering decision has to be made, all full-blooded Noorthi withdraw from the outside world and come together to discuss it."

"I could see that, but why ignore me?"

"Is it supposed to be all about you?" Fen asked gently.

"No. Yes. Maybe. I just wanted to know what I did wrong, so I can fix it."

"A noble thought, Ratha, but you can't fix this. Time is a good healer."

"I don't get it. You keep telling me I'm a Noorthi, and now you kick me out?"

"Exactly. You don't get it. You've left us with a dilemma, and now we have to make a decision we're not ready to make."

"Is this about where to live? Look, if it's such a problem, live where you want to. I don't care."

"But you do care, J, and therein lies the problem. You have come into our midst, and we are conflicted. The decision is now not as simple as it would have been."

"Well, tell them from me that when I visit Juno, if they don't let me in, I'll kick the fucking door down."

At least Fen smiled, and it was an image I knew I would take with me to the end of my days. "Um, look, I'm leaving in a few days to take Tars home. In case I don't see you..."

"By the time you get back, the *tantuu* should be over. I look forward to seeing you when you return." Fen left me, and I watched her walk over the top of the rim and disappear from my sight.

"Yeah," I whispered, "when I return." If she only knew. But I couldn't dwell on what was to come; there was too much to do before then. I turned and went to the second landing site and hopped on a speeder to go in search of Sasha. I found her where I thought she would be. The excavation site. Sasha had nothing in common with the Noorthi, so she tended to hang around the men.

"Hey, Sash," I called out from the speeder as it dropped down the escarpment.

"Yeah?" She looked up at me on the rapidly descending vehicle.

"I've got a job for you, if you're interested."

"Sure." If she were like me, she'd jump at the chance to get off this lump of dirt called Heaven for a while. "Who have I got to kill?"

The saliva in my mouth slid into my throat and made me cough loudly. I knew it was just a coincidence, but still. "Uh, nobody. I just need you to deliver a package."

She groaned. "That sounds so boring."

"Well, if you're not interested, maybe one of the boys would enjoy a leisurely cruise into Consortium space."

"Consortium?" I heard the excitement in her voice. Adding a little danger to the job could sway Sasha in a heartbeat.

"Yep. Still not interested?"

"Can a Jinduan hidge swallow its own tail?"

"I'll take that as a yes." But I planned to keep the nature of the package a secret until the last possible moment, because I knew it was going to cause trouble. "Great. Can you be ready in an hour?" I started to ascend the wall. "Oh, and take your ship," I yelled. Now I went in search of the package.

I found my package still arguing, right where I left him. It was time for him to go home.

"Gorin." I entered the laboratory as the two men were having one of their lengthy "healthy discussions." How an argument could be a discussion was beyond me. All I knew was I'd be grateful for the peace and quiet after he was gone.

"Jordana," he replied, interrupting his rather colorful description of Floric's mother.

"You're going home."

"Really?" By the sound in his voice, I don't think he was expecting to ever go home. "I said once you'd done your work, you could go home. Well, you've done your work. It's now time for you to go home."

"One would think you don't want me around here." He tried his best to sound affronted.

"I'm not a cold-blooded killer like Vel, you know."

"But you will be," Floric said softly.

"Please, don't start. It's hard enough as it is."

"Then don't do it." Floric stared at me.

"It's not that simple, and you know it. This is something the Consortium can't fix. Don't you see? If I don't do this, we may never get another chance." It was as if I was trying to convince myself.

"We?" Floric asked. "Or you?"

"Me, because I'm the only one who could get close enough to her."

"She's got a point."

"Thank you, Gorin. Now, kindly gather your belongings and meet me on the landing pad in an hour."

†

I intercepted Gorin as he was making his way up the steep path to the plateau. There was a question I needed an answer to before he left.

"Ah, Jordana, I was hoping to see you before I left."

"Are you going to tell them?" I asked.

"I suppose I should."

"You'd betray us?" Maybe I was wrong about Gorin.

"No. What are you talking about?" He glanced at me quickly before returning his gaze to the uneven path before him.

"Are you going to tell the Consortium about us?"

"You? No. Grimm? Yes."

277

"It's time they stepped in. My only worry is that they've left us alone until now. Will this be an invitation for them to occupy here as well?"

"I can't speak for them, Jordana. I suppose it's a matter of the lesser of two evils. Maybe my plea will go unanswered."

"Someone high up in the Consortium is a traitor, Gorin. If Vel has the neural net, she had to get it from somewhere."

"That makes it even more difficult. Who do I trust?"

I thought for a moment as we were about to reach the summit. "Who gave you the order to see Grimm?"

"It came from the Council."

"A messenger?"

"No, actually one of the councilors came to see me himself. I didn't think it was strange at the time."

"Do you know this councilor well?" The hackles on the back of my neck rose. Suddenly this seemed more than just a mere grab for universal domination.

"Only by reputation. We sertechs don't have a lot of contact with the council."

"If you are able, Gorin, see if a distress call was ever received from Grimm. You may have your man."

"And what about Juno?"

"Approach the whole Council all at once. Don't talk to this councilor."

"Rebbah."

"Councilor Rebbah. Don't go alone. Protect yourself with as many witnesses as possible."

"You two finished yakking?" Sasha yelled impatiently.

I grabbed Gorin's hand and shook it firmly. "Good luck, and thank you."

"Good luck to you, too." He then grinned devilishly at me. "And what's to stop me from turning you in?"

"Well, I still have that neural net. And I have a few friends in all sorts of places." My eyebrow rose in warning. It wasn't a threat, exactly, but more a friendly reminder of what I knew.

"You'd use that?" Suddenly he was nervous.

"That depends on you." I let him sweat for a moment longer before smiling.

"Come on, you two. Time's a wasting."

"Yeah, yeah. Keep your shirt on," I called at Sasha before I turned my attention back to Gorin. "Have a safe trip."

"I wanted to give you something before I went."

He handed me a small pellet. "What's this?"

"The poison."

My hand shook as I held it.

"Don't worry, it's safe," he said with a certain amount of amusement. In my opinion, Gorin enjoyed his work just a little too much.

"So what am I supposed to do with it? Ask Vel to oblige me and swallow it?"

"Something like that. You put the pellet in your mouth—"

"Are you nuts?"

"As long as you don't break it, it won't dissolve. If you can get it from your mouth to hers, and then somehow break it..."

"Oh, sure. How much easier can it be?" The glove idea was sounding better and better all the time.

"The capsule is a ceramic alloy, so it should be acceptable."

"Acceptable." I was tempted to ask him to test it for me first. "Then that makes it all right." For now, I put the capsule in a hidden compartment in my belt buckle.

Gorin watched me put the capsule away. "Won't Vel search you?"

"Probably, but I'll just have to give her something else to think about."

"Like what?"

"I haven't figured that part out yet."

"You know, when you first kidnapped me, I thought you were the devil."

"And now?"

"Now? You've confirmed my first impression of you." He turned on his heel and walked toward the ship, laughing loudly at my expense.

"Sasha," I said.

"Yeah?"

"A moment before you go."

Sasha jogged over toward me. "I have a bone to pick with you," she said.

"I want you back here as fast as you can."

"Believe me, I'll be pushing my gal to the limit to get out of there. I'll remember this, Laren. Sticking me with him."

"I needed someone who could get him there safely. It's important. Then get your ass back here." My voiced dropped to a low murmur. "I'm taking the Noorthi woman back to Juno."

"Are you nuts? Do you have a death wish?"

"I need you here if something goes wrong. Get the Noorthi to safety. Do it for me."

"Why return her at all?"

"It's all part of a plan."

"Jordana, you should give this some extra thought."

"Take care of Bessie for me." I was beginning to sound like my Last Will and Testament.

"J, now you're scaring me."

"Get going. Contact me when you're able." I pulled her into a hug and slapped her on the back. "Thanks."

"Okay." Sasha looked me in the eye, and she was thoroughly confused and intensely concerned. She left me and walked toward her ship, looking over her shoulder at me a number of times.

"We'll meet at Ix," I called.

She didn't say a word but held up her hand in affirmation. Would this be the last time I saw her? I hoped not.

"What's going on?"

The adolescent voice of Malt made me jump. "Hey. What have you been up to?"

"I finished the cam-thingie."

"Camouflage?" I knew that wasn't what this was about. She had been looking for me to find out what I was doing.

"Yeah, that. I wanted you to be the one to try it."

"Sure. Let's go." I glanced over my shoulder at the disappearing ship as it headed off to the stars, then threw my arm over Malt's shoulder. We got to the valley floor when she stopped me with a hand on my arm.

"What's going on?"

"What are you talking about?" One thing I had learned about Malt was that she was persistent. If she wanted to know something, she asked and asked until you just gave in to get some peace and quiet.

"Sasha is flying off in a hurry."

"She's taking Sertech Gorin back home. You know very well that she hates him."

"Then why didn't you take him home?"

"I'll be heading off soon to take Tars back to Juno."

"Can I come?" There was a hint of excitement in Malt's voice.

"Sorry, kid, there won't be any passengers on this trip."

"Why?" Malt looked pleadingly at me, knowing damned well she could make me give in with that look.

"It's just a quick trip. Fly in, drop her off, and fly out. There'll be no stopping off for shopping on this one."

Malt's eyebrows knitted together.

"What?" I asked.

"You're not coming back, are you?"

I could hear the sadness in her voice. Was there any point in lying to the kid? "I need you here, Malt. If things go wrong, Rales and Sasha will need your help to get the Noorthi off this rock and to safety."

"But—"

"No 'buts.' Please, just do this for me, okay?"

"Okay." She didn't sound very convincing.

"I mean it. This is something I want you to do because it's important." I grabbed her shoulders and drew her gaze to me. "This is no longer a game. Someone is going to die, and I'm going to try damned hard to make sure it isn't me. I can't do that if I'm trying to keep you safe. Can you understand that?"

"But I can help. Really." Now she was pleading with me, shamelessly using my affection for her to change my mind.

"I'm sure you can." I pulled her into a hug. "But you've finally found a place that you can call home. Here's a chance to live life, to find love and, if you're lucky, to raise a family. Don't throw it away on a foolhardy expedition to Juno."

She pulled far enough away to look up at me. "Isn't that what you're doing?"

"I suppose I am, but this is something I have to do. I know you don't understand any of this, but—"

"I understand. But my family isn't here. It's you. If you're gone, Jordana, who do I have left?"

I sighed. "I'm nothing but a broken-down bum living life on the edge. You need a better role model. And besides, who's going to look after Bessie?"

I don't think Malt was amused by a flippant attitude. She glared at me, turned around, and walked away, not once glancing over her shoulder at me for one last look.

Chapter Twenty-Two

Now or Never

As soon as Sasha contacted me, I went in search of Tars. Her return to Juno needed to be done now. If I thought too much about it, I wouldn't go at all. I made light of my departure, promising I would return soon. But Rales was argumentative, forcing me to make him promise to look after the women. His reaction sort of surprised me. He, of all people, should have understood my position.

Beri, however, was sad, like she had the power of insight. She looked into my eyes, and I knew I wasn't fooling her for one minute. I think we both knew what I was contemplating had to be done, and I appreciated her silence as I left, though I wanted to hug her and not let go.

As the small ship lifted off, I looked down on the serene scenery and remembered my reaction when I first saw it. Heaven was a diamond in the rough and something I didn't know the true value of until I was about to lose it.

For the sake of trying to keep our location secret, Beri got hold of one of Grit's sleeping potions and I slipped it into Tars's drink. She fell asleep in the copilot's seat. "At least you're going home," I said, though she didn't hear me.

I flew the vessel over the secondary landing spot to get my final view of my girl. Bessie sat there, her broken antenna still not fixed despite my best intentions. Oh, well. This would be how I would remember her, broken antenna and all.

I gave the valley and the cave one final glance and muttered, "Have a good life, my friends." Without looking back, I flew toward the stars and whatever my fate was.

As I left the outer stratosphere of Heaven for the last time, sadness gathered in my chest, almost painful with its weight. I had now set myself on a course from which there would be no return. Not that I had regrets. This had probably been the easiest decision of my short miserable life, and all I could hope for was that my death wasn't wasted. My job was to get Vel, and I would settle for nothing less.

I reached up into the tiny compartment in the ceiling over the pilot's chair and took out the vial that would be my weapon. I was still concerned about using it, but I also knew Vel wouldn't let me within spitting distance with anything that resembled a deadly device. I took the pellet out of my top pocket and held it in my other hand. Which method would I use? Would I try both the glove and the capsule in case one failed?

The tincture was an extreme solution, even for someone like Vel, and therein was my problem. Was I any better than Vel by using something so abhorrently torturous? Would I get the chance to kill her with anything else? I suppose I knew the answer all along, but I was hoping for an alternative to suddenly appear at the last moment. The only hope I could hold onto was that maybe Gorin and Floric got it wrong and it wasn't as devastating as they had said.

Tars was propped up in the copilot's seat, unconscious, while I maneuvered the ship to the far side of the galaxy. It was a leisurely trip, taken at sub-light speed so as not to alert anyone, but it was also the most boring thirty-six hours of my life. I suppose I could have hyperjumped all the way to Juno, but I wanted to make sure when I approached the planet I gave the impression I was coming from a different direction.

I must have overdone the potion. Tars slept the whole time. Regardless, I needed to contact Grimm about the return of his wife, so I lined up the vid screen so that Tars couldn't be seen before I signaled him to contact me. It didn't take too long. Now I would find out the answer to the final question that had eluded me.

"Grimm," I said in a sober tone.

"I should have expected it was you," he answered angrily.

"You didn't leave me with a lot of choice. After all, you tried to fry my brains, remember?"

"Get to the point."

"Not in the mood for idle chit-chat?" Before he had a chance to swear at me, I said, "The bottom line is Tars wants to come home, so if you behave yourself, I'll tell you where to find her." Now, I'm not a stupid woman. If I were, I wouldn't have lasted this long. He was going to try to follow me, and I would allow him, up to a point.

"What's the catch?" He was all business now, putting his simmering hatred for me on the back burner until he got his wife back.

"One hundred thousand credits." I had intended to give her back gratis, but a little spare spending money would help keep the Noorthi comfortable for years to come.

"I won't pay it."

"Okay, it's your loss. I'll just go back and tell her you didn't think she was worth a hundred thousand credits."

I was about to switch off the screen when he spoke again. "All right. You win." He didn't like being screwed again. "What's the arrangement?"

"Twelve o'clock, at the far end of Juno spaceport. That's two hours. Put the credits in metallic cases for pickup. Once I'm away and confirm that I'm not being followed, I'll send you the coordinates for your wife." Was I taking one risk too many to secure a legacy for the Noorthi? Our credit reserves were nearly gone, leaving us to survive on what we could scratch out of the soil. No, damn it. We deserved better than that. He owed us. No, not me. The Noorthi.

"Fine." But he said it too readily. I could see by the expression on his face that he was already imagining limitless possibilities of traps and ambushes.

"No tricks, Grimm. If I don't deliver the goods to a pickup point then no wife. I have good friends who are very inventive at storytelling, and they'll tell her how you were more interested in the credits than in her well-being." I could hear his teeth grinding. "Oh, and tell Vel and Andrissa to stay away, too." Knowing Vel as I did, telling her not to do something would only make her want to do it all the more.

"No Vel and Andrissa. Understood." Would he tell them just so they would act on the threat? Would he use them to capture me, then if something went wrong, he could blame them for interfering? Hell, if it were me, I would. "And if you harm one h—"

I cut Grimm off in mid-threat. There was really no point in wasting precious air threatening me when I already knew what he would do if he captured me. This was probably the one time I was hoping it was Vel who caught me.

I glanced over at Tars in the copilot's seat, and I thought I had enough time for one more communication before she woke up. "Sasha? I've got another job for you."

†

The plan was now in motion, and I had just passed the point of no return. I let the ship hover for a while as I leaned back in the chair and studied the stars. It really was beautiful out there, and I had taken it all for granted. How many star systems existed? No one really knew. How many civilizations? Species? Lives?

It's funny how facing your probable death—again—can turn your thoughts outward. Maybe it was because this time was different. This was a death of my own choosing, not one thrust upon me. Grit's words came back to me, and I realized that now that I had accepted I was going to die, calm settled over my body like a blanket and I felt at peace.

"Little stars shining bright..." I sang softly. "Bathed so gently in ethereal light." It was one of my favorite nursery rhymes when I was a kid. My mom used to sing it to me, and after she died, Dad tried to keep up the tradition. His burred voice sang it off-key but I still remembered him taking the time to sing it. That was when I knew my dad really loved me, because instead of going to the bar with his war buddies, he was home tucking me in and singing nonsense nursery rhymes until I fell asleep.

"Twinkling in the dark so clear."

Tars began to move as I sang, her lips smacking together as she slowly woke up.

"Wha—what's going on?" She sat upright as her senses took in where she was.

"You're going home," I said calmly.

"Really? What did you do to me?"

"Just a sleeping potion so you can't give away our position."

Tars said nothing, not even to deny such a thought. It was enough to draw me away from my little ditty and look at her. Did she know something I didn't?

"Where's Juno?"

"It's out there. Somewhere. But first I have to ensure that a certain transfer is made safely." There was no point in telling her about the little transaction until it was absolutely necessary. If she knew there were credits involved, she might make things difficult for me. It was better for her to think I was doing her a favor and have her cooperation. "I don't want to be fired upon while trying to deliver you to Grimm."

"He wouldn't do that."

"Ah, yes, that's right. He values you so highly that he wouldn't risk you to get at me," I said sarcastically. But I knew better. I think he hated me more than he loved her, so it would be a fine line between saving her and blasting me out of the sky. "You were a bit tough on Beri."

"She has no right condemning me." Tars's voice still held some hostility, and it peeved me. I was feeling mighty protective of Beri these days.

"But it's okay for you to do it, is that right?"

"I beg your pardon?" She sounded genuinely offended.

"You are such a hypocrite," I said. "Where in the Noorthi handbook does it say you can marry a man and have three children by him? Those women tried their damnedest to stay true to the Noorthi way while trying to survive on a planet where the outside temperature averaged one hundred and twenty degrees. And where

287

were you? Safely tucked away in a nice cool building with three meals a day and all the water you could drink."

"And who are you to criticize me?" Tars's voice steadily rose in volume.

"I'm their Ratha, and I'm doing my job. What I want to know is why you're so hostile toward your fellow sisters or, more important, Beri? What has she done to offend you?" When Tars said nothing, I continued, "Or is it because you have a guilty conscience?"

"I have no such thing."

"Did you marry Grimm for love or as a way to save yourself?" I knew it was a loaded question. Either way she was screwed.

"Love? Are you questioning my sincerity?"

"Then answer the question. Which is it? Love or security?"

"I will not dignify that with an answer."

"Just as I thought. You're a coward." She was really starting to annoy me, making me question whether sending her back was worth the effort. Then again, they deserved each other. "You strung him along because he loved you, and you used him to protect you from Vel." She just glared at me. I put my feet up on the console, leaned back in the chair, and put my hands behind my head. "And by the looks of you, you gave up the secret pretty easily, too."

"Do not insult me this way."

"I see no signs of torture on your body. Can you deny you told him what he wanted to know even before the torture began?" The more I found out about this woman, the more I wanted to pound her into next week.

"I was a holy woman. He did not want to harm me."

"Then your crime is all the more heinous. He had no qualms about putting the rest of the sisterhood on a barren planet for them to die slowly. What makes you think he would be concerned about torturing you? Unless, of course, you told him what he wanted to know, then appealed to his baser instincts."

I could nearly feel her fear in the air. It certainly resided in her eyes. "I had to survive."

"And you have no shame in what you did?"

"Of course, I feel guilty," she finally admitted.

"But not guilty enough to stop you having three children with him."

"He forced me."

"And yet you condemn Beri. Your attitude has undermined her confidence and put the very foundation of Noorthi tradition in jeopardy because you have a guilty conscience."

She stared at me. I finally made her speechless.

"It's all too late now, though. How about a caffeine synth?" I asked. "I don't know about you, but I could certainly use one." I stood up and stretched before moving out of the cockpit to the small corridor behind the wall. I activated the replicator and requested two hot caffeine synths. "How do you take it?" I called.

"Plain," Tars called back. She sounded a little more at ease now that she thought the arguing was all over. I didn't think it was over. She needed a serious reality check, but I let the matter rest for now. I reached into my pocket, took out a small flask, and poured a drop or two of the contents into the caffeine.

As I walked back into the cockpit I took a sip of my own caffeine, deftly handing over the remaining mug to Tars.

Over the rim of my mug I watched Tars drink her caffeine, a smile crossing my lips as her eyes slowly dipped until they were closed. I lunged for the mug before it slid out of her hand and lowered both her and the mug to the floor. Who would have thought she would fall for the same trick twice?

I reached the outer limits of Juno without much trouble, catching the beginning of the clutter of ships making their approaches to the spaceport. As I approached, I tried to calm myself, but adrenaline ran full throttle through my body. Half an hour before the meeting, I dropped Tars off on the far outskirts of the city and left her sleeping on the side of a dusty hill. Maybe that was mean, but I wasn't taking any chances with Grimm. My ship climbed steadily back into Juno traffic, and I wasted time wending my way through the floating junkyard. The ship's scanners, on full sweep, showed nothing more than the mass of ships slowly descending in an orderly fashion to Juno. But I knew they were there somewhere, watching my every move as I maneuvered to hover over the far end of the spaceport.

The cases sat out in the dustbowl that constituted the outer landing area of the spaceport. As far as I could see, the area was empty, but that didn't worry me. My focus was on the glittering prize on the ground. I also had a trick or two of my own. I activated a magnetic bar on the bottom of the ship to catch the cases without having to land for them. That accomplished, I accelerated away. I looked down at the ground and saw a number of figures running around and jumping up and down. They'd have to be a lot smarter to catch me. It was a crude move on their part, and therefore doomed to fail.

I moved the ship into the mass of ships over Juno and slowed down to keep pace with them. While the autopilot was running, I left the cockpit to check out the credits. The cases sat in the cargo bay, and I was almost afraid to approach them. Maybe they were booby-trapped, or worse, empty. I never doubted at least one of these was tagged, which was why I had one of Malt's scanners in my pocket.

I scanned the boxes and, sure enough, found tags. Each box had one and was locked. If they thought it would stop me, they had another thing coming.

The automatic pilot beeped at me as the ship approached the meeting point. Sasha's ship was waiting for me, casually drifting in and out of the ships crawling along in the mass of heavy traffic. I slid back into my seat and switched the autopilot off. "Hey, Sash. You there?" It was a stupid thing to say; it was obvious she was there, but I couldn't come up with something witty.

"Nah, it's Beri." Sasha thought she was a comedienne.

I ignored her, but in a weird way, I did wish that. "I'm coming in to dock. The cases are tagged and locked."

"And you didn't think they would be?"

"We'll need the usual tools, okay?"

"Ready when you are."

There was a loud metallic bang as the airlocks connected. I waited for the familiar "rap tap tap" that was Sasha's signal but nothing happened. Maybe the ships weren't aligned. I started to check the control panel when Sasha's signal sounded, so

I hit the airlock button and the door slid open. "Something wrong?" I questioned.

"Just foolin'." Sasha grinned at me.

"It's not like I'm in a hurry or anything," I commented sarcastically. "Come on, do your magic." I stepped aside so Sasha could come on board. Some things I did better than her, some things we did equally well, but a few things she did better than I could. Sasha excelled at cracking locks.

As she hunkered down in front of the cases, I looked into her ship and saw she wasn't alone. "Rales? Damn it, what the hell are you doing here?"

"I couldn't let my little girl come here alone," he said in a tone that didn't leave much room for argument.

"I wanted you back with the Noorthi in case Grimm finds them."

"There's no chance of that," he said. "Stop worrying."

"I'll stop worrying when Grimm and Vel are taken care of." Rather than think of the fate I figured I'd meet, I changed the subject. "What are you going to do when this is all over? Return to Aldronicus?"

Rales thought a moment. "Sasha and I have talked about it. We kind of like it on Heaven. It's different, but in a nice way." He laughed. "Who would have thought, huh?" His gaze met mine.

"And if the sisters go back to Juno?" I asked.

"Well, hmm."

"He'd follow them," Sasha said as she worked on the lock.

"Uh-huh." I gave him a look. Had he been messing with the Noorthi? "Anyone I know?"

"There isn't anyone," he said defensively.

"I've seen him talking to Grit now and then," Sasha called over her shoulder.

"Grit? Well, well. I would have thought that after all this time you would have remembered they're celibate." And probably not interested in men, I added, but not aloud.

"You're both nuts. Like I said, there isn't anyone," he said gruffly.

"What about the boys? What are their plans?" I asked.

"They're thinking of setting up there, too. They'll work off-world, but it's somewhere they can come home to. As Denneck said, it's somewhere to raise a family."

"Denneck said that?" Could I imagine that giant of a man with a baby sitting on his massive thigh? Yes, I could.

"Got it," Sasha said. "Give me a few seconds to get the other ones."

Rales shifted uneasily. "Jordana, you can't do this."

"Why not? The Noorthi can use the credits."

"No, not the credits," he said quietly. "What you're about to do. Is it worth your life?"

"To keep them safe, yes."

"The tags are in the box linings." Sasha told me nothing I didn't already suspect.

"Let's get to work, then."

Rales passed woven baskets to us into which he and Sasha and I tipped the credits. Once the cases were empty, Sasha reencrypted the locks. "Now get out of here," I said.

Sasha and Rales looked at me from their ship, indecision in their eyes.

"Don't even think about it." My lips tightened in frustration. "Why is it that everyone has to argue the point?" I said it more to myself than to the two in the adjoining ship.

"We can help you," Sasha said.

"Please, just once, will you do what I ask without arguing? The Noorthi need your help more than I do."

"But, J—"

"The longer you argue with me, the more Grimm is going to suspect something is going on. Just get the hell out of here, okay?"

Sasha nodded and prepared to close the door.

"Sash? Thank the boys for me, will you? Give them each a bonus for a job well done."

She opened her mouth to say something but closed it again and just nodded, then turned and walked away, deeper into her ship.

Rales and I were left to face each other alone.

"Do you really have to do this?" he asked.

"I'm open to suggestions that would give me the same result." His brow wrinkled in concern that was soon replaced with a look of sadness. "I wish I had one. Almighty Carn, I wish I did."

"This was how it was meant to play out." I stepped through the hatch to Sasha's ship and pulled Rales into a hug. "Goodbye, dear friend." No, at a time like this it didn't sound right so I spoke again. "You've been like a dad to me. I hope you know that."

"And you've been like another daughter to me. Please don't say 'goodbye.' Just say 'see you later.'"

I didn't argue the point and withdrew back into my ship. "Now get going before Grimm chases your asses, too." My last image of Rales broke my heart. A lone tear rolled down his face as the outer hatch door closed. Now I was on my own.

I sat in the pilot's chair and watched Sasha's ship disappear into the mass of vehicles surrounding us. I kicked the ship into life and negotiated the junkyard in front of me. Vehicles of all shapes, sizes, and ages made the journey to Juno for bartering, so weaving around them was part skill and part prayer. I only hoped that nothing broke off one of them and came through my window. I entered the Juno atmosphere and glided around until I found a group of ships leaving the planet. This was as close as I wanted to get to the planet, so I didn't waste a moment any longer than I had to in Juno airspace.

I broke out of the pack and hesitated, waiting to see if Grimm had found me yet. The ship's scanner picked up six vessels rising quickly from the surface and heading in my direction. When I thought there was enough distance between me and Grimm's ships, I accelerated and headed away from Heaven.

The small fleet of ships accelerated also, and the game began. There was no way I could outrun them. The cruisers had far superior and more powerful engines, but I had the advantage of knowing they were there. After all, my intention was to eventually

293

get caught, but not before I had them chasing their own tails for an hour or two.

I had a reasonable lead on them and stayed within range of their scanners. There was no point in weaving about, so I headed straight for the tiny planet Calceter and dove down low over the junk pile that made up this rock in space. I skimmed over the razor-sharp metal in the hope of enticing the cruisers to do the same. Would they take up the challenge or wait until I either exploded or emerged unscathed from the death run?

It took a few minutes before I had my answer. A flash of bright light appeared behind me, illuminating the metal graveyard for a moment before it faded. I looked up and saw two cruisers parked in orbit, obviously waiting for me.

Meanwhile, I caught a glimpse of a cruiser coming over the horizon, heading directly for me. These pilots were good. Really good. I made a hurried calculation for a jump into hyperspace. Doing a jump straight out of planetary departure wasn't a good idea, but they were giving me no choice. Besides, if I gave up this easily they would know something was up.

I increased my speed and zigzagged over derelicts and pods in an almost cavalier manner. When the speed was right, I angled the ship into space, getting enough momentum to make the jump. The cruisers moved into position to capture me, but in a split second I was gone.

"You've got to do better than that," I said to no one in particular, but somehow, it wasn't the same. Bessie at least would have answered me with an all-knowing, "Don't get too cocky, Jordana." Not this ship. It was as cold as the void outside. It would have been nice to make this last run in Bessie, riding the skies together one more time. But the thought of her being incinerated or damaged stopped me from using her. At least one of us should live past this day.

As I considered my next move, the scanners picked up five vessels coming out of hyperspace behind me. One down, five to go. I studied the holomap of the area and found what I was looking for. "Let's see how good you really are."

The engines whined as I ramped up to maximum speed. The cruisers would catch me eventually, but not before I reached the obstacle I'd chosen that would test their maneuverability to the limit. I closely watched the scanners as the field of broken rock came into view. It was a risk, I knew, but the object of the game was to make life difficult for Grimm's ships.

I entered the asteroid field unafraid, powering the small ship around large chunks of rock and small floating bits of debris. I could see the scanner in my peripheral vision and saw some movement in it. My attention was forward as I was trying not to crash into an errant boulder, so I couldn't see clearly what was going on. The scanner beeped at me, and I eased up on the throttle. When I had a bit of open space to move, I looked. Two of the cruisers were boldly trying to follow me while the remaining three parked themselves outside the field. While I looked, one ship disappeared from the screen, exploding into oblivion as the field claimed one more victim.

I couldn't see the remaining cruiser, but I knew it was there. I checked my chronometer and made a decision. I'd give them one more hour of chasing my tail until I let myself get captured.

I had given the poison a lot of thought. They would anticipate some sort of retaliation from me or, if it were me, I would anticipate something. Vel was no fool, and I suspected Andrissa wasn't either. What if I used both the gloves and the pellet? Sacrifice the poisoned gloves in the hope of getting a chance at Vel with the pellet? It was a huge risk, sure, but it was a necessary risk.

I took the pellet from my buckle and looked at it. The decision about when to put it in my mouth was a big one. As far as I could see, the only opportunity would be when I went down the stairs to the interrogation room. But I was making an assumption here. What if Vel decided to meet me at the front door and shoot me where I stood? The only other solution was to put it in my mouth when I was captured. But what if I was unconscious? Would I accidentally swallow it? Maybe it was the thought of dissolving into a puddle that guided my hand to put the pellet back into the belt buckle. No, somehow I would have to find that opportunity just before meeting Vel.

It was surprising how quickly time passed when trying to avoid getting hit by debris. The cruiser that had been sent in to get me had wisely backed out of the field after its companion had been destroyed. I was alone in the minefield, and it was only a matter of time before I emerged.

I maneuvered the ship to exit the asteroid field to the left of the small fleet. There was no doubt in my mind that they knew exactly where I was, but I had to at least make it look like I was trying to get away.

It was all over before I even had a chance to bring the ship up to speed. One of them was equipped with a tractor beam, and it trapped me as I flew out of the field. I sat back as the cruiser came closer, the ship out of my control. They finally had me cornered, and now all that had to be done was board me. Calmly, I reached up into the overhead locker and took out the vial. A metal clunk echoed through the ship. Any second now, troopers would flood through the hatch and into the ship.

I pulled on the metallic gloves, kneading the pliable material until it felt like a second skin. The tiny bottle was in my hand and I looked at it. Should I? Shouldn't I? Did I have any other choice?

My hand reached into my pocket and pulled out the pellet. I had a second to make a decision.

"You'd better be right, Gorin."

My plan was now in motion, and there was no going back. I was placing all my bets on the gloves and that once the poison was discovered they would relax and think I'd been caught. But would they fall for it?

When voices filtered through to me, and I realized time had run out, I opened the vial and poured a tiny pool of poison into one palm. Once the bottle was closed, I replaced it in the tiny locker above my head. As the troopers reached the door to the cockpit, I rubbed my palms together.

"Well, boys." It was all I could manage before the butt of a laser rifle connected with the back of my head.

†

I don't know how long I was out, but I found myself seated in a very comfortable chair with my hands manacled to the armrests. In a way, I was thankful; my eye was itchy, and I wanted to scratch it, an action that was now fraught with danger.

I flexed my hands and finally realized something was missing. Where were my gloves?

"Missing something?" The hiss of the "s" told me all I needed to know about who the speaker was.

"I wondered where you'd gotten to, Andrissa." I tried to focus on her, but her image was a little fuzzy.

"You've been a naughty girl, Jordana." She held up my gloves and waved them in front of my face.

"What are you talking about?"

"We found your little surprise. Or should I say, one of the guards found your little surprise. They're cleaning up the mess right now."

"Really?" I was pleased they had discovered the gloves. My only wish now was that they were satisfied with that and didn't look further.

I was pleased to see the old Jordana was back, ready to be witty at a moment's notice. Maybe it was because I had nothing to fear from Andrissa. Whether it was Vel or Grimm who ultimately got me, I'm sure she was told to keep her hands off. "Where are we?"

"Approaching Juno."

Juno? I must have been knocked out harder than I thought. "And the ship?"

"In tow." At least they didn't blow it to pieces.

"You know, you've got your credits back. How about you let me go, and we call it quits?"

Andrissa laughed. It was a strange sort of laugh, sounding more like a gargle. It probably had something to do with her tongue. "You're joking, right?"

"Me? I never joke," I said. "Unless it's funny, of course."

"And this is all a joke to you?"

"No. If it was a joke it would be 'a Human, a Crysean, and a Rogan walked into a bar—'" My head reeled as she hit me across the temple. "No, that's not the punchline." Crack! Her other hand delivered another blow, this time across the back of my head. "Enjoying yourself?" At this point I was grateful the capsule was in my belt buckle and not sitting inside my cheek.

"Immensely. Want another one?" Her gaze was pleading with me to smart-mouth her again.

"I think I've made my point."

"We're about to land," a voice announced.

Andrissa took her seat opposite me and fastened her seatbelt. She gazed at me with obvious venom.

"What did I do to you that you hate me so much?"

"You're a smart-ass."

"That's it? That's the reason?" The cruiser rattled gently as we passed through the stratosphere into the atmosphere of Juno.

"Yes. You go through life like the universe owes you a living."

I didn't think I had such an attitude, especially since Vel stepped back into my life, but arguing the point would probably only get me another slap. Maybe she was just baiting me. "Well, doesn't it?"

Andrissa's skin was slowly becoming orange, starting at a cool green and then fading to yellow. She was a living mood ring.

"Nah, I don't think that's it. You hate me because Vel does. She's probably been spreading vicious rumors about me. Then again, I suppose I was always a little larger than life." Talk about telling lies, Jordana, you old bitch. I could now see how these rumors got started. No, I think Andrissa would have hated me no matter what I did. The vessel touched down lightly on the ground, and I found myself back where I had been two weeks ago: on Juno and in Vel's clutches.

"Stand up," Andrissa ordered with an extra long hiss.

I did and stayed silent. If she was expecting some comment from me, I wasn't going to give it to her. But her skin was a mottled green-gray, which made me think she wasn't angry at all. Maybe she knew what my fate would be, too.

I looked at the guards, who smiled smugly at me as I walked toward the hatch. Once or twice, I got a push in the back for my trouble, but only because they knew they could do it without retribution. Was this how they treated the citizens of Juno? But now was not the time to get all worked up over whether they did or not. I had a plan, and it required my complete attention.

As I stepped down onto Juno soil, I could tell it was going to be another hot day. I looked around the field and saw activity near a number of cruisers. Heavily armed troopers were boarding them in an orderly line, and I felt the cold finger of fate touch my soul. This was important.

"Where are they going?" I asked.

"I have no idea," Andrissa replied, "but you have more important things to worry about than troopers."

"You know, Andy, you've become a real bore since shacking up with Vel." I was antagonizing her, I know, but I knew she couldn't touch me. I was Vel's plaything, not hers.

Andrissa hissed violently.

"Problem, Andy?"

"You're asking for trouble," she replied, her scaly skin changing color from a cool green to brown, to orange, and then to red. I was pissing her off nicely.

"Trouble? How much more trouble can I be in?"

"I could make your journey to Vel very uncomfortable indeed." The look in her eye told me she wanted me to push her to the limit so she had an excuse to hit me again. Or do even worse things.

"I don't think Vel would appreciate you damaging the goods. By the way, I should thank you for looking after my ship Bessie. She spoke very highly of you."

"Next time I see it, I'm going to blast it out of the sky."

"That's too bad. She likes you, and I'm sure you like her."

"I always thought you were a crazy bitch. I can see I was right."

"Me? Crazy? I'm not the one working for a psychopath here. If I were you, Andrissa, I'd be careful."

"You don't know what you're talking about."

"Fine. But don't come crying to me when she stabs you in the back."

"You won't be around that long to see it."

"So you admit you don't trust her."

Andrissa hissed at me, and I shut up. I think I had reached that line in the sand where if I stepped over it I would probably regret it.

Andrissa got into a waiting vehicle, sat down, and indicated I should do the same. It would get me to Vel faster, but at least I didn't have to walk all the way.

"So the troops are on the move, and Vel hasn't told you? Who trusts who, now?"

She didn't reply, instead confining her interest to the masses in the streets going about their business.

"If I were you, I'd ask for a raise or something. Better yet, ignore her and go directly to Grimm. After all, it's him you work for, not Vel."

Her interest came back to me, and she stared intently into my eyes. My thoughts wandered as she continued to stare at me. Did she possess the ability to hypnotize her prey with a look? I had heard stories about her kind but had never come across it in my travels. Maybe it was all a myth, just like the Noorthi were supposed to be a myth, but lately I'd been discovering that some myths had a kernel of truth to them.

It took a lot to tear my eyes away from her, but I managed to. I turned my vision to the dust and the heat before closing my eyes for a few seconds to gather my scattered thoughts. I wondered if I had been under her influence any longer whether she would have planted a subliminal order for me to carry out.

"In fact, I'm willing to bet you don't know anything. Vel doesn't think enough of you to include you in her plans." Andrissa was making me work hard for whatever I could find out, but she remained silent. "So you've got nothing in that head of yours?" I should have seen it coming, but she struck like the viper she was; her tongue lashed out and hit me across the face.

"I suppose I deserved that."

"Yes, you did," she snapped. If Andrissa had a tail, it would've been twitching right about now.

"Now what?"

"Now you sleep." She smiled that sort of 'I know a secret and you don't' smile and I didn't like it.

"What are you not tell—" I then passed out cold.

Chapter Twenty-Three

Big Bang Theory

I sat up abruptly and tried to get my bearings. I looked around and saw the vehicle was sitting in front of the Great House steps. Andrissa was gone, and two guards stood waiting, I suppose, for me to wake up.

"Come on," the taller one said gruffly, while his colleague reached in and grabbed my arm. He pulled roughly, but whatever Andrissa had hit me with sapped my energy. She sure packed a punch.

"Where are we going?"

"Somewhere where no one will hear you scream," the shorter guard said and then smiled.

"Again?" We began the descent down the staircase to a very familiar room. The stairs were not very wide, forcing us to move one behind the other. The guard behind me prodded me in the back with his pistol just in case I got any ideas about escaping.

This was my chance. My hand slid to the buckle, and I pulled out the pellet. Hiding the move to my mouth by scratching my cheek, I slipped the pellet under my tongue and shifted it slightly to get a more comfortable fit. My heart rate went up with the thought of that little bit of death sitting there so close to my skin.

The guard behind me prodded me again. Little did he know I had no intention of escaping, at least not until my job was done. However, I'm not the sort of woman who would sacrifice herself unnecessarily so if the opportunity presented itself after that, I'd be running like hell out of there.

We reached the bottom of the stairs that led directly to what had basically been an underground storage area or, as I had come to consider it, the interrogation room. I had run out of time. Vel was talking to Andrissa, who seemed a little agitated. Her skin was a pale green, tinged with yellow, so she wasn't quite angry, but she wasn't happy, either.

"Get out of here," Vel said imperiously to Andrissa. When Andrissa hesitated, Vel spoke more firmly. "Now."

I could hear the hiss from where I was standing as Andrissa expressed her displeasure. She turned on her heel and walked by me to the stairs. As she passed me, I said, "I told you so." She punched me in the arm, and I staggered back from the impact.

"Leave her alone," Vel snapped. "She's mine." Vel took a few steps toward us. I saw the look in Andrissa's eyes that she had used on me, and I watched for Vel's reaction. Surprisingly, Vel showed no obvious signs of being under the influence of Andrissa's hypnotic stare. Quite the opposite. Vel's jaw twitched as she tried to impose her will on her subordinate. "Get out."

"Are you going to tell me what's going on?" I asked Vel.

"Andrissa is going to kill those Noorthi bitches you have such a fondness for."

"So that's the nefarious scheme, huh?" I said to Vel.

"And since when did you know what 'nefarious' means?" Vel asked me.

"I've got a whole new vocabulary since we first met. Kind of weird, but I think it's really helped with my conversational skills."

"It's going to be a shame that you won't get to use it in the future, because you don't have one." Vel turned her attention to Andrissa. "Are you still here? Get going."

Vel watched me as I watched Andrissa leave. "You're not interested in where she's going, are you?"

"Wherever it is, you won't find the Noorthi there."

"Not even the third moon of Telgan?"

My heart rate increased from anxious to downright terrified. How the hell did she find that out? How was I going to warn them? Even if I survived this, I still couldn't protect them. I was faced with a dilemma—kill Vel or try to warn the Noorthi. I glanced back at Vel. I'd come this far. I might as well get her out of the way and deal with the next thing after. If I had the opportunity. Suddenly, it became entirely necessary for me to survive.

"Oh, come on, J. You wanted to play this game, now it's your turn to come up with some pithy remark."

"You won't find them there, either," I said with as much conviction as I could muster.

"That's not very pithy, or inventive, either." Vel had a smug expression on her face.

"What do you want?"

"I want you to die, but there's nothing in those rules of yours that says I can't have some fun with you before that."

"Fun? Killing a hundred women is fun to you?"

"Of course it is. It's about power. It's intoxicating."

Any doubts I had about using Gorin's death drug dissolved. Vel surpassed even my expectations of her inherent evil. My muscles tensed as I considered when to strike, but Vel moved away, turning her back on me. She walked toward the cell in the corner. I casually looked from side to side to see what the guards were doing and estimated my chances of getting to Vel before they got to me.

"Come," Vel said. The guard pushed me in the back, and I staggered forward. "You're not interested in how I found out where they were?"

"Why ask? You're going to tell me anyway."

"True, but I was hoping you would oblige me."

"Drop dead." Venting my anger would serve no purpose other than making me feel better.

"Let her be." Vel held up her hand. I couldn't see, but by her reaction, I suspected one of the guards was about to hit me. "I thought you would at least ask if that Noorthi bitch got home safely."

Something had happened. Vel was way too happy about the fact for it to be good news.

"After she told me what I wanted to know, she kept whining about being a holy woman. She seemed to have this absurd idea that she was untouchable, so I had to show her the error of her ways." A sly grin spread over Vel's lips.

"So where is she now?"

"With Grimm." Vel's grin turned wicked.

"And where is he?" I had a bad feeling.

"Somewhere where he won't need that trick arm of his anymore." Vel laughed.

"You've left the kids without parents."

"No." She stared intently into my eyes. Vel told me with a look what had happened to those children, and my guts froze. Kids? She'd get rid of kids, too?

"So, that's it, huh?"

"Yes. You're now looking at the new 'Count.'"

"You know I'm going to have to stop you."

"I don't think you have a firm grasp of the situation," she said sarcastically.

Vel nodded at the guards behind me. A hand landed in the middle of my back and pushed, shoving hard enough to move me into the cell. A low hum filled the air as the force field activated.

"What are you waiting for?" I asked, trying to goad her.

"I want you alive when I deliver the news of the annihilation of the Noorthi."

I turned around and faced the wall. There was no way I would give her the satisfaction of seeing my reaction. My blood pressure rose, and my heartbeat thumped loudly in my head. I had never felt as impotent as I did now. My friends were in trouble, and I was unable to defend them.

Vel laughed as she walked away, leaving me alone to contemplate the Noorthi's demise. "Craz!" I slumped onto the bed and lay down. What was I going to do? Wait. I remember some sort of emotional connection when I was last in Vel's clutches. A Noorthi had supported me when I needed help. Would she feel something if I tried to send a message to her? At this point I had nothing to lose.

"Fen?" I whispered, "I hope you can feel me, because I really need you to warn the others. You are in grave danger and need to evacuate Heaven. I'm sorry that we didn't get to know one another better."

As an extra measure, I sent a mental note to Beri. "You turned out to be a dear friend, B, you know that? Take care of Rice for me, okay? Remember me kindly to the kid."

I felt nothing in return. I had no idea if it worked or not, and I just lay in silence, utterly lost.

†

"It's all over," Vel announced.

I looked at my chronometer. Four hours had elapsed since I touched down on Juno. My heart broke at the thought of all those people dead, especially those I cared most about. But I wouldn't let Vel see my pain.

"So, you've won."

"More than you know." Vel nodded at a guard who shut down the force field around the cell.

She obviously wanted me to stand, so I obliged her. I took a few steps toward her and away from the cell. "It ends here, Vel." The two guards came up on either side of me, ready for anything that I might try to do.

"You're right, for once. You have been a thorn in my side for long enough."

Vel approached me, each of her steps timed to my heartbeat. The guards stood alert, and I knew that I would only get one shot at this.

"Your weapon," she demanded of one of the guards.

Vel was intent on making sure I was dead this time. Her arm rose with the pistol, and without hesitation, she pulled the trigger.

Pain shot through my gut and blossomed outward. The smell of burnt flesh once again assaulted my senses. My legs gave way as my body started to shut down. The ground approached rapidly, and I barely put my hands out to stop my face hitting the dirt. Was this how it was supposed to end? Had all this talk about destiny come to nothing?

I rolled onto my back and looked up at Vel standing over me.

"You should have gotten away when you had the chance, J."

"It's not over yet," I whispered.

"What?" She looked at the nearby guard. "What did she say?" I extended my hand upward for a moment before it became too heavy to hold. I motioned Vel to me. "I have something..."

Vel just had to know what I said. She knelt down beside me and lowered her ear to my lips. Before she could react, I did the only thing I could do at a time like this. I kissed her. The kiss was long and lingering. Maybe Vel didn't want my last action to be my own, because she took over the kiss, making it hot and demanding as her teeth latched onto my lower lip and bit hard. Her tongue invaded my mouth, and I felt the capsule move from under my tongue. When I had enough control, I pushed the pellet into her mouth.

"What?" She drew back and positioned the capsule between her teeth. I ignored the pain and clenched my stomach muscles, balling my bound hands into fists and slamming them into her face.

Vel landed on her ass, her hand vigorously wiping her mouth. Nothing happened. Had Gorin and Floric been wrong? Did I just leave the Noorthi to stand alone against Vel?

I looked at her, waiting. Suddenly, a tiny bit of blood appeared on her face. It was just a drop at first, running from her nose. She must have felt it, because she wiped it away. At first, she was puzzled. And then something like fear appeared in her cold eyes. Vel looked from the blood on her to me, and back again. "What did you do?"

"Killed you."

She started to kick me, which only made the poison work faster. Blood was now seeping from her eyes and ears. She stopped kicking me and turned around and screamed at the silent walls in frustration.

Something touched my shoulder, but I was too weak to look or even care. If Vel had still been kicking me, I wouldn't have felt it at all. But now there were hands under my armpits, and I was being dragged back toward a wall. I looked around, but no one was there. I looked down and couldn't see myself, either.

"Shh." The warning was barely audible above the sound of me being dragged away.

"You will tell me." Vel turned around. "Where is she?" She looked at the two men who were supposed to be guarding me. "You idiots. You let her escape?"

The older of the two guards stared at her, then glanced around the room.

"She couldn't have gotten very far. Find her and bring her back. I want to watch her die, do you hear me?" Vel's voice rose to a tight screech. "She must die."

I couldn't see my rescuers, but whoever they were, they were packing my wound. I tried to swallow the scream building inside me.

Vel stopped pacing and listened. A hand came over my mouth, and I tried to get control of the noise I was making. The pain inside immobilized me. The rag returned and was applied with some pressure to the hole in my gut. A moan escaped my throat, and Vel moved closer.

"Who's there?" She ignored the blood that ran down her face and dripped on the floor. "No more games. Have the courage to face me at the end."

I was so tempted to do as she asked, but the touch on my shoulder told me whoever was rescuing me didn't want me to fall into that trap.

Vel's hands clutched at her stomach, and she uttered a gut-wrenching groan that echoed up the stairwell.

"Let's go," I whispered. Whoever this was, I didn't want her to see what would happen next. Hell, I didn't want to see what would happen next.

There must have been two people, because I was bodily hauled to my feet, two hands under each arm. The cloth was tucked into my clothing to hold it in place before two shoulders tried to prop themselves under my armpits. It wasn't easy because of the manacles, but they managed. I knew one of my rescuers was Sasha, because that was the sort of gal she was.

"I thought I told you to protect the Noorthi," I whispered. Each word pressed on my abdominal muscles, and it hurt like hell.

"Stop worrying," said the disembodied voice next to my armpit.

"Damn it." Now was not the time for arguing, but I didn't know how much time I had left.

"Shut up, would you? I called on a few buddies."

I did. It was slow progress across the floor to the stairs, made all the more uncomfortable by the moans, screams, and begging of Vel. At the bottom of the stairwell, I was moved aside as guards came running down the stairs.

I nudged my rescuers along, taking one step at a time up to freedom. The odds were probably against me, but could I cheat death once more? I thought I had used up all my good luck already.

Vel continued to cry out, but it became more and more strangled and unintelligible, until it finally stopped altogether. Out of morbid curiosity, I suddenly wanted to see what had happened to her, but I was in no state to go back down the stairs. No, my imagination was doing an admirable job of picturing her dying.

I had always considered my death as an abstract condition. It was something I had talked about and convinced myself to accept, but here was the hard evidence it would probably happen. Dying didn't scare me. I had known it was a distinct possibility when facing Vel once more, but I still got a shot of adrenaline in spite of the extent of my injury.

The front door was closed. My rescuers had their hands full with holding me up, and I didn't have any spare energy to disengage the lock. I was struck dumb when the lock miraculously unclasped and the door eased open.

Vel's frantic cries had stirred the household, and people rushed down toward the interrogation area, ignoring the door.

We squeezed through the opening and staggered across the courtyard until I stopped. "I can't go much farther." My energy reserves were just about spent, but there was something more that needed to be said.

"A few more steps," one invisible body said.

"Sasha," I said, gasping, "we have to contact Heaven."

"I've already done that."

"But... Vel."

"Yes, yes," the other one said. "Vel did send a fleet of ships to Telgan. I know. I was there."

"Malt?" I giggled half-hysterically. That answered how the door got opened.

"Yep."

Malt was getting way too cocky for her own good. "Evacuate?"

"After I dropped off the old guy at Consortium," Sasha said, "I made a few calls. By the time the cruisers arrived, we had a fleet of ships of our own."

"And why is Malt here?"

"I couldn't let you go alone," Malt said.

"You are in so much trouble. Why didn't you stay put like I said?" It hurt to talk.

"Because you needed me."

I did, in more ways than one. This kid had gotten under my skin and into my heart, and nothing short of a heart replacement was going to get her out.

"Look, you two," I said, wheezing, "thanks for rescuing me, but I'm not getting out of here alive. I want you to leave and save yourselves." I was losing strength.

"I won't leave without you," Malt said, a little too loudly.

"Shh. They'll hear you," Sasha warned.

"I don't care."

"All right, all right. Let's go." It seemed I would have to live a little longer to save these two from themselves.

We were outside the walls of the Great House, leaning heavily against the cool courtyard wall. In the blink of an eye, we all became visible, Sasha and Malt now disguised as Grimm's troopers.

"What happened?" A unit leader approached us and looked at me. Was I a trooper as well? It was too late to find out, so I did what I do best. I lied.

"We were attacked," I said. "Inside."

He waved his unit onwards toward the house. "You," he said to me, "get some medical attention." He left us to join his unit in the compound.

"Aye, sir," I yelled as best as I could.

Malt and Sasha carried me out of the compound to the troop barracks. They found a speeder, and Sasha hotwired it. They lowered me gently onto the back seat. Just as Sasha brought the speeder to life, the air was filled with the sound of laser fire. I was flat on my back with my head resting in Malt's lap and unable to see what was happening. "What's going on?"

"Looks like the Consortium forces are here," Malt said over the revving of the speeder as it flew toward the spaceport.

Good on you, Gorin. The old man had proven his loyalty, both to the Consortium and to us.

Explosions rocked the area, forcing Sasha to weave to and fro to avoid flying debris. I was jostled in the back despite Malt's support, but I was unable to do anything about it. All I could hope for was that Sasha and Malt would get to safety. I suddenly felt cold and struggled to hold back a shiver. I was running out of time.

One strike nearly overturned us, but Sasha held the craft upright. She had no alternative but to take a sharp right turn down a side street and head off in a different direction.

"Where are we going?"

"Consortium troops heading this way. Have to take a detour," Sasha said in clipped tones.

I looked up at the sky and saw an errant laser strike or two from the cruisers hovering overhead. Grimm's empire was unraveling at the seams, and I took great satisfaction from that.

"She doesn't look so good," Malt said to Sasha.

"Huh?" I couldn't seem to concentrate.

"Jordana, please." Her hand stroked my hair but I barely felt her touch. "Don't leave me." She reached for my hand.

Sasha yelled over her shoulder. "J, hang in there. We're nearly at the ship."

"I need you. I don't want to be alone again."

I was finally able to get Malt into focus, and tears were running down her face.

311

"Don't cry." The words felt like dust in my mouth. I managed to wipe away a tear. The pain that had filled my body faded, and I floated in a haze of peace and calm. This must be it, then.

My hand covered Malt's. I looked up into those trusting eyes, swimming with tears, and smiled. "You be a good girl, okay?" Sasha appeared in my line of sight, standing behind her friend. "You keep an eye on her," I directed. Sasha nodded after I spoke.

"Jordana." Malt sputtered and her tears flowed like a river down her face. "You're the only family I have."

"The sisters are your..." The light faded from my vision, and the universe disappeared into darkness. My last thought was how sad Malt sounded when I heard her howl in the air. Then there was nothing.

Epilogue

Jordana, please! I need you!
The plea was so agonizing I couldn't ignore it. But it was dark, and I couldn't see. The words echoed down what sounded like a long hall. My body moved, and yet I wasn't aware of walking. I searched and searched, but I couldn't find the source of the heart-wrenching entreaty.
I can't go on without you!
The voice was familiar. I couldn't let this tortured soul suffer any longer, so I intensified my search. The darkness faded, slowly at first, going from completely black to a dark gray. Where was I?
"What do we do now? It's been nearly three weeks."
The conversation around me slowly became clear, and I was finally able to understand.
"We've done everything we can. Now all we can do is wait and see." The masculine voice was also familiar.
I opened my eyes a fraction, allowing in the light. It was too bright, and I closed them again.
"I think she moved," a young voice said excitedly.
"Malt, don't be silly. She's unconscious."
"No, Sasha. I'm telling you, she moved."
"Well, she's not moving now."
"You two take your argument outside." This was a voice of an older woman, and I think she was supposed to be someone I knew. I listened to the conversation around me, waiting to hear the voice that had guided me back. I tried opening my eyes again.
"See?"
"J? Jordana?" There it was. The voice in my dreams.

313

"Ahh." It was more an exhale than a word. My mouth was so dry that my tongue stuck to its roof.

"Water," someone ordered.

Who was that? I tried to focus on the short middle-aged woman trying to give me water. A few drops hit my lips, and I gladly licked them up.

"Where..."

"Heaven."

"I'm dead?"

Laughter. What was funny?

"Everyone leave her alone."

"Aww, Grit."

Grit. I knew that name. Through half-closed eyes, I looked at each face and put a name to it. Epi, Fen, Malt, Sasha, Rales, Floric. But it was the person sitting next to the bed and holding my hand who had my attention.

"I knew it was you," I whispered.

A single tear slid down Beri's cheek. "I thought I had lost you."

"Wait. Heaven?"

"It's safe," Sasha said quietly as she reached in and patted my arm. "The Consortium armada intercepted the troop ships heading for Locar. Unfortunately, this means the Consortium has moved into our universe, at least for now."

"We're all staying here, J," Rales said. "The Great House on Juno was destroyed by the Consortium attack. Me and the boys will begin building some dwellings for us all to live in, then I suppose we can get around to putting up a Great Hall."

"The Great Hall comes first," Grit said.

Rales shook his head. "I refuse to sleep in a Great Hall."

"And we won't allow you to," Grit said.

I ignored the dispute. "Are you okay?" I quietly asked Beri.

"I should be asking you that." Beri's dazzling smile went straight to my heart, and suddenly, everything became clear. "I knew you were in trouble," she said.

"Come on, now." Grit started pushing people out of the cave. Fen stopped at the entrance and looked back at me. She winked and nodded, and her eyes glanced at Beri for a second. It was like she had known all along. Was it one of those mysterious Noorthi things they seemed so apt at producing out of the blue? One day I would ask her, but for now, there was only Beri and me. Alone.

"Yeah?" I withdrew my hand from hers and placed it on her stomach. "And the baby?"

The hand that had been holding mine rested on top of my hand on her stomach. "Fine, now."

"Have you told them yet?" I patted her skin to indicate the baby.

"I didn't know how."

"Then we will tell our sisters together." Obviously, the thought of revealing her pregnancy to the Noorthi was a source of anxiety for her. "There's nothing to fear."

"But—"

"Grit already thinks I'm some sort of hero. Believe me, they'll all be happy." I didn't like seeing her so sad. "So I'm still alive?" A stupid question really, but I should have died twice.

"We told you to have faith, Jordana Laren." Beri said my name lovingly, and it sent a shiver through me. She had never said my name like that before. I liked it.

"I know, but I'm not one to invest heavily in faith."

"Even after all that's happened?"

"It's going to take some time to sort out this stuff in my head. But I think I'm staying, for you and for the baby. You've given me a gift I can't even begin to thank you for." All this talking had tapped what little energy reserves I had. I could feel my body pulling me back to sleep.

She leaned in close and murmured, "Then welcome home."

I lifted my hand with difficulty to her face, and I cupped her cheek. Beri had been in front of me all this time, and I hadn't seen her. Not in this light. I really liked it. Exhaustion overwhelmed me, and my eyes closed of their own volition. "Yeah," I said with a sigh. "Home."

About the Author

Erica Lawson is a "dinky di" Aussie, born and raised in Sydney, Australia, 58 years ago. She has worked as a secretary for most of her working life in a variety of interesting fields from a government scientific organization, the fire brigade, the film industry and finally, for the last 20 years, with a psychiatrist. Many of her friends will attest to the fact that she finally found her niche in the last job, gaining many helpful hints for her own state of mind.

Her first book, "Possessing Morgan", was released in December 2009. It is a winner of the 2010 GCLS award for best thriller/mystery novel. Her second book "The Chronicles of Ratha: The Children Of The Noorthi", a science fiction adventure, was released in December 2010 and a finalist in the 2012 GCLS Awards. Erica's third novel, "Soulwalker", released in 2012, won both the Rainbow Award for Best Sci-Fi of 2012 and GCLS Best Speculative Fiction in 2013. Her fourth novel, "Reflected Passion" won Best Historical Fiction at GCLS in 2014.

Erica has two novels published with Affinity eBooks. "Miss-Match", co-written with A.C. Henley, in April 2013. Her first solo effort for Affinity, "Out Of Retirement", came out in April 2014.

Erica now writes solely for Affinity eBooks and her previous novels, first released through Blue Feather Books, are being reissued by Affinity. They are available through Affinity eBooks website, Amazon, Barnes and Noble, and Bella Books.

Romance type: Lesbian romance. I qualify that with adventure, thriller, science fiction and historical settings.

Erica Lawson also writes under the name "Aurelia" on online fan fiction.

Website Link: http://www.ericalawson.com
Yahoo Group: Aurelia's Musings

http://groups.yahoo.com/group/aurelia_fan
Publisher: Affinity eBook Press
http://www.affinityebooks.com

Other Books from Affinity eBook Press

Nesting—Renee MacKenzie Macy Stokes, a divorced mother who is struggling with her sexual identity, jumps at a once-in-a-lifetime opportunity to help her friends. She doesn't foresee it will put her in jeopardy of losing her son, Jeremiah. Fresh out of high school, Cam Webber travels to Augusta, Georgia, to reconcile with her aunt. When she learns that's impossible, she determines to gain acceptance from her aunt's partner, Sharon. Meanwhile, Cam sets her sights on Macy, but Macy has other ideas. Kenny Brewer is a good old boy who loves his wife, Dorianne, even when he thinks she's gone totally off her rocker. Dorianne gets it in her head that a local woman is her long-lost half-sister. But soon, her obsession with that is eclipsed by medical problems that involve them all. Set in Augusta, Georgia, *Nesting* explores the age-old issues of guilt, regret, and redemption, and the part they play in driving people to create and protect family-at any cost.

Reece's Faith—TJ Vertigo In the return of the main characters from the bestselling novel *Private Dancer*, we see the blossoming relationship of bar owner, Reece Corbett and actress, Faith Ashford. The two women explore new, uncertain territory together, using sexual intimacy as a glue of comfort, helping them become strong and whole. A trusting Reece shares with Faith the sordid tale of how she became *The Animal* and Faith finds herself newly empowered by Reece's ongoing trust and support. Jealousy arises when Faith has to kiss a man on her TV show and two amorous women stalk Reece. When Faith is outed on her television show, things get crazy. With arrival of her parents on the scene, the craziness escalates. As Faith tries to justify her lifestyle and defend her love for Reece, she discovers that nothing about her parents is as she once believed. This, not to be missed passionate and erotic romance, will have you begging for more.

Starting Over—Jen Silver   Ellie Winters, a successful potter, is living on a remote hilltop farm inherited from her parents. Her well-ordered life is shaken apart when her past meets her present. Robin Fanshawe, Ellie's philandering long-term lover, has a fragile truce with Ellie. The arrival of women from Robin's present threatens to break that tentative pact. Charming Dr. Kathryn Moss, an archaeologist and an old lover of Ellie's, arrives on the farm searching for a new site to dig. When she discovers a previously unknown Roman settlement and ancient burial site on Ellie's farm, Ellie allows her to start an archaeological dig of the area. Will Ellie also allow the rekindling of an old romance or will she stay with Robin? Can that long term relationship, albeit tentative, recover from this collision or will an old romance trump everything she knows? Will Robin, seeing the interaction between Ellie and Kathryn, leave her womanising ways behind? Will she take a chance on giving herself wholly to the woman she loves? These questions and the mystery of whose royal resting place is disturbed at Starling Hill are answered in this classic romance of simmering passions, anguished loss, and the wonder of love.

Twisted Lives—Ali Spooner   A twist of fate leaves Bet and her daughter Kylie stranded at the entrance of the home of Alex Graves, as she flees the control of an abusive husband. When custom –homebuilder Alex arrives to find steam boiling from Bet's car and a beautiful child asleep in the passenger seat, her heart goes out to them. Alex offers shelter to the pair setting off a chain of events that bring both mother and daughter close to her heart and danger to her door. A heartwarming story of true love that will keep you smiling long after you've finished the book.

Malodorous—Del Robertson   Sequel to **My Fair Maiden** Something in Fairhaven stinks. Other than the mutton stew, that is. Gwen thought life after being a virgin sacrifice would be a bed of roses. Bodhi was just looking for a wench to bed. Neither less-than-dashing hero nor not-quite-so-pure maiden imagined they would meet again, much less be trapped together in a city the likes of the ill-named Fairhaven. There's a killer on the loose. Fairhaven's on lockdown, its citizens fearful for their lives. The local guards are corrupt. And, Bodhi's been accused of murder...

Desert Blooms—Dannie Marsden Luce's story continues in DESERT BLOOMS... When we last met Luce Velazquez in Desert Heat, she went through hell and back to salvage her soul and reputation. Hoping to get her life back on track with lover Beth Ryan, a woman who understands her pain and can relate on every level. Instead, Luce is in the hospital, and Beth in protective custody. Jessica Sullivan, Luce's friend and ex, has big doubts about the sincerity of Beth's love, and is in no hurry to release her from custody. Can Luce's new found happiness last, or is Jessica correct in her doubts? A heart stopping romance that will fill you with the wonder of friendship, anger of betrayal, and the everlasting vision of love.

HER—Lisa Ron Fox has been looking for that one person who will make her feel complete-her perfect match. Together with her friends, Megan and Tree, Fox continues her quest while dodging exes and clingers, laughing a lot along the way. When she meets Madeline, she instantly knows that she finds HER. Madeline has her own problems-notably a domineering husband. Can Fox win her heart? Can they make a life together? This story will make you laugh, cry, and hold your breath as the story unfolds. With the right person love can conquer all.

Bayou Justice—Ali Spooner Hell hath no fury like a woman scorned. When Kara, Sasha's, new lover is taken hostage as a diversionary tactic to allow the drug dealing Bellfontaine brothers to escape justice, Sasha springs into action. Kara is released physically unharmed, however, her emotions, and budding career in the District Attorney's office are left in shambles when she is held blame for their release, Appalled, by the failure of the criminal justice system, Sasha exacts her own brand of justice for the acts committed against her lover. From the Bayou's of Louisiana to the jungles of South America, Sasha plots her revenge.

Out of Retirement—Erica Lawson Melanie Stokes was a doctor—a very good one, or so she hoped. She was calm and cool under pressure, and very little fazed her. Until…Caitlin Joseph ran a small retirement home for older women in need. The fact that everyone in the house was gay was a coincidence, although it did cut down the number of women agreeing to live there. Mel took up an offer to do some relief work for a local community center when their regular doctor was away on holidays. As soon as she arrived at the home she knew something was different about the place. Was it the little old lady chasing the paper boy down the street or the sign saying "Dykes Retirement Home"? But there was something about the place that also appealed to her. Sure, Caitlin was cute as a button, but it was more the fact that she took very good care of her charges, despite their rather bizarre behavior. The older women seized the opportunity to introduce a woman into Caitlin's lonely life, using any means possible to keep Mel coming back. Their plans were boosted by the introduction of another woman into the house, who set hearts a fluttering and blood pressure rising. Now if she was a lesbian it would have been perfect…

Letting Go—JM Dragon A failed relationship puts Stella Hawke's life on the brink of chaos. When her grandmother falls gravely ill in Ashville, Stella ends her army career to take care of the woman during her last weeks. Little does she know that an old army comrade, socialite Reggie Stockton, whose family owns the local newspaper, also lives in Ashville. Will she allow herself to accept Reggie's help to turn her life around and let go of the past? This is a journey where both women re-evaluate what they want out of life. Will that path lead to happiness or to a parting of the ways?

Through the Darkness—Erin O'Reilly Becca Cameron is a loner—by choice. She lives in a hundred year old farmhouse built by her great grandfather. A tragic accident in her home a year earlier drove away her lover, and Becca tries to accept what she cannot change and hang on to the belief that love can conquer all. Chase Hunter, had a meteoric rise in the Eastman Corporation and was, at thirty-four, the youngest vice-president. To Chase, her work was all consuming leaving little time for friends or lovers. There was simply no place in her life for anything but her job. When Becca and Chase meet at their work place, the attraction is spontaneous. Life begins to look brighter for both women as work takes a second seat to romance. Unknown to either woman, someone is watching their every move…Will passion outweigh doubt? Can love conqueror fear?

Beginning of the End—Alane Hotchkin What happens when life doesn't go exactly as you planned and you must protect others from your own fate? Escaping a horrific childhood, Nikki longed to find happily ever after in adulthood. What she found was Hell. Or did it find her? Finding the courage to break the cycle of betrayal, she opens her heart one last time. Alex lived a childhood others dreamed of. Her father never once denied the young rebel a thing. All her life she dreamed of protecting others; to follow in her father's footsteps. Soon though she learned sex and fists made the most powerful of weapons. Alex controls the women in her life through fear and sex, will breaking the cycle be too much to overcome? Will loving Nikki be enough to change her, or is Alex beyond help? Alex would give Nikki the world, but at what price? When a person's tightly controlled reality snaps what then…? This is the Beginning of the End for one of them and the ultimate sacrifice for the other. But who is who in this game of life?

Till There Was You—S. Anne Gardner Julia is a woman used to power and is not afraid to use it or impose her will to get her way. She appears to have the world but a part of her is empty and cold as a frozen tundra. Julia rides in the mornings to clear her head and to make plans for what she is about to set in motion. Theodora, known as Teddy, is trying to put together a marriage filled with uncertainties. She felt once upon a time that she would have a great love but that has eluded her. One morning these two women meet and from the first instance, it is explosive. The attraction is undeniable, the fears very real and the end without question will change them both forever.

Denial—Jackie Kennedy Time spent in Somalia has Doctor Celeste Cameron accustomed to living and working in a war zone. Coming back home to America, Celeste is glad to see the end of the peril she has been in—or so she thinks. Danger seems to follow Celeste and she finds it in the shape of Amy. What Celeste feels for Amy scares her more than anything she has faced in war zones. Amy has the same feelings, but is in denial and vows to marry Josh, Celeste's twin brother, no matter what. When fate brings them together again, will they give in to their mutual attraction or will they once again deny what they feel.

An Affair of Love—S. Anne Gardner From a dark past, a forbidden love, a secret comes. Among the confusion and the chaos of an unwanted reality, two women find something they neither want nor can deny.

Desert Heat—Dannie Marsden For Luce Diamond, an undercover policewoman, her life is in shambles. Her longtime lover left her and an automobile accident that resulted in a child's death haunts her.

E-Books, Print, Free e-books

Visit our website for more publications available online.

www.affinityebooks.com

Published by Affinity E-Book Press NZ LTD
Canterbury, New Zealand

Registered Company 2517228